"What about you, Agent Buc
How did you bec
retrieval spec

"I have a knack fo
making them belie
I make the bad guy
thing and then I do e the opposite of what he
expects."

He chuckled—couldn't help himself. This was a
woman who enjoyed her work.

"Well, Agent Buchanan, it's a pleasure to make your
acquaintance." He thrust his hand at her.

She grinned and gave it a shake. "Ditto, Agent
Flynn."

Now if they could only get themselves out of this
thorny situation, maybe he'd ask her out to dinner.

A frown furrowed his brow. The beef jerky
obviously hadn't done its job or he wouldn't still be
thinking about food.

Then again, maybe it wasn't food on his mind.

He peeked at the lady lying so close.

Too dangerous, he reminded himself.

Maybe another time when they weren't both
targeted for execution.

SECRETS SHE KEPT

USA TODAY BESTSELLING AUTHOR
Debra Webb &
Carol Ericson

Previously published as *The Safest Lies*
and *Undercover Accomplice*

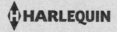

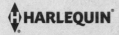

ISBN-13: 978-1-335-42471-6

Secrets She Kept

Copyright © 2021 by Harlequin Books S.A.

The Safest Lies
First published in 2019. This edition published in 2021.
Copyright © 2019 by Debra Webb

Undercover Accomplice
First published in 2019. This edition published in 2021.
Copyright © 2019 by Carol Ericson

Recycling programs
for this product may
not exist in your area.

This edition published by arrangement with Harlequin Books S.A.

For questions and comments about the quality of this book, please contact us at CustomerService@Harlequin.com.

Harlequin Enterprises ULC
22 Adelaide St. West, 40th Floor
Toronto, Ontario M5H 4E3, Canada
www.Harlequin.com

Printed in U.S.A.

CONTENTS

Debra Webb is the award-winning *USA TODAY* bestselling author of more than one hundred novels, including those in reader-favorite series Faces of Evil, the Colby Agency and Shades of Death. With more than four million books sold in numerous languages and countries, Debra has a love of storytelling that goes back to her childhood on a farm in Alabama. Visit Debra at debrawebb.com.

Books by Debra Webb

Harlequin Intrigue

A Winchester, Tennessee Thriller

In Self Defense
The Dark Woods
The Stranger Next Door
The Safest Lies
Witness Protection Widow
Before He Vanished

Colby Agency: Sexi-ER

Finding the Edge
Sin and Bone
Body of Evidence

Faces of Evil

Dark Whispers
Still Waters

Visit the Author Profile page
at Harlequin.com for more titles.

THE SAFEST LIES

Debra Webb

This book is dedicated to
my two beautiful daughters. Like the heroine
in this book, you are strong, amazing women!

Chapter 1

Winchester, Tennessee
Friday, August 9

Sadie Buchanan had never been to Winchester before. The closest she'd come was Tullahoma and that had been years ago when she was first assigned to the Nashville area. A joint task force conference at the Arnold Air Force base had required her attendance for a day. Frankly, it was unusual for an agent to end up in this area, much less request a retrieval. The kind of trouble that required her participation rarely happened in small towns. Most of her assignments took her to the larger metropolitan areas around the state or deep into the desert or the mountains.

In any event, whenever an agent was in trouble, she went in.

She parked in front of the Franklin County sheriff's office. Extracting agents from dangerous situations hadn't exactly been a part of her plan when she started her career, but within two years of her first field assignment she found herself doing exactly that after one particular mission. The assignment as well as the agent involved had been high profile, garnering her the full attention of the powers that be. During that fateful mission she as well as the Bureau discovered her knack for getting in and out with particular ease. From that point forward, she had been focused on training for moments like this one. It wasn't the sort of task just any agent felt comfortable doing. Success required a very particular skill set.

Go in, attain the target and get out alive.

Her father always said that everyone had a gift. Evidently, this was hers. It hadn't failed her yet. She had no intention of allowing it to start today.

Inside the brick building that housed the sheriff's department and county jail, a female desk sergeant greeted her.

"Special Agent Sadie Buchanan." Sadie showed her credentials to the other woman. "I'm here to see Sheriff Tanner and Agent Ross."

"Good morning, Agent Buchanan. Down the hall and to the left," Sergeant Rodriquez said with a gesture toward the long corridor beyond her desk. "They're waiting for you in the conference room, ma'am."

Sadie thanked the sergeant and headed in the direction she'd indicated. One thing she had noticed about Winchester already and it was barely ten o'clock in the morning—it was a couple of degrees hotter than Nashville. The town was attractive in a quaint sort of way, surrounded by a lake and bordered by hills and woods. Most folks would see those hills and woods as nature's perfect landscape. What Sadie saw in all that natural beauty were places to hide. Lots and lots of potential hiding places.

Not a good thing when attempting to locate a target.

She opened the door to the conference room and walked in. Four people waited for her but only one that she recognized: Special Agent Deacon Ross. He, too, was assigned to Nashville. They'd only worked together on one occasion, but he had a stellar reputation. The last she'd heard he had taken an extended leave of absence.

Maybe the rumors that he might not be coming back were just that—rumors. He certainly appeared to be involved in this case.

"Agent Buchanan," a tall, dark-haired man at the head of the table said as he stood, "I'm Sheriff Colt Tanner. We're glad you could come." He extended his hand.

Sadie gave his hand a shake. "Happy to help, Sheriff."

"This is Chief of Police Billy Brannigan." Tanner gestured to another man. This one had brown hair and eyes and looked as much like a cowboy as the sheriff.

Brannigan extended his hand across the conference table. "Good to meet you, Agent Buchanan."

"Likewise, Chief." Sadie accepted the gesture and turned to the next man in the room. "Agent Ross." She offered her hand.

Ross gave her hand a shake and then turned to the woman at his side. "This is Cecelia Winters."

Sadie extended her hand once more, this time toward the petite woman with the fiery mane of red hair. "Ms. Winters."

Winters brushed her palm briefly against Sadie's but didn't speak. Since she had the same last name as the target, Sadie assumed she was a wife or other family member.

"Why don't we have a seat and get started," Ross suggested.

Sadie pulled out a chair and sat down as the others resumed their seats. A couple of files and a stack of maps lay on the table. Not exactly the typical setup for a tactical mission briefing but she'd gotten the impression this one was different than her usual assignment. She didn't have a problem with different. As long as it didn't get anyone killed. Sadie was yet to lose a target once she had attained him or her.

"I imagine," Ross said, "you were briefed on the situation we have."

"I only just returned to Nashville late last night from an assignment in Memphis. I'm afraid the details I received are sketchy at best. I assumed I would be fully briefed when I arrived."

This would certainly be her first briefing with a civilian present who was totally unrelated to the official aspects of the investigation. She had a feeling this assignment was going to become more and more unusual.

"A particular group of extremists in the Franklin County area was pinpointed more than two decades ago. Gunrunning was suspected to be a major part of this group's activities. Over the past few years suspicions of their involvement with kidnapping, possibly related to human trafficking, have surfaced. My former partner, Jack Kemp, investigated this group when it was first discovered but at the time there was not enough substantial evidence that the members were involved in anything criminal or illegal to pursue any sort of operation. Just over nine years ago that status changed, and Jack came back for a second look. During the course of that assignment he disappeared. Recently, new information about what happened to him has come to light. In part, that information was obtained through a civilian informant. Like most of us, Jack worked with a number of civilian informants."

"One of those informants is Levi Winters," Sheriff Tanner added. "Levi has recently gone missing and we suspect this group may be involved."

Brannigan didn't add anything. Sadie was undecided as to whether his continued silence was a good thing. Perhaps his involvement was only for informational purposes. The target was likely outside his official jurisdiction.

"Is the Bureau opening a new case in the area?" Seemed a no-brainer. But Sadie was not up to speed on the happenings in Franklin County. The more Ross talked, the more she understood that he had friends in high places and that was why she was here. "Or is this one off the record?"

The men in the room exchanged a look, which answered the question without anyone having to say a word.

"To a degree," Ross admitted, "the retrieval is off the record. There appears to be some hesitation about reopening the case involving the group known as Resurrection. Personally, I think we're caught in the middle of a war between the Bureau and the ATF, leaving us blind. We're hoping any information Levi may have will help pull this all together. But," he qualified, "finding him is our primary goal."

Making it doubly important that she brought him back alive. Sadie considered the other woman at the table. The hope in her eyes was impossible to miss. Right now, Sadie could walk away and that decision would not adversely affect her career since this mission was off the record. She could stand up, walk out that door and never look back rather than risk her life for some informant whom she did not know and had no idea if he was actually credible.

Chances were, if she made that decision, the informant would die.

And though that decision would not prove unfavorable to her career, it would prove immensely unfavorable to her conscience.

"Let's have a look at what I'm up against."

Tanner went first. He explained that he had not encountered any trouble with members of this group—at least none of which he was aware. The members of the so-called Resurrection group were anonymous. Any who lived amid the community kept quiet about their involvement. Neighbors, friends, possibly even family had no idea about their participation. The tactic was actually fairly common and had been used for centuries by one secret group or another.

Brannigan spoke for the first time, agreeing with Tanner's summation. The Winchester Police Department had not run into trouble with anyone who claimed to be or who was thought to be involved with this extremist group. The crime rate in the county was comparatively low. Rumors regarding the group known as Resurrection leaned toward the idea of extreme or doomsday-type preppers. Part of the problem was that there appeared to be an offshoot fringe group known only as the *others* who were far more dangerous. More primitive and violent.

Ross took over from there. "We've contacted a source within the ATF but we don't have anything back from him just yet. He can only help us so much without crossing a line. Whatever else we do, we can't keep waiting and risk losing Winters. Ultimately, the hope is that the Bureau and the ATF will initiate a joint task force, along with local law enforcement, to look more thoroughly into what this group is doing. As I said, for now, our immediate focus is on extracting Winters."

Sadie understood perfectly. "If the Resurrection or this offshoot group has him, we need to get their attention. Obviously—" she scanned the faces at the table "—you don't have the location where he's being held."

Tanner tapped the stacks of maps. "There are certain areas we feel are the more likely places but, no, we don't have a damned clue."

"And there's no time to conduct the kind of search required to locate a needle in a haystack," Sadie suggested. "Time is our enemy." She set her gaze on Ross's, knowing he would understand the goal. "We need their attention. I would recommend a news bulletin about a missing federal agent last seen in the Winchester area. Keep it ambiguous for obvious reasons. Give my description but not my name." She shifted her attention to Tanner. "I'll start with the most likely place and beat the bushes until they find me."

"You want them to find you?" Tanner looked uneasy as he asked the question.

"We don't have time to locate and infiltrate any other way. Prompting them to find me will be much faster and far more efficient."

"Isn't that far more dangerous, as well?" Brannigan asked.

"Yes." Sadie saw no point in whitewashing the answer. "But it's the only way to accomplish our goal in a timely manner."

"Agent Buchanan is highly trained for exactly these sorts of situations," Ross assured all present.

Judging by the expressions Tanner and Brannigan wore, his assurance did little to alleviate their reservations.

"You're suggesting going in without backup," Brannigan argued. "The only thing I see coming of that is two hostages needing extraction."

Sadie acknowledged his assessment with a nod. "That is a possibility. But, Chief, you can trust me when I say, if I wasn't experienced and completely confident about this situation, we wouldn't be having this conversation. I know what I'm doing. I understand the risk and, based on what I've heard so far, I am not overly concerned."

"I may be able to help."

All gathered around the table turned to the woman who had spoken. Cecelia Winters looked directly at Sadie even as the men in the room started to argue with her announcement.

"Not happening," Ross stated unconditionally, tension in his voice, his posture and the set of his jaw.

"He's right," Tanner agreed with a firm shake of his head.

"This whole thing is far too risky as it is," Brannigan added.

Sadie ignored them all. Instead, she focused on the woman who had made the statement. "How do you believe you can help?"

Cecelia blinked at Sadie's question. "The people in this town know me. They know what happened to me—to my family. Nothing is secret anymore. If I spread the news, they'll believe me. They will pass it along far more quickly than something reported in the news. Not everyone around here trusts the news."

"Cece," Ross argued, "your getting involved could only complicate matters."

Sadie got the picture now. Ross and Cecelia were a couple. He didn't want her anywhere near the line of fire. A personal connection more often than not spelled trouble when it came to an assignment like this one.

"Help from most any source can be useful, but Ross could be right," Sadie said, not to change the woman's mind but because it was true.

The hard look Ross sent her way shouted loud and clear that he wasn't happy with how she had responded to the offer. Too bad. He wanted Sadie to do a job, an extraction—a very risky extraction. Why wouldn't she use any available resources?

"Levi is my brother," Cecelia said. "I want to help." She glanced at Ross. "I need to help."

"You understand that when this is over, there could be a backlash?" Sadie needed her to comprehend the long-term ramifications of any step she might opt to take. Sadie didn't like getting civilians involved but it seemed as if this one was already eyeball deep in the situation.

"I do. The past decade of my life has been one long backlash. I think I can handle a little more."

Ross obviously didn't think so.

Sadie stared directly at him. "Is this going to be a problem for you?"

She didn't like problems. Especially those that came from the people who were supposed to be on her side.

He held her gaze for a moment before saying, "I guess not."

"Good." Sadie turned back to Cecelia. "You tell whomever you believe will get the word out the fastest that the agent who was working with your brother showed up and was going around town asking questions." She shrugged. "Trying to help, but now she's suddenly gone missing and you're worried about her."

Cecelia nodded. "I can do that."

"The most likely starting place?" Sadie asked, looking from one man to the next.

"The church," Ross said. He glanced at Cecelia as he spoke. "We have reason to believe the Salvation Survivalists were working with the primary group in some capacity. They were housing weapons most likely intended for the Resurrection group, but we don't have solid evidence of that conclusion. The ATF is looking at that aspect along with numerous others but, as we've established, they're taking too damned long and they're not sharing."

"But you're certain the two are or were connected."

"We are," Ross said.

Tanner and Brannigan agreed, as well.

"Then that's where I'll start." To Cecelia she said, "You put the word out about me asking questions." She shifted her attention to Tanner. "Make sure the local news reports a missing federal agent. No name, just a description," she reminded.

Tanner nodded. "I can make that happen."

"I'd like to familiarize myself with maps of the area, particularly around the church."

Ross spread the maps on the conference table and started the briefing regarding landscape. Sadie took her time and carefully committed the maps to memory. One of the things that made her good at her job was her ability to memorize maps and recall landmarks. For a girl who grew up in the city, she was a damned good tracker. As good as any hunter she'd ever worked with and she'd worked with a few.

More than anything, she paid attention. The old saying that it was all in the details was more often true than not. The details were crucial. One didn't need a photographic memory to recall the details. She just had to pay attention.

"What about the church?" Sadie considered the map of the area around the church, which appeared to be well outside town. "I need some additional history on the church."

"My father started the church about thirty-five years ago," Cecelia explained. "He was a very cruel man, capable of anything. He had many devoted followers who turned to my older brother, Marcus, after our father's murder. There are those who still believe one or both to be messiahs of a sort. I'm confident the most deeply devoted know far more than they've shared. If they hear about you, you better believe the word will go where you want it."

Ross pushed a folder in Sadie's direction. "This will give you a good overview of what we know. It's not complete by any means, but it's as much as anyone knows."

Sadie opened the file and skimmed the first page. "I'd like some time to go over what you have and then I'll drive out to the church, hide my car and start digging around. If I'm lucky, someone will come looking for me in short order."

"For the record," Chief of Police Brannigan spoke up again, "I still think this is a bad idea."

Sadie wished she could convince him otherwise but to an extent he was correct. This was most likely a bad idea.

But their options were limited. Sometimes the bad ideas were the only feasible ones.

Chapter 2

Dusk was settling way too fast. Sadie had knocked on doors in the vicinity of the church—not that there were that many. She'd asked straightforward questions, calling the group she sought by name. Then she'd driven to the now-defunct church of the Salvation Survivalists and she'd started poking around.

Breaking in had been a breeze. The ATF and the FBI had gone through the building numerous times and though every entrance had been secured, the lock on the back door was damaged. All of ten seconds were required to rip the crime scene seal away and finagle the thing open. As easy as taking candy from a baby.

It was possible a couple of days might be required to garner the attention she sought. Not good for her target. Levi Winters might not have a couple of days. On the other hand, it was possible he wasn't a hostage at all and was happily ensconced among friends deep within this suspicious group. His sister, Cecelia, was convinced he was a hostage, but sisters didn't always know the whole story.

Sadie's sister certainly did not.

She and her sister had never been friends. Maybe it was the ten years that separated them in age or the fact that her sister had chosen a path Sadie despised. Pricilla Buchanan was a criminal defense attorney. Her entire existence was focused on undoing what law enforcement personnel like Sadie risked their lives to do. Of course their mother insisted they were both angels, but she was wrong. Their mother wanted to see good in everyone. Pricilla was not good. She was self-centered, self-serving and indifferent when it came to justice.

Sadie kicked aside thoughts of her older sister as she strolled the halls of the extremist church whose followers still refused to speak ill of their most recent infamous leader. The man, Cecelia Winters's older brother as it turned out, had been hiding smuggled guns. He'd sworn he had no idea how the weapons had ended up in the secret underground hiding place beneath the church. He'd gone so far as to attempt to claim the weapons had been there since before his father died almost nine years ago. Talk about a scumbag. Then again, apparently his father had been an even bigger lowlife.

Ross and the others suspected Marcus Winters had been holding the stockpile of weapons for the Resurrection. Despite the seriousness of the charges he faced, Winters refused to spill his guts. Whomever Marcus Winters was protecting he was too damned afraid to make a deal, even for the promise of a new life in witness protection.

The moment he'd been arrested he had shut down like a dying cell phone battery and hadn't spoken since.

Anything that might provide clues about a connection between the church and the gunrunning extremist prepper group was long gone. The tunnel between the church and the Winters home was set for demolition. Cecelia mentioned that she intended to sell the place the moment it was released from evidence. She wanted to wash her hands of that ugly past as soon as possible and who could blame her? Based on what Ross had told Sadie, the woman had already paid a high price for standing up against her family.

Sadie followed the directions she'd been given to find the tunnel area. Mostly she was killing time. The longer she hung out in the area the more likely she was to run into what she was looking for. At least that was the hope. If she were really lucky things would happen as quickly as she hoped.

Ross had given her a piece of information to use as leverage once she had infiltrated the group. His contact from the ATF insisted this would be immensely useful. She'd gone into missions with less, but this felt a little slim by any measure.

The entrance to the tunnel was barricaded. Sadie turned and headed back in the direction she'd come. She took the stairs two at a time and returned to the church's main sanctuary.

There was nothing else to be done here. She turned for the front entrance and stalled. A man sat on the very back pew. His hair was gray—not the white gray, the silver gray. It poked from beneath a fedora. A full beard did a hell of a job of camouflaging his face. He wore overalls and a button-down, long-sleeved shirt, no matter that it was as hot as hell outside. It was difficult to assess if he was armed. Her view of him from the chest down was blocked by the back of the pew in front of him. From a merely visual perspective he appeared reasonably harmless.

Sadie, however, was too smart to assume any such thing based on appearances.

"You must be that missing fed."

Though he said this in a low, rusty-with-age voice, it seemed to echo in the hollow sanctuary. Not particularly threatening and yet with simmering power.

"That's me. Sadie Buchanan."

"I hear you and a fed friend of yours have been looking for me."

Obviously, he meant Deacon Ross. "I don't know about anyone else and I definitely don't have any friends around here, but I've been looking for someone. That's a fact. Can't say whether that someone is you."

She dared to walk toward him, one step at a time down that long center aisle. The rubber soles of her hiking boots were quiet on the wood floor.

"What is it you think you're looking for, Ms. Buchanan? Or should I call you Agent Buchanan?"

Sadie sat down at the pew in front of him, turned in the hard seat to face him. "Sadie is fine. After yesterday, I doubt that anyone considers me an agent anymore—except maybe for the purposes of prosecution."

The story that she was an agent on the run was the best cover she could come up with given the circumstances and the shortness of time.

"Nine years. Stellar record. Up for promotion," he

said, his gaze steady on hers, "the way I hear it. That's a lot to give up for whatever it is that brought you here, Sadie."

So the man had friends in the right places. Only a handful of people in this town knew her name and none beyond the four with whom she had met in the sheriff's conference room were aware of her background. She shrugged. "I should have gotten that promotion two years ago. And you're right, nine years is a long time to watch men like my SAIC write his own definition of justice. Besides, my daddy was a firm believer in a man—or woman—having the right to live his life the way he wanted and to bear arms. I suppose I have him to thank for my hardheadedness."

The man's gaze hardened. "As interesting as this conversation might prove to be, I don't like wasting my time, Sadie. Why don't you tell me what it is you think I need to hear?"

"I appreciate that you looked me up, Mister...?"

"Prentiss," he said, "Rayford Prentiss."

"Mr. Prentiss," she acknowledged. "The trouble is— and I mean no offense to you—I really need to speak with the man in charge. It's urgent. We don't have a lot of time."

He held her gaze for a long moment of thickening silence. "You don't look like the sort with a death wish," he finally said.

Sadie smiled. "Not if I can help it. What I have, Mr. Prentiss, is some information about a joint task force mission that will prove more than a little devastating to the Resurrection. If you and your friends take me in, I'll give you the heads-up you need to survive the storm that's coming—assuming you know what I'm talking about and have the authority to take me where I need to go."

A crooked smile lifted one corner of his bearded mouth. "First, I know precisely what you mean and I have all the authority I need. The real question is, why on God's green earth would I believe that foolish story?"

"Well, my motive is somewhat personal, Mr. Prentiss. I will tell you that I've gotten myself into a bit of trouble and I don't see any ready way out, so this looks like as good an option as any other. My daddy always said planning for the future was smart business. I need to disappear for a little while, Mr. Prentiss. I think you and your friends can make that happen. You do me a favor and I'll do one for you."

Prentiss chuckled. "I really am flummoxed, Sadie. You appear quite sincere and yet I'm not certain I believe you. Be that as it may, we'll play your little game. After all, it took considerable courage to start this thing." His gaze settled heavily on her and this time there was no mistaking the promise there. "Rest assured, whatever this is, if you're lying to me, you will not like how this ends."

"Great." Sadie pushed a smile into place and sat up straight. "Then we have a deal."

Another of those long moments of silence elapsed with him staring at her. "It appears we do."

He raised a hand and people seemed to come out of the woodwork. Four men, all armed. "My friends will see to your transportation. Goodbye, Sadie."

When he stood and walked away, she couldn't help wondering if this mission would end right here, right now. These guys could kill her and no one would ever know exactly what happened, much less who did the deed.

Wasn't that the way it always was?

The door closed behind Prentiss and she stood, glanced from fierce face to fierce face. "So, who's driving?"

"Take off your clothes," the one nearest her said.

She laughed. "I never take off my clothes on the first date."

He aimed his weapon at her. "Take them off now."

One of his pals stepped forward and tossed a bag on the floor at the end of her pew.

"There are clothes in the bag," the one who appeared to be in charge and who held his aim steady on her announced.

"Well, if you insist."

Taking her time she toed off her boots, peeled off her socks, then unbuttoned her shirt. When the shirt, the boots and socks were in a neat pile next to the provided bag, she shucked her jeans and added them to the pile next.

When she reached for the bag, the man with the gun at the ready protested, "Everything comes off."

She figured that would be his next order. Sadie reached behind her and unhooked her bra. She allowed it to fall forward and drop to the pile. Then she swooped off her panties and added them unceremoniously to the rest.

The man nodded and she reached for the bag. Inside was a pair of gray sweatpants and a white tee. No underwear. No socks. Thankfully there was a pair of plastic flip-flops. The cheap kind found in bins near the checkout counter at discount stores. She donned the provided outfit and slipped her feet into the flip-flops.

The man who'd brought the bag grabbed her things and put them into the empty bag. She hated that her cell phone was in that bag. Besides a gun, it was the asset she depended upon most.

Oh well.

"Let's go." The man with a bead on her motioned with the barrel of his weapon toward the back of the church.

"What about my car?" she asked as they marched toward the rear exit.

"A friend will pick it up and dismantle it for parts."

She stalled and glared at the man. Was he out of his mind? "Wait just a minute. That car cost—"

"You won't need it where you're going."

The drive to their destination took half an hour, give or take a minute.

Sadie had counted off the seconds and minutes, in part to distract herself from the sorts of thoughts that wanted to crowd into her brain. But mostly because it was important to maintain a sense of location. Half an hour from the church was a reference anyone coming to her rescue could use to facilitate the task.

Except there was no one coming. This mission was basically off the books. Ross and his friends would get worried when they didn't hear from her in a couple of days but there wasn't a whole lot they could do other than beat the bushes and rattle a few cages looking for her. Finding her would be difficult if not impossible. The tracking devices in her cell phone, in the soles of her shoes and in her bra were who knew where. Unless someone had been watching her and followed this caravan, she was probably out of luck as far as backup was concerned.

Frankly, she had been surprised by their vehicles. She'd expected big four-wheel-drive trucks caked with mud and decked out with gun racks. But that wasn't the case at all. The two vehicles were both new top-of-the-line SUVs. Sure, they were four-wheel drive, but they were sleek and almost elegant looking—unlike the men inside.

The younger of the group had been tasked with her personal security. He'd secured her hands behind her back and dropped a cloth bag over her head. He sat in the back seat with her. Another one drove. The other two men were in the second vehicle, with Prentiss, no doubt. No one in this vehicle had said a word en route. Music had played just loud enough to prevent her from noting another reference—any sounds in the areas they drove through. Animals, trains, construction, whatever.

When the vehicle rolled to a stop and the engine cut off, the music died. The doors opened and low voices rumbled around her. Beyond the voices was quiet. No city sounds. No traffic sounds. Not even any animals.

Fingers wrapped around her upper arm and tugged her from the center section of the back seat. A hand guided her feet so she wouldn't break her neck climbing out. When she was steady on the ground the sack was dragged from her head.

Her first thought was that she had gone back in time. The towering stone walls made her think of the ones surrounding a castle she'd visited in Edinburgh, Scotland. The walls were massive, at least thirty feet high. There were what appeared to be guard towers built into the wall. A large, square stone structure stood in the center of the expansive grounds that were like a quad on a college campus without all the fancy landscape. Like the primitive keeps she'd seen in her travels, the windows were tiny in proportion. There were other buildings beyond the larger one, but she could only see the rooftops in the distance.

She stared overhead. Frowned. There was no sky.

She scanned what should have been the sky for as far as she could see. Steel and some sort of panels stood high above her. Reminded her of a massive warehouse. But no clouds or sun or anything else that said *sky*.

Wherever they were, they were not outside. But the SUVs had rolled to a stop right here. She glanced over her shoulder at the one she'd only just emerged from. The ride had seemed to stay on level ground. There had been no downhill or uphill movement. The ride had been smooth but not so smooth that she wouldn't have noticed a change in elevation. There could have been an elevator somewhere that brought them below ground. But that didn't seem right, either, since they hadn't stopped long enough to roll into any sort of elevator until a minute ago, when the engines shut off and they got out.

The man behind her nudged her forward with the muzzle of his weapon. She took in as much of what she could see as possible, committed it to memory as they moved forward. Wherever they were, the place was certainly fortified for battle. If they were underground as she suspected, she supposed the purpose was for surviving a nuclear attack. Additionally, being underground would explain why the feds and local law enforcement hadn't already spotted the compound from the air.

By the time they rounded the corner of the largest building she'd seen so far, only two of the men remained with her. Prentiss and the other two had gone in a different direction. The one with the gun at her back kept her moving forward with the occasional nudge. Beyond the large building were increasingly smaller ones. Along the east side of the wall the smallest structures were numbered. They sat in a long row like cabin rentals at the lake. Only there was no lake—not that she'd seen so far anyway—and this was no vacation. The long, low building that stood the farthest west from the center of the grounds had no windows and appeared to be their destination. The squat roofline told her it was one story. She saw only one entrance along the front, assuming what she was looking at was the front.

The second of the two guards unlocked and opened the door. Number one nudged her to go in. The guards followed close behind her. An immediate left took them down a long white corridor lined with doors on either side. No windows on the doors, either. Midway down the corridor, they stopped at a door and number two guard unlocked it with a few clicks of the keys on the control pad. Once the thick door pulled outward, Sadie understood this would be her accommodations for now. Until they decided what to do with her, she imagined.

"I'm supposed to be meeting with the man in charge," she reminded number one.

"Tomorrow."

The door slammed in her face.

She turned around. A dim light came from around the perimeter of the room. There was a steel cot, a toilet hanging on the wall with a sink formed in the tank. Just like the ones she had seen in the few prison cells she'd visited.

With a quick drawing back of the covers, she checked the mattress, ensured the sheets weren't tainted with anything she could see or smell. Fabric smelled clean enough. She paced the small room and considered her options. There had been four men with Prentiss. She hadn't seen any others when they arrived but that didn't mean there weren't hundreds around here somewhere. There was no accurate body count for this group.

If the Resurrection was like most of these extremist groups, there would be several hundred on-site. This was obviously a headquarters. The setup was too good to be anything else. The Bureau had been gathering information on extremist groups like this for decades. But this one had somehow managed to stay under the radar. The members didn't talk. Fear, she imagined. It was human nature to talk about the things in which one was interested. Being a part of something like Resurrection would typically provide bragging rights for those who had a penchant for the extreme. But there was no bragging from these members.

Their silence made them even more dangerous. Restricted the available intelligence to gather, making the jobs of Sadie and others like her far more difficult. Law enforcement personnel depended upon informants and the information garnered on the streets. When information stopped flowing, it was impossible to find footing in a given situation.

Sadie braced her hands on her hips and moved around the room again, this time more slowly. She considered the walls, thought about the door when it had opened. The walls were likely made of concrete just as the door was. Thick concrete, eight inches at least. The floor and ceiling of this building appeared to be the same as the walls. The smooth, cold finish of the concrete was interrupted only by the small blocks of light around the walls near the floor. The cot was metal, the sheets a thin material more like paper than fabric. No good for constructing a hangman's noose. She turned back to the door. The lock wasn't the usual residential sort. It was electronic and required a code.

Getting out of here wouldn't be easy. If she was really lucky, Levi Winters was in this same building. Assuming he was a hostage. Hopefully, he would know a way out and would be willing to go with her.

That was the problem with being underground or, perhaps, burrowed into a mountainside. Getting out was generally somewhat complicated.

She'd been in tighter spots, Sadie reminded herself.

All she had to do was find her target and she would locate a way out of here.

It was what she did.

Chapter 3

The woman was trouble.

Smith Flynn studied the screen monitoring her movements. She paced the six-by-eight cell as if the journey might end some other way the next time she turned around. She hadn't stopped since being placed inside. This restless behavior was for the benefit of anyone observing.

He had watched her arrival. She had walked into the compound, shoulders back, chin held high, all the while discreetly surveying everything in her field of vision. Sadie Buchanan was neither afraid nor uncertain. Her arrival at this compound was not by accident any more than was the timing of her appearance. She was on a mission.

Whatever she was doing here, unfortunately she was his issue now.

He did not like unexpected issues. Even fearless, attractive ones like Sadie Buchanan.

"What's your take on this new development?"

The voice drew Smith from his musings. He turned to Prentiss. The older man had been running the group known as the Resurrection for a very long time. He rarely had much to say but when he spoke anyone within hearing distance listened—not because he was so articulate or interesting, but because they wanted to live. Prentiss did not take disrespect well.

"She has an agenda," Smith said, not telling the other man anything he didn't already know. "It'll take some time to determine what that agenda is."

Prentiss nodded, his attention fixed on the screen. "I don't like killing women. There's something innately wrong with a man killing a woman. It's a sin like no other, except for killing a child. Any man who would kill a woman or a child is lower than low." His gaze swung to Smith. "But, if you tell me she's lying, I will kill her."

Smith didn't waste time pretending to consider the situation. "I can tell you right now that she *is* lying. No question there." He turned his attention back to the screen. "The question is why. We'll need that answer before you kill her."

Prentiss nodded. "You're right. Until we have the answer, she belongs to you. Do with her what you will, just get the truth for me."

"I always do."

The old man stood and headed for the door. Smith waited until the door closed before turning back to the screen. He wondered if this woman had any idea just how much trouble she was in. Whatever she thought she'd come here to do, she had made a most regrettable mistake.

He exited his cabin, locking the door behind him, and crossed to the detention center. No one questioned his movements. They knew better. The door was unlocked and opened for him as if he was a king. Once inside he said to the guard, "I'll be using interview room two for an hour or so. Bring me Levi Winters."

"Yes, sir."

The guard hustled away to do Smith's bidding. Smith took the short corridor on the right and then an immediate left where six interview rooms waited. Each room was equipped with very specific instruments for persuading answers from those who had the misfortune of ending up in one of the spaces. Before going to interview room two, he stepped into the observation room and checked the monitoring system.

Two minutes elapsed before the guard entered interview room two. He settled the prisoner Levi Winters into the chair on the side of the metal table facing the hidden camera. Once Winters was secured to the bolt in the concrete floor, the guard exited. Smith considered Winters for a longer moment. He was younger than this woman who'd gotten herself invited to this ultrasecure place.

More important than any other aspect of this prisoner, he was scared. Scared to death.

They were probably going to kill him now.

Levi's whole body felt as cold as ice. There was no telling what they had planned for him this time. That bastard Flynn had done things to him, made him talk when he didn't want to talk.

Levi closed his eyes and lowered his head. He was doomed. All he'd wanted was to find the truth. To prove to his sister that he wasn't a bad guy like their brother, Marcus. He'd let her down so badly already it hurt to think about it. Even under the circumstances. He hadn't helped Cece the way he should have so he'd decided to prove the whole truth about their daddy and all that he and Marcus had done, like ordering the death of the FBI guy, Jack Kemp.

Jack had been good to Levi. He'd made him feel like his life mattered—like he mattered. Levi had wanted to be like him. And then the guy had disappeared.

What nobody knew was that Levi remembered the night their mother had died, no matter that he'd been nothing but a little kid. She and that bastard who was their father had been arguing so loudly and so desperately—arguing, screaming and crying. Then suddenly the arguing had stopped. Levi had crept out of his bedroom and to the top of the stairs. Their momma had lain at the bottom of the stairs. The crying had started again, only that time it was Levi. The only thing he remembered after that was Cece holding him and their grandmother screaming. Eventually she had calmed down and taken them home with her.

The certainty and hatred that had sprouted that night had grown and grown but before Levi could work up the courage to do what needed to be done, their younger sister, Sierra, had killed the old bastard. It should have been Levi. He should have killed that devil and taken care of the family when their older brother, Marcus, had not. But Levi had been weak. He'd been weak and afraid. He'd let Cece down and now he was going to die without having made up for the past.

He wished he could see Cece one more time and tell her how sorry he was. She had paid the price for all of them.

The door opened and Levi froze. It would be him—the one the other prisoners called the Interrogator. Levi's body shuddered at the idea of what he might have planned for him this time. Why had he screwed up so badly yet again? All he wanted at this point was to go home. To show his sister how much he loved her and to start doing the right thing with his life.

He wasn't like his father or his older brother. Evil didn't swim in his blood.

He just wanted to go home.

Smith Flynn walked into the room. He had the lightest gray eyes, almost transparent. That and his blond hair almost made him look like some guy from Norway or Sweden or something. He didn't look like anyone from around here. He was tall, six-four at least. And strong. You could tell he pumped iron. But he hadn't laid a hand on Levi. He had other ways to induce pain. He used equipment and his words. He knew the things to say to strike terror in a man.

Before Levi could stop himself, his gaze flitted to the far end of the room where the metal cabinets stood. Inside those locked doors were instruments he hoped to never see again. Evidently he wasn't going to be so lucky. Flynn wouldn't be here otherwise.

The worst part about the whole damned mess was that this guy wanted some truth from Levi, but he didn't have anything to trade for his life or even for a little more time free of torture. Levi had nothing. He had come to this place to prove something. All those years ago when he'd first joined the Resurrection so Jack Kemp would see how smart he was, he'd made a mistake. Truth was he'd let Jack use him. He'd needed that father figure Jack represented so badly. Levi would have done anything to impress him. But he'd gone too far.

All he'd done was gotten into trouble. Now he was likely going to get dead the same way Jack had.

Levi would end up in hell with his damned daddy.

"We have a new problem, Levi."

Fear tightened around his neck. Even the man's voice had a way of terrifying anyone who happened to be stuck in the room with him. Deep, dark, dangerous. Fear twisted inside Levi. Why didn't this Interrogator just kill him and get it over with? He didn't want to die but he couldn't take this much longer.

"I already told you I don't know anything. I only came here to find the truth about an old friend. I swear that's it. The whole story. The truth. There's nothing else."

"Jack Kemp," Flynn said. "You told me that before. Tell me again why you think Kemp came here?"

"He was from the FBI," Levi said. No point pretending he could hide anything from this bastard. The Interrogator had ways of digging stuff out of him. "He asked me to help him get information about the group called the Resurrection, but I went too far."

"Meaning you joined the calling all those years ago? Nine or so years ago, am I right? You did this to help your friend."

Levi nodded. "But Jack disappeared before I could tell him anything. I figured y'all found out what he was up to and got rid of him."

"Your brother, Marcus, was responsible for what

happened to him, Levi. If you had seen the news recently, you would know this. He confessed."

Levi was surprised that Marcus confessed to giving Jack to those crazy people. The only way he would have admitted to anything was to save his sorry ass. Hurt twisted in Levi's chest. "What about my sisters? Did you see anything about my sisters?"

Flynn directed that icy glare at him. "Do I look like I would waste my time keeping up with your sisters?"

Levi blinked, bit his tongue so hard he tasted blood. He wanted to hurt this guy. But he'd heard all about him—the Interrogator. The one who got the answers for the Council. The one who knew how to cause pain. Fear snaked through Levi. He shouldn't have come back here. He'd wanted to help…but he'd just made another mistake. Jack was dead by now, no question. Marcus was in jail. God only knew about Sierra. Hopefully Cece was okay.

Flynn placed a photo of a woman on the table. "Do you know her?"

The woman had black hair and eyes nearly as dark, like a raven. Her skin was dark, like she'd lain on a beach all summer. She was pretty but he hadn't seen her before. He shook his head. Prayed that was the right answer because it was the only one he had. "No. She doesn't look familiar."

"Are you certain? Think carefully, Levi. If you lie to me, it will be much worse for you."

"I swear to God I don't know the woman. I have never seen her before."

Flynn said nothing for a long moment. Levi's chest felt ready to explode with tension. Why the hell didn't the bastard just go ahead and tell him he was a dead man? If death was coming, he'd rather know now and brace for it. He was sick of these games. He did not know this woman. He did not know any other information related to the FBI or this damned place or any damned thing else that mattered. His foot started to bounce, making his shackles rattle. He forced himself to still. Losing it wouldn't help his situation.

"I believe you, Levi." Flynn withdrew the photo, tucked it away in a folder. "My true concern is that she appeared here only a few days after you."

Agony welled inside Levi. "I don't know why. I don't know her. Why don't you ask her?"

"Not to worry, I certainly will. I think I might know why she's here but I need to be certain."

Levi blinked. He didn't have a damned clue where this was going or what this woman had to do with him. He just wanted to go back to his cell and be left alone. He didn't want the Interrogator opening up those cabinets over there the way he'd done before. Pulling out his torture tools and making Levi nearly piss his pants.

Ever since he was a teenager, Levi had thought that to some degree he was brave. He'd thought he was the kind of man who did the right thing. A sort of hero. At least he'd wanted to be. He'd hoped he could be a hero for his sister Cece and help her prove her innocence... but he hadn't helped. And he damned sure wasn't a hero. He wasn't even brave.

He was a coward.

Nothing but a stinking coward.

"Can I count on your help, Levi?"

Levi snapped his focus back to the man. He swallowed back the bile that had risen in his throat and tried to slow his pounding heart. "Yeah, sure. What do I have to do?"

"I haven't worked out all the details just yet. We'll talk again soon."

The man stood and walked out.

Levi sagged in his chair. Squeezed his eyes shut and thanked God he'd survived a second encounter with the Interrogator.

Whatever he wanted, Levi could do it. He would do it. At this point obedience was probably the only way to stay alive. Cece would want him to stay alive. She would. He knew this without question. His sister would absolutely want him to do whatever necessary to stay alive.

Even if he was the worst kind of coward.

Smith returned to his cabin and turned on the security feed to watch the woman.

She had stopped her pacing. Had decided to conserve her energy. He suspected she was above average in intelligence. Certainly she was cockier than the average agent. Her dark hair and eyes, the olive skin, gave her an exotic appearance. Beyond the superficial, she looked strong. Undeniable curves, but not soft. Lean. Toned muscle. This was a woman who worked hard to be prepared.

Her claim of possessing useful information was not a particularly original tactic. Her methods of getting their attention, however, were damned original. To garner the attention of Prentiss himself, then get herself picked up by members and brought here this way was ingenious. And extremely risky. Whatever she wanted, it was important. Important enough to risk her life.

Reconnaissance teams had been doubled and were out there now, patrolling and watching for trouble. No matter that the team that had brought her here had ensured they weren't followed. Her clothes and personal items had been removed before she left that godforsaken church. That level of motivation demanded careful consideration.

It was possible a tracking device was implanted somewhere on her slim body but the initial scan had not picked up on anything close to the surface. Her clothes and cell phone had been cleaned. As he'd anticipated, her phone was more or less a blank slate. Anything incriminating had been wiped. It had been reduced to a mere tracking device. This was a very well-trained agent.

Rather than take the risk the initial scan had missed something, he picked up a secure internal line and called Medical. "Run deep scans on Prisoner Buchanan. Send the results to me ASAP."

Smith ended the call, his attention still focused on the woman. He watched as she whirled around at the sound of her cell door opening. She didn't resist when the guard cuffed her hands behind her back and then escorted her out of the confining space. Smith followed the monitors, watching her move down the long white corridor and out onto the quad. The two crossed the common area and entered the smaller medical building. Smith switched to another camera and followed their movements inside.

The guard took a position at the door leading to Imaging while the waiting technician assumed custody of the prisoner.

"Remove your clothing," the tech ordered.

Buchanan glanced around the room, noted the imaging equipment and then did as he asked without question. The top came off first, revealing high, firm breasts and a narrow waist. As the sweatpants slid down her hips and thighs, Smith's gaze followed. Despite his own training, his body tightened. Her shape was undeniably attractive. Gently rounded hips and long legs sculpted by hours of running. Her long hair hung around her shoulders, the only remaining shield she possessed.

The quality he found most surprising and interesting was that she stared square at the male technician without the slightest flinch. She was not shy or afraid.

Smith continued to observe as the scans were accomplished. On a second screen, he monitored the results. There was no indication a tracking device or other electronic object had been inserted or implanted. She was clean.

His curiosity roused. This woman—this Federal Bureau of Investigation agent—had walked into a compound filled with heavily armed and well-trained extremists. In truth, the people here were more mercenaries than preppers. She had done this while completely unarmed and with no way to call for backup or hope to escape.

Sadie Buchanan was either telling the truth about her agenda for being here or she was completely insane.

He would know the answer soon enough.

Chapter 4

Sadie opened her eyes. Darkness crowded in around her, jolting her heart into a frantic run.

For a moment her brain couldn't assimilate where she was. Air refused to fill her lungs.

Then she remembered. Compound. *Resurrection.* Trouble.

She froze.

What had awakened her so abruptly? A sound. The slightest brushing of fabric against fabric as if someone had come far too close to her huddled position on this rock-hard cot.

She dared to take a breath and the subtle scent of leather and wood whispered against her senses. Adrenaline burned through her once more.

She was not alone.

Forcing herself to relax, she peered into the darkness. Slowly but surely her eyes filled in the dark form sitting on the edge of the thin mattress, barely centimeters away. Whoever it was sat perfectly still, didn't even breathe.

Someone had come into her cell, had walked the half-dozen steps across the small concrete room and sat down on the edge of her cot. The door opening should have awakened her but it had not. Had they put something into her food?

She never slept so heavily.

"What do you want?" She said the words then waited for a response, holding her breath for fear she would miss some part of the answer, assuming an answer came.

"Why are you here, Sadie Buchanan?"

Male. His voice was intensely deep, and...*dangerous*. She couldn't stop the shiver the sound elicited.

Grabbing back her usual unflappability, she fired back, "You already know the answer to that question."

A grunt was his immediate reaction.

She ordered herself to relax. Where was her usual fearlessness? It was something for which she didn't typically have to search. Granted he had startled her from sleep in the middle of the night. Then again, she couldn't be sure what time it was. It could be morning for all she knew. Without a window with which to judge, she couldn't make an accurate assessment. There had to be something in the food she had dared to nibble at. She had known better but hunger sometimes overrode experience.

"Why are you here, Sadie Buchanan?" he said once more.

The words were harsher this time. His patience was thinning, and he obviously didn't like repeating himself. Well, she didn't, either.

"Like I told your friends, I have information that could help your cause. I came to make a deal."

He laughed. There was zero humor in the rough noise. "If you were half as smart as you apparently believe you are, Sadie Buchanan, you would know that people like us don't make deals."

The full depth and breadth of her courage finally reared its head. About time. "Well, now, that's not entirely true, Mister...?"

"Flynn. Smith Flynn."

Her brain instinctively searched her memory banks. No Smith Flynn was found there. "Perhaps you're unaware of the deals those in charge make quite often. Deals with a certain South American gunrunning cartel. The recent shipment was detained by the feds and local authorities right here in Winchester—assuming we're still in the Winchester area. And that's only the beginning of your troubles. Things are not going to go so well for your friends if you refuse my generous offer of help."

He appeared to contemplate her warning for a time. If she was really lucky, his curiosity would trump his logic.

"What happened recently," he said, his voice still somehow disturbing to her senses, "was an unforeseeable stroke of good fortune for *your* friends, but it won't happen again."

Sadie was the one who laughed this time. "You really believe all those stored weapons were found in those underground tunnels at the church by accident? A lucky break for the feds?"

His tension shifted to the next level; she felt it in his posture even if she couldn't see him in the darkness. Though their bodies weren't touching, tension crackled between them. He was as edgy as she was. She squinted, peered harder through the darkness. Her eyes had adjusted more fully to the darkness allowing her to see that he had lighter hair. Blond, she calculated. Maybe gray. She couldn't say for certain.

"You have proof it wasn't?"

The next step was a risky one. Other than Levi Winters, she had no names of members except the one she was saving as the ace up her sleeve. "I know what the local authorities said. A heads-up took them to the church. The Winters family meltdown was secondary. They were already going there anyway. The church had been on their radar for a while. The goal was to hit when it counted. We both know how that turned out."

He considered her statement for long enough to make her doubt herself.

"I can't decide, Sadie Buchanan, whether you actually have relevant information or if you simply have a somewhat complicated death wish. If exiting this world is your goal, putting your service weapon to your temple would have been far easier."

"I can assure you, Mr. Flynn, I do not have a death wish." She was winning this round. "What I have is information you and your friends can use. But I can't force your interest." She relaxed into the thin mattress as if she'd said all she had to say.

"I will be watching you, Sadie Buchanan. If you're

lying, you will regret your actions far more than you can imagine."

She reached out, her hand landing on what felt like his upper arm. The muscles there were like steel but she suspected that had nothing to do with him not being relaxed and everything to do with serious workouts.

"Tell me about you, Smith Flynn. What's your story? What are you running away from?"

He snagged her hand, clutched it in his own. "Why would you think I'm running from something?" His thumb found her palm and stroked the tender flesh there. "You don't know me."

His touch unnerved her, which was the point. "How can you be certain I don't know you? No one is invisible, Mr. Flynn."

The mattress shifted and fabric rustled as he leaned close. His face came so near to hers she could feel his breath on her skin. Her own ability to breathe stalled.

"I know this because you have never seen my face. A name is only a name. It's the face—the eyes—that tell the story, and I will know yours."

With every ounce of courage she possessed, she forced herself to turn fully toward him, putting their mouths mere millimeters apart. "Then show me your face and we'll know for certain."

She felt his smile. "You are very brave, Sadie Buchanan. Or perhaps you are more naive than I thought."

"I thought you had me all figured out, Mr. Flynn."

"So did I."

He drew away and she dared to breathe again.

"You have a command performance this morning, Ms. Buchanan." The mattress shifted again as he stood. "I hope for your sake you pass the series of tests you are about to encounter. If some part of you recognizes that you're in over your head, you might consider quitting now. I'm confident the Council would be willing to permit a quick, merciful death if you confessed the truth before wasting more of their time."

"I'm not a quitter, Mr. Flynn." Sadie dropped her feet to the floor. "If you knew me at all, you would know this."

The next sound she heard was the door closing and then locking.

Just to be sure he was actually gone and not waiting in the darkness, she stood and moved around the walls of the room, reaching out to ensure he wasn't standing in the center of the dark space.

She leaned against the door and closed her eyes. He might be right about one thing—there was a very strong possibility she was in over her head.

The guard ushered her out the exit. This one, like the ones yesterday and the men who had accompanied Prentiss, wore a camouflage military uniform. The boots were military style, as well. Outside, Sadie squinted at the light. It seemed so bright she had to remind herself it wasn't the sun. There was no sky because this place was underground somehow.

"Where is this place?" she asked the man ushering her along. "Underground? In a cave?" If it was a cave, it was a really large cave. Maybe it was built into a mountainside. That would explain how they'd driven directly in and why the facility had not been located by any sort of aerial surveillance.

As usual, the man ushering her along said nothing. Even when he'd opened her cell a few minutes ago, he hadn't spoken. She had gotten up from the cot and walked out, grateful to escape the concrete box.

"If we're underground…" Sadie stopped, causing him to almost trip over her. "Technically I don't need these cuffs. Where would I go if I ran?"

He glared at her, grabbed her by the upper arm and steered her forward.

"Where are we going?"

Still not a word.

The smaller buildings, almost like cabins, captured her attention again. Living quarters for those in charge, she surmised. Somewhere around here there would be a barracks for those members like the one escorting her this morning. She wondered about the man who had come to her cell sometime during the night. He probably lived in one of those private quarters.

"Were you on duty all night?"

Still no answer. He walked forward, his gaze straight ahead.

"A man came into my cell." She almost stumbled trying to look back over her shoulder at the mute guard as she spoke. But she was glad she did. He made the slightest little flinch in response but quickly schooled his face. She couldn't decide if he'd felt a fleeting hint of concern that she might fall or if the idea of the man who visited her unsettled him somehow.

"He tried to scare me."

No reaction.

"But he didn't scare me. If he'd intended to kill me, he would have."

"There are worse things than dying."

His fingers wrapped around her upper arm once more and ushered her toward a building on the left.

The sign posted by the door read Clinic. She wanted to question him about the comment, but he ushered her through the entrance and walked away before she could. A woman wearing a white uniform took charge of Sadie.

"The guard will wait for you outside," the nurse, doctor, whatever she was, explained.

The woman, her black hair slicked back in a tight bun, led the way to a plain white room with an exam table as well as a side table loaded with medical equipment. Sadie decided the woman was a nurse or technician. She checked Sadie's temperature and then led the way back into the corridor.

In the next room, there was yet another examination table. A stack of neatly folded sweatpants and a tee sat on the table. Beyond that was a curtain—the type that would hang over a shower.

The nurse pulled a key from her pocket and removed the cuffs, then gestured to the curtain. "Take off your clothes and shower. Use the soap in the bottle."

Sadie didn't argue. She took off her clothes, got into the shower and washed her hair and body as instructed. When she'd finished and stepped out of the shower, the woman—nurse, whatever she was—waited by the exam table. She wore an apron, a face mask and gloves. Stirrups now extended from one end of the table.

"We'll do your exam now."

No point in arguing. Sadie climbed onto the exam table and placed her feet in the stirrups. A close physical examination followed. She rolled Sadie onto her side and checked her back and buttocks. She scanned her arms and legs, hands and feet. Her face and scalp. Then she did a pelvic exam.

Sadie grimaced. "You looking for anything in particular?"

They had scanned her thoroughly yesterday. This seemed a bit overkill.

The woman peeled off her gloves and tossed them into a trash receptacle. "Put on your clothes."

Sadie complied. When the fresh sweats and tee hung on her body, the nurse recuffed her and led her back out the front entrance to where the guard waited. From there, he led Sadie toward yet another building, this one about the same size as the clinic. The sign on the door read Council. The building was like all the rest, gray, like concrete. Austere. This one was a one-story like the clinic and the detention center.

As soon as they stepped inside the building Sadie understood this was a place of importance. The floor was carpeted. Something commercial with low pile, but enough to quiet footsteps. The walls weren't a stark white as all the others had been. This was more of a beige.

"What did you mean when you said there were worse things than dying?"

"Wait here." He steered her toward the waiting bench. "Maybe you won't have to find out."

Sadie sat on the bench against the wall and watched as he walked away. She ignored the idea that he had a point about there being some things worse than dying. For now, she preferred to focus on more optimistic scenarios. She had a feeling she was on a dangerous precipice. Whatever happened in the next few minutes would determine her future. One slip either way and she could go over the edge completely.

Minutes passed. Three, then four and five. Eventually ten. Sadie crossed her legs, uncrossed them and then crossed them again. She swung her foot up and down. Someone in this place was watching her. She might as well show them how thoroughly unimpressed and utterly bored she was.

A door on the opposite side of the corridor, a few yards beyond where she sat, opened. A different guard—she recognized the camo uniform but not the face—strode to her, pulled her to her feet and shepherded her toward the door he'd exited. The room was fairly large. A long table stood across the far end; seven, no eight men were seated on the other side. One chair sat on this side of the table. Sadie suspected that chair was for her. The guard nudged her forward, confirming her suspicion. When she'd taken a seat, he waited behind her.

Most of the men were old and Caucasian. Not a particularly big surprise. There was one, however, who was not so old. A few years older than Sadie. Maybe forty. Blond hair. Piercing gray eyes. He stared at her, as did the others, but there was something about his stare that penetrated far deeper. They wore civilian clothes. Jeans, short-sleeved shirts—some button-down, others pullovers—and hiking boots. Except for one.

Of all those present, the only person among them she had seen before was the man named Prentiss. He wore the same style overalls and long-sleeved shirt he'd worn in their first meeting. No fedora this time.

He spoke first. "Agent Buchanan, you've created quite a stir around here." He glanced side to side, acknowledging his colleagues. "We're mostly in agreement as to what should become of you. There's a single holdout, preventing a final decision."

Sadie made a face. "I'm not sure I understand, Mr. Prentiss. You haven't heard what I have to say. Maybe you're not interested in protecting your assets and followers."

He stared directly at her, his glare as deadly as any weapon she'd ever faced. "I don't think you understand, Agent Buchanan. We have no interest in anything you have to say. We have our doubts as to the worth of anything you might have to offer and we've decided we have no patience for whatever game you're playing."

Not exactly the reaction she'd hoped for. Time to throw out the ace up her sleeve. "Mr. Trenton Pollard." She scanned the faces as she said the name, looking for a reaction or some indication that one or more of those present recognized the name. Everyone seated at the table—except the younger man—had shoulder-length hair, a full beard and mustache, hiding a good portion of their faces, but not one of them outwardly flinched, grimaced or so much as batted an eye.

"The Bureau and the ATF," she went on, "have targeted Resurrection with the intention of taking down those in power, starting with you, Mr. Prentiss. They consider you the weak link in this group. The necessary information to accomplish this feat will be provided by Mr. Pollard. It's my understanding there's more than simply your location, far more, he plans to share."

All eyes stared at her.

Good or bad, she'd shown her hand—her only hand. Now the ball was in their court.

She had nothing else.

Except what she could make up as she went along. She'd always been fairly good at improvising.

The men whispered among themselves, save the younger one. He sat staring at Sadie without saying a word or even glancing at anyone else. That he still watched her so closely had begun to get under her skin. She kept her attention on the others, hoping all that going back and forth was in her best interest.

Finally, a hush fell over the group and Prentiss settled his attention on her once more. "Agent Buchanan, we still have reservations about your decision to come here with this so-called warning. Though I will give you this, you have our attention. Still, my question to you is what could you possibly hope to gain?"

Now for the improvising. "I screwed up." She shrugged. "I had an opportunity to pad my bank account and I took it. I see no reason to share the dirty details. Sadly, two days ago I found out an investigation had been opened and my assets were about to be frozen. I moved a few things around but there was no way I was going to be able to disappear quickly enough. I needed someplace to go ASAP. Someplace they wouldn't be able to find me. Since they haven't been able to find you in all this time, I figured we could help each other out. The information would buy my way in. Then I found out Pollard is about to spill his guts. I'm assuming your organization has a backup plan for disappearing."

"I fear you have overestimated your worth, Agent Buchanan."

Well, hell.

"I regret that you feel that way." She stood.

There it was. The no-go she had hoped wouldn't be

thrown out. Still, he had mentioned a holdout. Maybe, just maybe the game wasn't over yet.

When no one said anything else, she offered, "Since there's no place for me here, I guess I'll just have to take my chances trying to outrun the Bureau's reach. I wish you well in doing the same. They are coming, Mr. Prentiss. Trust me on that one."

A remote smile tugged at the old man's face. "Perhaps you should have done your due diligence when weighing your options, Agent. You see, once you're here, there's only one way to leave."

She didn't need a more detailed explanation.

The Council had decided her fate.

Death.

Chapter 5

"What happens now?"

As usual, the guard said nothing while he steered Sadie out of the building. She hadn't actually expected him to answer her question, but she needed to try. He was the one person who had spoken to her besides Prentiss, even if it had been only once.

And there was the man who had visited her in the dark of her cell.

Definitely wasn't the guard. His voice was different. He smelled different, too. This close it was obvious her guard wasn't freshly showered like the man who'd sneaked into her cell. The stranger who'd made that middle-of-the-night appearance had smelled clean, like soap—the kind of soap used by a man who cared how he smelled. His hair had been lighter, as well; a blond or maybe a gray.

Frankly, she hadn't encountered anyone else who met the smell-good criteria. She thought of the blond man in the room where her appearance before the powers that be had taken place. He had seemed nearer to her age. Considering his light-colored hair, he could have been the one, though she hadn't been close enough to him during the questioning to pick up on his scent.

Didn't matter, she supposed. They hadn't bought her story so living past this moment was growing more and more unlikely. Not exactly the way she had seen things going. She was still breathing so no need to give up just yet. There might be time to turn this around.

"Are you supposed to kill me?"

Her guard just kept walking, shepherding her along as he went. He wasn't so old. Early forties, maybe. It was difficult to tell. He was tall, reasonably muscled. He looked fit. The woodland greens uniform molded to strong arms and legs and a broad chest. His complexion wasn't as pale as she would have expected considering this place—wherever the hell it was—appeared to be sheltered from the sun. Now that she thought about it, the old men who'd sat around the table, the younger one, as well, had good coloring. They either had tanning beds around here someplace or these people spent time in the sun outside these walls.

But where?

Gardens? Fields? Wasn't part of the doomsday prepper thing attaining self-sufficiency? They either raised their own food or bartered with others of like mind.

"If I'm going to die, why not talk to me? It won't matter in a little while anyway, right?"

Despite her urging, he kept his mouth shut. He led her beyond the quad and all the buildings that seemed to circle the place where she'd been questioned by the group of elders or leaders. The final building they approached wasn't really a building. It was more like a massive carport. SUVs and trucks and a couple of military-type vehicles were parked beneath its expansive canopy. On the far end a long low building with half a dozen overhead doors connected to the covered parking. Vehicle maintenance, she supposed.

The guard didn't stop dragging her along until they were beyond the parked vehicles. Several small metal domes dotted the ground. At first she thought of underground gasoline tanks, but that didn't make sense since four huge tanks stood next to the maintenance building. Maybe the aboveground ones were water tanks. There had to be a water supply in here somewhere.

Her guard ushered her to the nearest dome and opened it. Beneath the metal dome was a steel wheel, the kind you would see on a submarine door. Grunting with the effort, he twisted it to the right and then raised the lid-like door upward. Beyond the door was a ladder that disappeared into the ground.

The guard straightened and reached for her secured hands. When he'd removed her restraints, he gestured to the ladder. "You go on now."

She looked from the hole in the ground to him. "What's down there?"

He stared at her a moment. "You'll see."

"Really? You couldn't think of anything more original than *you'll see*?" She ordered her heart to slow its galloping. This was that moment, the one where she had to decide if she was going to cooperate or make a run for it.

She glanced around. There was no readily visible

place to run. Her guard didn't appear to be armed but that didn't mean that others who were close by weren't. Besides, where the hell would she go? And there were those guard towers.

"Running won't do you no good."

He didn't need a crystal ball or to be a mind reader to recognize what she had on her mind. "Tell me what's down there and I'll get out of your hair."

With a big put-upon breath, he said, "There are people like you down there."

"Prisoners?" She stared him directly in the eyes.

He nodded.

"Are they dead or alive?" That was the big question now.

He shrugged. "Does it matter? Like I told you, there's some things worse than dying. This is one of them."

He said a mouthful with that. So much for rescuing Levi Winters. Then again, maybe he was down there, too. "Well, thanks for the heads-up."

It was now or never. If she was going to make a run for it—

"You see that hole in the wall to your right?"

His words yanked her attention back to him. "What hole?"

Even as she asked the question, a small square opened and the barrel of a rifle extended from the wall. Apparently there were guards monitoring the walls of this place from numerous vantage points, not just the obvious towers she had seen. Running would definitely be a waste of time.

"If you run, you're dead."

Made her decision considerably easier. "Got it."

Sadie put a hand on the ladder and swung one foot, then the other onto a rung. When she'd scaled down about four rungs, the squeak of metal on metal drew her attention upward as the hatch-type door closed. She drew in a big breath and let it go. Nothing to do now but see if there were any other living humans down here.

Thankfully it wasn't completely dark. Emergency-type lighting, dim though it might be, was placed along the downward path. When she reached the bottom of the ladder, a good twenty feet below the hatch, a long tunnel lay ahead of her. More of that dim recessed lighting kept the darkness at bay. The temperature was far cooler down here and there was that earthy, musty smell in the air.

Speaking of air, it was obviously pumped down here somehow. She took another breath. Hoped like hell it was anyway.

"You're the first female we've had down here."

Sadie whipped around at the muttered words. The man stood only inches from her. How had he sneaked up on her like that? Her instincts were generally far more in tune with her surroundings.

"Who are you?" She kept her shoulders square and met his curious gaze without flinching.

Unlike the men in the compound, this man was as pale as a ghost. His hair was a stringy brown and hung down around his hunched shoulders. His clothes were like hers, sweats and a tee, only his looked old and were filthy and ragged. His feet were bare and dirty.

"George." He licked his lips. "What about you? Got a name?"

"Sadie." She braced to make a run for it but decided to hold off until she got a better indication of his intentions. It wasn't as if there was any real place to go and George here likely knew the place like the back of his hand.

"Sadie." He rolled her name around in his mouth as if he were tasting it.

She glanced around again. "What is this place?"

"The big dig." He chuckled, the sound as rusty as his teeth.

She forced her lips into a smile. "Like in Boston. I gotcha. Where are you digging to, George?"

He shrugged one of those bony shoulders. "Wherever they tell us to."

"They tell you things?" She jerked her head up toward the hatch at the top of the ladder.

"Orders. Yeah. They send 'em down along with food and water."

Thank God. That was her next concern. "So they feed you. That's good."

Another of those spasmodic shrugs. "Enough to survive. Most of the time anyway."

Well, great. Just great. "What now, George?"

"Can't say for sure. You work until we hear different." He started forward into the tunnel.

"Work?" Sadie walked alongside him. The tunnel was wide, plenty wide enough for about three people to walk side by side. Overhead, wood and steel supports kept the ground from caving in. This was no slipshod operation. Some amount of engineering know-how had gone into what they were doing.

"On the dig, of course. We're working on a tunnel headed south to Huntland. Already got one finished to Winchester."

"Sounds like a sizable operation."

He croaked another of those rusty laughs. "The Resurrection's got big plans, Sadie."

Clearly. "How many workers are down here?"

"About twenty."

"They're all prisoners?"

"Yep. Some of us were part of them before we screwed up. I guess getting put down here was better than the alternative."

That remained debatable. "What about those who weren't part of the Resurrection?"

"Some were taken from the outside for their knowledge or skill and put down here."

"Knowledge?"

"Contractors. You know, builders. A couple ex-military guys who were assigned to the air force base."

A point she would need to pass along if she ever got out of here. "You have tools and equipment?"

"Sure." He glanced at her, his brown eyes sunken and hollow. "Lots of tools."

Sadie followed him down the length of the first tunnel and then they hit a sort of fork in the road, except there were about four different ways to go. He took the fork farthest to the left.

"Do you dig up to the surface, creating an egress or access point?" This could be a good thing.

He shook his head, deflating her hopes. "Only so far up. The rest is up to them. They do that part from above. We're not allowed to get too close to the surface."

Nevertheless, that meant those areas were closer to freedom. "Sounds like they've got it all figured out."

Her escort grunted an agreement.

The sounds of metal clanging and low voices rumbled in the distance. "We're almost to the dig where we're working now."

Ahead, the outline of bodies moving came into focus. Men wore helmets with attached lights. They swung pickaxes, hefted shovels and other digging tools. A battery-operated jackhammer rattled off. Sadie surveyed the cacophony of activity.

"This is what I'll be doing?"

George stopped and faced her. She did the same. "You give me those flip-flops you're wearing and I'll tell you."

She could do that. They were a sort of one-size-fits-all and pretty much worthless as foot protection went. "Sure."

As soon as she kicked off the footwear, he snatched the thongs and tugged them onto his grimy feet. When he'd finished, he looked directly at her and held up his end of the bargain. "We'll get the word—usually don't take long, I'd say between now and tomorrow—then we'll know whether you're a worker or supplies."

"Supplies?" A frown creased its way across her forehead. Deep inside she had a very bad feeling this was the worse-than-dying thing the guard had mentioned.

"Sometimes they stop feeding us. Like when we don't get as much done as they want. Some of us get sick and can't work as fast. They punish us then. If you're supplies, then you'll be the emergency food."

Oh hell.

He shrugged those bony shoulders again. "You'd be surprised how long even someone as skinny as you will last."

She glanced around. Said the only thing she could think to say in response to that unnerving statement.

"Doesn't seem as though you have any way to keep your *supplies* from going bad."

"No need. We wouldn't eat you all at once. We always keep supplies alive as long as possible. Take an arm or a leg, then another when that one is gone. It works out pretty good. By the time the supplies is dead, we can finish off the edible parts before they start to rot."

Made an eerie kind of sense, she supposed. Unless you happen to be the main course.

No one paid much attention to them as they arrived at the worksite. The man who'd served as her guide—George—handed her a pickax and motioned to a spot for her to start. Sadie walked wide around the other workers and started hefting the ax. She couldn't help glancing over her shoulder now and then just to make sure no one was watching her. Most of the group looked like the man who now sported her flip-flops. Baggy, ragged clothes. Long, stringy hair. Filthy. Pale and weary looking.

Now that she had arrived they didn't talk so the only sounds were the pecking and scraping at the earth. The rattling jackhammer. And in those rare moments of silence, the breathing and grunting. During the next few minutes several things crossed her mind. Where did they sleep? Relieve themselves? And if she was the only female to show up, would she be raped if she tried to sleep?

Maybe she would ask George the next chance she got.

A loud sound like the single dong of a doorbell echoed through the rhythmic poking and pecking and grunting. She glanced around, her attention settling on

George. He put down his shovel and started back the way they had come. The other workers looked from George to her before going back to work.

Apparently the news had arrived. Maybe dropped down from the top of that ladder the way she basically had been.

Her fingers tightened on the handle of the ax.

She supposed she would know soon enough if she was to be a permanent worker or emergency supplies.

Smith waited for Prentiss to show up.

He'd asked for a meeting with the man immediately after the Council questioned Buchanan. The old man had decided to take his time. He knew Smith was not happy with the decision and he wanted him to wallow in his frustration.

Smith crossed the Council's private meeting room and stared out the window. For more than three decades the Resurrection had been clawing its way into this mountainside. Back then there had been only whispers about a group of doomsday survivalists sprouting up in Franklin County. No one really knew or understood what they were. Smith wasn't sure if even those early leaders of the small group understood what they would become over time.

Smith shook his head. They had become something entirely different from what they once were—from what they were supposed to be. Preparing to survive mankind's destruction of himself was one thing, preparing for a war with those not like-minded was something else altogether.

But things had escalated in the past decade. Now it

was about power and greed for the few rather than the safety and survival of the many.

"Making you wait was unavoidable."

Smith turned to face the man who had entered the room. Rayford Prentiss was an old man now, but that didn't stop him from being utterly ruthless. Age had not mellowed him at all—in fact, it had done the opposite. He was as mean as hell and cared nothing for human life.

Prentiss poured himself a hefty serving of bourbon and lifted the glass to his lips. Smith watched, his patience thinning all the more with each passing moment. But he would not allow this bastard to see his mounting discontent. He couldn't let that happen until the time was right.

Soon, very soon. Sooner than Smith had anticipated.

The Buchanan woman's arrival and the name she had tossed about was a warning. Something was about to go down. Smith needed to prepare. To do that, information was required—information from Buchanan. Dropping her into the hole had been premature. The move was a blatant challenge against what Smith had suggested.

"You're displeased with my decision about the woman," Prentiss announced as he poured himself a second drink.

"She obviously has connections. Those connections could prove to be valuable."

Prentiss sat the bottle of bourbon back onto the credenza and belted out a laugh. "Because she spouted the name of a man who has been gone from here for years? If she had connections, she would know that Pollard is likely dead and buried. Of no use or threat to anyone."

"Maybe, maybe not. Either way, you're missing the big picture, old man." Smith strode toward him. "How much longer do you believe you can continue to rule these people like a dictator?"

"You believe you would be better as the head of Council."

It wasn't a question. Smith purposely made no bones about his feelings. He wanted Prentiss to know that his days were numbered. Far more so than he realized. Smith had to bite back the smile. Everything was going to change and this greedy bastard had no idea what was coming.

"You're the only one left who believes in your vision. No one on the Council agrees with your methods. They merely tolerate you out of respect for what once was."

Anger sparked in the old man's eyes. "You mean your father? I've gone too far beyond *his* vision of what the Resurrection was?"

Smith gritted his teeth for a moment. "Don't compare yourself to my father."

Prentiss moved in closer, glared up at Smith, his fury barely held in check. "You were gone for ten years. You only came back when you heard he was dead. If he hadn't named you to the Council with his dying breath, you would be in the tunnels where you belong."

The one thing that had gotten Smith through the past two years was knowing that in the end—when this was all over—he would be able to look Rayford Prentiss in the eyes and tell him the truth that no one else could know. The shock alone would likely kill the old son of a bitch.

Smith lived for that day.

Prentiss cleared his face of emotion. "You would have me change my decision about the woman."

Another statement. "You can do as you please, including change your mind."

No one questioned Prentiss. At least no one except Smith. His first month here, Smith had drawn the line in the sand. So far, Prentiss had not crossed it. He blustered and stomped all around it, but he was careful not to push too far. There were too many who remained faithful to the memory of Avery Flynn. Prentiss wouldn't risk a rebellion. Not at this crucial juncture.

"And why would I change my mind?"

"Buchanan could prove useful," Smith said. "She didn't pull that name out of thin air. Consider how few people know what that name stands for."

Smith had him there and he knew it. Trenton Pollard had been an ATF agent. He was the only one to burrow in so deeply without being discovered. Fury roared through Smith at the memory. Pollard had burrowed deep into Resurrection. Almost took them down and then he disappeared. Except he hadn't gone far. Like the FBI agent Jack Kemp. He'd ended up buried not far from here. But Prentiss didn't know that for sure. No one except Smith knew. Although Kemp had been a casualty of the Winters family, he and Pollard had been after the same goal: the end of the Resurrection.

They weren't the first but they were the most memorable—the ones who had infiltrated the deepest.

Until now.

Prentiss made a face of dismissal. "I have my doubts as to any potential use she might prove to have."

"Are you willing to take that risk?" He wasn't. Smith was well aware that his bravado was merely for show.

Particularly now that the possibility had been publicly brought to his attention. He would never give Smith that kind of ammunition to use against him if he turned out to be wrong. "At the very least she could prove a valuable bargaining chip in the future."

"Very well. For you, I will change my mind. But the risk is yours. If she becomes a liability, she will be your liability."

The two stared at each other for a long moment. Smith imagined Prentiss wished him dead. The feeling was mutual.

But not just yet.

"One day, old man, you'll learn to trust my judgment."

Prentiss made a scoffing sound. "Perhaps."

The old man walked out, leaving Smith staring after him. Rayford Prentiss would know soon enough.

Smith summoned the guard who had been assigned to Buchanan's security. He wondered if she would ever understand that she owed her life to him. If the two of them survived what was to come, he would see that she recognized what a serious error in judgment she had made coming to this place.

What the hell had she been thinking?

What had the Bureau been thinking?

He supposed it was possible this was some sort of rescue mission. Maybe for Levi Winters, though Smith didn't see him as a valuable enough target to risk the life of an agent.

Whatever had brought her here, she had put a kink in his timeline.

Now he was left with no choice but to make drastic

adjustments. Otherwise everything could go wrong. The past two years of his life would be wasted.

That could not happen.

Chapter 6

Sadie did as she had been ordered and kept digging but part of her attention remained on the man coming toward her. Most of the other workers glanced her way but none dared to stop and stare. They wouldn't risk being caught slacking. The men in charge, George and three others, didn't mind bopping a slacker on the head with a shovel or nudging them in the kidneys with an ax handle. Judging by the scars on some of the workers, things could get a lot worse.

Whether it was survival or just the hint of control that came with being in charge, George and his peers appeared to take their positions very seriously. Maybe there were perks not readily visible. Obviously it wasn't clothes or a good hot bath or more to eat. Everyone in this hole looked the same as far as their state of health, ragged attire and level of filth went.

George stopped a couple of steps from her. "Come with me."

The best she could estimate she'd climbed down that ladder about two hours ago. Already blisters were forming on her hands and her muscles ached from hefting the ax. As much as she didn't look forward to days or weeks or months of this sort of hard labor, she would take that any day of the week over becoming the rest of the crew's dinner.

"Why?" Might as well know now. The whole crew would hear the news soon enough. Why keep everyone in suspense?

"They want you back up there." He jerked his head upward.

Sadie's knees almost gave way on her. "I have to go back up the ladder?"

She framed the question in a less than optimistic manner since the rest of the workers were listening. No need to rub in the idea that she was out of here. If she sounded hesitant or worried maybe they wouldn't feel so bad that they weren't the ones climbing out of this hole. Then again, there was no way to guess what waited for her up there.

There are some things worse than dying.

Still, she preferred continuing to breathe over the alternative.

"Let's go," George said rather than answer her question.

She tossed her pickax to the ground and followed the man back through the long, dimly lit tunnel. He didn't speak, just walked along, his newly attained flip-flops clacking in the silence.

When they reached the ladder, he squinted his eyes

to look at her. "Somebody up there must have plans for you. Once you're down here, you don't usually go back up."

She thought of the man who had visited her in the dark and then of Prentiss. If either of them wanted her back, it couldn't be good. She would know soon enough, she supposed. If Levi Winters was still alive, he was obviously up there. She hadn't seen him down here.

"Guess so." She shrugged.

He nodded toward the ladder. "Thanks for the flip-flops."

She resisted the urge to tell him that if she had anything to do with it, he and the others would not be down here much longer. But she couldn't take the risk. Not to mention, at this point she couldn't guarantee anything. So far this mission had been an epic failure.

"Sure."

She climbed the ladder. As she reached the upper rungs the hatch-type door opened. The guard—the same one from before—waited for her. She blinked repeatedly, then squinted against the brighter light. Maybe it was coming up from the dim lighting, but she realized that the lighting was very similar to sunlight. More so than she had realized. Maybe there were solar tubes or some other discreet way of pumping in sunlight without being easily detected by anyone flying over the area.

The guard closed the hatch and glanced at her feet. He didn't ask what happened to her footwear. He probably had a good idea.

He ushered her away from the small field of domes. She decided since she'd only seen one access point while she was down there, all the other domes must be for pumping air into the tunnels.

"Where am I going now?"

He probably wouldn't tell her but it didn't hurt to ask.

As she'd expected, they continued forward without him responding. When they reached the detention center, they kept walking. Once they were beyond the Council building where she'd been questioned, they reached the area with the row of smaller buildings. He steered her toward the one marked with a number nine. At the door, he knocked and waited.

Sadie's fingers and palms burned and she wished she could wash her hands. The blisters stung. Her gaze drifted down to her feet. And they were filthy. Her pink toenails looked out of place on those feet.

The door opened and the blond man from the group who'd questioned her today stood in the threshold.

He nodded and the guard walked away. "Come inside."

This he said to Sadie. His voice was deep, curt. His silvery gaze unflinching.

Sadie did as he ordered, crossing the threshold and entering unknown territory. Nothing new. Encountering the unexpected was a major part of her mission history. If she and Levi Winters were lucky, this mission would flounder its way to success while they were both still breathing.

Her host closed the door behind her. The cabin-like structure was basically one room. A bed, table and chairs, and a small sofa were the only furnishings. On the far side of the room was a small kitchenette. A door beyond the kitchenette likely led to a bathroom. Next to the bed was a smaller table that appeared to serve as a desk since a laptop sat atop it. All the comforts of home, she mused.

He pulled out a chair from the larger, round table. "Sit."

She sat.

Rather than secure her in some manner as she'd expected, he moved to the other side of the table and sat down, his clasped hands settled on the tabletop.

"You present quite the quandary, Sadie Buchanan."

She had been told this more than once, usually by a superior at the Bureau. The words rarely turned out to be a compliment. More often, she was reminded of proper procedure and other prescribed protocols.

"Tell me what I need to do to rectify whatever the problem is." She placed her hands on the table, wanted him to see the blisters. "I'd like to know I have a place here."

He stared at her for a long while without saying more. She decided he was even closer to her age than she'd first thought. Thirty-five or thirty-six, maybe. He was tall, looked strong and his skin was unmarred by scars, unlike many of those she'd seen above and below ground in this compound. Obviously, he'd never been in a lower-level position.

"I don't trust you."

He said this in scarcely more than a whisper and still the sound startled her. He hadn't spoken in so long, she was caught completely off guard. And there was something else. The harsh whisper was somehow familiar. She studied his blond hair and then she leaned forward, putting her face closer to his, and she inhaled deeply, drawing in his scent.

It was him.

The man who had visited her in the darkness. *Smith Flynn.*

She eased back into her seat. "If it makes you feel any better, I don't trust you, either, Mr. Flynn."

He smiled. The expression was so scant she might not have noticed had she not been staring at him so intently.

"You would be wise to be grateful for my intervention on your behalf."

She met his intent stare with one of her own. "So you're the one who had me yanked back out of that hole." She hummed a note of surprise. "Interesting."

Made sense, she supposed, since she'd been brought directly here.

"Is that your way of saying thank you?"

She stared directly into those silvery eyes for a long moment before she answered, opting to give him a taste of his own medicine. "Should I be thankful?"

He glanced at her blistered palms. "I can send you back, if you prefer. The rest of the Council recommended you for emergency supplies."

Damn. She moistened her lips, tried her best not to show how immensely grateful she was not to still be in that hole. "That won't be necessary. I am thankful you rescued me, Mr. Flynn. I suppose I'm a little worried about why you would go against all the others."

"You need a bath, Agent Buchanan."

He pushed back from the table and walked to the door. When he opened it, her guard still waited on the other side. "Get her cleaned up and put back in her cell," Flynn ordered.

"Yes, sir."

Sadie didn't wait to be told what to do next. She pushed to her feet and headed for the door. When she stood next to this man who had saved her for now, she hesitated. "Will I see you again?"

"If you do as you're told, you will see me again."

She walked out, followed the guard in his camo uniform. As usual, he said nothing. Relief sagged her shoulders. She was tired and hungry. Maybe after the bath she would be allowed to eat.

She decided to go broke on information. "I haven't seen Levi Winters. Is he in solitary or something?"

The guard didn't respond.

"He's been here longer than me," she went on, as if he'd spoken. "Maybe he's already assigned to a job. I didn't see him at the big dig."

At the door to the detention center, he finally looked at her. "You don't need to worry about anyone but yourself. That's the way you stay alive. You do what you're told and you don't ask questions."

She nodded. "Got it."

Inside, he took her to another room, not her cell, and ordered the female in the white uniform there to see that she got cleaned up. This was only the second time she'd seen another woman. When her guard had left, Sadie turned to the other woman. "Hi."

The woman looked her up and down. "After your bath we'll do something for those blisters."

Sadie followed her to a large room that was mostly a huge shower. Three freestanding tubs sat to one side. Hooks along the wall were likely for towels. The other woman turned on the water in one of the tubs and then she left the room. More than ready for cleaning up, Sadie walked over to the tub and started to undress.

The woman returned with a towel, more of the ugly sweats and a pair of sneakers. "Size seven?" She glanced at Sadie's feet as she asked the question.

Sadie nodded. "Yes, thanks."

"Don't linger too long," the woman said. "When you're done, come back to my office."

Sadie nodded and thanked her again. The woman disappeared.

The extra-warm water felt amazing as she stepped into it. She ignored the burn when it covered her hands. A sigh slipped from her lips as she permitted herself a moment to relax. She had earned it by God. The woman had said not to linger so she didn't. She washed her hair and smoothed what appeared to be homemade soap over her skin. When she was finished, she dried off and pulled on the clothes. Still no underwear and no socks, but she was grateful for something more than flip-flops.

She exited the shower room and walked in the direction she'd come. The only other door went into the woman's office. It looked more like an exam room. The woman got up from her desk and gestured for Sadie to sit in the only other chair.

Sadie watched as she gathered gauze, tape and some sort of salve. "You're a nurse?"

The woman glanced at her. "I am."

She was young. Midtwenties, Sadie decided. "They let you go to nursing school?"

The woman paused in her work of applying salve to Sadie's palms.

Damn, she'd obviously asked a question she shouldn't have. "Sorry. I was just curious."

"I had just finished nursing school in Tullahoma when they brought me back here."

Sadie held her gaze. "Oh."

The other woman's attention flitted away as she wrapped gauze around Sadie's right hand. "I thought I didn't want to come back but then they told me I'm getting married this year." Her face lit with a smile. "I was happy then."

Sadie moistened her dry lips. The young woman had gotten a taste of freedom during nursing school and she hadn't wanted to come back so they had dangled a carrot. "Who's the lucky guy?"

"His name is Levi. We met a long time ago but then he left. I never forgot him. I always told my father I missed him."

"Levi Winters?" Was that possible?

She nodded. "You know him?"

Sadie gave her head a slight nod rather than flat-out lie. "Who's your father?"

"Rayford Prentiss." She beamed another smile. "The head of the Council. He has many children here. Of course, we're all grown up now. My father says it's time for more children."

The picture cleared for Sadie. The Resurrection numbers were dwindling and Prentiss intended to plump up the population.

"Are there lots of married couples here?"

"Some, yes. But more are getting married this year. Some of us will be moving out, integrating into the outside communities. It's—" She snapped her mouth shut and her face paled as if she'd only just realized she had said way too much to a prisoner.

"I understand," Sadie said quickly. "It's a great plan. Mr. Prentiss is a visionary."

The other woman's smile returned. "He is. I didn't want to see it when I was younger, but I see it clearly now."

Sadie wondered if the powers that be at the Bureau and the ATF had any idea what Prentiss was planning.

The man had his sights set on far more than this compound.

Smith ran hard, pushing for another mile. There were times when he left the compound for Council business but this was the only way he left the compound on a daily basis. He ran six miles every day. Did the rest of his workout in the rec center at the compound. But when he ran he needed the freedom he couldn't get within the center running around and around a track. To find that freedom he ran through the woods. He had a route that took him through the areas where he was less likely to run into another human. Only once had he encountered another man and he'd been a hunter with no desire for small talk. He'd been on a mission that involved prey of the four-legged kind.

Smith made his usual quick stops. Leaned against a tree in one location and pretended to check his right shoe. There was nothing on the ground at the base of the tree. Nothing tucked into the moss. Then he moved on. His next stop was the sparkling stream that bubbled out from the mountainside. He knelt on one knee and cupped his hand for a drink. The water was crystal clear and cool despite the heat of the late summer days. He scanned the rocky bottom of the stream as he drank. Nothing. He sipped the water and then moved on. There was one final stop, the rocky ridge where he stopped again. This time he tied his shoe. There was nothing tucked between the stones.

No message.

He had been certain there would be something. A warning of some trouble headed his way. Or of some planned rebel uprising. The one time that had happened had secured once and for all his position on the Council. This time, however, he'd expected news of Sadie Buchanan's true mission. Some word of other trouble he should anticipate. But no message had been sent.

There could be only one explanation. Buchanan's mission was off the books, in all probability unsanctioned.

She was on her own.

Damn it. He couldn't take care of a rogue federal agent and complete his own mission. He was already on thin ice with Prentiss.

The memory of Avery Flynn carried a great deal of weight, as did his warning when a rebel faction had planned a takeover. But Prentiss remained more respected. If a choice had to be made between the two of them, Smith would not likely come out on top.

There was one other thing he could do. He could go down to the church and find the most recent newspaper. A message went into the classifieds only if there was no other option. If his contact had felt he was being watched in the woods, he would not leave a message at any of the regular drops.

Smith headed in that direction at a steady pace. His destination was just over three miles so less than half an hour was required to make the journey. He would have been able to go much faster if not for the winding, rocky paths through the woods. The paths were ones used by hunters and hikers, nothing made by anyone who belonged to the Resurrection.

He and the others were careful not to make new paths and to stay on the ones made by others. Slowing as he approached the church, Smith surveyed the area to ensure no one was about. The church was now defunct. Marcus Winters and his sister Sierra had been outed by their sister, who had recently been released from prison.

That was the way of secrets. They could only be kept for so long before they were found out.

His secret wouldn't keep much longer. He could not accommodate this unforeseen hitch. There was no leeway in his schedule for Sadie Buchanan and whatever trouble she had dragged in with her.

The church was empty as he'd expected. He walked to the road and checked the paper box that hung beneath the official mailbox. With the local newspaper in hand, he strode back to the church and sat down on the front steps. He opened the paper and carefully skimmed the classifieds. Nothing.

But the name Trenton Pollard had been a clear warning. He tossed the paper aside and stood. Something was happening and he needed to be able to prepare for whatever that something was.

What if his contact had been compromised?

There was no way to know.

Smith heaved a breath and returned to the woods. He picked his way back to a familiar path and jogged for a couple of miles. In the two years since going undercover he had not been faced with a situation like this one. But he'd understood this time could come. His contact could be compromised. The man was older; he could very well have fallen ill or died. Time would be required for a replacement to be situated.

The only question was whether or not Smith had the time.

He slowed to a walk when he was within a mile of the compound. For now there was little he could do beyond moving forward as if Sadie Buchanan had not suddenly appeared.

The Levi Winters issue had apparently been rectified. Prentiss had decided to use him as a breeder. Smith still found that abrupt decision strange. Had that been the beginning of whatever was happening? Perhaps Sadie Buchanan was not the real problem. Maybe it was Winters.

His brother, Marcus, had been a reliable ally for many years. Levi had been an on-again, off-again dabbler. He had been involved with Jack Kemp—yet another reason Smith couldn't understand Prentiss's sudden decision to keep him for any purpose.

Smith ensured he was not being followed as he ducked into the camouflaged pedestrian entrance to the compound. Whatever Prentiss was up to, he would keep it to himself until he was ready to move. He never shared a strategic move that involved security with any of the other Council members, much less Smith. He was far too paranoid.

There was nothing to do but remain vigilant and see how the situation played out.

Prentiss was a very astute man. He had not hung on to his position as leader of the Council by being naive or weak.

Smith supposed he should be grateful he had managed to abide the man this long. Certainly he could claim at least one record.

No one else had ever lived a lie right in front of Rayford Prentiss for this long.

Chapter 7

"Where are we going now?"

Sadie felt grateful for the bath and the clean clothes and in particular for the salve and the bandages on her hands. But she still had a mission to attempt completing. She needed to find Levi Winters. Obviously he was still alive if Prentiss had planned his marriage to one of his daughters. Sadie decided not to try to figure out if the woman was his biological child. The idea that the old man could have dozens of children by different women made her feel ill, especially if the women had not been willing participants in the endeavors.

"The cafeteria."

Her attention slid back to the man at her side. The rumble in her stomach warned that it had been way too long since she had fueled up. No question. But maybe the trip to the cafeteria was about a new job for her.

Just because she was being taken there didn't mean she would be allowed to eat.

"To work?" she asked since her guard seemed a bit more receptive to answering questions now.

"To eat."

This time her stomach growled loud enough for him to hear, too.

He grunted. She supposed that was as close to a laugh as he would permit, but she didn't miss the glint of humor in his eyes.

They entered the detention center. This time their journey took them to the left when they reached the connecting corridor that led to the cells on the right. At the end of the left corridor a set of double doors stood, the word *Cafeteria* emblazoned across the pair.

At the doors he hesitated. "Go to the serving line. Get your food and sit down. Eat and don't get into trouble. I'll be back for you in fifteen minutes."

She nodded her understanding and walked through the doors. Her guard didn't follow. There was probably a separate cafeteria for the people who belonged. There were maybe a dozen people, all wearing the same attire as she did, seated around the four tables. When she stepped up to the serving line, the man behind the counter grabbed a plastic tray and dumped beans, bread and something not readily identifiable but green in color onto the tray.

Sadie accepted the tray and walked toward the tables. Stainless steel water pitchers and cups sat on each table. The other prisoners were male. Not surprising since the number of females she had met were few and far between. The other prisoners eyed her suspiciously as she passed. She caught snatches of conversation about working in the fields or the laundry facility. There was one who sat alone at the table farthest from the serving line. He stared at his plate, visibly forcing his spoon to his mouth, chewing and then repeating.

Relief swam through Sadie. It was Levi Winters. Even in the baggy sweats and with his head bowed, she recognized him. She headed for his table, pulled out a chair and sat. Before she spoke, she reached for the pitcher and poured herself a glass of what appeared to be water. Just plain water, she hoped. Hopefully not laced with some drug to keep them under control. She still believed the man—Flynn—who had come into her room in the middle of the night had only been able to do so without her knowledge because she had been drugged with a mild sedative.

When she had downed a bite of bland-tasting beans and dry bread, she glanced at her tablemate. "You okay, Levi?"

He glanced up at the use of his name, stared at her for a moment. "Do I know you?"

She shook her head. "My name is Sadie. Your sister Cece sent me."

Hope lit in his eyes. "Is she okay?"

Sadie smiled. "She's doing great. Her name has been cleared and they've sorted the truth about what really happened when your father was murdered."

Cece had given Sadie a specific message for Levi. "Cece wanted you to know that everything is fine and none of what happened was your fault. She just wants you safe and back home."

His hopeful expression fell, and he stared at his plate once more. "They'll never let me go."

"Do you want to marry the girl?"

His head came up, his fearful gaze colliding with Sadie's. "I don't even know her. Prentiss said when I was a kid my father promised me to him for one of his daughters. He said if I didn't do exactly what was expected of me they'd put me in the tunnels." He shook his head, shuddered visibly. "I've heard about what happens to the folks who end up down there."

Nothing good. Sadie knew this firsthand. She glanced around. "Don't worry. I'll get you out of here. Just stay calm and trust me."

A frown furrowed his brow. "I don't know who you are but you're crazy if you think we'll get out of here alive. No one does. You either do what they say, or you're never seen again."

Sadie gave him a reassuring smile. "Like I said, just stay calm. Do as you're told until I tell you different."

His eyes rounded, his attention shifting over her shoulder.

Sadie glanced back just in time to see a man coming toward her. He didn't look happy. In fact, he looked angry. She stood, putting herself between Levi and the threat. "You have a problem, pal?"

The man stopped, evidently surprised that she stood up and faced him. He glared at her. "I'm going into the tunnels, because of you." He stabbed a finger into her chest. "You're damn right I have a problem."

He called her one of those truly ugly names that no woman ever wanted to be called and then he spit in her face.

Sadie swiped away the spittle with the sleeve of her sweatshirt. "I hate to hear that, but I didn't make the decision. Mr. Prentiss probably did. Why don't you take it up with him?"

His face blanched at the mention of Prentiss's name. Sadie gave herself a mental pat on the back for the quick thinking.

The man glared at her a moment longer, then walked back to his table. Sadie dragged her chair around to the end of the table and sat where she could see the rest of the people in the room. She snagged her tray and pulled it down to where she sat and forced herself to eat. Food was necessary to survival. She tasted the water—it seemed okay so she drank it down, quenching the thirst that had been dogging her since she arrived.

One by one the other prisoners in the cafeteria got up, tray in hand, and readied to leave. On their way to the tray drop, they passed Sadie, flinging whatever food they hadn't eaten at her.

She ignored them, kept shoving beans and bread into her mouth. From time to time when the food hit her in the face she flinched, but otherwise she showed no outward sign of discomfort or fear. They were all ticked off at her now. She had been pulled back from the tunnels and one of them was going in. They likely believed it was only because she was a woman. The truth of the matter was, Sadie had no idea why she'd been pulled out of the tunnels. Luck? Not likely.

"I wish I was as brave as you."

Sadie glanced at Levi. She gave him a reassuring smile. "You're doing pretty damned good, Levi. Cut yourself some slack. And don't worry, we'll be out of here before you know it."

He shook his head. "You don't understand."

Judging by his defeated expression he was more worried than relieved to know she was here. "What is it that I don't understand? I came here to find you and get you out. I will make it happen."

He swallowed hard, his throat seizing with the effort. "They're listening. I couldn't tell you. I had to do what I was told." He stood, picked up his tray. "I'm sorry. Really sorry."

As Levi walked away Sadie wondered how she had allowed her defenses and her instincts to fail her so thoroughly. She'd made an elementary mistake. One that would likely carry a heavy cost—like her life. She should have considered that Winters would have been brainwashed or indoctrinated to some degree by now.

"Well, hell."

She stood to take her tray to the drop zone but her guard appeared. "Leave it," he said, his expression as unreadable as his tone.

Sadie deposited the tray back on the table and followed the guard out of the cafeteria. The corridor was empty. The prisoners who had thrown food at her had either returned to their cells or were back at work. The guard led her back to her cell. He held her gaze a moment before he closed and locked the door. She could swear she saw a glimmer of regret in his eyes.

If the guard was feeling sorry for her, she was definitely screwed.

Smith stepped out of the shower and dried his body. There had to be a reason he hadn't been given additional intelligence about Sadie Buchanan via his contact. The name she had tossed out, Trenton Pollard, was a code phrase warning that trouble was headed Smith's way. But there was nothing else. No message at any of the usual drop sites.

He pulled on clean jeans and a freshly laundered shirt. The dress code was fairly simple for Council members. They wore whatever they liked. Most moved back and forth between the compound and the outside community. But not Smith. He stayed here. Didn't take chances by lingering in the community.

The guards wore the camo while the workers were issued the sweats. Only those in supervisory positions or who served on the Council were allowed to wear civilian attire. The clear distinction was one of the things Flynn hated most about this place…this life.

No one should be made to feel inferior to others. One's way of life should be based on choice, not a dictatorship led by one insane, self-centered man. How the hell had so many been drawn into this life? Then again, the world was changing, and those interested numbers were dwindling.

A knock at his door drew his attention there. He finished lacing his boots and stood. "Enter."

The door opened and one of Prentiss's personal bodyguards, this one named Mitchell, stepped inside.

"Mr. Prentiss would like to see you in his private quarters."

The old man rarely summoned Smith unless there was a Council meeting…or trouble. Smith's gut said this was the latter.

"Tell him I'll be there shortly."

Mitchell gave a quick nod, then left, closing the door behind him.

Smith walked to his desk and checked the monitor on his laptop. Buchanan was in her cell. Her bandaged hands and clean sweats told him she'd behaved herself during her cleanup. There were no posted complaints of trouble involving her.

She presented a conundrum. Did he tell her who he was or did he wait for her to admit why she was really here? Her provided story wasn't cutting it for him. There was something more she was hiding.

Prentiss hadn't swallowed it, either. Smith's move this morning had bought Buchanan a little more time, but he couldn't be certain how long that time would last. He had hoped to receive word from his contact this morning to give him some sense of direction. His best course of action at this point was to hold out for any intelligence that filtered in over the next few days, assuming the trouble he worried was coming didn't show first.

Taking his time, he walked to the final cabin on Council Row and knocked on the door. When his father had been alive, he had lived in cabin one. Prentiss didn't like the idea of being that available. He wanted the rest of the Council in front of him, like a wall, protecting him from any danger that forced its way into the compound.

The bastard was a coward.

"Come in."

Smith went inside. The old man sat at his table, a steaming cup of tea in front of him.

"Join me," he offered with a wave of his hand.

Smith pulled out the chair opposite him and settled into it. "I'm good, thanks," he said, declining the tea.

Prentiss sipped his tea for a half a minute before saying, "The Council has had a change of heart."

Smith remained still, his face clean of tells. "Has there been a vote I wasn't informed about?"

Of course there had been. This was how Prentiss conducted business when he wanted something his way. He didn't bother arguing his point, he simply left out the people he felt would vote against him.

"It was an emergency and you weren't available." His gaze locked with Smith's. "Apparently you were on a run or a hike. Some communing with nature."

"I do the same thing every day," Smith reminded him. "Today was no different. You're well aware of my personal schedule."

"Except something occurred while you were out," Prentiss countered. "Your new pet project, Sadie Buchanan, confessed her real reason for being here and it was not that she required sanctuary. She has infiltrated our walls under false pretenses. She represents a threat to our security."

Dread coiled inside Smith. Buchanan hadn't looked as if she'd suffered any torture for information. He couldn't see her voluntarily coming forward with this new and startling information, particularly if it cast her in a negative light.

"Really. That's an interesting development. Why don't you tell me what happened?"

"She told Levi Winters that his sister had sent her here. Buchanan was tasked with coming here to rescue him. The information she fed us was nothing more than a distraction to cover her real mission."

"I'd like to question her again," Smith said. He stood as if the recommendation had already been approved. "I'm confident I can get her full story."

Prentiss held up a hand. "No need. A final decision has already been reached. We're turning her over to the *others*. Levi Winters, as well."

Smith kept his surprise to himself. "You selected Winters for your daughter—"

"The choice was premature. He failed his final test. We don't need his kind here."

"We do need more females. Buchanan wouldn't be the first one we've swayed to our way of thinking." It was the best argument and the most logical one he could come up with at the moment.

The old man eyed him for a long while before he spoke again. "You've been her champion since she arrived. Are you suggesting you've selected her as a wife?"

Before he could answer, Prentiss went on. "You've snubbed each of my daughters, but you would have this traitor? This outlander?"

"As I said—" Smith ignored his suggestions "—she may prove useful in a future negotiation. I have not considered her as a wife, only as a bartering asset."

Prentiss announced, "The Council wants her out of our midst."

"I don't agree, and I have an equal say on Council matters." Smith held his ground. He had a vote in all matters. Prentiss understood this, no matter that he despised the idea. The bastard would not force his hand.

Prentiss stood and walked over to his desk. He picked up a document. "It is decided. The decree is signed, and the message conveyed to the *others*. There is nothing further to discuss. You missed a great deal by being out of pocket this morning, Smith. Perhaps you should rethink your schedule in the future."

"Decrees can be overturned," Smith said, dismissing the other man's declaration. "I'll speak to the Council members."

"There will be no further discussion on the matter. You will escort Buchanan and Winters personally. Tomorrow morning."

Smith stared long and hard at him. "What are you up to, old man?"

He held Smith's gaze, then he smiled. "We make our own beds, Smith. And in the end, we have no one to blame but ourselves for the lack of comfort."

The slightest hint of uneasiness trickled through Smith's veins. This was something more than Sadie Buchanan or Levi Winters at play here.

"At sunrise in the morning you will depart," Prentiss repeated. "You should be back before dark."

Smith didn't waste any more time arguing. Instead, he left and walked straight to the detention center. The guards didn't question him as he entered, nor did anyone attempt to stop him when he walked straight to Buchanan's cell and unlocked the door.

Buchanan turned to face him. She stood on the far side of the small cell as if she'd been pacing the too-confined space. Before she could school the reaction, uncertainly flared in her dark eyes.

He went straight to the point. "What happened today?"

There were ears everywhere on this compound but questioning her was not going to change what had already been done. As a Council member he had a right to know all the facts.

"What do you mean?" She shrugged. "I was pulled back from the tunnels, given an opportunity to bathe and then taken to the cafeteria."

His irritation flared. "Do not waste my time. What happened?"

Her arms folded over her chest. "I ran into an old friend. Gave him a message from his sister. She's been worried about him."

"What exactly did you say?" Fury had him clenching his jaw to prevent saying more than he should.

She heaved a big breath as if he were the one trampling on her last nerve. "I told him who I was and that his sister had sent me to rescue him. I also told him not to worry because I would be getting him out of here."

Well, that sure as hell explained a lot. He stared directly into those dark eyes. "So you lied. Your story was a cover for your real mission."

She gave a succinct nod. "I lied."

"Get some sleep. We leave at sunrise."

He turned his back on her but before he was through the door she asked, "Where are we going?"

He didn't bother glancing back. "To trade a mole for a lost rabbit."

Chapter 8

They knew.

What was worse, she had told the enemy herself.

Sadie closed her eyes and shook her head. She had royally screwed up this one. Flynn had called her a mole. He was taking her from the compound today to trade her for a lost rabbit. One of the Resurrection's own, obviously, who had been taken by another group or some other faction involved with their mutual black market business dealings.

Considering she was FBI, it was possible the lost rabbit was in holding with some branch of law enforcement. The local cops? The feds? She had gotten the impression that as far as Winchester and Franklin County law enforcement were concerned—at least until the takedown at the Salvation Survivalist church—the Resurrection was more a local legend than anything else. A bunch of local yokels with guns they picked up at gun shows and MREs they ordered from the internet.

But that was not the case at all. The Resurrection was a long-term, well-planned and -operated organization with powerful contacts and an extensive reach. At this point, local law enforcement was well aware that gunrunning was involved. In Sadie's experience, drugs and human trafficking oftentimes went hand in hand with the smuggling of weapons. Maybe these daughters of Prentiss's weren't his biological children. Maybe they were stolen children he'd raised in this damned compound.

Sadie paced the few steps to the other side of her concrete cell. She had to finagle an escape. There were people in this place who needed rescuing. There was Levi and the ones in the tunnels. And possibly all the women. Though she had only seen a couple, she suspected there were more. She exhaled a big breath. This situation was far bigger and more complicated than she or anyone else had initially speculated.

It was possible another federal agency, like the ATF or the DEA, knew more than the Bureau about this group. The sharing of information was limited to a need-to-know basis for the safety of any ongoing operations and embedded agents.

She needed more information. She exhaled a resigned breath. What she really needed was backup.

The swish and whir of the lock snapped her attention to the door.

Sunrise had arrived.

The door opened and Smith Flynn met her gaze. He didn't mince words. "Let's go."

She walked toward him, expecting the broad-shouldered man to step aside so she could move through the door but he didn't. He held his ground, staring down at her.

Apparently he had more to say before this party got started.

"From this moment until I tell you otherwise you will do no thinking for yourself. You will do exactly as I say, when I say. Understood?"

Anything to get out of this prison. "Understood."

"We walk out of here, you don't look at anyone, you don't say anything. You follow me and you do exactly as I tell you."

"I can do that."

He turned and headed along the corridor. She followed. As they left the cell behind and reached the exit of the detention center, she didn't spot her guard or any others for that matter. Outside was the same. Her instincts urged her to look back over her shoulder, to look around, but she resisted the impulse. Flynn had told her not to look at anyone. She decided not to test him this early in today's game. Whatever was going to happen from this point forward, she needed to proceed with extreme caution.

She had resigned herself to the idea that she might not be able to escape this place on her own. If she couldn't get out, she couldn't get Levi out. At least if she managed to lose Flynn at some point, she had a chance of getting help back here to rescue Levi.

At this point she was more than a little surprised that Flynn hadn't restrained her hands. They headed

in the direction of where she had spotted all those vehicles parked. The tunnels were in that direction, as
well. Her heart instantly started to pound. She did not
want to end up back down there. If that was what was
about to happen, she had to do something. At least try
to escape. A final ambitious effort even if she was shot
for her trouble.

She bit her lips together to prevent asking him if
that was his intent, simultaneously bracing for fight
or flight. He'd said she was being traded. Surely that
meant they were leaving the compound. Then again,
the guy in the cafeteria had been fired up because he
was being sent to the tunnels in her stead. That was a
trade, wasn't it?

Damn it. A rush of dread roared through her veins.

She was stronger than this. If she allowed the dread
and uncertainty to get to her now, she would lose all
semblance of control over the situation. She might not
have much as it was, but she was still hanging on to
a sliver. Whatever happened, she had to cling to that
modicum of control.

When they reached the motor pool, he opened the
rear passenger door of a black SUV. He reached inside
for something. When he drew back he had two things,
nylon wrist restraints and a black hood like the one
she'd worn on the way here with Prentiss and his thugs.

Movement inside the vehicle had her leaning forward just a little. Someone was already in there. The
black hood concealed everything from the shoulders
up, making it impossible to say if the passenger was
male or female.

Flynn held out the nylon restraint and she offered
her hands, wrists together, for him to do what he had

to do. When her wrists were bound tightly together, he dropped the hood over her head. A hand rested against her upper arm, ushering her toward the open SUV door. She climbed in and settled into the seat.

"Where are we going?" the other prisoner asked.

Sadie recognized the voice. *Levi.* Apparently, he either hadn't received the same lecture she had or he chose to ignore the order.

The door closed and a few moments later the front driver's-side door opened, the SUV shifted slightly and then the door closed again. She resisted the urge to lift her hood and make sure it was Flynn who had climbed behind the steering wheel. He'd secured her hands in front of her so she could certainly do so but, again, she resisted the impulse. If the situation went downhill from here it wasn't going to be because she gave it a shove.

She wanted out of here far more than she wanted to satisfy her curiosity. That Levi was with her was a genuine stroke of luck. If she could salvage this rescue operation, all the better.

The vehicle started to move. About a minute later there was a brief stop, then they were moving forward again. Sadie imagined they had stopped long enough for the doors or gate or whatever to open, allowing them out of the compound. Though she couldn't see to confirm the conclusion, her heart hammered at the idea that they could very well be beyond those suffocating walls.

For the next ten minutes by Sadie's count, they drove fairly slowly. The ride was smooth, making her judgment of the speed not as reliable as it could be. Again, the urge to lift the hood and look around nudged her. She wrestled it away.

At least for now.

"Get down on the floorboard!"

The shouted order startled Sadie and for a split second she couldn't move.

"Get down!"

She tugged at Levi's arm and then scrambled onto the floorboard. Thankfully he did the same.

The shattering of glass and the pop of metal warned they were under assault.

"Stay down as low to the floor as possible," she whispered to Levi. She felt his body flatten in an attempt to do as she said.

The SUV's engine roared and the vehicle rocketed forward. The momentum of the driver's evasive maneuvers swung their weight side to side, made staying down increasingly difficult.

"Stay down," she urged the man hunkered between the seats with her.

The SUV barreled forward, swaying and bumping over the road. Sadie concentrated on keeping her body as low and small as possible. This vehicle likely wasn't bulletproof. The shattered glass she'd heard earlier all but confirmed as much. A stray bullet could end up killing one of them.

If the driver was hit…they would probably all die.

The SUV suddenly braked to a hard, rocking stop.

Another shot exploded through the rear windshield and then a detonation of new sounds. Ripping, cracking, scratching…then a hard crash.

The SUV suddenly lunged forward.

"You can get up now."

Flynn's voice, definitely his voice though it sounded muffled. Sadie recognized it was the blood pounding in her ears that smothered his words. She scrambled upward, swept the glass she felt from the seat and then righted herself there.

"We okay now?" she asked. After what they had just gone through, she figured the rules had changed. Asking if they were out of danger seemed reasonable.

"For now."

"What's happening?" Levi demanded, his voice high-pitched and clearly agitated.

"We're okay," Sadie told him, hoping he would calm down rather than grow more distressed.

She felt his arm go up. She grabbed it, hung on. "Don't do anything until he gives the order," she reminded. "We need to get through this."

At this point, she trusted Flynn on some level whether he deserved that trust or not. But they weren't in the clear yet. She couldn't be sure of his ultimate intent. There was a strong possibility that she and Levi were only valuable if they were still alive. His risky protection measures might be self-serving.

The SUV braked to another sudden stop. Sadie's pulse sped up again.

The hood covering her head was abruptly yanked off. "Get out," Flynn ordered.

He whipped Levi's hood off next and issued the same order to him. Sadie hurried out of the SUV. Levi came out behind her rather than getting out on the other side. The road was not paved. Dirt and gravel. Muddy. It must have rained last night.

She looked up, squinted at the rays of sunlight filtering through the thick canopy of trees overhead.

They were deep in the woods but they were out of that damned prison. The dirt road seemed to cut around the edge of the mountain. To their backs was the mountainside, in front of them was a steep drop-off. As she and Levi watched, Flynn stood outside the driver's-side door and guided the still-running SUV to the edge of the road. He jumped back as the engine roared and the vehicle bumped over the edge of the road, crashing through the trees.

Exactly like the one that had been firing at them, she realized, as the familiar sounds echoed around them. That was the reason for his sudden stop back there. The other driver instinctively attempted to avoid the collision, whipped the steering wheel and ended up going over the edge of the road and down the mountainside.

Sadie watched the man walking toward them. It wasn't until that moment that she noticed the backpack hanging from one shoulder. She didn't have a clue what was in that backpack, but what she did know was that they had no transportation.

She asked, "What now?"

"Now." He pulled a knife from his pocket and sliced through the restraints on her wrists and then did the same to Levi's nylon cuffs. Flynn's gaze locked back on hers. "We run."

The Council had voted.

Fury roared through Smith as he moved through the dense underbrush as quickly as he dared. Buchanan had no trouble keeping up with him, but Winters was slowing them down more than anticipated.

"Keep up," he shouted over his shoulder. Buchanan shot him an annoyed look.

He imagined she had some idea that they were in trouble but he doubted she fully comprehended the magnitude of the situation. The Council had decided to terminate Smith's position within their ranks and, apparently, him. They would want him and the people with him dead as quickly as possible. No loose ends. No way to trace the murders back to them.

This was Prentiss's doing. No one else on the Council would have dared to speak against Smith. The old man had grown worried that the rest of the members preferred Smith's style of progressive leadership.

He had suspected this was coming. Smith had kept his cover intact far longer than anyone expected. Funny thing was, it wasn't until Buchanan showed up that Prentiss found the perfect leverage to use toward this very end.

Smith had two choices: save Agent Sadie Buchanan's life or attempt to salvage his cover.

His cover was shot to hell.

He led them deeper into the woods. Merging into the landscape was the only way they would make it off this mountain alive. For now, they had a head start. The three-man crew Prentiss had sent after them was down. If one or more survived, it was only a matter of time before he climbed up that ravine and called for backup. Staying on the road was out of the question. There were lookouts at certain points along this stretch of road and there was no other drivable egress in the close vicinity. Disappearing between scout stations was the only option. Moving back and forth and in a zigzag pattern was their only hope of outmaneuvering the enemy.

Reinforcements would come like panthers after

prey. Until then, they needed to put as much distance between them and this location as possible. Prentiss would send his team of trackers and they would bring the dogs. Time was of the essence.

Smith knew these woods. He had grown up here and he'd spent most of his time cutting paths through this dense foliage. Over the past two years he had planned for this very moment. There was never any doubt about this moment. It would come and he would need an emergency egress. He just hadn't expected to be bringing two others along with him.

There were answers he would need eventually but there was no time for that now.

"Where exactly are we headed?"

Buchanan pushed up behind him. She was strong, fit. The only good thing about the additional luggage with which he was saddled.

"You'll know when we get there."

"Those were your friends back there, right?"

Before he bothered with an answer, she fell back a few steps. "Hang in there, Levi. We have to keep going."

"Why the hell are we following him?" Winters shouted. "He's one of them."

"That's a good point."

It was the total lack of sound after Buchanan's statement that warned Smith the two had stopped.

He did the same and swung around to face the latest hurdle in this unfortunate turn of events. He visually measured Buchanan before shifting his focus to Winters. "Do you know your way out of here?" He waved an arm to the junglelike growth around them. "We're a lot of miles from the nearest house. You'll need water. I have water. A limited supply, but I have it."

Buchanan glanced at Winters, who now stood beside her. Then she looked up, probably searching for enough of the sky to see in which direction the sun was rising.

"We're heading south," Smith advised. "And we have a long way to go. When my *friends* back there—assuming there are survivors—get a call through to Prentiss… Even without survivors, he'll be expecting a check-in. When that call doesn't come, they'll pour out in droves to find us and they'll bring the dogs. We have to move as fast and as far as possible before that happens."

"Why should we trust you?" Buchanan asked.

She was no fool. She was ready to go but she held out, no doubt to prove to Winters that she was ultimately on his side. She hoped her support would gain his cooperation. If rescuing him had been her original mission, she likely wanted to make that happen. Understandable.

Smith shrugged. "You have no reason to trust me. But I'm going. I know the way. I have the necessary supplies. You can either follow me or you can find your own way. Makes no difference to me."

He pivoted and continued his trek through the shoulder-deep underbrush.

Fifteen seconds later he heard the two coming behind him. They were moving fast, trying to catch up. Whatever Buchanan had said to Winters, she had lit a fire under him. Good. Smith had no desire to end up dead before he'd finished his own mission.

They walked for another three hours before he felt comfortable allowing a water break. There was a small overhang of rocks just up ahead. They would duck under there. It would be cooler close to the earth beneath the outcropping and their position would be hidden from anyone who might be catching up to them. So far he hadn't heard the dogs but that didn't mean someone wasn't out there on the trail. Prentiss would use every method available to him. Losing more control was not an option. Smith almost wished he could see the bastard's face.

He had his doubts about the physical condition of the three who had gone over the mountainside in the other SUV. He doubted any one of them would be capable of giving chase. A call for backup would require time. Forty minutes to an hour to prepare and reach the point where the three of them had abandoned the SUV.

He scanned the trees beyond their hidden position and listened intently. By now, it was more likely than not that search parties were out there. The dogs would ensure they moved in the right direction. The head start Smith had gained was the one thing he had on his side.

Smith downed the last of his water and tucked the empty bottle back into his pack.

"Where are we going?" Buchanan asked.

"To the river. The water is low this time of year but that will work to our advantage. We'll use the water to throw the dogs off our scent."

"I haven't heard any dogs," Winters argued. "Wouldn't they be after us by now?"

"When you hear them," Smith warned, "it'll be too late." He pushed up from the rock he'd used as a seat. "Let's get moving."

He held out his hand for their water bottles. He

tucked each one into his pack and headed out. Buchanan didn't hesitate. Winters did but not for long.

Rested, Smith pushed a little faster. He wanted over this ridge and to the water's edge within the hour. He wouldn't rest easy until they'd put a mile or so wading through the water behind them.

Mosquitoes swarmed when he pushed through the foliage. He ignored the occasional bite. Behind him he heard his followers swatting at the irritating insects. The ground was rockier here, making him less sure-footed. Still he pushed as fast as he dared.

By dark he would reach the safe place where he would be able to use the emergency device that would summon backup. Smith had nothing against local law enforcement in Franklin County, or the neighboring counties, for that matter, but he had an obligation to ensure there was no breach in security. The only way to do that was to use the communication device he had hidden and to call his contact and no one else.

The rumble of curt conversation droned behind him. He didn't slow down or bother to look back. He couldn't force either of them to follow him. More important, he could not share who he was or his mission with either of them, either. If they were captured, Buchanan might survive torture without talking but Winters would not.

Besides, Smith saw no reason to share that information until absolutely necessary for his own protection, as well.

"Why did my sister send you to find me?" Winters asked the woman two or three steps in front of him.

Evidently, Winters had decided to question all aspects of his good fortune. Some people just couldn't be satisfied by merely being rescued from certain death.

Buchanan kept her voice low as she answered the question. Smith didn't catch all that she told the ungrateful man. Something about his sister being worried and the local police being concerned that the Resurrection group were a more considerable threat than they had estimated.

Smith could tell them exactly how big the threat was, but he had to get out of this situation first.

"Why you?" was Winters's next question.

Smith slowed, diminishing the distance between them. He would like to hear the answer to that one.

"That's what I do," Buchanan said, practically under her breath. "I rescue other agents or assets who get themselves into trouble."

Well, well, he'd known the lady wasn't the average federal agent. Interesting that she was a rescue and retrieval specialist.

"I guess this time isn't working out so well," Winters said with a dry laugh. "Just my luck."

"We're not beaten yet," she protested. "I've never failed before. I don't intend to start now."

Smith hoped the lady was right.

Failure would mean a very bad end for all of them.

Chapter 9

They had been walking for most of the day. Her sneakers were still wet from the slog through a mile or more in that narrow river. The water level had been low but hopefully it was enough to throw the trackers and their dogs off their scent.

The sun was going down and the trees were thick but it was still as hot as hell. Sweat beaded on Sadie's forehead. Her legs ached. She was in damned good physical condition but this went way beyond her usual workout. This was grueling. They'd been going up-hill until the past hour. The downhill journey wasn't much better, just used a different muscle group. The under-canopy brush remained thick and the landscape was rocky.

She had tried to keep Levi calm and focused on moving forward but he was resisting more and more the farther they went on the desperate journey. She wasn't sure how much longer she could keep him cooperative. His misgivings were understandable, reasonable even. But they had little choice. Keeping ahead of the enemy had to be their priority.

So far they hadn't heard any sign of the dogs Flynn had worried about. Thank God. Their stoic leader had stopped several times and listened for anyone who might be following them. He hadn't heard or spotted anyone yet. She hadn't, either, and she was keeping her eyes and ears tuned in as keenly as possible. She did not want to be captured by those bastards. Chances of surviving beyond the trip back to the compound were way less than zero.

If they were caught, they were dead.

"How far now to the destination you've targeted?" She had to admit, she was damned tired, not only physically but of blindly following orders. But she would keep going until they reached some semblance of safety or until she found reason to do otherwise.

"It's a ways yet."

Flynn said this without looking back.

Something about his nonchalance bugged the hell out of her. "Define *a ways*."

He stopped. She almost bumped into his broad back. He wheeled around, his glare arrowing in on her and she stumbled back a step.

"We've been lucky so far, let's not screw that up now. We'll get there when we get there. Just keep moving and stay quiet."

He gave her his back and started forward again.

So much for getting an update. Sadie trudged after him.

"I'm done." Levi glanced covertly at her. "I know

where we are now. I just want to go home." He jerked his head toward the faint path Flynn left in his wake. "We can't be sure what he's got planned. I'd feel better taking my chances on my own from here. I can do it. You should go with me."

Sadie slowed, keeping pace with Levi. She glanced at the man disappearing deeper into the woods. "You sure about that, Levi? If they catch us, it's doubtful we would survive. Let's get through this night and we can decide how we want to move forward in the morning."

"Just let me go." He started backing away from her. "Hell, the best I can tell, he's leading us away from Winchester. My sister and the people I trust are that way." He jerked a thumb to his left.

"Let's catch up with him and confront him about your concerns." She had a bad, bad feeling about this. "We'll figure out the best option. We're safer in a group."

Levi shook his head and took off in another direction. West, Sadie decided. She went after him. As curious as she was about whatever Flynn had in mind, Levi was the one she'd come to rescue. She had a duty to keep him safe, even when he made it difficult.

She wanted to call out to Levi but she couldn't risk that the enemy was close. The last thing she wanted was to draw Prentiss's people.

She pushed harder to catch up with him. All this time he'd dragged behind. Apparently he'd gotten his second wind. They hadn't made it far when she heard someone behind them. Adrenaline fired through her veins. She glanced over her shoulder and spotted Flynn.

Levi ran harder. Sadie did the same. But Flynn was gaining on them.

In the next moment Sadie had to decide whether to keep going with Levi or to distract Flynn, giving the younger man an opportunity to reach his sister and help. If Flynn had no real interest in what happened to them, why come after them? Why not just let them go?

Something was wrong with this scenario.

And if Levi was familiar with the area and knew the way home, why not give him a chance to make it?

Decision made, she zigzagged, heading south once more. She held her breath until Flynn shifted his direction and came after her.

She ran harder still, determined not to make it easy for him to catch her.

She sidled between two trees; her shoulder scraped hard against one. She cringed. That would leave a mark.

Keep going.

Maintaining her balance at this speed and along this rough terrain as she plowed through brush and dodged the bigger trees was not an easy task, especially downhill.

No slowing down! He was close. Only steps behind her. She could hear him breathing.

Damn, she needed to go faster.

Fingers grabbed the back of her sweatshirt. Yanked her off her feet.

They went down together, rolled in the brush. A limb poked her cheek. She grimaced.

Flynn landed on top of her, his bigger body grinding her into the brush and dirt.

"What the hell are you trying to do? Guarantee we end up dead?"

She tried to scramble away. Screaming was not an

option. If there was anyone out there on their trail, they would hear.

Better the devil she knew…

"Get off me," she growled.

He glared at her for a long moment, those silver eyes icy with fury.

Then he got up, pulled her up with him and kept a death grip on her arm. He had no intention of allowing her to run again.

"That little move you pulled back there, allowing your friend—your rescue target—a chance to run, likely put a bullet in his brain or worse."

Uncertainty trickled into her chest as she struggled to catch her breath. "He knows how to get home from here. He said you're taking us in the wrong direction. Is that true?"

Frustration hardened his face. "That depends on where you think the right direction is. He's going home to Winchester? To his friends?" He laughed, shook his head. "I hope he makes it, but that's highly unlikely. They have watchers in town. Those watchers will be on the lookout for all of us. The possibility that he'll make it to help before someone nabs him right off the street is about the same as Santa paying him a visit early this year. He won't make it. Do you hear me? He. Will. Not. Make. It. Which is why we're not going directly to Winchester. I have a safe place to wait for help."

That trickle of uncertainty turned into a river. "Then I have to go after him."

When she would have headed back in the direction she'd come, he held on to her more tightly.

"You're going to draw them right to us. We have to

go. We've wasted too much time already. The only way you can help Levi now is by doing exactly what I say."

She stared at him, tried to see beyond that iron mask of his. "Who are you?" She had no real reason to trust this man and yet every instinct screamed at her to do exactly that.

"You already know the answer to that question. Right now, I'm the man who's trying his best to save your life."

"How can I be sure?"

She waited for an answer, held his gaze. He needed to give her something concrete. Why would a man so high up the food chain in the Resurrection organization suddenly throw everything away and run just to save her or anyone else?

"You answer a question for me and I'll answer one for you," he countered.

"Quid pro quo," she suggested.

He gave a succinct nod.

She could do that. He pretty much already knew all there was to know about her anyway. She'd owned being a federal agent. She'd made the mistake of spilling her true mission to Levi. Beyond her last boyfriend, this guy probably knew everything there was to know about her, including her favorite college professor's name.

"All right." She braced for his question.

"Why did you use the Trenton Pollard cover story? Where did you get that name?"

"That's actually two questions," she pointed out.

He gave her a look that said he was running out of patience.

"That was the name I was told to toss out if I needed more leverage in a dicey situation."

"Who gave you the name?"

"My point of contact."

More of that frustration tightened on his face. "He or she has a name?"

She nodded. "But I'm not giving that name to you until I see where this journey ends."

He shrugged. "Fine. Let's get moving."

"Wait a minute. I get a question, too."

"So ask your question so we can go."

"Why does the Pollard name mean so much to you?"

"He's a friend of mine and I don't see how you or your point of contact could know him."

Done talking, he started forward again. She glanced over her shoulder. Hoped like hell Levi knew what he was doing. She followed Flynn. If Flynn was truly on the run, her money was on Prentiss and his people coming after him first. Finding him and Sadie was likely far higher on their priority list than finding Levi.

Hopefully that would work in his favor until he reached help.

Either way, he'd made his decision and she'd done the only thing she could: helped him escape an unknown situation.

They were close. Smith was relieved. He wasn't sure how much longer Buchanan would last. She'd held up far longer than he'd expected as it was. She was strong but they were both tired.

The safe place he'd prepared wasn't far now.

"Give me a minute."

Smith stopped, sized her up as she leaned against

a tree. He shrugged off the pack and removed the last bottle of water. "We can share this one," he offered, passing the bottle to her.

This last one would have been for Winters but he'd cut out on them without any supplies. Smith wondered how far he would get before a member of Prentiss's posse caught him. Not all the way into town for sure.

He watched as she opened the bottle and downed a long swallow. When she came up for air, he said, "We're almost there."

She choked out a dry laugh. "That's what you said an hour ago. I'm beginning to think you're lost, Flynn." Her gaze locked with his. "I hope that's not the case."

"Being lost is one thing you do not have to worry about, Buchanan."

He knew this place inside and out. He'd explored every square mile in his youth. Always looking for something different, something else. He'd never found it here. Leaving had been the only way to escape this life and the people he had grown to hate. His father had been the only voice of reason among the group of preppers who had started the Resurrection. When Avery Flynn had fallen ill, Prentiss had taken over and changed things without his knowledge. He'd started to dabble in criminal activities. Smith's father had never wanted to cross that line. There had been fringes of his followers who'd gotten caught up in the black marketing of weapons and even in transporting drugs, but he'd always weeded them out in time.

But when his father lost control, it all went to hell.

Smith hadn't come back to make things right. It was too late for that. Too many of the old-timers were gone and too much of the younger blood was greedy and power hungry. The extremists without conscience had taken over. He'd come back to take them down. It wasn't what his father would have wanted but his father had been wrong. Anywhere those with extreme attitudes and beliefs gathered, nothing good came of it.

Ever.

"Fifteen minutes," he assured her. "We'll reach our destination in fifteen minutes—barring any unforeseen events."

She screwed the cap onto the water bottle and tossed it to him. "I'm holding you to that."

He downed a long swallow and put the remaining water away. Before he could stop himself, he licked his lips and savored the taste of her. Sadie was different from any woman he'd ever met. She was stronger, determined, loyal. Intelligent. Unconditionally fearless. She stirred his interest in numerous ways.

Shaking off the distraction, he started moving forward again. "Let's go. We don't want to fall behind schedule since you're holding me to it."

She laughed again. He liked the sound of it. "You're a smart guy, Flynn."

Maybe. He hadn't considered himself smart in a long time. The truth was, he hadn't even considered the future until very recently. He had resigned himself to the idea that he would likely die getting this done.

Still could. It wasn't over yet.

The underbrush was thinner here in the rockier soil. Made going a little easier. Being physically exhausted, however, made just moving a chore. It had been a long day. Buchanan wasn't the only one who was beat.

They made the fifteen-minute timeline with a couple of minutes to spare. He pointed to a copse of trees that hugged the mountainside maybe ten yards below their position. The relief on Buchanan's face was palpable.

The overgrowth was thick around the cave opening. He carefully pushed the limbs aside and ducked inside first. There were times when a man should go first—like when he needed to ensure there were no wild animals, no den of snakes holed up in his safe place. Buchanan would likely argue the point with him but there were some things his father had taught him that stuck. *Always protect those under your care.*

Something else she would argue. Fiercely, no doubt.

He tugged the flashlight from its holder on the side of his pack and scanned the small shelter. Clear. No sign of animals. As often as he could get out here he sprayed the area with repellant to ward off animals but some critters weren't so easily put off. Thankfully the place was clean, no animal droppings. No snakes.

"You can come in." He held back the limbs, ensuring he didn't break any. Those limbs acted like a curtain, providing a layer of camouflage.

Once she was inside, he used his flashlight to locate his stored supplies. The cave was only about fifteen feet deep and the last five or six feet narrowed down to the point where crawling was the only option. He'd banged his head plenty of times. At the very back, he carefully moved the stacked stones he'd gathered in the immediate area. All looked exactly as if they'd always been right here in this pile. He'd gone to a great deal of trouble to ensure no one who might stumble upon this place noticed his stored goods.

Beneath the stack was a nylon bag, pale gray in color, nearly as large as his pack. It was sealed in a clear plastic over bag. Inside he kept his emergency supplies. The plastic was to better protect them from the elements and to ensure the bears and wolves didn't pick up on any scents.

His gut growled as he set the ready-to-eat packets aside. They'd only had a couple of protein bars today. It was time for something a little more substantial.

"What's all this?" Buchanan moved in next to him, sat back on her knees.

"Dinner. A burner phone. Weapon. First-aid supplies." Not so much of the latter but enough to get by in a minor emergency. A packet of blood-clotting agent, a suture kit. Antibiotic salve and a few bandages. "Water. A small blanket. Emergency light. You know, the usual."

There was also a backup plan, which he pocketed without mentioning. He tucked the nine millimeter into his waistband and loaded most of the other supplies into his pack. "You want beef or chicken?"

She studied the two packs of ready-to-eat meals. "I'll take the chicken."

"Good choice." He passed it to her and grabbed the beef.

He moved back to the roomier portion of the cave and opened up the small emergency light. He sat it on the ground. The lumens were low but he didn't want it glowing beyond the cave opening. It was enough. He tossed his guest the thin blanket. It wasn't much but it was better than nothing when one was sleeping on the ground.

"You can use that tonight. I'll use my pack for a pillow. I don't mind sleeping on the ground."

"So we're staying the night here?"

He shrugged. "If that's what it takes."

While she opened the food pack and ate, he fired up the burner phone. Once it was on, he moved to the cave opening to get better service. With a few taps, he sent the necessary message. The phone's battery was way too low. He'd charged it the last time he was here. With it turned off it should have maintained the charge. When the message had been delivered, he relaxed. He returned to where Buchanan sat and settled in for however long they had to wait.

He opened his meal pack and ate slowly, more slowly than he wanted to but it would satisfy him better that way. Buchanan did the same. She'd likely had similar training and understood the need to adapt to extreme change. Being a field agent required a degree of flexibility. That she consumed every bite of the less-than-tasty meal confirmed his conclusion.

When she'd finished, she said, "Tell me about the message and why we may be here all night."

"The message goes into a pipeline of sorts. It takes a while to get to the intended recipient. Once he has it, he'll make arrangements for a pickup. When the pickup is ready, we'll go to the designated location. There are several good options within two miles of our position."

She sipped on the packet of water. "The contact is aware of this location?"

He shook his head. "No one knows this location. It's a security precaution in case there's ever a breach in our communications. I selected this location based on my knowledge of the area and the best egress routes. We agreed upon designated pickup points. The gap allows for a degree of separation between me and any trouble that might crop up. As I'm sure you're well aware, advance preparation is key."

She nodded but then frowned. "What if you're injured? You might not be able to make it to the pickup point."

"That's where my backup plan comes into play." He patted his pocket. "I have a beacon, the same technology skiers use. If necessary, I turn it on and they can find me."

Her expression told him she was impressed. "You've got all the bases covered."

He focused on his food for a while, let the silence fill the space. It would be dark soon. Since there was no way to know what time they would have to move, it would be best to get some sleep now while they had the opportunity.

When he'd finished his meal, he put the packaging into his pack. "Sleep if you can. We may have to move again at any time."

He checked the screen on the burner phone before sliding it into his shirt pocket. With the phone on vibrate and the pack as a pillow, he stretched out for a quick nap, braced his arms over his face. He hoped like hell the charge lasted until he had a response.

He listened as Buchanan spread the thin blanket out on the ground and did the same. She lay there quietly for about a half a minute. He was surprised she lasted that long.

"What are you, Flynn? If you tell me you're just a run-of-the-mill member of that group we escaped, I'm going to know you're lying."

At this point he didn't see any reason to keep her in the dark. "I'm like you."

She rolled onto her stomach. He felt more than saw the move. "Only way different."

He chuckled and lowered his arms. "Not so different."

"Come on. You don't work for the Bureau or I would know. The ATF didn't claim you. Neither did the DEA. Since when does Homeland Security embed agents in the middle of nowhere like this?"

This time he outright laughed. "I'm not with Homeland Security. I'm with the ATF."

She lay there for a moment seeming to mull over what she'd learned. It wouldn't be unusual for an embedded agent to be denied for the purposes of protecting the mission. Like the military, need to know was the motto for most federal agencies.

Finally she asked, "How did that happen? Did someone recruit you?"

"No. I recruited myself."

She waited for him to go on but he didn't. He should have realized she would want his story as soon as she knew the truth about who he really was, but he wasn't sure he wanted to share it. It felt too intimate.

Or maybe he was afraid it would turn the *moment* into something intimate. It was essential that they stayed focused. Emotions could not get tangled up in this precarious situation.

"I'm waiting for the rest of the story, Flynn. Don't leave me hanging like this."

"I grew up in Franklin County. My father was one of them, only not like what you see today. It didn't start out that way. But I watched it happen and I hated it, hated the men who made it happen. I made my way into the ATF for the sole purpose of coming back here and taking Resurrection down. For years I pretended that wasn't my motive. I tried to be a good agent, take the assignments given. Do the job to the best of my ability—whatever that job might be. But I couldn't forget. Two years ago when my father died, I approached the top brass with an offer. They accepted and I came back to do what needed to be done."

"Wow. That's a hell of a story, Flynn. You must have incredible restraint. You've had to pretend to be one of them for two whole years."

He rolled over her comment for a time and then he said, "I've always been one of them. I'm just not like them. That's the difference."

She nodded. "I get it."

"What about you, Agent Buchanan? How did you become a rescue and retrieval specialist?"

"Growing up in Montana I always said I wanted to work where the sun shines all the time and there's no snow so I ended up in Miami. I was so new it was painful but because of my obvious Hispanic heritage, I was needed for a particularly high-profile assignment right off the bat. They wanted me to get inside and evaluate the situation with a deep-cover agent who had gone silent. Getting in was easy. I have a knack for putting people at ease and making them believe what I want them to believe."

"You do." If it hadn't been for her using the Trenton Pollard name, he could have fallen for her story. She was good.

"Not only did I find the guy but I got him out using my favorite bait-and-switch tactic. It almost never fails."

"Is that right?"

"That's right. I make the bad guy believe he's going to get one thing and then I do exactly the opposite of what he expects."

He chuckled, couldn't help himself. This was a woman who enjoyed her work.

"Turns out my target was the grandson of a former director. He was so impressed with my work, he urged the powers that be to make better use of my skill set. So here I am. This was basically a favor. An off-the-record mission."

"Well, Agent Buchanan, it's a pleasure to make your acquaintance." He thrust his hand at her.

She grinned and gave it a shake. "Ditto, Agent Flynn."

Now if they could only get themselves out of this thorny situation, maybe he'd ask her out to dinner.

A frown furrowed his brow. The beef jerky obviously hadn't done its job or he wouldn't still be thinking about food.

Then again, maybe it wasn't food on his mind.

He peeked at the lady lying so close.

Too dangerous, he reminded himself.

Maybe another time when they weren't both targeted for execution.

Chapter 10

The way Flynn kept checking the burner phone, Sadie was reasonably confident he was worried more than he wanted her to know that there had been no response from his contact and the phone's battery was dying.

He hadn't said as much but she was no fool. There was no way a crucial reaction to a critical situation would take this long. She pulled her fingers through her hair, wished she had a brush. She shifted her position a bit—this rock was not made for comfort. Being stuck in this cave all night was even less so. She was thankful for the protection from the elements and the enemy but even when she slept, fitfully to say the least, she was aware of *him* next to her. The smell of his skin, the heat emanating from his body. Not helpful when trying to sleep. At least not when she wanted desperately to do something entirely unrelated to sleeping.

Not smart, Sadie.

The situation wasn't completely unexpected. She had been so focused on her career for years now that she'd totally ignored her personal life. Sure, she had the occasional date with some guy a friend insisted she so needed to meet. Very rarely did that develop into physical gratification. Apparently, that was an issue. She was like a starving animal now, desperate…

She rubbed her hands over her face and wished for a long, hot bath. Maybe a trip to the spa the way she'd done years ago—before her career took over her life. There, she decided, was the real source of the rub. All her female friends—the ones with whom she'd done lunch and spa days—were married. Most had children. They all thought because Sadie was approaching thirty-five that she should be doing the same. It wasn't really because they were old-fashioned or had narrow views, it was just human nature. The heightening urge to procreate as one reached thirty.

Sadie had passed thirty several years ago and not once had she thought about a permanent relationship, much less kids.

She worked. Work was her constant companion, her best friend, her lover.

Her traitorous eyes stole a glance at the man packing up their sparse campsite. But this man had her dwelling on her most basic instincts. Of all the times for an attraction to form, this was the absolute worst possible one.

The guy was a stranger—no matter that she now

knew he wasn't a criminal—and their situation was dire at best.

Before daylight he'd gone outside their hiding place and checked the area. When he'd returned, she had taken a turn slipping out of the cave to go for a necessary break, as well. Flynn was good at concealing his concern but she hadn't missed his mounting tension. It was in the set of his broad shoulders, the lines across his handsome forehead.

He was worried.

Which made her worry.

It was possible, she supposed, that there had been a delay due to some unpredicted issue. But they had gone well beyond that possibility now. This was not just a delay, this was a total breakdown in the link between a deep undercover agent and his primary support contact.

When Flynn pulled on the pack, she asked the question burning in her brain. "What's the plan now?"

"No response from my contact. The phone's battery is dead. We move on. Staying here any longer would be a mistake. As well hidden as we are, the dogs could pick up our scent again."

"Agreed." For the first time this morning she thought of Levi. She hoped he had made it to someplace where he could call someone he trusted. Things would have been a lot simpler if he'd stayed with them. She glanced at the man towering over her. A lot simpler on numerous levels.

"Stay close," he reminded her, "and move as quietly and quickly as possible. We'll head off this mountain and into town via trails that keep us out of sight and away from where we would most likely run into people."

Which meant they would be hiking a lot of miles, taking the longer, tougher routes. The blisters forming on her feet ached. They weren't as bad as the ones on her hands, but they were getting there. She glanced at the bandages, considered discarding them but decided against it for now.

At the opening that would take them out of the shallow cave, he hesitated. "We'll save the backup plan for later. I have no way of knowing what's gone wrong with my communication link so I don't want to give anyone our location until we know whether the one who receives the signal is friend or foe."

So, she'd been right.

He parted the thick foliage and made his exit. Sadie followed.

Whatever happened now, they were on their own.

Smith had no choice at this point but to admit that his contact was either dead or he'd turned.

He had known the man who was his primary backup for a decade. He found it difficult to believe he could be turned. Odds were, he was dead. The mistake was Smith's. He had insisted on only one person having knowledge of his egress options. He should have known better than to rely on only one man. Humans were not immortal. Accidents happened, health issues cropped up. One or both stealing lives at inopportune moments. Things happened, infusing desperation, weakening even the strongest man.

Choices at this juncture were extremely limited but at least they still had a couple.

Smith had decided that they would keep moving. Yesterday had been spent traveling in wide circles up and then down the mountain. No express routes. Today would be somewhat more direct. He would use a scatter pattern to prevent leaving a straightforward trail to follow. However hard he tried not to leave signs of their presence, it was impossible not to break the occasional small branch or trample plants.

Their path wouldn't be difficult for a trained tracker to follow. The dogs wouldn't need anything but their scent.

Frankly, Smith was surprised he hadn't heard the dogs at some point yesterday. Particularly after Winters separated from them.

This, too, was cause for concern.

Was Prentiss so certain he would win that he didn't bother sending a search party?

The idea hadn't crossed Smith's mind until his contact failed to come through and time had continued to lapse without trouble finding them.

Now that he considered the possibility, Prentiss had been the one to insist Smith take Buchanan and Winters to the *others*. If he'd discovered Smith's secret, why not kill him at the compound? Was the old bastard's intent to make an example out of him? Show his followers who their true protector was?

This was more wrong than he had realized.

There was a mole all right, but it wasn't Buchanan. It was someone on Smith's home team. Someone in the ATF with clearance to this mission. Only a handful of people knew about this cleanup and infiltration detail. Still, that didn't mean someone with the opportunity hadn't found a way to access the files. The world was one big electronic filing cabinet these days. Nothing was unattainable if one knew in which drawer to look and possessed the skill to open it.

Had Prentiss turned someone with that kind of know-how?

The only way to be sure was to get Buchanan to safety and then for him to return to the compound for Prentiss. This was a finale that required an up close encounter.

He had spent the past two years of his life digging deeply into the Resurrection. He was not going to walk away without eliminating the organization, even if that meant taking matters into his own hands.

The compound had been built into the mountainside. It was completely camouflaged and protected by the earth itself. Over and over he had mentally plotted where and how the explosives would need to be planted to destroy the place—to bring down the entire mountainside. The problem was, as gratifying as that result would be, it wouldn't change anything. Some of the powers that be lived outside the compound. They hid themselves among the locals to stay aware of whatever was going on in the rest of the world. Having everyone with power, reach and contacts in the same place at the same time for elimination would be virtually impossible.

Smith had toyed with that scenario a thousand times.

Once the compound was destroyed, those who survived would go into hiding. He knew them all—every single one. But sending them to prison for their criminal activities required solid evidence, none of which he possessed outside that compound. Even lining them up for vigilante-style termination would require an army. The moment one was taken out, the rest would scatter like crows. Since he didn't have an army prepared to commit cold-blooded murder, he needed a better plan.

A laugh tugged at his gut. In two years he hadn't been able to come up with a workable strategy.

He could sever the head of the snake, Prentiss, but another one would sprout in his place.

Unless…he found a more lethal snake willing to swallow up the competition entirely.

A new plan started to form. Smith had a feeling this one might even work. But to make that happen he would need to enter the territory of that lethal snake.

It was a good plan. He thought of the woman right behind him. Rather than attempt to explain the intricate details and to persuade Sadie to go along, he decided to keep her in the dark. She would be mad as hell when she found out, but if he accomplished his ultimate goal, she would forgive him.

He hoped.

Altering his course, he headed for dangerous territory. He readied for trouble, exiling all distraction in order to focus fully on his surroundings, listening and watching. Within the hour they would cross into territory ruled by another group. They couldn't really be called an organization since they weren't technically organized. These people didn't even have a name, much less a motto. Anyone who knew them merely called them the *others*. The one thing Smith knew for certain about them was that they were dangerous. Cunning and methodical.

Maybe clinically insane. Certainly crazy by anyone's measure.

Crazy was what he needed at the moment.

All he had to do was find it without getting Buchanan or himself killed.

They were traveling in a different direction now. Yesterday he had done the same. Flynn had wound back and forth around this mountain. She'd figured his goal was to make their path more difficult to find and follow. With no response from his contact and no sign of Prentiss's people or dogs, she had expected he would take a more direct route today.

Maybe not.

She wanted to ask him about his plan, but he'd reiterated that silence was particularly important today. Rather than risk making too much noise, she'd kept her questions to herself for now and followed his lead. If she had to find the way out of here they would likely end up bear bait in these damned woods.

Not that she'd spotted any bears or bear tracks but there could be bears, coyotes or wolves, to name a few predators who would present a problem.

There was the gun he'd had hidden in the cave. But she didn't have any idea how much ammunition Flynn had on him. Maybe only what was in the weapon. Maybe not enough to survive if they were attacked by man or beast.

But they had their wits, no shortage of determination and Flynn's extensive knowledge of the area.

The situation could be a lot worse.

A muzzle jammed into the back of her skull. Before her brain had time to analyze how it happened so fast without her noticing someone was closing in on her, her body instinctively froze.

"Don't move."

Somehow she had known the person—man obviously—on the other end of that barrel was going to say those two words.

Smith spun around, his weapon leveled on the threat. "Back off," he warned.

Before his growled words stopped reverberating in the air, three more men stepped forward, rifles aimed at him.

Sadie blinked, startled when she'd thought nothing else could shock her. The men wore paint, like body paint—nothing else as far as she could tell. They had melted into the landscape and only when they moved had their presence become visible. She blinked again to ensure she wasn't seeing things.

"Back off," Flynn repeated. "Aikman is expecting me."

If these were more of his friends, it would have been nice if he'd given her a heads-up before the one behind her startled the hell out of her.

One of the three fanned out around Flynn stepped forward, moving closer to him. "Drop the gun."

Sadie held her breath. Agents were trained never to relinquish their weapons but sometimes there simply was no other choice. An agent learned through experience when it was time to forget the classroom training and do what had to be done.

Flynn tossed the weapon to the ground and raised his hands. "My name is Smith Flynn. Take me to Aikman."

The guy behind Sadie shoved a bag at her. "Put this on."

Sadie took the bag and tugged it onto her head. The

last thing she saw before the black fabric fell over her eyes was Flynn with the business end of a rifle stuck to his forehead.

The nearest muzzle nudged her back. "Start walking."

She did as she was told, hoping like hell she didn't trip over a tree root or a rock. No one talked but she heard the faint sounds of their new friends moving through the underbrush. She suddenly wondered if the painted guys wore shoes or boots or something on their feet. She hadn't noticed. The guy behind her was probably painted, too. He was, she decided as she recalled the arm that had thrust the bag at her.

The only good thing was that Flynn appeared to know who these people were. This Aikman, she assumed, was someone in charge. Hopefully someone high enough up the food chain to keep them from becoming "emergency supplies."

Her toe snagged on a root or a rock and she almost face-planted. Thankfully, she managed to grab back her balance. Her sudden stop to capture her equilibrium won her another nudge from the muzzle.

Sadie counted off the seconds and minutes. By her estimate, they walked for half an hour. The terrain didn't change much. Brush, rocks, moving sometimes up, sometimes down. The scent of food cooking told her they had reached a camp of some sort. She doubted it was noon yet but it was past midmorning. No matter that she'd had a protein bar very early that morning, her stomach sent her a warning that she needed to eat again soon.

And coffee. What she would give for a big, steaming cup of coffee.

She wondered if this group would have a compound built into the mountainside like the Resurrection. She had to admit, the idea had been ingenious. A hand suddenly rested on her left shoulder. She stopped, braced to either fight or run like hell. The bag whipped up and off her head.

She blinked twice, three times, and surveyed the area. There was a canopy of green overhead. A combination of trees and vines and other plant life she couldn't readily identify. Sunlight filtered through, making her blink with its brightness after wearing the bag. There were shacks made of branches, twigs and brush. This didn't look anything like a compound. These were like primitive huts that flowed seamlessly with the brush and trees. She looked upward again, spotted similar builds in the trees. The tree houses were also constructed with limbs and other pieces of the surrounding natural resources, making them almost like an extension of the trees.

Another nudge in the back and she started walking again. Flynn walked ahead of her, a painted man on either side of him. They moved deeper into the trees. Finally they reached an area that looked very much like the place against the mountainside where they'd slept last night. Brush and branches hid a narrow cave opening. They were escorted inside where two more men, these wearing dark clothes similar to SWAT gear, took over escort duty. The man who'd been behind Sadie all that time and his friends slipped back out the way they had come.

Beyond the opening, the cave widened into a room. There were lights in the cave but not electric lights. The lanterns looked like the old oil type. The cave floor was rocky. Water trickled from the walls here and there. Smelled musty. No more food smells. Whoever had been cooking, they were outside in the rustic camp they'd passed through.

This cave was far larger than the one they'd called home last night. The ceiling zoomed several feet overhead and the width of the space was five or so yards. They moved downward from there. Maybe a more elaborate compound had been built deeper in the cave.

The wide tunnel divided and they took the left fork. A few yards in they passed another wide room-size section on the left. Rows of rustic tables filled that space. Dozens of oil lamps lit the area. People dressed in white coveralls like painters and wearing paper face masks were frantically packing some sort of product.

Oh hell.

Drugs.

Her stomach sank. This was one of those things you couldn't unsee. People in this business didn't allow outsiders to see their work and walk away.

This was bad.

She hoped like hell Flynn knew what he was doing. She also hoped he knew these people really well—well enough to share dark secrets.

Otherwise they were goners.

Once they had moved beyond the workers in the white suits, they passed a number of large round stones that sat on either side of the corridor. The lead man stopped. With obvious effort he pushed one of the stones aside, revealing a hole in the rock wall, like a large round doggie door without the flap.

Not exactly a user-friendly entrance to wherever they were going next.

"Inside." The man looked at Sadie as he said this.

She glanced from him to the hole. Was he serious? She shifted her gaze to Flynn. "I'm supposed to go in there?"

"For now. Don't worry."

He couldn't be serious.

The man with the gun waved it as if he was running out of patience.

Great. She squatted, then dropped onto her hands and knees. She poked her head far enough through the opening to see what was inside. Nothing. As best she could determine it was just an empty, small, cube-like rock room. She crawled inside. Squinted to get a better look at the space. She shifted, scanning all the way around while there was still light filtering in from the open hole. In the corner to the left of the hole she'd just entered her gaze snagged on a form. She crawled closer, her eyes adjusting to the even dimmer light.

Bones.

Not just bones. An intact skeleton.

The rotting clothing suggested the owner of the bones had been male.

She swallowed back a sound, not exactly a scream but something on that order.

The noise from the stone rolling in front of the hole once more rumbled around her. She sat down on her bottom and stared at the only exit from this new prison. A dim outline of light from the lanterns in the corridor slipped in past the stone now blocking that exit.

Her gaze shifted back to the bones. She couldn't really see them now but her brain filled in the details from the picture seared into her memory.

Whoever had been stuck in here before had died in this place.

Without water or food it wouldn't take that long.

She thought of the lack of tissue on the bones. The person had been trapped in this place for a very long time. Years. Maybe as much as a decade considering the deteriorated state of the clothing he wore.

Sadie sat in the middle of that musty, dark space and replayed the past decade of her life. She had graduated with a master's degree and some big plans. Two summer internships with the Bureau and she was accepted as soon as she reached the age requirement. Her parents had been so proud. Her mother had been a little concerned about her daughter going into law enforcement, but she'd come to terms with the decision after the first year. Maybe it had been Sadie's excitement that had won over her mom.

Sadie had ended the relationship with her hometown boyfriend before entering training. The long-distance relationship had basically been over since undergrad school anyway. They were going in different directions with changing objectives. Why prolong the misery by watching the relationship they had once believed would go on forever shrivel up and die? Strange, she never once considered when the relationship ended that it would be her last one.

Dates, never more than three, maybe four with the same guy. Her social calendar consisted more of bridal showers, weddings and baby showers for friends than dates for herself.

If she died in this dark, dank place her parents would be devastated.

A life half lived.

Not true, she decided. If she died in this place, she would be dying young, for certain. But it wasn't a life half lived. She had lived every single day to its fullest. She had loved the hell out of her work. She had helped to bring down numerous bad guys and she had rescued more than her share of good guys.

"Get over it, Sadie. You are not going to die in this hole in the ground."

She pulled up a knee and rested her chin there. She would find a way out of here. It was what she did. And she was really, really good at it...usually.

As soon as Flynn finished his meeting with this Aikman person and was brought here, they would put their heads together and come up with an escape plan.

Flynn had a contact with these people. He hadn't appeared worried when they were captured. She shouldn't be worried, either. Then again, Flynn's record with his contacts hadn't actually been a reassuring experience so far.

Maybe it was time to get worried.

Chapter 11

Smith had waited a half hour. The cuckoo clock on the wall counted off every second with a loud tick-tock. Any minute now the bird would slide past its door and count off the hour: 11:00 a.m.

He forced himself to relax. He possessed as good an understanding of these people as anyone. They did things their way in their time. Making him wait was a way of showing dominance. As long as he was still breathing there was reason to believe an arrangement could be reached.

This move had been a risk. A risk he was wagering everything would work out. Unfortunately, the wager involved Buchanan's life as well as his own. If things didn't work out as he intended, her death would be on him. That was the one part that didn't sit well with him. But they were in a no-win situation. As a trained agent, she would understand the need to take drastic measures.

Smith drew in a deep breath and reminded himself to be patient. To play the game.

The tunnel where Buchanan had been secured had forked again, leading to the outside once more. Another campsite had been built against that side of the mountain. Again, using elements that blended in with the environment to keep them off the radar of reconnaissance flyovers.

Aikman's office was like any other with a desk, chairs and electricity. The electricity was furnished by a generator. The primary difference between this place and that of the Resurrection as far as Smith could see was the absence of electronics. The *others* didn't use electronics with the exception of burner phones, which they used sparingly. They stayed as far off the grid as possible.

The door behind Smith opened and Aikman entered, minus his usual bodyguards. They no doubt waited outside the door. No matter that he was well aware that Smith was unarmed, he would never take the risk of being alone in a room with a known follower of the Resurrection without backup close by.

"You got some nerve coming here after what you did, Flynn." Aikman sat down behind his desk. "I was expecting you to deliver two packages yesterday. Prentiss and I had a deal. First, you don't show, then I get word you've dropped off the grid. Now you waltz in here with only one package." He shook his head. "This is not good."

Draven Aikman was younger than Smith. His rusty-brown hair was kept skinhead short but his beard was long, at least ten or twelve inches. He wore the same dark uniform as his soldiers. He'd killed the old man who held the position as leader before him. The story was that the old man was sick, practically on his deathbed and making bad decisions. Aikman claimed he took care of the failing part for the good of the whole. Whatever his motive, he now held the highest position among this closed, clannish group known only as the *others* by the few who were aware of their existence.

Aikman propped his feet on the desk and leaned back in the chair, eliciting a squeak of protest from the base. The desk and chair, like the rest of the furnishings, might have been unwanted castoffs picked up from the side of the road on garbage day. The *others* had a reputation for living free of excessive material burdens. Survival of the coming human self-annihilation was their singular goal. Still, they were only human and not completely immune to power and greed. In any group there was always someone who couldn't resist the temptation of *more*.

"You suddenly develop a death wish?" Aikman asked. "Coming here, throwing my name around like we're friends. I could get the wrong idea."

"The deal Prentiss made is off. I'm here with a different offer."

Aikman lifted his brows. "This better be good."

"There are other names on my list," Smith warned, "but I chose to bring this offer to you first."

The other man's gaze narrowed. "What kind of offer?"

"We both know the Resurrection is your primary competition. We've blocked your every attempt to expand your operation into other areas. You've been stuck making the drugs no one else wants to make unless they have no other choice. We've pushed you out of the arms business. Basically, we've kept you down for decades."

"If you're supposed to be buttering me up for some proposition," he laughed, a rusty sound, "you're falling way short of the mark."

This was the mistake most people made. To look at the *others* and how they lived, one would automatically think uneducated, backwoods hillbillies. But that was not the case at all with the ones like Aikman. According to Smith's sources, the man had a master's degree in business administration. He was smart. Allowing you to believe he wasn't automatically put you at a disadvantage in any negotiation.

"I'm sure you get my meaning," Smith said, ignoring his dig. "I've decided it would be in both our best interests to join forces. We both have our resources. If we pool those resources, we could expand our operations and take over the Southeast."

Aikman dropped his feet to the floor. "You want me to believe that you're ready to abandon your loyalties to the Resurrection—an organization that runs in your blood? You would trample on your daddy's memory?" He grunted a sound of disbelief. "Pardon me if I don't believe you. What're you up to, Flynn?"

This was the risky part. It would have been easier for Smith to keep walking. To climb down this damned mountain and turn himself over to local law enforcement. He would have been sent back to where he belonged ASAP. The mission would have been over and the goal he'd dedicated his entire existence to for the past two years would have been lost forever.

He would have been alive, safe and free of this nightmare.

Except Prentiss would have gotten away. He and his Council of ruthless killers would have relocated and continued doing whatever they pleased with no care of the human cost. No worry about what the guns and the drugs were doing to society.

Smith was left with one option—finish this in the only way possible: light the fuse of the Resurrection's number one enemy.

Start a war.

"Prentiss sold me out," Smith confessed. That part was true. Rumor of the shake-up would get around soon enough if it hadn't already.

There was no other explanation for the trio who'd showed up behind them on that mountain road after they left the compound. Prentiss had intended to wash his hands of Winters, Buchanan and Smith. End of story. To believe they had appeared for any other reason would be foolish. Somehow Prentiss knew. Which would also explain the sudden drop in communications with Smith's contact.

Whatever had gone wrong, Smith was on his own. He had few options if he wanted to finish his mission and this was the best one.

Aikman reared his head back and considered the announcement for a moment as if he didn't quite believe what he'd heard. He pursed his lips then rocked forward, propping his forearms on his desktop. "You actually expect me to believe that Prentiss dared to attempt a coup so he could be rid of you?"

"Believe what you want." Smith turned his palms up. "I came here to give you the first dibs on *my* coup.

If you're not interested, then I overestimated your ability to see the bigger picture. I won't waste your time. I have other options."

Aikman's gaze narrowed once more. "What other options? We own this mountain. My people and yours. There's no one else."

Smith smiled. "If that's what you believe, then I really did overestimate you, Aikman."

The statement was a direct insult but it also made the other man think. "You're talking about that Hispanic gang, aren't you? They've been inching their way up the food chain for years, but they're not organized enough or financially flush enough to be more than a nuisance." He hesitated. "What is it you know that I don't?"

There was no time to go there. "We have to act fast, Aikman. We can't sit around discussing the politics of the region. Prentiss is out there looking for me right now."

Aikman scrubbed a hand over his jaw. "What is it you've got to offer?"

"You get me and my friend off this mountain and I'll give you everything you need to take down the Council. Locations, security codes. Everything. The Resurrection and all it entails will be yours for the taking."

"Where do you come back into the picture?" He shrugged. "Doesn't sound like we're doing anything. Sounds more like I'm doing and you're cutting out."

Smith shook his head. "I'll be back. There's a personal matter I have to take care of first."

Aikman grinned. "Are you referring to the woman?"

Tension slid through Smith. "I am."

Aikman scratched at his thick beard some more. "You see, that's where we have a bartering issue."

Smith's instincts stirred. "What does that mean, Aikman?"

He leaned back in his chair, his hands on the worn arms. "To tell you the truth, things get a little lonely out here from time to time. Sure there's women, but not one I've cared to take for more than a little bump and grind. There's definitely none like her. I need someone who presents a challenge. The ones I've run up on so far bore me."

Smith's gut clenched at the idea of what this bastard had in mind. The *others* were known for staying to themselves. They had no use for those who were different, whether that difference was as simple as skin color or went way deeper. The man's fascination with Buchanan would be short-lived and then she'd end up a curiosity or, worse, a sex slave.

"I don't see how that's my problem. This is business. Important business," Smith warned. "You should keep that in mind as you decide your next move."

Aikman grinned. "I'm making it your problem, Flynn. You brought this problem between you and Prentiss to my door, now I'm bringing mine to you. I want the woman. You give me the woman and we'll have a deal."

"Not happening." Smith stood. "Let's not waste each other's time with games. We'll be on our way to the next prospect if this is your final answer."

The other man stood, leaned over his desk, bracing his hands on the worn surface. "Do you really think I'm going to let you just walk back out of here?" He moved his head slowly from side to side. "This was a no-turning-back meeting, Flynn. You don't get to sit in my office and then just walk away. You think Prentiss would watch me walk away if I paid him a visit?" Aikman angled his head and studied Smith. "Then again, he might if I told him I had a gift for him. What you think you're worth to the old bastard?"

Smith smiled. "Not nearly as much as you are."

Aikman reared back, then laughed as if Smith's statement hadn't startled him. "I gave you a chance, Flynn. I guess you aren't as smart as you think. What woman is worth dying for?"

"I could ask you the same thing."

Aikman didn't flinch, but Smith saw the glimmer of uncertainty in his eyes before he blinked it away. "My people appreciate tangible proof they're being protected. With that in mind, from time to time a public display is required to keep them reassured. At dawn, we'll give them something to feel good about. Maybe the two of you will be worth all the distraction you've caused after all. You wouldn't believe what organs go for on the black market."

Smith ignored the threat, turned his back and walked out of the man's office. The guards grabbed him by the arms and jerked him forward.

Not exactly the news he'd hoped to take back to Buchanan.

Sadie had moved around the entire space and found no openings, not even a crack, except for the small round opening she'd been forced to crawl through to get in here. She couldn't help wondering if the owner of the remains in the corner had done the same thing—

searched for some way to escape, wondering what would happen next—before he died here.

Whatever he'd had planned, it hadn't worked out for him.

For the first time on a mission, her mind wandered to her folks and she tried to remember the last time she'd spoken with her parents. Had she said the right things? Told them she loved them? She couldn't see her sister being there for them in their time of grief if Sadie never made it out of this place.

Don't even go there, Sadie.

Moving around the perimeter of the room once more, she closed her eyes and listened for any sort of sound. The soft whisper of words slipped beyond the crack between the stone that made a door and the hole in the wall that it covered. She couldn't say if the voices were those of the guards outside the room or people walking past in the long corridor.

The lives of these people likely revolved around the preparing and packaging of drugs. Survival. They lived to please their leader, this Aikman that Flynn asked to see. There was no logical reason why they would concern themselves with her or her survival.

Lines creased her forehead, nagging at the ache that had begun there. How long had Flynn been gone? An hour? An hour and a half? He could be dead by now for all she knew. She hugged her arms around herself, feeling oddly chilled. It would be bad enough to be stuck here with him. The concept of ending up alone in this hole—her gaze drifted across the darkness—was far worse.

Movement near the small opening drew her attention there. The rock rolled away and light poured in.

Sadie stood back and waited to see what would happen. She held her breath, hoped it was Flynn and not the guards ready to drag her away to some torture chamber.

When Flynn popped up through the hole, relief rushed through her and she drew in a lungful of air.

Before he could speak, she asked, "What happened? Did you talk to Aikman?"

The stone was rolled back over the hole, blocking all but that narrow crack of light. Flynn hesitated, waiting for the guards to lose interest and wander back to their posts.

"I did. He was intrigued by my offer."

His tone told her that wasn't the whole story by any means but it might very well be the best part of it. "What was your offer?"

"The information he would need to take over the Resurrection."

No surprise there. Flynn was worried that Prentiss would get away. He didn't want that to happen. "What did you ask for in return?"

"Safe transport off this mountain."

Made sense, she supposed. If his ultimate goal was to stop Prentiss and his followers, giving away his secrets to an enemy would certainly do the trick. Not exactly the usual protocol for a federal agent, but desperate times called for desperate measures. She couldn't fault him for wanting to see his primary mission accomplished no matter that his cover was blown.

She sat down on the floor. No need to keep standing. She'd walked this space a thousand times. Exhaustion and hunger were nagging at her. "When do we leave?"

He didn't sit. Instead, he kept moving around the

space as if he was agitated or frustrated. Either would be understandable under the circumstances.

"Watch for the bones on the left of the door," she warned.

Still, he said nothing, just kept moving through the near total darkness. After five minutes, his movements had grown unnerving with her sitting so still. Finally, she stood and demanded some answers. "So what's the rest of the story?"

He stopped, turned to her. She couldn't see his face, certainly couldn't read his expression, so she waited for him to explain.

"I took a calculated risk coming here. I put my offer on the table and it didn't go the way I expected."

"Can you be a little more specific?" He'd told her a considerable amount with those two statements and yet nothing at all.

"The only way he's prepared to accept my offer is if he gets *you* in the bargain."

Sadie barked out a laugh. "Are you serious?"

"Unfortunately, I am." He heaved a frustrated breath.

The idea of where they were and those bones over in the corner slammed into her midsection like a sucker punch. "How did you respond?"

On one level she could see how he might want to agree. After all, at least one of them needed to get out of here alive. It was the only way the people expecting their return would ever know what took place on this mountain. No matter that she comprehended the logic, she struggled to maintain her objectivity. Agreeing to the man's terms would be the reasonable thing to do.

At least that way Flynn could go for help. Assuming she survived whatever came after that, she could still be alive when help came.

But on a whole other level, she wanted to kick his ass for coming up with this insane idea in the first place. Fury burst through her.

As if he'd read her mind or felt her mixed emotions, he said, "I told him no way. If I go, you go."

Her heart skipped and then sank just a little. "What good does it do for both of us to be stuck here?" Or end up like the guy in the corner? She exhaled a chest full of exasperation and crossed her arms. "Tell him you changed your mind. Tell him," she added firmly, "he has a deal. You go and I'll stay."

"No way."

His hands were on his hips and she could feel his glare even if she couldn't see it.

"It's the right thing to do, Flynn. One of us needs to get down this damned mountain."

She hoped Levi Winters had found help. Maybe she would have been smarter to go with him. Except it was better that she and Flynn drew the danger away from him and let him get away. At least he could tell Ross and the others all that he knew. That was something.

"I got you into this," Flynn said, his voice low, fierce. "I'll get you out."

"How do you plan on doing that?"

He moved in closer, put his face near enough to hers that his lips brushed her ear. She shivered in spite of her best efforts not to react.

"He's not going to pass on this deal. He just wants us ready to do whatever he asks when he pretends to have a change of heart."

The feel of his breath on her skin made her want

to lean into him. She pushed the idea away. "What do you think he'll want us to do?"

"He'll want us to act as a distraction while he carries out his coup."

"What kind of distraction?"

"The kind that gets captured and taken back to the compound and to Prentiss."

She jerked away from him. "What? Why the hell would we do that?"

"Because he's not a fool. He knows it won't be easy getting in even with the information I can give him. If that's what he requires, we have to be prepared to go. Are you with me?"

She wasn't so sure this plan was any better than the first one he walked in here telling her about.

But that was irrelevant.

"I'm in," she said finally. "At least we won't end up like the guy in the corner."

How had this mission turned so completely upside down?

Chapter 12

Sadie woke, her body shivering. A moment was required for her to orient herself.

Cave. Aikman. The *others*.

She sat up, scrubbed at her cheek where her face had been pressed to the cold ground. She'd been curled into a ball on the cold rock floor. She peered through the darkness, scanning the room as best she could. Listening for any sound, including breathing, she heard nothing.

Where was Flynn?

Memories of him pulling her against him in the night invaded her thoughts. She'd shivered from the cold invading her very bones and he'd pulled her against his big body to keep her warm. Several times during the night she had awakened to the feel of his protective arms around her, his shoulder like a pillow and the length of his body radiating heat into hers.

"Flynn?"

She got to her feet, dusted herself off for the good it would do. No answer. She ran her fingers through her hair. Apparently she'd slept through him being taken away.

Had Aikman summoned him for another meeting?

Her heart kicked into a faster rhythm. Maybe they'd already taken him off this damned mountain. Maybe she wasn't going anywhere.

Aikman had requested to keep her.

She chafed her arms to create some heat with the friction. Flynn would never go for it. He'd said so last night. He wasn't going without her.

Then again, it was possible he hadn't been given a choice this time.

For a few minutes she walked around, warming up her stiff, aching muscles. She really needed to use a bathroom but she doubted she would be permitted to leave her small prison. A few more minutes and she decided she couldn't wait any longer. She chose the corner the farthest away from the remains and re-lieved herself. The dead guy had likely been forced to do this for days or weeks before his body could no longer resist death.

Another ten or so minutes elapsed with her walk-ing back and forth across the center of her prison cell when the stone suddenly rolled away from the open-ing. She moved to the wall and braced for whatever trouble might be coming. If one of the guards came in for her, she could fight him off for a while. As weary as her body was, the battle might not last long.

"Out!"

The voice was male but not one she recognized. She didn't move.

"Come out!" the man demanded. "Time to eat."

Her stomach rumbled. Getting out of here was better than staying. If it involved food, that was all the better. She pushed away from the wall and moved to the opening. On her hands and knees she scurried out as quickly as possible and shot to her feet. She didn't like being in a vulnerable position. She looked up, and two men—guards she presumed—stared down at her as if she were some sort of alien.

She blinked repeatedly to help her eyes adjust to the light. It wasn't that bright but it was a hell of a lot brighter than inside that hole she'd been stuck in all night. The two stared at her for a moment longer, then gestured for her to go to the left. Her gait was a little off at first but she soon found her rhythm. One of the guards ambled in front of her, the other behind her. They led her back the way she'd originally come into this cold, dark place. Once they were outside the cave, she squinted against the way brighter light. The sun was up but it was still early. She was escorted to one of the twig shacks and ushered through the primitive door.

A woman waited inside the shack.

"Take off your clothes and get into the tub."

She stared at Sadie, waiting for her to obey the issued command. Her hair was long and dark like Sadie's but her skin was pale. If a bath was on the agenda, Sadie wasn't about to argue with her. She stripped off her clothes and toed off her shoes. Once she was in the tub the woman peeled the bandages from her hands and ordered her to sit. Sadie complied.

It was at precisely that moment that she considered maybe she was to be the morning kill. Maybe she was breakfast. She jerked her attention to the left just in time for a pail of water to be poured over her head. Surprisingly it was warm. A bar of soap was tossed into the tub with her and she went to work washing her face and body. It felt so good. More water poured over her and the woman started washing her hair. Sadie didn't complain. It felt amazing to have her scalp massaged. She could sit here and savor the attention for hours.

Then came more water, only this time it was cold. When she was thoroughly rinsed, the woman helped her towel off and provided a pair of blue cotton shorts and a white tee. Sadie had no idea where the clothes came from but they fit and she was glad to be out of the days-old sweats. She tugged on the same shoes she'd been wearing since her time at the compound. They were finally dry after their trek through the water. The blisters on her hands and feet were still tender but there was nothing she could do about that.

The woman ushered her over to a table and chairs and prepared food for her. The plate was metal, more like a pie tin. Scrambled eggs and toast were heaped onto the plate. A tin of water stood next to it. Sadie didn't wait to be told—she dove in. She was starving. She hoped Flynn was given food before he was taken to wherever he had gone. The food suddenly felt like a lump of cement in her stomach. She felt guilty about the nice bath and the hot food considering she had no idea where he was or what might be happening to him.

Focus, Sadie. You can't stay strong and be of any use to anyone if you don't eat.

As she forced bite after bite into her mouth, first one and then another woman came into the tiny shack and climbed into the tub of water she'd used. After five women had bathed, they shared the duty of carrying out pails of the dirty water.

Sadie understood the concept of conservation but she was immensely grateful she'd been first this morning.

The woman with the long dark hair led her back outside. One of the guards who'd escorted her from her cell was waiting. He led Sadie through the woods and to yet another shack-like house, this one larger. Once they were inside, she could see that this one was built into the mountainside and the interior was more like an actual house. A long corridor led to another door. The guard opened this door and urged her inside.

"And here she is. The woman we've been waiting for."

The man behind the desk stared at her, a grin on his face. Another man stood, rising above the chair that had prevented her from seeing him.

Flynn.

The relief that gushed through her made her knees weak. He was still here. More important, he was alive.

Rather than aim her question at Flynn, she stared directly at the other man. "What happens now?"

"Now, the two of you head out."

So Flynn had been right. This man—Aikman, she presumed—had never intended to keep her. The threat was nothing more than leverage to garner their cooperation.

"We'll take you as far as the road where you dumped the SUV. You'll be on your own from there." Aikman turned to Flynn. "As you know, I'll have eyes on you at all times. Once you're inside, I'll wait for your signal to make my move."

Sadie kept her thoughts to herself. There was no point in asking questions until she and Flynn were alone.

Flynn nodded. "On my signal."

Aikman nodded and with that gesture they were escorted from the man's office and back outside his rustic dwelling. Two all-terrain vehicles waited. One guard climbed aboard each vehicle and ordered Sadie and Flynn to do the same. Once she climbed on behind a guard and Flynn did the same with the other, a third guard dropped the black cloth bags over their heads. Aikman intended to keep their location a secret.

The vehicle bumped over roots and rocks and God only knew what else. Sadie held on tight no matter that she'd just as soon not touch the guy driving. Holding on to the enemy was better than risking a potentially fatal injury from bouncing off this rocky ride. She focused on counting off the minutes.

Half an hour later the vehicles stopped.

"Get off," the driver shouted over his shoulder at her.

Sadie reached up and removed the bag, then climbed off the ATV. The guard snatched the hood back from her as if he feared it might carry his fingerprints. She smoothed a hand over her hair as she watched the two drive away, bouncing and bumping over the terrain.

When they were out of sight, she scanned the area. Woods. So thick they almost blocked the sky.

She turned to Flynn. "You're still sure about this plan?"

"I don't have an option."

She turned all the way around, surveyed the woods once more. Nothing but trees and brush. "The way I see it, we can go in whatever direction we like." Her gaze settled on him once more. "You don't have to finish this if it means you'll end up dead."

Flynn held her gaze for a long moment before he finally spoke. "You go. Stay south and you'll find your way to the main road running into Winchester. If I still had the emergency beacon you could use that, but they took it so you'll be on your own. Keep your movements quiet and you'll be fine."

Sadie was shaking her head before he finished talking. "Either way we go, we go together."

"They have Winters," he said, his tone grave. "I have two hours to show up or he's dead."

Son of a bitch. Frustration, then fury tore through Sadie. "He should have listened to you." To both of them for that matter.

Flynn shook his head. "Doesn't matter. Prentiss had learned my identity before I left the compound with the two of you. We were never getting off this mountain without doing this or something like this."

"In that case, I guess we should get moving." Damn it all to hell. "We have a timeline we have to stick to." When he would have issued another protest, she held up her hand and shook her head.

Obviously not happy about her decision, Flynn led the way to the narrow rutted road. It split through the forest like a dusty brown snake. Sadie shuddered. She was extremely thankful they hadn't run into any creepy creatures. At least not the kind without legs.

When the silence had dragged on about as long as she could tolerate, she said, "You know, I thought you left me this morning." Might as well make conversation while they walked toward their doom.

He glanced at her. "You still don't trust me?"

"It wasn't about trust." In fact, she hadn't considered the idea of trust in a while now. She had instinctively trusted him. "I assumed you weren't given a choice. Then they took me for a bath, gave me clean clothes and fed me. The next thing I knew I was in Aikman's office with you."

His gaze traveled down the length of her, pausing on her bare legs before shifting back up to her face. "I noticed."

His attention swung back to the road. She smiled. Funny how such a simple, offhanded compliment could give her a moment's pleasure even at a time like this. But then, when you might not live beyond the next few hours it didn't take much.

As cold as she'd gotten in that cave last night, it was already hot enough to make her sweat this morning. The humidity was off the charts. Made the uphill journey even more of a slog.

Since Flynn had given her a sort of compliment, maybe she would give him one. "Thanks for keeping me warm last night." She flashed him a smile. "That was very gentlemanly of you."

"I thought you were keeping me warm."

Her jaw dropped, then he grinned. "You're a real comedian." She laughed. "Seriously, though, I appreciate it. I woke up shivering after you were gone but I remembered you keeping me warm through the night."

"You're welcome, but it was a mutual exchange."

Combined body heat. "What's going to happen when we get there?" As much as she would like to pretend they wouldn't really have to return to that damned compound, she knew there was no way around it outside the cavalry showing up out of the blue to take over the situation.

No one even knew their exact location. They were on their own and the chances of either one of them surviving were about nil. If they walked away, Levi, her target, would die. No matter that they would likely all three die anyway, she couldn't just walk away and leave him without attempting to do something. She glanced at the man beside her. She couldn't just walk away and leave Flynn to deal with this on his own, either.

"I have one sibling, a sister, and my parents." Sadie wasn't sure why she made this abrupt announcement. Just seemed like the thing to do. They might as well enjoy each other's company until they were taken prisoner again.

He said nothing for a while, just kept walking. She did the same.

"No siblings. Parents are long gone. It's just me."

So he was completely alone. "No wife or kids or best buds?"

He shook his head. "The job fills those slots."

This she understood all too well.

"Same here. Although my parents aren't going to be happy if I don't come back."

Another span of silence.

"I guess I'll have to make sure that doesn't happen."

She glanced at him again and this time he was looking back. They smiled simultaneously. It was foolish, she knew, but the shared smile had butterflies taking flight in her stomach. "I'm sure they would appreciate that. I know I would."

The conversation waned from there. What was there to say? They both had at least a couple of choices. If they chose not to go through with this, Levi would die. If she walked away and left Flynn to go on his own and he and Levi didn't make it out, she would have to live with that decision. Levi was not Flynn's problem but he was choosing to take that responsibility. No way was she leaving him to do her job. Walking away wasn't an option.

An hour later, the road was scarcely more than a path now. They were close. Sadie remembered the terrain. The memories sent a chill over her skin. Whether it was self-preservation or utter desperation, she suddenly stopped.

"There has to be something else we can do." She surveyed the endless woods. "Someone who lives out here who has a phone or a vehicle."

There was no one. She was aware of this. Not anywhere close by at any rate. Still, she couldn't *not* ask the question again. Being ambushed was one thing but walking into a death trap was just plain crazy. Of course, that was exactly what she'd done to get into the compound in the first place.

What did that say about the two of them? Maybe they both had death wishes that they explained away with their careers.

"There's no one for miles." He stopped walking

and turned to face her. "I understood the risk when I started this. There's no way out."

Sadie moved in on him, taking the three steps between them. "Are you doing this for you or for your father?"

He looked away from her but not before she saw emotions cloud his eyes. "Does it matter?"

She folded her arms over her chest to prevent reaching out to him. One of her instructors had warned her about a place exactly like this. The place you find yourself when you've lost all sight of the difference between your life and your work. When work becomes more important than anything else—even surviving.

"This is the job, Flynn. This isn't about you or your father. This is the job. Justice. Doing the right thing. Taking down the bad guys for the greater good, not for your own personal reasons. Like maybe revenge."

He laughed, shook his head. "Did you spend the last hour thinking up that speech or did you suddenly remember it from your agent-in-training handbook?"

She had definitely hit a nerve. "Don't be a smart-ass. I'm only trying to help. To make you see that we've both lost sight of what we were trained to do. What we swore to do when we started this journey."

"I don't need a lecture, and the only way you can help is to walk down that mountain to safety while I do what I have to do."

Now he was just being arrogant. "Levi Winters is my target. He's my responsibility. I have just as much right to walk into this trap as you do."

He stared at her long and hard. "It's only a trap if you don't see it coming."

"We need a plan, Flynn. We shouldn't just walk into this, whatever you want to call it, without a plan."

"I have a plan."

That was the moment she remembered what Aikman said. The memory had rocks forming in her gut. "What did your friend mean when he said he would wait for your signal?"

"Let's go."

When he would have turned to start walking again, she grabbed him by the arm. "We're in too deep for you to blow me off at this stage of the game."

He stared at her, his own anger blazing in his eyes.

"It means just what he said, I give the signal, he and his people invade. I've given them the access codes along with the guard locations. Now let's get moving."

Did he really think she was going to let it go? "What's the signal?"

Since they didn't have a cell phone, beacon, flare gun, air horn or any damned thing else, just how the hell did he expect to give anyone outside the compound a signal?

The stare-off continued. Ten seconds, fifteen, twenty.

Enough. She made up her mind then and there. She grabbed him by the shirtfront and jerked his face down to hers. Then she kissed him. Kissed him hard on the mouth. Kept her lips pressed to his until he reacted. His fingers plowed into her hair and pulled her more firmly into him, deepening the kiss, taking control.

She poured herself into the kiss, into the feel of his mouth, his lips and his palms against her face. When the need for air forced them apart, he looked her straight in the eye and said, "I'm still not telling you."

The answer to the question was suddenly as clear as shiny new glass. He had no way of sending a signal.

"They have someone inside, don't they? That's the person who'll give the signal when you've done whatever it is Aikman has asked of you."

He looked away.

She shook her head. "All this time they've had someone inside. Why the hell do they need you?"

"We're running out of time. Let's go."

She grabbed him by the forearm, kept him from turning away. "No. Not until you tell me the truth."

Fury tightened the lips she had only moments ago kissed. Wanted to kiss again, damn her.

"You don't have a need to know, Agent Buchanan."

A sharp laugh burst out of her. "Don't even try playing that game with me." She held his gaze, silently demanding an answer. She saw the answer without him having to say a word. The determination as well as the resignation. Her heart stumbled. "You're going to kill Prentiss, aren't you? That's the signal Aikman will be waiting for."

He snapped his gaze away from hers and started to walk once more, but not before she saw the defeat in his eyes.

Prentiss's bodyguards would kill Flynn.

There was no way he would survive.

She had to figure out a way to turn this around.

Chapter 13

Smith started walking. He could not allow her to sway his decision. She didn't understand. Aikman would have killed her after doing other unspeakable things if Smith hadn't agreed to his terms.

There was no other choice. No way out.

It was true that at this moment there was some measure of leeway. Quite possibly they could take off and maybe get down this damned mountain before they were caught. But that would be like putting a gun to Levi Winters's head and pulling the trigger. If that wasn't bad enough, Prentiss would no doubt disappear.

This—right now—was the one chance Smith had of stopping him.

"You're a fool."

He ignored her, which wasn't easy to do. She had surprised him when she kissed him. He'd felt the mutual attraction almost from the beginning, couldn't have missed it if he'd tried. The intensity of it was his own fault. It had been way too long since he'd allowed himself basic human pleasures. She made him want to indulge those ignored needs. It was difficult for a starving man to ignore a buffet right in front of him.

"This goes against your training. We both understand what needs to happen. This is a textbook example of a no-win situation. We need backup."

"You feel strongly about following the rules, is that it, Buchanan?" She was as bad as him. She'd walked into a deadly situation without so much as a blink and damned sure without any backup. She had no right to judge his actions.

"It's not the same," she argued.

"It's exactly the same."

She stopped and turned to him. He bumped into her shoulder.

"I didn't walk into that compound prepared to kill a man."

Anger clenched his jaw. He struggled to utter an answer. She couldn't possibly understand. "He deserves to die."

She nodded. "Maybe so but not because you want to put a bullet in his brain. What you're talking about is premeditated murder. Are you a murderer, Flynn?"

He bit his lips together to prevent denying the charge. Maybe he was a murderer. He had never wanted to kill another man the way he wanted to kill Prentiss.

"If you are, what makes you any better than him?"

A part of him wanted to refute her words. To explain his reasoning. But did any of it really matter? He wanted to watch Rayford Prentiss die. He couldn't wait to see him take his last breath. Equally important, he wanted the bastard to know that he—Smith Flynn, the son of Avery Flynn—had been the one to bring his ruthless reign and his life to an end.

"Nothing," he admitted.

He walked on. They were close to the compound. The watchers would spot them and send out a team to bring them in. It wouldn't be long now.

The answer he'd given to her last question kept her quiet for a few minutes. She was searching for some other rationalization for why he couldn't do what Aikman had ordered him to do. He could practically hear the wheels in her head turning. She wanted to help him.

But she couldn't.

No one could. Not at this point. It was too late.

As much as he regretted what he had become and all the things he'd had to do, if necessary he would do it all again to stop Prentiss.

"Once we're inside, give me some time," she suddenly said, her voice low as if she feared the trees had ears. Most likely they did.

"Time for what?" He asked this without looking at her. He didn't want to look at her. Not simply because she was attractive and alluring and made him want things he shouldn't. But because she reminded him of all that was good—of the reason he became an agent in the first place. She made him want the career he'd had before this journey started. She made him wish things had been different.

Could he be that man again? Did the good part of him even still exist? He had worked for two long years to erase that guy. To make him immune to the emotions that would only get in his way.

Buchanan had made a valid point. He was a murderer. He'd killed the man he used to be. What he was now was no better than Prentiss.

He doubted there was any going back.

She stopped again, moved in close to him, making his body yearn to pull her close. "Once we're inside, give me time to create a distraction. We can turn this around, Flynn, make it work for us."

The hope in her eyes made him want to believe her. Made him want to grab on to the life raft she offered and hang on for the ride.

But what if she was wrong?

"He won't be fooled so easily this time. He knows he can't trust either of us. How do you expect to manipulate him in any way to buy time or anything else?"

She was an optimist. A woman who wanted to stand by the goodness and justice she believed in. She needed him to believe, too, but he'd lost the ability to blindly believe in anything.

"Trust me, Flynn. You would be surprised at the tricks I have up my sleeve."

He shouldn't agree to the idea. He should do what he had to do and be grateful for the opportunity.

But she made him want to do the right thing.

"I'll give you as much time as I can."

She grinned. "That's all I can ask for, partner."

Despite the worry and uncertainty nagging at him, he smiled back at her. Maybe they could turn this around.

He just hoped she lived through it. He had never expected to survive this assignment, but he didn't want to be the reason she lost her life.

As they ascended the next ridge, troops came out

of the trees. Seven, no eight. The group swarmed out and surrounded their position, weapons leveled on his and Buchanan's heads.

Smith held perfectly still. "I need to see Prentiss."

"He doesn't want to see you."

Smith knew this soldier. He was an ambitious man. He would want to prove he was somehow responsible for Smith's capture.

"Take me to him," he said to the younger man, daring him to argue. Smith was now listed as an enemy but there would be those who had their doubts. Those who feared turning their backs on him since it was not out of the question that he could be restored to his former position. After all, he was Avery Flynn's only son.

The soldier gave a nod to one of his minions. "Search them both."

When he and Buchanan had been patted down to the man's satisfaction, he ordered his team to move out. The soldiers stayed in a tight ring around Smith and Buchanan as they continued on to the compound.

The compound was only a mile or so away at this point. He glanced at Buchanan. Somehow he had to find a way to keep her from ending up dead no matter that she refused to cooperate.

She'd asked for time, which likely meant she had a plan. Maybe he should listen to her reasoning. She wasn't emotionally tangled up with this situation and he was. Her reasoning might be clearer than his own. He'd been guilty of a lot of mistakes over the years but he didn't have to make one today.

Prentiss waited alone in the meeting room.

Of course he wouldn't want any of the other members of the Council present when he said what he had to say. The secrets and lies he had kept over all these years were not the sort he wanted anyone to know, particularly those who looked to him to lead them. There was not a bigger con artist alive. The man was capable of anything if it gained him what he wanted. But the other members of the Council, the followers, none of them would ever believe he was anything other than a selfless leader who protected their way of life.

Smith had barely resisted the urge to take a swing at one of the guards when he prepared to separate Buchanan from him. As two guards dragged her away she had shouted for him to remember what she said.

He did remember.

For what it was worth, he would try his best to give her some time.

Smith was shackled and escorted to a chair, where he was forced to sit before the shackles around his ankles were anchored to the floor. Prentiss didn't speak until the guards had left the room. Only the two of them would ever know the whole story if Prentiss had his way.

"Is it true?" the old man asked as if he could hardly believe the reality of what had occurred.

"What would you know about the truth?" Looking at him sickened Smith. How had he managed these past two years?

"I know enough," Prentiss warned. "I know a mole when I see one. A traitor. A man whose entire existence is a betrayal to his own people."

"Doesn't matter now," Smith mused, deciding on a delay tactic that might just work. "You're finished."

The old man's gaze narrowed. "I don't believe you.

If the feds had anything on me, they would be here now arresting me and pinning medals on you." He glanced around the room. "I don't see or hear anyone coming to your rescue. Perhaps you should pray about this dilemma in which you find yourself."

Smith chuckled. "I don't need to pray, old man. I've spent two years feeding information to those feds. They have what they need, they're only waiting for the perfect moment. Believe me when I say that moment is close at hand."

"If that's true, then why were you and your friend still wandering about on this mountain? Why haven't your comrades rescued you? Or have they forsaken you as you have forsaken me?"

"I refused a rescue. I want to watch from right here." He smiled. "I want to witness them dragging you away in shackles." He shook his head. "Too bad the other members of the Council are going down with you. They are only guilty of following your orders. How fast do you think one or more of them will roll over and start spilling his guts about the executions and the shipments?"

Prentiss stood and moved toward him. He looked even older and more than a little frail in those overalls and worn boots. But there was nothing frail about this bastard. He was dangerous. Ruthless. Cunning as hell.

"I will know what you've told them," he warned as he braced his hands on the arms of the chair and leaned in close to Smith. "I will know every secret and every name you've shared. And then you will die a slow, agonizing death."

Smith allowed a wide smile to slide across his lips once more. "I shared them all. Every single name, every single secret. They know about your partners in South America. They know your next incoming shipment and the distribution channels you intend to use. They know *everything*."

"I want names," Prentiss demanded. "Who are your contacts?"

"You can't stop this, old man. They're coming and you and all this will fall."

Prentiss drew back sharply as if he feared catching some contagious disease. "Your father would be sickened by your actions. He would kill you himself."

Smith leaned forward as far as his shackles would allow. "My father was not like you. He would be grateful to me for stopping you."

Prentiss held his ground. "Maybe you're right. Avery had grown weak in his old age. He failed to see what was best for the security of our people. Progress is necessary. As is extending our reach. He was blind to those needs."

"But they followed him. Looked up to him. Not you," Smith reminded him. "You were always in his shadow."

Prentiss was the one smiling then. "And yet I'm still here and he is gone."

"How much longer do you think you can hang on when your people learn you failed to see the traitor in their midst? Or maybe they'll see you as the traitor."

"They already know what you are. You're just like your father. Weak. Shortsighted. A stumbling block to survival."

Anger ignited deep inside Smith. "My father was not weak. His vision was far greater than yours. You will never be half the leader he was."

"Before I order your public execution perhaps it's time you were told what really happened."

Smith stilled. His father suffered a heart attack. "I'm well aware of how he died."

On some level he would always believe that his decision to leave had been part of the burden that weighed upon his father, making him a prime candidate for a sudden heart attack. He couldn't help wondering if he'd secretly discovered what Smith had become, a traitor to all his father believed.

"His heart stopped true enough." Prentiss reared back, his thumbs hooked into the side splits of his overalls. "It was the only way to protect what we had achieved. He would have ruined everything."

Something cold and dark swelled inside Smith. "What does that mean?"

"It means," the bastard said, obviously enjoying the moment, "that he wanted to pull back. When he found out about my deal with the cartel, he demanded I leave. He intended to put me out after I had dedicated my life to the cause." Prentiss shrugged. "It was him or me. He was too sick to understand what he was saying and doing. So, as you can see, it wasn't me."

Shock radiated through Smith. "You killed him?"

"I did," Prentiss confessed. "Just like I'm going to kill you."

Sadie didn't bother struggling. Prentiss had ordered her to the tunnels. Her friend Levi, Prentiss had warned, was already there, unless he'd ended up as dinner earlier than expected.

No wonder Flynn wanted to kill the man. He was

a ruthless degenerate. Every minute he drew breath, someone else suffered.

The dome was pulled back by one of her guards, revealing the ladder that led deep under the ground. Sadie went along, feigning uncertainty. She had a plan and having it start in the tunnels would work to her advantage.

When she reached the bottom of the ladder, George was waiting. He still wore those flimsy flip-flops he'd bartered out of her.

"Wasn't expecting you back," he said. "I heard you ran off."

"I missed you and decided to drop by for a visit."

He stared at her a long moment, her light sarcasm seemingly lost on him. Finally, he nodded. "Anyway, your friend is down here, too. He ain't faring so well."

"What's wrong with him?"

"I guess he don't like the idea that if an emergency happens and we run out of food, he'll be the backup."

Levi was supplies. Prentiss had enjoyed telling her that, as well. Before George could turn and start walking away, she said, "We should probably talk before joining the others."

He frowned. "You know the drill down here. What do we have to talk about?"

Sadie looked around as if to make sure no one else was nearby. "They're coming today. If all of you are still here, you'll end up in jail, too."

Confusion flashed in his eyes. "Who's coming?"

"The feds, local law enforcement. They're coming to take Prentiss and the Council to jail. They know everything about this place."

He shrugged. "They've boasted about taking Prentiss down before and it never happens. He's way too careful."

"Trust me, George. I'm with the FBI. They know everything. You were nice to me so I'd like to help you and the others down here. But there isn't a lot of time. We should get out of here while we still can."

"What?" He drew back as if her words had attacked him.

"You know how to get out. You've dug egress routes. You know where they are and how to use them. Don't pretend you don't, George."

"I think we should get to work." He started walking deeper into the tunnel.

Sadie didn't move. She stayed next to the ladder. She wasn't going anywhere until she got George thinking about how easy it would be to escape this tunnel and flee to someplace well beyond the reach of the Resurrection. Not that the group would have any power left when this was done. She decided on a new tactic.

"Prentiss and the rest of the Council are leaving. You think they're going to let you guys out of here before they evacuate?" She shook her head. "They'll leave you to die. The authorities can't question the dead."

He stalled, shook his head at her. "You're lying."

"I'm not lying, George. I have no reason to lie. I just don't want to die and that's what will happen if we don't get out of here."

He started walking again. She followed.

"The feds are coming to take Prentiss and his Council down. They'll be here before nightfall. We don't have time to waste. Prentiss and his cronies are going to get away clean and all of us down here won't."

He stopped and glanced back at her again. "If what you're saying is true, what do you expect us to do?"

"You told me about the egresses you've prepared. Let's go to the closest one and get out of here before it's too late. Before Prentiss orders any and all loose ends cleaned up."

"There will be guards waiting at the egresses," he argued. "They'll shoot us."

She shook her head. "They'll be gone. They're afraid. They're not going to hang around once word about what's coming gets around."

George kept moving until he reached the work area. Sadie trudged along behind him. Levi was there and he looked in reasonably good condition. No visible injuries. Relief rushed through her. Maybe this would be a second chance to get him safely out of here. This time she wasn't allowing him out of her sight. She fully intended to deliver him to his sister.

With his shovel in his hand, George joined the others. Sadie wanted to shake him. Why the hell wasn't he listening? She needed something to happen soon if she was going to help Smith.

"Hey," she shouted at him. "Didn't you hear what I said? We have to get out of here or we're all going to die. Why aren't you telling these people?"

Several of the men glanced at her and then at George but made no move to stop what they were doing.

"Levi!" She waited for him to look at her. "Come on. We're getting out of here."

He looked around at the other men. Just when Sadie was certain he would keep working, he threw down his shovel and walked toward her.

Another wave of relief swept through her. "Who else is with us?"

She scanned the dirty faces. All stared at her, their expressions weary, defeated.

"Tell them, George," she urged. "Tell them what's about to happen up there. We have to run while we still can."

George stared at her for a long moment, then he threw down his pickax and stalked toward her. She held her breath, not certain whether he intended to yank her over to take his place or if he intended to join her.

When he reached her, he turned back to the others. "We'll need shovels and axes. It'll take us at least twenty minutes and if they see us on the cameras, they'll come down here and make us wish we hadn't listened to her."

"We can do this," Sadie urged, not wanting his warning to dissuade them. "We'll work faster than we ever have before."

George surveyed the men now watching him. "Grab your shovels and the axes. We're out of here."

Much to her immense gratitude, George led the way. Sadie and Levi followed. At least twelve more hustled along the corridor behind them. She glanced at the cameras placed overhead approximately every fifteen yards along the seemingly endless corridor. They wouldn't have a lot of time.

The alarm was sounding by the time they reached the closest egress. Six of the men climbed the ladders and started to dig. Six more formed a wall across the tunnel in anticipation of the guards who would no doubt come.

The sound of boots pounding on the ground echoed

through the tunnel. George and his friends were shouting at each other to hurry. Sadie dragged Levi closer.

"As soon as that egress is cleared," she murmured close to his ear, "we have to get out of here and go for help."

He nodded his understanding.

Shouting in the tunnel echoed some ten yards away. *Hurry.* Sadie looked from the wall of bodies standing between the coming guards and their position to the men jabbing and poking overhead.

"Go!"

Sadie jerked her attention toward George. Sunlight suddenly poured into the tunnel. Three of the men were already scrambling out.

"Let's go." Sadie nudged Levi forward.

They rushed up the ladders and climbed out. Two guards who had been taking a smoke break suddenly turned toward them. George and the others were on top of them before they could get their weapons into position.

Others were clambering out behind Sadie and Levi.

Sadie didn't look back. She held on to Levi's hand and ran through the woods as fast as she could.

She had no idea how far they were from help but she had to get to wherever that was as quickly as possible.

Smith's life depended upon it.

Chapter 14

Sadie kept a firm grasp on Levi's hand as they ran through the woods, branches and undergrowth slapping at her bare legs.

The crack of gunfire behind them forced Sadie's heart into a faster cadence.

She charged forward with a new burst of adrenaline-inspired speed. Levi managed to keep up though he was barefoot and stumbling with exhaustion. He would pay for the lack of shoes or boots later. She imagined he had blisters on his hands just as she'd had after her time in the tunnel, though hers were partially healed now.

If the guards got off a good shot, the two of them would have far more than blisters to worry about.

"This way." Levi tugged at the hand she had clenched around his.

He knew the area and she didn't. She might as well

trust him. He had as much reason to want to escape this mountain as she did. Staying alive was always a strong motivator no matter which side of the equation one was on.

Levi deviated into a different direction. Plowed through the jungle of trees.

By the time they slowed Sadie could barely get her breath.

"Hold on a minute." Levi leaned against a tree and struggled to catch his breath, as well.

Sadie propped against the nearest tree and took slow, deep breaths. When she could string words together, she asked, "How far to civilization?"

"If we keep going this way—" he hitched a thumb in the direction they'd been headed, south Sadie thought "—we'll hit the valley in about a mile and a half. There are a few houses in that area. We can probably use a phone there."

Sadie nodded. Worked for her.

When they headed out again they moved considerably slower. Sadie's muscles burned from the hard run and the abuse they'd suffered the past several days. She would need weeks to recover from the way she'd mistreated her body on this mission.

Assuming she survived. She glanced over her shoulder to ensure no one was coming. Clear for now.

As they moved downward the underbrush grew less dense. Even the trees weren't so thick. Up ahead beyond the tree line an open pasture came into view. She and Levi hesitated at the edge of the woods to have a look at what lay beyond.

Sadie spotted a house and barn in the distance. Judging by the cows in the field and the farm equipment scattered about, someone lived there. There were other houses beyond that one. Acres of open pasture rolled out between the houses. She glanced behind her once more. Moving through those open areas would be risky if the enemy on their trail caught up with them.

Sadie turned to the man at her side. "Do you know any of the people who live on this stretch of road?"

Levi shook his head. "All we need is to use the phone, right? Surely one of them will let us do that whether they know us or not."

Sadie nodded. "We'll tell them our car broke down. If we mention the trouble on our heels, they may not let us in the house. Some people don't like to get involved."

"Yeah." He surveyed the expanse of green space in front of them. "You're right. We can't tell them what's really going on."

Sadie scanned the woods behind them. She listened for several seconds. "Maybe we lost those guards."

More than a dozen people had escaped the tunnel. Most went in different directions. Hopefully, the two guards she had spotted as well as those who had come up from the tunnel had followed some of the others. Not that she wished that unlucky break on anyone, but she was only human.

"Let's try that first house," she suggested. "The sooner we get to town the sooner we can send help for Flynn." Her stomach twisted at the idea that he could be dead already. She had urged him to buy some time. To do his best to drag out the inevitable. She hoped he was successful. As long as he didn't allow his emotions to take over, he would be okay. He was a well-trained agent. Hopefully that training would kick in and keep him thinking smart.

With one last backward glance, she and Levi dashed across the pasture. Part of her braced for the crack of a weapon firing at them but it didn't come. As they neared the house a cow raised its head and stared at them.

They bounded up onto the front porch. Levi reached the door first. He knocked. Sadie kept a watch on the tree line to ensure no one came rushing out after them. All they needed was a phone. One call.

Her pulse pounded as Levi knocked again. No television sound, no footsteps moving about. The house sounded empty. Worried that was indeed the case, Sadie peered through the nearest window. *Kitchen.* There were drying dishes on a towel on the counter. If no one was home now, they had been earlier.

"Somebody lives here." She checked the tree line and pasture again.

A loud thump drew her attention to the door. Levi backed up and body-slammed it again, using his right shoulder.

Sadie winced as he slammed it a third time before it gave way and burst inward.

She exhaled a big breath and followed him across the threshold. Breaking and entering wasn't such a bad thing considering they were running for their lives.

"Phone's over here," Levi said.

Sadie went to the side table beneath the big front window. "Have a look around and make sure no one's in the shower or something. We don't need an armed homeowner thinking we mean harm to him or his property."

She sure as hell didn't want to escape armed killers only to end up shot by a terrified farmer or his wife.

Levi nodded and headed into the hall. The house was a brick rancher, not so large. It wouldn't take him long to have a look.

Sadie entered 911 into the handset. As soon as the dispatcher finished her spiel, she identified herself and asked to be connected to Sheriff Tanner.

Tanner was on the line in under twenty seconds.

Sadie sagged with relief. "Tanner, we're..." Hearing footsteps, she turned to ask Levi exactly where they were.

Gun.

She froze.

Levi stood in the cased opening between the living room and the hall, his hands high in the air. An older man wearing a cap had the business end of a rifle jammed into the side of his head. Levi's eyes were round with fear.

"I tried to tell him we need help," Levi explained.

"Put the phone down," the man demanded.

Damn. "Sir, I'm on the phone with Sheriff Tanner." She thrust the phone at the man. "We're unarmed. Speak to the sheriff and he'll explain everything."

The man backed away from Levi but kept a bead on his head. He took the cordless phone receiver from Sadie and backed a few steps farther away in order to keep them both in his line of vision.

"Sheriff Tanner, this is Cord Hawkins." Hawkins gave the address and then listened as Tanner spoke.

Sadie couldn't make out what he was saying but she heard the rumble of his voice. Judging by the way the man lowered the barrel of his weapon, he understood Sadie and Levi were no threat to him.

"I'll do it," Hawkins said. He offered the receiver to Sadie. "Sheriff wants to talk to you again."

"Thank you." Sadie took the phone and pressed it to her ear. "Tell me you're on your way. We don't have much time."

As Tanner passed along orders via another phone line, Sadie was vaguely aware that Hawkins had brought cans of cola from the kitchen. He passed one to Levi and offered one to her.

Sadie summoned a smile and murmured a thank-you. She popped the top and downed half the can before Tanner turned his attention back to the conversation with her.

"Sit tight, Agent Buchanan, we're on our way to you. We'll have that mountain covered within the hour."

Sadie ended the call and drank more of the cola. Levi leaned against the wall and slid to the floor as he guzzled his cola. Sadie closed her eyes against the weariness dragging at her. She had never been so tired in her life.

"Are those friends of yours?"

Sadie jerked her attention back to the here and now and rushed across the room to the big window. Hawkins pointed at three men running across the same pasture she and Levi had sprinted across. She peered across the distance to make out their faces. One was George, she decided. She didn't need to recognize the faces of the other two. All wore the dirty sweats and sported the greasy hair and dirty faces of tunnel workers.

"They were prisoners just like us." She turned to Hawkins. "They're not the bad guys."

His fingers tightened around his rifle. "You sure about that, ma'am?"

She nodded. "I'll go out and talk to them."

"I'll be watching," Hawkins assured her.

"Thank you."

Sadie stepped out the front door as the three men bounded up the porch steps. "Did they follow you?" She hadn't seen anyone else coming out of that tree line.

George shook his head. "We lost them."

"Hurry." Sadie opened the door. "Let's get inside. The sheriff is on the way with help."

Hawkins passed out colas to the three and dug up a couple of big bags of chips. The men ate as if they hadn't eaten in days. Probably hadn't. She kept her attention on the tree line and said a prayer for Flynn.

He was still at that compound. On his own.

"The sheriff's here," Hawkins announced.

A whole parade of official vehicles arrived. Uniformed deputies and officers poured into the house. Paramedics insisted on giving Sadie, Levi and the other three a quick check while she and George provided information about the compound, the people there and the precarious position in which they'd left Agent Smith Flynn.

Winchester's chief of police, William Brannigan, was already on the phone with the ATF. The state police and the Bureau had been notified en route. Through the window Sadie spotted Agent Ross and Cece Winters, coming up the porch steps.

"Levi." Sadie turned to the young man who had resumed his seat on the floor. "Someone's here for you."

He pushed to his feet at the same time that his sister

and Ross entered the house. The reunion of brother and sister was the one good thing that had happened this day. Sadie was grateful to be a part of it.

Cece Winters hugged Sadie next. "Thank you for rescuing my brother."

Sadie glanced at Levi. "I think it was a mutual rescue."

He smiled. "Maybe."

Special Agent Deacon Ross shook Sadie's hand. "I appreciate what you must have gone through to make this happen."

"We're not finished yet," she warned. "There's a war about to happen on that mountain. The Resurrection and the *others* are going head-to-head. Agent Flynn is caught in the middle of it. He could be dead already. We have to hurry."

George suddenly stepped forward. "I know the one access road to get to that compound. Know the codes, too. I'll take you there."

The other two who had come with George echoed his offer.

They all wanted to see Prentiss go down.

No one wanted that more than Sadie.

"Ms. Winters will take you back to my office," Tanner said to Sadie.

She shook her head. "No way. I'm going with you."

Tanner started to argue but he must have seen the absolute determination in Sadie's eyes. He nodded. "All right, then, let's move out."

Smith struggled to focus.

He hung from a hook attached to the ceiling, his feet dangling several inches off the floor. He'd been stripped to the waist and tortured for hours. He'd lost track of the time.

The beating he rode out without much more than a flinch. The shock torture had become tedious the last half hour or so. This was nothing he hadn't endured before. But it was the burns that were about to be inflicted with a branding iron he would just as soon skip.

Prentiss, the son of a bitch, watched from a safe distance across the room as the irons turned red amid the fiery coals. Smith knew the soldier tasked with the job of inflicting the torture. The man didn't appear to feel bad about having to torture an old friend. Maybe Smith had made more enemies than he'd realized during his time here. Or maybe the guy was just glad to be the one inflicting the torture and not the one receiving it.

Who could blame him?

The one thing Smith knew with absolute certainty was that providing he survived long enough he would kill Rayford Prentiss if it was the last thing he ever did.

The bastard had admitted to murdering his father.

Prentiss was responsible for the deaths of countless other people with his gunrunning and drug trade. And that was only the beginning.

As if his thoughts had summoned him, Prentiss dared to venture closer. He surveyed Smith, enjoying the blood dribbling from his mouth and nose, the swelling of his face and eyes as well as the bruises forming on his torso. All these things gave him pleasure. This bastard had tortured and murdered many. But Smith would be his last, one way or another.

Whether Smith survived this day or not, Buchanan would ensure the bastard got what he deserved.

If she had survived.

Smith closed his eyes against any other possibility. She was too smart and too determined to fail. Prentiss had been called out of the room once, a couple of hours ago. Smith hadn't been able to hear all that was said but he'd picked up on the gist of the conversation. There had been an escape. Ten or twelve people had dug out of the tunnel and evaded the posted guards.

She would be one of them, Smith felt certain.

Go, Sadie.

A smile tugged at his damaged lips. He liked her name. *Sadie.* He liked her sassiness and her courage.

He hoped he had the chance to get to know her better.

"What on God's green earth do you have to smile about, boy?"

Smith opened his swollen eyes as best he could. "I was just thinking how you'll rot in prison with all your friends. Oh wait." He managed a rusty laugh. "You don't have any friends. That should be interesting."

He'd expected Aikman to show up even though he didn't get a signal indicating Smith had taken care of Prentiss. With all the access codes and information Smith had provided him, he'd figured the man would make a move either way.

"I thought maybe you were worried about your own friend, or enemy as the case might be," Prentiss said. "Aikman, I believe his name is."

Smith clenched his aching jaw to prevent showing a reaction to the name.

"You see, I found out about his man inside. He was watching, nosing around in places he didn't belong today, so I guessed something was up. Unlike you, he sang like a bird with very little prodding. My people are on high alert. No one is getting into this compound today or any other. Strange." He rubbed at his beard. "I understand you were going to kill me. Whatever changed your mind?"

Smith smiled again, his split lip burning like fire. "I decided I'd rather know that you're rotting in a prison cell than give you an easy way out. I want you to live, old man. A very long time so you can enjoy what the future holds for you when justice is served."

Prentiss picked up one of the knives lying on the table with all the other torture instruments. He turned it over in his hand, pretending to inspect the stainless steel blade and handle.

Tension slid through Smith. He braced to lift his legs and kick him across the room. He'd been waiting for time alone with the guy administering the torture in hopes of using that move as a means to escape, but so far that moment hadn't come. Once he attempted any sort of maneuver, if he was unsuccessful steps would be taken to ensure he was unable to repeat the effort. So he had waited. Unfortunately, his strength was waning far too quickly. He'd have to make a move soon or find himself unable to do so.

The door on the other side of the room opened and one of Prentiss's private bodyguards rushed in. He whispered something in the old man's ear. Prentiss set the knife aside. His gaze settled on Smith as he listened to the rest of what the man had to say.

It was happening. Smith didn't have to hear the words. He saw the abrupt fear in the old man's eyes.

Prentiss looked to the other man in the room. "Finish him and clear out."

Oh yeah. Either Aikman and his people were descending on the compound or the backup Sadie had gone after was close.

Either option suited Smith.

Prentiss hurried out with his bodyguard.

Smith held very still as the man who'd beat and tortured him walked toward him for the last time. Mentally preparing himself to expend the last of his physical strength, Smith waited until the man was close enough to pick up that big-ass knife from the table. His fingers wrapped around the handle and he weighed it, hoping to add a layer of tension, to build the dread.

Smith made his move.

He wrapped his legs around the man's neck and squeezed. Struggling to free himself, the bastard lifted his right hand, aiming the knife at Smith.

Smith used his whole body to jerk to the right, snapping the bastard's neck. His eyes bulged. The knife fell from his slack fingers and clanged on the floor. Smith loosened his hold and the now-lifeless body followed that route, dropping like a rock.

Swinging his legs to the left, Smith grabbed hold of the table with his bare feet. He hung that way for a moment to catch his breath and to give his muscles a moment to recover. Slowly, he used his feet to drag the table closer. When he could kneel on it, he rested another moment. Finally, he pushed upward, lifting his bound hands from the meat hook that had held him suspended in the air. He collapsed into a kneeling position on the table. A few minutes were required for his arms to stop stinging.

He scooted off the table and found his footing on the floor. Where the hell was the key to these wrist shackles? He checked the table and the items that had been flung to the floor when he'd dragged it close. No key. Then he checked the dead guy who'd wielded the hours of torture. The key was in his right front pocket. Smith pulled the key free.

Collapsing into a cross-legged position, he focused on getting the key into the lock that held an iron bracelet around his left wrist. He dropped the key, once, twice before he managed to get it into the lock. He had to twist his right hand in an awkward position to turn the key but he finally managed. The lock on his left wrist fell open. Relief surged through him. He picked up the key and unlocked the bracelet on his right wrist. When the final shackle fell free, he rubbed his wrists and dragged in a deep breath. His damaged ribs ached with the move.

Pushing to his feet, he surveyed the room for a weapon.

Depending on who had arrived, he could be in for another battle for his life. He turned over the dead guy, snatched the gun from his waistband. He checked the ammo cartridge. Full. He shoved the gun into his waistband and went in search of his shoes. He finally found them in a pile with the shirt that had been cut from his body. The shirt he could live without but the shoes would be useful.

Now to find Prentiss before the bastard managed to slip away.

Smith stalled halfway to the door and went back to the dead guy for his cell phone. It was possible Prentiss would call to ensure Smith was dead. He no doubt wanted Smith dead as badly as Smith wanted him caught. A vehicle fob fell out of the guy's pocket. Smith took that, as well.

Running footsteps in the corridor outside the door snapped Smith's attention in that direction. He started toward the door. Halfway across the room it opened.

Smith leveled the weapon on the potential threat.

Aikman.

Chapter 15

"Well, well, if it isn't the man who failed his mission." Aikman shook his head. "*Tsk, tsk*, Flynn, I had you pegged for better than that."

Apparently the idea that Smith was the one holding the gun aimed at him didn't faze the guy. Aikman's weapon was in his hand but not aimed at anything other than the floor. Whoever else had been in that corridor with him had moved on to the next door. A bad decision any way you looked at it.

"I was working on it and the bastard found out you had invaded the compound. So he took off while I was still a little tied up."

Aikman glanced at the meat hook beyond Smith. "Ouch."

Smith wasn't sure whether the guy was trying to put

him off-balance or if he really wasn't worried about the weapon aimed at his head just now.

"You might want to put that weapon away," Smith suggested. "I don't want to get nervous and do something we'll both regret."

Aikman smiled, made a laugh/grunt sound. "Of course." He tucked the weapon into his waistband. "We've decided we prefer these accommodations over our own. So we'll be taking over the compound."

"You planning on killing everyone here?" Smith hoped like hell backup was close.

Aikman shrugged. "There are some I'd rather have join my team." He made a questioning face. "You interested, Flynn?"

He lowered his weapon and wiped his bleeding mouth. "Why not? As long as the terms are agreeable."

Aikman glanced around the room. "Where's your little friend? I was looking forward to seeing her again."

"I'd like to know the answer to that one myself." He started toward the door that Aikman currently blocked. "I'm hoping Prentiss didn't take her with him." Smith knew that wasn't the case but Aikman couldn't know.

Aikman turned his back to Smith and exited the room first. The guy continued to surprise Smith.

"We've rounded up all the Council members." Aikman glanced at him as they moved along the corridor. "Except Prentiss and you, of course."

Dread thickened in Smith's gut. "Did you kill them?"

Aikman shook his head. "Not yet. They no doubt have information I'll need going forward. Unless you have everything you think we'll need. In that case we can be rid of them right away."

"Prentiss was careful never to give all the power to one person. Each of us had our domain. We'll need them all."

This was a lie but if it kept Aikman from performing a mass execution, that was all that mattered.

There was just one problem as far as Smith could see. He couldn't be sure which of the Council members would be smart enough to keep his mouth shut about him being an undercover agent. If any of those who knew warned Aikman, this situation would do a one-eighty in a heartbeat.

He needed that backup to arrive now.

"I have them gathered in the conference room." Aikman glanced at him. "We'll join them and start the downloading of information, so to speak."

"I'll meet you there in fifteen. I need to wash the blood off my face and change clothes. We don't want them to see any sign of weakness. We need to present strength and unity so they'll understand the shift in power."

"Smart move. Fifteen minutes." Aikman suddenly stopped and turned back. "Ollie!"

One of his followers hustled up to join them. "Escort our friend Mr. Flynn to his personal lodging. Ensure he's in the conference room in fifteen minutes."

"Yes, sir." The man named Ollie turned his shaggy head to glare at Smith. "Let's go, Flynn."

Aikman didn't trust him as much as he'd let on. That made them even because Smith didn't trust him at all.

Outside was quiet. "Where is everyone?"

"They're in the detection center."

Smith was surprised the other man, Ollie, gave him an answer but he was glad he had. As much as Smith despised Prentiss, he did not want this day to turn into a mass killing of people whose only mistake was believing in the wrong man.

Walking across the quad was eerie. No sound. No movement. Nothing. The faces in the guard towers were unfamiliar to Smith. Aikman's people, no doubt. When they reached his cabin, Ollie went in, looked around and then waited outside, leaving the door open.

"If you go in the bathroom," he said to Smith, "don't close the door."

"Got it."

Smith grabbed fresh clothes and went into the tiny bathroom. He pulled the cell phone from his pocket, placed it on the sink, then did the same with the gun. When he'd dragged on the clean clothes, he looked to see that Ollie was still outside the door. He held the phone where it couldn't be seen from the door and sent a text message to 911. He had no idea if the 911 service in the area was able to receive text messages but, at the moment, it was his only available option. He couldn't risk making a call with Aikman's man right outside.

Once he'd sent the text, he deleted it. He set the phone to silent just in case the dispatcher tried to call him back, then slid it into his hip pocket. He shoved the weapon into his waistband at the small of his back, then washed his face.

His eyes and jaw were swollen, and he was reasonably sure he had a couple of cracked ribs, but things could be far worse.

He joined Ollie outside. "I'm ready."

The walk across the quad was the same as before,

too quiet. Too still. They reached the headquarters and entered. Two guards were posted outside the door to the conference room. Ollie walked right up and opened the door and entered. Smith followed him.

The scene in the room brought him up short. The members of the Council lay on the floor in a neat line. All were dead, all had been shot once in the head.

His gaze swung to Aikman, who stood in the center of the room. Behind him someone was seated in a chair but Smith couldn't see who it was since Aikman blocked his view.

"I thought we were going to interrogate them." He glared at Aikman, his fingers itching to reach for the weapon in his waistband.

As if Ollie had sensed his thought, he plucked the weapon from Smith.

"That was far too much trouble," Aikman said. "It seemed far easier to simply go to the head and learn everything straight from the source."

He stepped aside, revealing the person in the chair. *Rayford Prentiss.*

"You weren't expecting to see me, were you, *Agent* Flynn?" Prentiss laughed. "Looks like this game of double-cross is going to turn out just fine for me." He glanced up at Aikman. "New blood is always a good thing."

Sadie dropped to her haunches next to Sheriff Tanner. "Aikman and his people have taken over," she said, worry gnawing at her. "We can't wait, we have to move fast. The killing won't stop until we stop it."

The text message relayed to Tanner from the 911

dispatcher mentioned heavily armed men and numerous prisoners. Dozens were dead already.

Sadie's chest squeezed. The text had to be from Flynn, which meant, for now, he was still alive. She hoped he stayed that way until they could get in there and stop the killing.

The good news was, inside those walls were the leaders of the Resurrection and those of the *others*. This operation was going to stop two of the worst kind of extremist organizations in one fell swoop.

As much as she wanted to be grateful for that possibility, she couldn't help worrying about Flynn. She didn't want him to end up a casualty. She wanted to spend time with him. Time that didn't involve a mission or a race to stay alive.

Tanner nodded. "We're almost ready."

Sadie had been able to warn them about the scouts around the compound. Strangely they hadn't spotted any outside the walls. Had to have something to do with the takeover. Several bodies had been discovered.

Tanner put a hand on her arm. "We're moving." His gaze locked with hers. "But you're staying right here until we have the situation under control."

She drew her arm away from his touch. "No way, Sheriff. I'm going in with you."

He nodded to someone behind her and she shot to her feet only to come face-to-face with two female deputies.

"Ma'am," the dark-haired one said, "we'll go in as soon as we receive the all-clear signal from the sheriff."

Anger swirled through Sadie as she watched Tanner sprint forward. He'd double-crossed her. Dwelling on the reality would only distract her so she shrugged it off and focused on the events unfolding only yards away.

The two deputies moved in close next to her. One wore earbuds to listen in to the ongoing operation. The other watched through binoculars. Tanner hadn't left these two women with her because he didn't think women were as strong as men. Sadie had noticed seven female deputies. The other five had obviously gone in with Tanner. One of the women, she noticed, was very pregnant. She would have needed to stay away from live fire anyway.

Obviously she was fearless or she wouldn't be in these woods right now.

The echo of gunfire jerked her attention forward. The exchange was happening outside the entrance to the compound that had been built into the mountainside. Aikman no doubt had the entrance heavily guarded.

The sudden silence was more unnerving than the bursts of gunfire had been.

One minute turned into two and Sadie couldn't take it a second longer.

"Sorry, ladies, but I can't do this."

Sadie took off in a sprint. The deputy who wasn't pregnant rushed after her. Sadie ran harder. She disappeared into the thick trees and underbrush that camouflaged the entrance. The entrance stood open, dead followers lying on the ground.

Inside, Tanner's deputies had fanned out and were entering buildings.

Sadie palmed her weapon and headed for the headquarters building. As she neared the entrance, Tanner and the female caught up with her.

He pulled her next to a vehicle that had been parked there.

"What the hell are you trying to do, Buchanan?"

"They'll be in there." She jerked her head toward the building that was the headquarters. "This is where all the decisions are made. Where the Council meets."

"And you're certain Flynn will be in there."

His words hit like a blow to her midsection. She wasn't certain. She was guessing. Speculating. Concluding the most likely scenario.

"It makes the most sense." Sadie suddenly felt completely unsure.

Tanner used his radio to divert resources to their position. Sadie's heart thundered in her chest. What if she was wrong?

A single shot exploded beyond the walls of the headquarters building. Sadie might not have heard it if one of those moments of absolute silence hadn't settled around them beforehand. And the entry door stood open.

Tanner was the first to move. He burst through the open entrance.

Sadie was right behind him. The other deputy behind her.

With Tanner's glance at her, Sadie moved ahead of him and led the way to the conference room where she had been questioned by the Resurrection Council.

At the door Tanner gave her the signal to wait.

His next signal had Sadie and the deputy dropping into a crouch. Tanner banged on the closed door.

The door opened and a guard walked out.

Tanner rammed the muzzle of his weapon into his temple and pulled him aside.

Another guard rushed out. Sadie handled him.

"Well, well, it appears we have the proverbial stand-off."

Sadie recognized the voice. Aikman.

"Do come in," he said. "Agent Flynn and I were just discussing our next move."

Leaving the two guards under the careful watch of the female deputy, Tanner and Sadie entered the conference room.

"Drop the weapon," Tanner ordered.

Sadie moved to one side of Tanner, who had a bead on his target. When her brain absorbed the image before her, her heart sank to the floor.

Aikman had Flynn on his knees. His weapon was pressed against Flynn's forehead. Nearby Prentiss sat in a chair, the bullet hole between his eyes leaking blood.

On the floor to her left was a line of dead bodies.

The Council members.

"I'll drop the weapon when I'm safely on my way out of here," Aikman argued. "I'll turn Agent Flynn loose at that time, as well. Otherwise, I'm going to do the same thing to him that I did to Prentiss and the members of his esteemed Council."

As Tanner negotiated with the man who wasn't going to change his mind, Sadie made a decision. She lowered her weapon. "Take me instead. The Bureau is far more flexible in these negotiations than the ATF. Did we mention that both are here?"

Something flashed ever so briefly across Aikman's face. Flynn's was far easier to read: he was not happy with her offer.

"Back off," Tanner muttered to her.

Aikman grinned, obviously enjoying the dissention.

"Well, aren't you the brave one? Come on over here and I'll let your friend go."

Sadie stepped forward.

"Don't do it, Buchanan," Tanner warned, his attention zeroed in on Aikman.

"It won't be my first bait and switch, Sheriff." She looked directly at Smith as she said this but quickly shifted her gaze to Aikman. "I'm not afraid of this guy."

Aikman smirked. "That's an astounding statement considering the dead bodies lining the room."

It was in that moment—that fraction of a second when Aikman thought he had to prove how scary he was—that Flynn made his move.

He twisted and dove into Aikman's knees.

Sadie dropped to the floor.

As if he'd been in on the plan from the beginning, Tanner fired one shot straight into Aikman's right shoulder. The fool's weapon fell from his suddenly limp fingers as he was propelled backward by Flynn.

Flynn grabbed Aikman's weapon and pushed to his feet. Aikman clutched at his shoulder, right where that major nerve center would be, and howled.

"Good shot," Flynn said to Tanner.

Sadie pushed to her feet but her knees had gone so weak she had no idea how she would remain upright.

Tanner took over the prisoner and Flynn walked toward her.

Her breath caught at the injuries to his face or maybe just at the sight of him moving toward her.

He was alive.

She was alive.

And they were getting out of here.

Flynn wrapped his arms around her and hugged her. The weapon in her right hand slipped to the floor. Her arms went around him.

"Thanks for coming back to rescue me," he murmured against her hair.

She turned her face up to him. "It's what I do."

He smiled then grimaced.

"Your face looks like hell," she pointed out.

"Feels like it, too."

The next several hours were filled with rounding up prisoners and getting medical attention to those injured, as well as identifying the dead.

Flynn refused to bother with being checked out until the work was done. By the time they were off that mountain, Sadie was ready to drop.

George was in the DA's office making a deal. Sadie was glad. He'd paid in that tunnel for whatever he'd done wrong. Aikman was trying to work out a deal, as well. As it turned out the remains in that rock hole at Aikman's compound were those of Jack Kemp. The FBI had waited a long time to learn this information but both Ross and Tanner assured Sadie that Aikman wouldn't be getting any sort of deal beyond the possible setting aside of the death penalty.

Aikman was like Prentiss; he didn't deserve a deal. He deserved a long life behind bars where he'd have plenty of time to reflect on his bad judgment.

Deacon Ross had accompanied Levi Winters for his statement.

The place was crawling with federal agents.

Sadie's SAIC had called and made sure she was okay. Flynn had been sequestered to one of the interview rooms for his debrief. She had called her parents just to hear their voices. There was really no reason at this point for her to stay. She had done what she came here to do. She could go home. Maybe even call her sister.

Maybe if she told herself a couple more times there was no reason to stay she would talk herself into walking away without waiting for a chance to say goodbye to Flynn. He'd already thanked her for rescuing him. Goodbye wasn't actually necessary.

Except it felt necessary.

"Agent Buchanan."

Sadie looked up at the sound of her name. Cece Winters smiled as she walked through the door of the sheriff's office where Sadie had taken refuge. It was about the only room in the building that wasn't filled with agents and deputies. Tanner had told Sadie to make herself at home.

"Hey." Sadie returned the smile. "I'm sure they'll allow Levi to go home soon. This part takes a while sometimes."

Cece nodded as she sat down in the chair next to Sadie. "I wanted to thank you again for saving my brother not once but twice."

"He did his part," Sadie told her. "He's a good guy. A little confused maybe, but a good guy."

"Deacon and I plan on seeing that he gets back on the right track."

Sounded like the two were definitely a couple. Sadie had gotten that impression.

"Ladies."

Sadie's attention swung to the door once more. Flynn stood there, still looking a little worse for the wear.

Cece got to her feet. "I should see how Levi's doing."

She slipped out of the office and Flynn walked in. He closed the door behind him. Sadie looked from the closed door to him, her pulse starting to pound.

"I was afraid you'd left already."

"I was just getting ready to go." She tried to think what to say next. "It'll be good to get home."

He nodded. "I don't want to keep you." He exhaled a big breath. "But I was hoping we could get a bite to eat first. I don't know about you, but I'm starved."

As if her belly had just realized how empty it was, she nodded. "I could eat. Sure."

"Good."

They stood there for a moment without saying more. Sadie suspected he felt as awkward as she did. Neither of them was the kind of person who did this well.

"We both live in the Nashville area."

"Home sweet home." She felt heat rush to her cheeks. What a totally dumb thing to say.

He smiled, grimaced. "Yeah. Anyway, I hoped we might spend some time together. You know, get to know each other better."

She felt certain the grin that spread across her face said way too much about how happy his words made her. "I would like that very much."

"It's been a long time," he admitted, "since I've met anyone who understood this life…who made me want to get to know them better."

She was certain it would be entirely dorky for her to say the same thing. Instead, she put her hand in his. "I'm ready."

"I could take you home," he offered. "I heard you lost your car."

She laughed. "I would love for you to take me home."

That was all she needed to say. The rest would take care of itself.

* * * * *

Carol Ericson is a bestselling, award-winning author of more than forty books. She has an eerie fascination for true-crime stories, a love of film noir and a weakness for reality TV, all of which fuel her imagination to create her own tales of murder, mayhem and mystery. To find out more about Carol and her current projects, please visit her website at carolericson.com, "where romance flirts with danger."

UNDERCOVER ACCOMPLICE

Carol Ericson

Prologue

He ducked into the cave and swept the beam from the weak flashlight around the small space. Releasing a frosty breath, he slid down the wall of the cave into a crouch and faced the entrance, balancing his weapon on his knees.

After he'd helped Rafi and the others fight off the intruders who'd attacked their village, he took off for the hills—but not before he'd arranged another meeting with Pazir.

The last time he'd tried to meet with Pazir, it had led to the death of an army ranger, the possible death of one of his Delta Force team members and his own decision to go AWOL. He hoped for a better result this time.

A bush outside the cave rustled and he coiled his thigh muscles, getting ready to spring. His trigger finger twitched.

A harsh whisper echoed in the darkness. "Denver? Major Denver?"

He rose slowly, his jacket scraping the wall of the cave, the light from his flashlight illuminating a figure on hands and knees at the cave's entrance. "If you have any weapons, toss them in first. If you're not alone… you soon will be."

Pazir sat back on his heels and tossed a small pistol onto the dirt floor. He rummaged through the clothes on his body and flicked a knife through the air. It landed point down on the ground.

"That's all I have." Pazir continued forward on his knees, his hands in the air. "I had nothing to do with the ambush at our previous meeting. I barely got out of there with my life."

"The other Delta Force soldier? Asher Knight? Do you know what happened to him?"

"He survived."

Denver almost sank to the dirt again as relief coursed through his rigid muscles. "You know that for sure?"

"I know that he and the others are challenging the story that's out there about you."

"They are?" Denver's spine stiffened, and he lined it up against the cave wall again.

"Your men are loyal to you, Denver."

"But they haven't cleared me yet?"

"They're getting close. My sources tell me there's a battle raging about your guilt in the highest levels of government."

"You have good sources, Pazir." Denver gestured with his weapon. "Sit. What else have they told you? What do you know about those weapons at the embassy outpost in Nigeria? What do you know about the car bomb at the Syrian refugee camp?"

"Al Tariq."

Denver cleared his throat and spit. "Too small. I know that group and there's no way they could pull off what they're doing."

"They're the front group in the region. They're being used to do some of the grunt work. They're being used to track you down."

"By whom? Who's behind this and what do they want?"

"As far as I know, it's an international group, moles from different government agencies working together. They want weapons, and they're close to getting their hands on a nuclear device."

Denver swore, finally loosening the grip on his weapon. "That's what I was afraid of, and now you've just confirmed it."

"Has to be more than a rumor, Denver."

"I wanna know who's at the top. It's not good enough to finger Al Tariq."

Pazir scratched his beard and squatted across from Denver. "I know Al Tariq wasn't responsible for kidnapping that CIA agent."

"That female?"

"She was getting too close to the truth—just like you."

"They released her."

"She escaped."

"And you think the people who kidnapped Agent Chandler are the same ones pulling the strings for Al Tariq and trying to get their hands on this nuclear device?"

"I know it, Denver. Don't ask me how."

"Then I need to figure out who kidnapped Chandler."

"From here?" Pazir threw out one arm.

"I have to stay in hiding. You don't."

Pazir snorted. "I can't exactly run around the globe and travel to Washington, either."

"No, but you can get a message out for me, can't you?"

"Yes." Pazir reached into his pouch and pulled out a piece of flatbread. He ripped it in half and thrust one piece at Denver. "You want me to try to send a message to Agent Chandler?"

"I want you to send a message to one of my Delta Force team members. Hunter Mancini worked with Chandler on a covert mission once, and they got… close. You get a message to Mancini, and he can contact Chandler. Maybe she has some insight into who held her and what she was working on, but she's afraid to say anything."

"I can do that." Pazir pulled a pencil and pad of paper from his bag. "Give me the details."

As Denver chewed through the rough bread, he rattled off instructions to Pazir for contacting Mancini. "I don't have to tell you not to let this fall into the wrong hands."

"I give up nothing."

"Shh." Denver sidled along the wall of the cave and peered out the entrance. "We're not alone."

Pazir lunged for his weapon. "We'll fight them off together."

"You go." Denver grabbed a handful of Pazir's jacket. "I'll distract them. Get that message to Mancini if it's the last thing you do."

Chapter 1

Sue slipped the burner phone from the inside pocket of her purse. She swiped a trickle of sweat from her temple as she reread the text and ducked into the last stall in the airport bathroom. Her heart fluttered in her chest just like it always did before she made a call to The Falcon.

He answered after one ring. "Seven, one, six, six, nine."

The numbers clicked in her brain and she responded. "Ten, five, seven, two, eight."

"Are you secure?"

The altered voice grated against her ear as she peeked through the gap between the stall door and its frame at several women washing their hands, scolding children, and wheeling their bags in and out of the bathroom, too concerned with their own lives to worry about someone reciting numbers on a cell phone.

Their nice, normal lives.

"Yeah."

"You got the name of the barbershop wrong. There's no Walid there."

"That's not possible."

"You misheard the name…or they purposely fed you the wrong one because they made you."

Sue swallowed and pressed her forehead against the cool metal door. "They didn't."

"Because they would've killed you when you were with them?"

"That's right." Sue yanked off a length of toilet paper from the roll and stepped in front of the toilet to make it flush automatically. "I've been doing this for a while. I'd know."

"That's what I like about you, Nightingale. You're a pro. You've already proven you'll do anything for the cause."

She swallowed the lump in her throat and sniffed. "Next move?"

"We need the correct barbershop."

"I can't exactly call up my contact and ask him."

"You'll figure it out. Like I said, you're a pro."

The Falcon ended the call before she could respond.

Sighing, she pushed out of the stall and washed her hands. On her way out of the bathroom, she almost bumped into her stepmother.

"Where have you been? We need to get to our gate. I can't wait to get out of this place. I hate D.C."

Sue dropped to her knees in front of her son, re-gretting that she'd spent their last precious minutes together on the phone with The Falcon—regretting so much more. She grabbed Drake's hands and kissed the tips of his sticky fingers, inhaling the scent of cinnamon that clung to his skin. "Be a good boy for Gran on the airplane."

Drake batted his dark eyelashes. "You go airplane, too, Mama?"

"No, cupcake. Just you and Gran this time, but I'll visit you soon."

Linda fluttered a tissue between the two of them. "Wipe your hands, Drake."

"That's not going to help, Linda. He had a cinnamon roll for breakfast. He's going to have to wash his hands in the restroom." Sue waved her hand behind her at the ladies' room.

Pursing her lips, Linda snatched back the tissue. "Cinnamon rolls for breakfast? You spoil him when he's here. I'll get him a proper lunch once we get through security, if he still has any appetite left."

He will unless you ruin it.

Sue managed to eke out a smile, as Drake was watching her with wide eyes. "Nothing spoils Drake's appetite. He could eat a horse and ask for dessert."

"We don't eat horses, Mama." Drake giggled and Sue pinched the end of his nose. "Give me another hug."

Drake curled his chubby arms around her neck, and Sue pressed her tingling nose against his hair. "Love you, cupcake."

"Love you." Drake smacked his lips against her cheek. "Can I live here?"

"Not yet, my lovey, but soon." Blinking the tears

from her eyes, Sue straightened up and placed Drake's hand in her stepmother's. "Give my love to Dad."

Linda sniffed as she yanked up the handle of her suitcase. "I don't know why some people have children if they can't be bothered to take care of them."

"Linda." Sue ducked toward her stepmother and said through clenched teeth, "I told you. This…arrangement won't be forever, and I don't appreciate your talking like that in front of my son."

Linda's pale eyes widened a fraction and she backed up. "I hope you're not going to be landing in trouble every other month, or you'll never have Drake with you. You were right to leave him with your sister. Children need stability. You should give up this crazy job and find yourself a husband to take care of you, a father for Drake, and settle down like your sister."

Sue opened her mouth and then snapped it shut. She'd promised herself not to argue with Linda—besides, her stepmother had a point. As it stood now, Sue couldn't keep her son with her and raise him properly—even if The Falcon had allowed it.

And he hadn't.

"It won't always be like this. I plan to transfer to another position, and then I can have him with me all the time. I'll contact you tonight for some face-to-face with Drake. Ask Dad. He knows how to do it."

"I know, I know. Your father knows everything."

"Thanks, Linda. Safe travels." Sue blew a kiss to Drake as her stepmother hustled him toward the line for security.

She waved until they got to the front of the line. Knowing her father would be stationed at the airport in South Carolina to pick them up was the only thing that allowed her to turn away and leave the airport. Drake lived with her sister, Amelia, and her family, but they were in the Bahamas and Sue hadn't wanted Drake to go along, so she sent him to Dad and Linda.

Linda could take care of Drake's physical needs and keep him safe, but she trusted only Dad to meet Drake's emotional needs. Her stepmother didn't have the capacity for that job, as Sue suspected she trash-talked her to Drake whenever she got the chance.

If Sue had one more incident like the one she'd faced in Istanbul, she had no doubt her stepmother would move against her to take Drake away from her completely and declare her an unfit mother.

Sue clenched her teeth and exited the airport. She'd just have to make sure she didn't have any more of those close calls.

After she fed her parking receipt into the machine and the arm lifted, Sue flexed her fingers on the steering wheel of the car and glanced in her rearview mirror. With Drake's visit over, she could finally breathe... and find out who was following her. The possibilities were endless.

She navigated out of the airport and drove straight to her office. She had to confront her supervisor, Ned Tucker, about her suspicions. She'd already been debriefed after the kidnapping. Why was the CIA still dogging her? And if it wasn't the CIA, maybe Ned could help her figure out who it was. She hadn't wanted to tell The Falcon about this new development.

He thought she was a pro who could handle anything. She could, but handling everything on her own all the time had gotten old. Sometimes a girl just needed a shoulder to lean on. She'd had that shoulder…once.

She rolled up to the parking gate of the office and held her badge out the window.

The security guard waved her through, and she parked her car. Slipping her badge lanyard over her head, she marched toward her office building. She'd taken the day off to drop off Drake and Linda at the airport, but she couldn't wait any longer to get to the bottom of this mystery tail.

She punched the elevator button and almost bumped into one of her coworkers coming out.

Peter held up his hands. "Whoa, what's the hurry?"

"Sorry, Peter." She stepped to the side.

"Thought you were out today."

"Half day. I need to talk to Ned."

"I think he needs to talk to you, too."

"Why? Was he looking for me? He knows I'm out today."

Peter shrugged. "You might wanna turn around and go home."

"Why?"

Peter pivoted away from her and called over his shoulder, "Take someone's advice for once, Sue."

If Peter thought his cryptic warning would send her home, he didn't know her very well. She dropped her hand from holding open the elevator doors and stepped inside.

Good. If Ned wanted to talk to her, maybe he wanted to explain what the hell was going on.

The elevator deposited her onto the fifth floor, and she badged the door to the cubicles. The hum of low voices and keyboard clicks created a comforting welcome.

As she turned the corner to her row, she stumbled to a stop. A man she didn't know was hanging on to the corner of her cube and Ned's head bobbed above the top.

She bit the inside of her cheek and continued walking forward.

At her approach the stranger turned, and his eyes widened. "Chandler."

She stopped at the entrance to her cubicle, her gaze darting from Ned to a woman sitting at her desk, accessing her computer.

"Wh-what's going on here, Ned?"

Her boss ran a hand over his bald head, his forehead glistening with sweat. "I thought you were out today, Sue."

"So, what? You figured you and a couple of strangers could get into my computer in my absence?"

The guy to her right straightened up and pulled back his shoulders. "Ms. Chandler, we've noticed some irregularities on your workstation."

"Irregularities?" She shot a look at Ned, who refused to meet her gaze. "I don't understand."

The woman sitting in front of her computer twisted her head around, a tight smile on her face. "I found another one."

"Another one what?" Sue stepped into her cube, hovering over the woman seated at her desk.

The man placed a hand on Sue's arm. "Perhaps it's best we talk in Ned's office."

Sue had noticed a few heads popping up from other cubicles. She lifted her own chin. She knew damn well she didn't have any irregularities on her computer. The Falcon would make sure of that—unless these were communiqués from him.

"Let's go, then." She shook off the man's hand and charged out of her cubicle and down the aisle to Ned's office in the corner.

She reached Ned's office before the two strangers, with Ned right behind her. She swung around, nearly colliding with him. "What's going on, Ned?"

"They received an anonymous tip about you forwarding classified emails and documents to your home computer."

"What? You know I'd never do anything like that. I've been in the field myself. There's no way I'd put anyone in danger."

"I know that, Sue." His gaze darted over his shoulder, and then he sealed his lips as the two investigators approached.

Sue shuffled into the room as Ned sat down behind his desk. "Take a seat, Sue."

"That's okay. I'll stand." Folding her arms, she squared her shoulders against the wall.

The two investigators remained standing, too.

The woman thrust out her hand, all business. "I'm Jackie Templeman."

Sue gripped her hand and squeezed hard, her lips twisting as Jackie blinked.

The man cleared his throat and dipped his head. "Robert Beall."

He didn't offer his hand and she didn't make a move to get it. She folded her arms across her chest and asked, "What did this anonymous email say?"

Templeman shot a glance at Ned. "To check your emails."

"You have no idea who sent it?"

"No." Templeman shook her head. "That's why it's anonymous."

Sue smirked. "Got it. So, you believe every anonymous email you receive and rush in to do an investigation?"

Templeman hugged her notebook to her chest, as if guarding state secrets. "Not everyone."

"Oh, I see." Sue shoved off the wall and plopped into the chair across from Ned. "Just the ones about me."

Beall finally found his voice. "Because of your… um…the incident."

"Funny thing about that incident." Sue drummed her fingers on Ned's desk. "You'd think the Agency would be kissing my…rear end, considering a leak on their part led to my kidnapping in the first place."

"And then you escaped." Templeman tilted her head.

"Yeah, another reason the Agency should be nominating me for a medal or something instead of combing through my computer."

"You escaped from a group of men holding you in Istanbul." Templeman's delicate eyebrows formed a V over her nose.

Sue snorted. "I guess that's hard for *some* people to believe, but *some* female agents aren't pencil-pushing computer geeks. Some of us know how to handle ourselves."

A smile tugged at Beall's lips, but he wiped it out with his hand.

"Besides, I was debriefed on that incident and the

case was closed. You still seem to be using it to go after me."

"The point—" Templeman straightened her jacket "—is that we *did* find anomalies on your computer. Enough for us to confiscate your machine and suspend you."

"Suspend?" Sue jumped from the chair. "Is that true, Ned?"

"Just until they can figure out everything. I think there has to be a mistake, and I told them that. We already know those emails implicating Major Rex Denver and sent to a CIA translator were fakes. I'm confident that this investigation is going to find something similar with these emails and you'll be in the clear, Sue."

"Suspension starting now?"

"Yes, we'll accompany you back to your cubicle if you want to take any personal items with you." Templeman pushed past Beall and opened the door.

"I don't have anything there I need." Sue smacked her hand on Ned's desk. "Let me know when this is over, Ned."

"Of course, Sue. Don't worry."

As she stepped through the door, Templeman tapped her shoulder. "Badge."

Sue whipped the lanyard over her head and tossed it at Templeman's chest, but it slipped through the investigator's fingers and landed on the floor. The woman couldn't even make a good catch. No wonder she had a hard time believing Sue had escaped her captors.

Sue strode out of the office, not looking right or left. When she stepped out onto the sidewalk, she took a deep breath of fresh air.

Maybe she sent her son away early for nothing.
Maybe her senses had been on high alert because the
Agency *had* been tracking her. Now that they'd made
their move and suspended her and confiscated her computer, they'd back off.

The thought didn't make her feel much better. The
CIA didn't trust her, and being falsely accused made
her blood boil. Of course, if the Agency knew about
her work with The Falcon, the accusations might not
be false. She didn't have to worry about that, though.
The Falcon would have her covered.

As she waited for the elevator in the parking garage,
her phone buzzed and she squinted at the text message
from her friend, Dani Howard.

Dani knew she'd sent Drake back home and figured
Sue needed some cheering up. Dani had no idea how
much cheering up she needed.

Sue texted her friend back. I'm up for cocktails tonight.

What the hell did she have to lose at this point?

Sue spotted Dani already sitting at the bar, and she
squeezed between the people and the tall tables to reach
her. "This the best you could do?"

Dani gave her a one-armed hug. "I just got here five
minutes ago. Haven't even ordered a drink yet."

Hunching over the bar, Sue snapped her fingers and
shouted, "Hey."

The bartender raised his hand. "Be right with you."

A minute later he took their order for two glasses
of white wine.

Dani sighed as she flicked back her hair. "It must be

your commanding presence that gets their attention. Did you see Drake off okay today?"

"I did." Sue rolled her eyes. "Of course, I had to put up with Linda's jabs."

"Our mothers should have a contest to see who can outshame the single moms." Dani picked out some pretzels from the bowl of snack mix on the bar and popped one into her mouth.

"Stepmother. At least Fiona's dad is in the picture."

"You say that like it's a good thing."

"Okay then, at least Fiona lives with you and you're not in constant fear of losing custody of her."

Dani folded back the corners of the napkin the bartender had tossed down when he took their order. "You know I'm planning to drive down to Savannah, and I'd be happy to drop in on Drake for you. Text me your parents' address, and I'll see if I can make the detour— just a familiar face from where Mom lives might make a big difference."

"That would be great, but I don't want to put you out."

"Happy to do it." Dani snatched their glasses from the bartender's hand and handed one to Sue. "Drink."

Sue took a big gulp of wine, but there wasn't enough alcohol in the world right now to drown her sorrows.

"Stop beating yourself up. You're saving the freakin' world." Dani tilted her head. "I suppose you can't tell me about this hush-hush assignment of yours."

Not only did she not have a hush-hush assignment, she didn't have any assignment—unless she counted the one to get the name of the right barbershop.

Sue put a finger to her lips and swirled her wine in the glass. "No questions about my job."

"Don't even ask about *my* job...except for the new resident who started his rotation." Dani winked.

"Not another doctor. You need to date outside the medical field."

"I need to date and I may have just found the answer to our prayers." Dani tilted her head to the side and twirled a strand of her red hair around one finger.

Sue put her glass to her lips and shifted her gaze above the rim toward a table to Dani's right, where two men had their heads together. "Are you sure they aren't gay?"

"Not the way they've been eyeing us for the past few minutes." Dani drew back her shoulders and puffed out her ample chest. "Besides, they have a table, and we're stuck here at the bar getting squeezed out."

One of the men had noticed Dani's move and he sat up, nudging his buddy.

An evening with Dani always ended in the company of men, and for once, Sue welcomed the distraction. She smiled at the eager suitors.

One of the guys raised his glass and pointed to the two empty chairs at their table.

"And score." Dani wiggled her fingers in the air. "I get the blond unless you have a preference. I'm just thinking about cute little strawberry-blond siblings for Fiona."

Sue's gaze shifted to the dark-haired man as she pushed away from the bar. At least he was her type. "Go for it, Dani."

The two men jumped from their seats and pulled out the chairs for her and Dani. She and Dani did a little dance to get Dani seated next to the blond.

He spoke first. "You two looked so uncomfortable

packed in at the bar. It seemed a shame to let these two chairs go to waste."

"Thank you. I'm Dani and this is Sue." Dani's southern accent always got more pronounced in front of men, and they seemed to eat it up.

Dani's future husband pointed to himself. "I'm Mason—" and then he pointed to his companion "—and this is Jeffrey."

They all said their hellos and launched into the inane small talk that characterized meet-ups in bars. Sue had no intention of winding up with Jeffrey or anyone else at the end of the evening and tried to keep her alcohol consumption to a minimum.

She failed.

Mason, or maybe it was Jeffrey, ordered a bottle of wine for the table, and then another. Although Sue continuously sipped from her glass, the liquid never dropped below the halfway point, and by the time she staggered to the ladies' room on her second trip, she realized the men had been topping off her wine.

She'd have to put a lid on that glass when she got back to the table.

As she wended her way through the crowded bar, she stumbled to a stop when she saw Jeffrey alone at the table. She clutched her small purse to her chest and took the last few steps on unsteady legs. "Where are Mason and Dani?"

"They left—together." Jeffrey lifted one shoulder.

Sue sank into the chair, snatching her phone from the side pocket on her purse. "Whose idea was that?"

"I think it was mutual." Jeffrey held up his hands. "Don't worry. I know we didn't hit it off like they did, and I have no expectations."

She scowled at him over the top of her phone. "I hope not."

Dani picked up on the first ring. "Hey, Sue, did Jeffrey tell you I left with Mason?"

"He did. Are you okay?"

"I'm fine." Dani giggled and sucked in a breath. "I'm sorry. I shouldn't have left you there with Jeffrey."

"That's okay. As long as you're all right. Do you have an address where you're going?"

"The Hay-Adams."

"Okay. Be careful."

Dani ended the call on another giggle and Sue shoved her phone back into her purse.

Jeffrey raised one eyebrow. "Your friend okay? Mason's a good guy."

"He'd better be." Sue raised her phone and snapped a picture of Jeffrey. "Just in case."

A spark of anger lit Jeffrey's eyes for a second, or maybe she'd imagined it. Then he tucked some bills beneath his empty glass. "Can I at least see you home?"

She shook her head and then clutched the edge of the table as a wave of dizziness engulfed her brain. She took a sip of water. "I'm fine, thanks."

"Really? You don't look fine. The booze was flowing as fast as the conversation tonight. You look… woozy."

Woozy? Someone had stuffed a big cotton ball in her head to keep her brain from banging around. After the day she'd had, she'd wanted to let loose, tie one on. Now she had to face the consequences.

"I didn't drive. I can just hop on the Metro, one stop." She staggered to her feet and grabbed the back of her chair. She'd be paying for her overindulgence tomorrow morning for sure.

Jeffrey jumped from his chair. "Are you positive I can't help you? I can walk you to the station or call you a taxi or rideshare car."

She narrowed her eyes and peered at him through a fog. Why was he so insistent? Why didn't he just leave her alone?

She raised her hand and leveled a finger at him. "Stay right where you are."

Jeffrey cocked his head and a lock of his brown hair slipped free from the gel and made a comma on his wrinkled brow.

Had she made sense? She tried to form another word with her thick tongue, but she couldn't get it to cooperate.

She resorted to sign language, raising her middle finger. Would he get the picture now? "Whatever." He plopped back into his chair. "Just be careful."

She swung to the side, banging her hip on the corner of the table, jostling all the empties. Putting her head down, she made a beeline for the door.

Once outside, she gulped in breaths of the cold air but couldn't seem to revive herself. Walking should help. She put one foot in front of the other and weaved down the sidewalk. Oncoming pedestrians gave her a wide berth, and a few made jokes.

Oh, God. Was she a joke? A drunk joke? She placed a hand flat against the side of a building and closed her eyes.

She hadn't been this drunk since college days, and she didn't intend to make the same stupid mistakes she'd made back then.

She shoved a hand into the pocket of her leather moto jacket and fumbled for her phone. Jeffrey had been right about one thing—she should call a taxi.

After she pulled the phone from her jacket, it slipped from her hand and bounced twice on the sidewalk before landing in the gutter.

She dropped to a crouch and stuck her hand over the curb to feel for the phone. The effort proved too much for her and she fell over onto her side.

Good thing her son couldn't see her now, passed out like a wino in the gutter.

She flexed her fingers toward her phone but lead weights had been attached to their tips—and her eyelids. DC Metro would pick her up and she'd lose her job for sure.

"Sue? Sue? You're coming with me now."

An arm curled around her shoulders and pulled her upright. Jeffrey. He'd followed her out to finish what he'd started.

She arched her back, but her gelatinous spine sabotaged the act and she collapsed against Jeffrey's chest.

He had her.

"It's all right. I'm taking you to my hotel."

Her lips parted and she uttered a protest, but just like everything in her life lately, the situation had already spiraled out of her control.

Her mind screamed resistance, but her body had already succumbed.

Sue stretched her limbs and rubbed her eyes, the silky, soft sheets falling from her shoulders. Then the memories from the night before tumbled through her mind in a kaleidoscope of images.

She bolted upright against the king-size bed's headboard, yanking the sheets to her chin to cover her naked body.

Had Jeffrey raped and abandoned her at the hotel? Was his name even Jeffrey?

The bathroom door crashed open and a large man stopped cold on the threshold. "God, you look beautiful even after the night you had."

Sue's mouth dropped open as she took in the man at the bathroom door, towel hanging precariously low on a pair of slim hips.

The man she'd betrayed and who still haunted her dreams…and it sure as hell wasn't Jeffrey.

Chapter 2

The look on Sue's face shifted from shock to disbelief, to horror, to pain and to a whole bunch of other stuff he couldn't figure out. And that had been his problem with Sue Chandler all along—he'd never been able to figure her out.

Those luscious lips finally formed a word, just one. "You."

He spread his arms wide. "In the flesh. Did you expect me to leave you in the gutter, like you left me?"

"As I recall, it was a luxury hotel." She patted the pillow next to her. "Somewhat like this one—and all I did was check out."

"Details, details."

She pointed at him. "Your towel is slipping. Not interested in seeing that package—again."

The years hadn't softened Sue Chandler one bit. He held up one finger. "Give me a second."

As Sue turned her tight face away, he crossed the room to his suitcase, tugged a pair of briefs from an inside pocket, dropped his towel and pulled on his underwear.

"There." He turned toward the bed. "Decent."

Her gaze flicked over his body, making him hot and hard, as only Sue Chandler could do with one look from her dark eyes.

The twist of her lips told him she'd noticed the effect she had on him.

"Maybe not decent enough." He yanked open a dresser drawer and pulled out some jeans. He stepped into them, feeling less cocky under Sue's unrelenting stare, but he had the upper hand for once.

"Now, are you going to tell me what you were doing last night stumbling along the streets of DC close to midnight?"

"I live here." Her jaw hardened. "What are *you* doing here and how did you happen to find me?"

"You're not exactly hard to find. You work for the CIA and live in DC, and I knew you weren't on assignment, not after…"

"You know about my kidnapping?" She drew her knees to her chest beneath the sheets, clasping her arms around her legs.

"Several special forces knew about it and were actively planning your rescue." He tilted his head to the side. "But you didn't need rescuing."

"Don't go throwing any parades. The kidnappers were not that bright." She blinked. "Is that why you're here? Have you been following me?"

"Whoa, wait." He tossed his towel onto the foot of the bed. "I followed you from your place to the bar last night. That's it. I just arrived yesterday."

She sank back against the stacked pillows. "Why'd you follow me? Are you here on official duty, or something? I've already been debriefed by the Agency."

"Official duty? Really? What would a Delta Force soldier have to do with the kidnapping of a CIA agent?"

"Don't try that 'Who, me?' stuff with me, Mancini. You didn't seek me out to profess your undying love. You had three years to do that—and not a peep."

He reached into the closet and jerked a shirt from a hanger, leaving it swinging wildly. "You're not gonna pin that on me. I got the message loud and clear that you were moving on. Did you expect me to chase after you?"

Sue opened her mouth and then snapped it shut. Then her eyes widened and she gathered the covers around her body. "I'm naked. How did I get naked?"

"I took your clothes off—sorry." He gestured to a pile of clothing in the corner of the room. "Yours were dirty. I didn't think it was sanitary to put you to bed in filthy clothes."

"How thoughtful." She snorted. "I fell on the sidewalk. I'm sure you could've brushed the dirt from my slacks and left my underwear alone."

He cleared his throat. "You vomited all over yourself when I got you to the room."

"Oh my God." She covered her mouth with both hands. "I don't know what happened last night. I—I apologize."

"Nothing I haven't handled hundreds of times before with my buddies. I'm sure we can send your clothes to the hotel's laundry or dry cleaning. I already cleaned off your boots and jacket."

"I don't know what to say. I'm embarrassed. I'm not sure what came over me. I did have a lot of wine last night, but I've never felt that way before."

"I'm thinking the fact that you upchucked saved you."

"Saved me from what?"

"Whatever was in your system."

"You mean besides the alcohol?" She twisted a lock of dark brown hair around her finger, not looking surprised at all. "What do you know? Why are you here in DC?"

He swallowed against his dry throat. He had to concentrate, but remembering Sue naked in bed had his thoughts scrambled.

Should he pretend he was here for her instead of trying to explain the real reason? He met those dark, shimmering eyes that seemed to see into his very soul. He couldn't lie to Sue—not that she'd believe him, anyway.

"I got a message from Major Denver."

"Major Rex Denver? AWOL Delta Force commander?"

"You know as well as I do that he isn't and never has been working with any terrorist organization against the US government. One of your own translators proved the emails she'd received implicating him were phony."

"I've heard all the stories, but if he's innocent, why won't he come in? Why is he sending messages to you instead?"

"He doesn't feel it's safe yet. He's already been the victim of a setup, and he doesn't trust anyone."

"Yeah, I understand that." Sue bit her bottom lip. "What was the message? What are you supposed to do?"

"Contact you?"

"What? Why?"

"He believes the people who kidnapped you belong to the same group he's trying to bring down, the same group that he believes is planning some kind of spectacular attack."

Sue clenched the sheets in her fists. "Why does he think that?"

Hunter's pulse jumped. Again, no surprised looks from Sue. "Something his informant told him. Why? What happened during that kidnapping? Did they ever give you any reason why they snatched you?"

"Wait." She massaged her temple with two fingers. "I can't take all this in right now, especially not huddled under the covers with no clothes on. I need a shower. I need breakfast. I need clothes."

"The shower's all yours. I can send your clothes out to the laundry right now, if you're okay with eating room service wearing my sweats and T-shirt." He took a step to the side and slid open the closet door. He reached in, his hand closing around the fluffy terrycloth of a hotel robe. "You can wear this into the bathroom."

"Thanks."

She uttered the word between clenched teeth, almost grudgingly, but he'd take it at this point. Her reception of him had been chillier than he'd expected, especially since she was the one who had ended their brief affair by leaving him in his hotel room with no note, no phone call, no explanation.

He placed the robe across her lap, dropping it quickly and jerking back. Being close to Sue again had proven to be more difficult than he'd expected when he first got Denver's message. Undressing her last night and putting her to bed had been an exquisite torture. His hands lingering on her smooth flesh had screamed violation, so he'd made quick work of it.

"I'm going to bag your stuff and call housekeeping. I'll put a rush on it, so your clothes will be ready by the time we finish breakfast." He pinched the strap of her lacy bra between two fingers and held it up. "Anything need special attention or dry cleaning?"

"Everything is machine washable." She flicked her fingers in the air. "Turn around, please."

Not like he hadn't already seen every inch of her beautiful body.

"Yes, ma'am." He turned his back on her and stuffed her clothing into the hotel's plastic bag for laundry, as she rustled behind him.

She slammed the bathroom door before he even rose from the floor with her bag of clothing dangling from his fingertips.

Blowing out a breath, he wedged a shoulder against the closet. He knew it wouldn't be easy reconnecting with Sue after what had happened in Paris, but she couldn't completely blame him for not contacting her, could she?

They'd met at a party of expats. He knew she was CIA, and she knew he was Delta Force on leave. They'd approached their relationship as a fling and had been enjoying each other's company until she'd turned cold. He'd assumed at the time it was because she knew they'd have to end their Paris idyll once he got deployed, even though he'd been ready to ask her to wait for him.

Maybe it hadn't been the wisest decision for him to get involved with someone so soon after separating from his wife, and maybe she got that vibe from him, although he hadn't gotten around to telling her about his wife. He hadn't wanted to open that can of worms until he'd gotten a signal from Sue that they had some kind of future. Once she'd shut that down, he'd shut down, too. He didn't need any more women in his life who couldn't accept his military career.

He pushed off the closet and grabbed the phone by the bed. He requested a laundry pickup and then room service, ordering eggs, bacon, the works. From what he'd seen of Sue's body last night, she still must work out and burn calories at a ferocious rate. With Sue's dedication to running, kickboxing and Krav Maga, he'd had no trouble imagining her escaping from a gaggle of hapless terrorists—even though others did.

He'd heard rumblings that Sue faked her kidnapping and miraculous escape but hadn't heard about any motive. Why would she fake a kidnapping in Istanbul? Glory? Sue wasn't like that. Didn't need that. The woman he'd met in Paris kept her head down and got to work. No nonsense. No drama.

And that's how she'd ended their affair.

The bathroom door swung open, and Sue poked her head into the room. "Can they do my clothes?"

"They haven't picked up yet, but they assured me they could have them ready by noon. Is that okay?" He glanced at the clock by the tousled bed. "You don't have to get to work?"

"I have a few days off. That's why I was out last night with my friend."

"When your friend left the bar with that guy, I thought maybe…" He shrugged.

"You thought I'd be leaving with someone, too?" She tucked a lock of wet hair beneath the towel wrapped around her head. "Queen of the one-night stands?"

"What we had wasn't…"

He choked to a stop as she sliced a hand through the air. "Don't want to discuss it."

"Housekeeping." The sharp rap at the door had him pivoting to answer it. He handed the bag to the woman. "I was told the clothes could be returned by noon."

"That's what I have on the order, sir."

By the time he turned back to the room, Sue had grabbed what she needed from his bag and retreated to the bathroom.

He ran a hand across his mouth. He didn't understand her anger at him. He hadn't been the one who abruptly left Paris without a word, without even a note on the pillow.

She'd hurt him more than he'd cared to admit, but he'd chalked it up to being dumped and accepted it as a sign that he shouldn't have gotten involved with someone so soon after Julia left.

Maybe Sue had expected him to run after her, pursue her, but he hadn't had the energy at that time for games and he'd let her go without a fight—clearly his loss.

She emerged from the bathroom again, yanking up the waistband of a pair of gray sweats that swam on her.

"I can turn up the thermostat in the room if you just wanna wear the big T-shirt."

"That's all right. I don't plan to run any marathons, or even leave the room."

The next knock on the door brought breakfast, and Hunter added a tip and signed the check. He lifted the cover on the first plate. "Eggs, bacon, hash browns. Is that okay?"

"Toast?"

"Under this one." He plucked a cover from a rack of toast. "Coffee?"

"Please."

She'd exchanged her ire for a cold civility. He couldn't decide which stung more. Over the years, he'd built up some ridiculous significance to their fling— Sue just set him straight.

He poured her a cup of coffee and nudged the cream and sugar toward her where she'd taken up a place across the table from him.

She dumped some cream into her coffee, picked up the cup and leveled a gaze at him over the rim. "Where did you sleep last night?"

His own coffee sloshed over the side of his cup. "The sofa."

"That small thing?"

"My legs hung over the edge, but I've had worse."

All the questions that must be bubbling in her brain and *that* one came to the surface first?

"Look, this is what happened." He slurped a sip of coffee for fortification. "I'd followed you to the bar from your place. I watched the entrance, waiting for you to come out, and I was going to approach you then."

"Why not sooner?"

"I told you, I'd just arrived in the afternoon, and I

didn't have your address right away. Figured you'd be at work, anyway. By the time I got around to finding your place, you were on the move. I didn't want to interrupt your evening. I thought about leaving you a note, but..."

"You figured I might not contact you."

"So, I followed you to the bar and waited."

"How'd you know I was with Dani? A woman? You mentioned seeing my friend leave with a man."

He cleared his throat. "I went into the bar."

"You were watching me inside the bar?" She stabbed at her eggs with a fork. "Creepy."

His lips twitched. "Sorry. I didn't stay long. Then I waited outside and saw your friend leave."

"Just in time to see me staggering out."

"Scared the hell out of me."

"Why?"

"It didn't look...normal, and I knew you weren't a big drinker, or at least you weren't in Paris." There he was, acting like some big expert on Sue Chandler.

"It didn't *feel* normal." She dropped a half-eaten piece of toast onto her plate. "If that guy I was with, Jeffrey, drugged me, what did his friend do to Dani? And why would they want to do anything to either of us?"

"Before we try to answer that second question, why don't you give Dani a call?" He crumpled his napkin next to his plate and grabbed her phone off the charger. "I found your phone charger in your purse and took the liberty of hooking you up."

"Thanks. Seems like you thought of everything."

"Except that change of clothes." He dropped the phone into her palm.

While Sue called her friend, Hunter shook out his napkin and listened. Everything sounded okay on this end. Maybe he'd been wrong about Sue being in danger.

She ended the call and tapped the edge of the phone against her chin.

"Everything okay?"

"Dani's already home. Seems Mason was the perfect gentleman. She passed out in his hotel room, and he checked out before she woke up. He left her a note telling her to order anything she wanted from room service and to take her time. And she woke up with all her clothes on...which is more than I can say for myself."

"Maybe Dani passed out before she had a chance to hurl all over herself."

"Don't remind me." She made a face and stuck out her tongue.

"That's good, then. Dani is safe at home with her virginity intact."

Sue covered her lower face with her napkin and raised her eyebrows. "I wouldn't go that far."

"But she's all right."

"She is."

"You don't sound relieved."

"I am relieved, but I'm puzzled." She swirled her coffee in the cup, staring inside as if looking for answers there. "Why did we both have such strong reactions to a couple bottles of wine? Dani knows how to get her drink on. I've never seen her more than a little tipsy, and I haven't gotten sick on booze since my college years, when we'd get an older classmate in our dorm to buy us a bottle of cheap rum and we'd mix it with diet soda."

"Now *I'm* feeling sick." He dusted toast crumbs from his fingertips into his napkin. "I don't know why you're confused. Just because Dani wasn't assaulted, thank God, doesn't mean the two of you weren't drugged."

"For what purpose? I just told you, Mason didn't molest Dani, and I passed out in the gutter like a common drunk."

"And I rescued you."

"What?" Her eyebrows created a V over her nose. "Rescued me from what?"

"I think I rescued you from Jeffrey." He held out his hand as Sue began to rise from her chair. "Just wait. Did you think he was going to haul you out of the bar in front of witnesses? Did he suggest walking you out or to your car?"

"Yes."

"Maybe he planned to make his move then."

"What move?" Sue hugged herself. "Now you're scaring me."

"I'm not sure, Sue. Those two men, Mason and Jeffrey, or whatever their names are, zeroed in on you and Dani. They slipped you some something and Mason was charged with getting Dani away while Jeffrey was supposed to take care of you."

"'Take care of'? What the hell are you talking about, Mancini?"

"You were kidnapped once and you escaped. What did your captors want with you? Did you think that was going to end just because you escaped?"

This time she did jump up from her chair, and it tipped backward with a thump.

"That was Istanbul. This is DC." She twisted her napkin in front of her.

He raised one eyebrow. "You ever hear of travel by airplane? It's a newfangled invention."

She fired her napkin at him. "Why are you joking? This is serious. You're trying to tell me the people who kidnapped me in Turkey are trying to recapture me here?"

"It's a strong possibility, especially in light of the message Denver sent me."

She stalked to the end of the room, spun around and stalked back. "You said you arrived in DC just yesterday afternoon?"

"Yeah, why?" His heart thumped against his rib cage. He recognized that look on her face—the flared nostrils, the pursed lips, the wide eyes, as if to take in everything in front of them.

"I felt—" she rubbed her upper arms "—like I was being followed the past few weeks. That wasn't you?"

"Nope, but it must've been someone. Your instincts are sharp." He rose from the chair and stationed himself by the window.

"They usually are." She aimed a piercing look at him from her dark eyes and he almost felt the stab in his heart.

He cleared his throat. "Then I think it's clear what we need to do."

"It is? And who's this *we*?"

"Me and you. We need to figure out why you were snatched in the first place and what it has to do with Denver." He rubbed his hands together, the thought of being with Sue, of working beside Sue, making his blood sing.

"I don't think so, Mancini."

"What? Why? Major Denver's life might depend on it, not to mention your safety."

"You and I working together? Spending days and nights together? Heads together?"

"Yeah." He couldn't stop his mouth watering at the prospect, especially when she put it like that.

"We both know that's a prescription for disaster."

"Why is that?" He folded his arms and braced a shoulder against the window, knowing damn well why she thought his idea stunk but wanting to hear it from her lips.

"I… We…" Her cheeks sported two red flags.

He'd never seen Sue flustered before. Could he help it if it gave him a prick of satisfaction?

A knock on the door broke the tension between them, and he silently cursed the hotel staff as Sue crawled back into bed.

The knock repeated, accompanied by a male voice. "Housekeeping. Laundry."

Hunter stepped away from the window, his gait slow. Once Sue got her clothes and got the hell out of here, he'd never see her again. He knew how she operated.

Denver had pegged the wrong man for the job if he wanted intel out of Sue. She wouldn't give him the time of day—even after what they'd shared three years ago.

He swung open the door. "Right on time."

The hotel worker charged into the room with Sue's clothes bagged and draped over his arm. As he brushed past Hunter, the plastic covering the clothing crinkled.

Hunter staggered back. "Whoa."

Before Hunter regained his balance, the clothes slid from the man's arm…revealing a weapon clutched in his hand.

Chapter 3

Sue stared down the barrel of the .38. Her jaw tensed, along with every other muscle in her body.

Hunter made a slight move, and the man with the gun leveled it at her head. "Stay back or I'll take the shot, and it doesn't have to end this way. We just want to talk to her."

"Who's *we*?" Hunter's voice came out in a growl that made the hair on the back of Sue's neck stand on end.

"You need to get lost. You don't want to be involved with her—trust me." The man's lips curled into a lop-sided sneer.

Sue's hands tightened into fists around the bed covers. She not only had to stop this guy from shooting her or abducting her; she had to stop him from outing her to Hunter.

With his words, the man had made it clear he didn't

have the slightest idea he had a member of Delta Force looming behind him. Good. They'd use that to their advantage. She had to hope the same thought had occurred to Hunter at the same time.

In one movement, Sue yanked the covers over her body and rolled off the bed, toward her would-be kidnapper's knees. She barreled into his legs at about the same time she heard the whiz of his gun's silencer right over her head.

The man grunted and kneed her in the side of the face. Then she felt him go down with a thud, followed by a sickening crack. She yanked the bedspread from her head and came eye to bulging eye with the intruder as Hunter choked off his breath.

The sleeper hold worked like a charm, and the man slumped to the side, his weapon inches from his useless hand.

Panting, Sue scrambled to her feet. "Good work. I thought you'd take advantage of the situation."

"And I'm glad you made that situation possible, even though he could've shot right into those bunched-up covers and hit some part of you." Hunter crouched beside the unconscious man and thumbed up one of his eyelids.

"What now? He's going to come to any minute." And she didn't want this guy talking. Sue dropped to her knees and reached across Hunter, grabbing the gun by the silencer.

The man's lids fluttered and he coughed. His eyes widened and his body bucked.

Sue brought the butt of the gun down on the back of the man's skull and he pitched forward again, a stream of blood spouting from his wound.

Hunter cocked his head. "That's one way to handle it."

"I'm the one he was aiming at. I didn't want to take any chances." She put two fingers against his neck. "I didn't kill him."

"We definitely don't want to leave any dead bodies behind." He pointed at the gun, dangling from her fingers. "You wanna take care of that?"

Rising to her feet, Sue kicked aside the last of the covers wrapped around her ankles and headed for the bathroom. She grabbed a hand towel from the rack and wrapped the gun in its folds.

She returned to the bedroom, placed the gun on the nightstand and knelt across from Hunter, who was rummaging through the man's pockets. "Any luck?"

"A little cash and…this." He held up a cell phone. Then he dropped it and tapped her cheek with his fingertip. "What happened? The side of your face is all red."

"He bashed me in the face on his way down." The throbbing of her cheekbone turned into a tingle under Hunter's gentle touch. "I'll get some ice on it. Phone."

"I'm assuming you have no idea who this guy is or what he wanted?" Hunter's blue eyes narrowed like a jungle cat's.

Had the man's words advising Hunter not to get involved with her registered with Hunter?

She shrugged. "No clue, but I'm guessing he's connected to Jeffrey from last night or maybe the kidnapping in Istanbul or maybe even my suspension from the CIA."

Hunter's head jerked up from the cell phone. "You didn't tell me you'd been suspended. Why?"

"Anonymous tips and emails. Sound familiar?"

"Same tactics used against Major Denver." He scratched his chin with the edge of the phone. "This is getting more and more tangled."

You have no idea, Hunter.

She nudged the inert form on the carpet with her knuckle. "How much time do you think we have?"

"That was a hard blow to the head. I think you bought us fifteen minutes at a minimum." He jabbed his finger at the pile of clothes on the floor. "At least he brought your laundry."

"And look how you tipped him."

He held up one hand. "I just choked him out. You're the one who delivered the lights-out."

Sue ripped the plastic from her slacks and blouse and clutched them to her chest as she backed up toward the bathroom. "I'm going to get dressed, and then we need to leave. I'm not going to explain this situation to hotel security."

"Neither is he." Hunter made a move toward his suitcase parked by the door. "I'll put the Do Not Disturb hanger on the doorknob to buy him some time. When he comes to, he'll want to hightail it out of here."

"You're right." She tapped her cheek. "Can you grab some ice from the machine for my face while I'm getting dressed?"

"I'm on it."

As she stepped into her slacks, she heard the door open and close, and she eased out a sigh. Who the hell was that in the other room? Was The Falcon right? Had she been made?

She wouldn't put those strong-arm tactics past the Agency, either, so it could be someone following up on her suspension. Her life was becoming more complex than usual—and the appearance of Hunter Mancini had just added to the mayhem. But what sweet mayhem.

Those blue eyes of his held the same hypnotic quality she hadn't been able to resist in Paris—even though hooking up with Hunter had broken all the rules. She hadn't given a damn then, and she didn't give a damn right now.

She needed someone on her side. Someone she could trust. Someone she could reach out and grab—unlike The Falcon, a nameless, faceless contact spitting orders at her.

The banging of the door made her jump. She smoothed the blouse over her hips and straightened her spine. Time to get to work.

She exited the bathroom and almost ran into Hunter, dangling a bag of ice from his fingertips.

"You looking for another black eye?"

"I don't think I'm going to get a black eye, but I can see a bruise forming on my cheek." She took the bag from him and pressed it against her face with a shiver. "You have toiletries in the bathroom."

"Thanks, I'll grab them, and then we'll get out of here."

"Did you check his phone?"

"Password protected." He patted the pocket of his button-up shirt. "We'll figure it out."

Sue stepped over their conked-out guest on the floor on the way to her boots. Perching on the edge of the bed, she pulled them on. "You have everything? Do you need to check out?"

Hunter stuffed his toiletry bag into his suitcase, along with the wrapped-up gun, and zipped it. "I'll call the hotel later and tell them I had a change of plans. I don't want housekeeping coming up here anytime soon, not until our friend wakes up and gets out of Dodge."

"Do you have another place in mind?" She strode to the credenza and grabbed her purse, her own weapon stashed in the side pocket.

"Your place?"

Her head whipped around and she swallowed hard. "No."

"From the outside, the place looks big enough for the two of us." He drew a cross over his heart. "I promise not to undress you and put you to bed anymore—unless you need it."

She snorted. "I'm not going to need it, and staying at my place would be a bad, bad idea. You don't think these goons...whoever they are...know where I live?"

"Your building looks secure and we're both armed." He tipped his head at the man on the floor. "I think we can handle anything that comes our way."

Hunter wouldn't be able to handle anything in that townhouse.

"I think it would be best if you found yourself another hotel." She hitched her purse over her shoulder. "I may even join you."

Hunter's blue eyes darkened. "Does this mean you're gonna work with me to figure out if the guys who snatched you are the ones working against Denver? 'Cause you were dead-set against that before this guy came along and pulled a gun on you."

"Exactly. He made me change my mind."

"Maybe I should thank him—or at least make him more comfortable." Hunter returned to the bathroom and came out swinging a hand towel.

He crouched beside the man and wrapped the cloth around his head, pressing it against his wound. Then he jerked back.

"We need to leave—now."

"Is he coming around?" Sue lunged for the hotel door and plucked the hanger from the handle.

"His color is coming back. It shouldn't be too much longer now." He stepped back from the body on the floor and grasped the handle of his suitcase. "Lead the way."

Sue held the door open for him as he wheeled his suitcase into the hallway. She eased the door closed and slipped the Do Not Disturb sign onto the handle.

When they got to the elevator, Hunter punched the button for a floor on the parking level.

"You have a car?"

"A rental. Do you have any suggestions for my next stop?"

"Is money a consideration, or no?" Her gaze flicked over his expensive suitcase, black leather jacket and faded jeans, which told her nothing except the man was still hotter than blazes.

"No." He lifted one eyebrow toward the black hair swept back from his forehead.

"Then I'd suggest the Hay-Adams. It's in the heart of everything, too crowded for us to stand out, too busy for us to be accosted at gunpoint in the parking lot, too expensive not to have security cameras everywhere."

"That's where your friend, Dani, was taken last night."

"Exactly. Maybe we can do a little research on those two guys from last night." She patted her purse. "I didn't tell you I took a picture of Jeffrey."

"A selfie of the two of you?"

Her brows snapped together. "Insurance in case he raped and murdered me."

"Quick thinking. I didn't get a good look at either one of them when I snuck into the bar last night for surveillance."

"Not very good surveillance, then." She clicked her tongue.

"I didn't want to out myself by staring."

The elevator dinged, and Hunter jabbed at the button to hold open the doors. "After you."

Once he loaded his bag into his rental car and pulled out of the parking structure, she directed him to the next hotel. He maneuvered through the busy streets like a pro, and they left the car with the valet in front of the hotel.

She hovered at his elbow as he checked in, drumming her fingers on the reception desk. She'd played up her fear over returning to her own place, as there was no way in hell she could have him inside her townhouse, but she'd have to explain somehow that she felt perfectly safe returning home on her own. She couldn't stay in this hotel with Hunter—not again.

She had very little self-control when it came to this man—and she needed her self-control.

"Thank you, Mr. and Mrs. Roberts. Let us know if you need anything." The clerk smiled as she shoved a key card toward Sue.

Sue blinked and then swept the card from the counter and pocketed it.

As Hunter wheeled his suitcase toward the elevator, she hissed into his ear, "Who the hell is Mr. Roberts? Or Mrs. Roberts, for that matter?"

"That would be us, dear." He winked at her. "You're not the only one who knows how to play spy. I have a whole new identity for my stay in DC. I told you that I'm not here on official duty and I don't want my actions to be tracked."

"You have all the credentials?" She tilted her head. "Driver's license, credit cards?"

"I do. Mr. Roberts even has a passport."

She held the elevator door open for him as he dragged his suitcase inside. "I feel so humbled now that I know how easy it is for anyone to fake a new ID."

"Spare me." He nudged her shoulder. "As if you don't know all about that. Half the time the Agency can't locate someone, it's because he or she adopted a new identity."

"Just like I'm sure Jeffrey on my phone is not really a Jeffrey."

"He must've followed us back to my hotel and notified the second shift…if he was in on it."

"I'm pretty sure that was no coincidence—passing out and then the attempted abduction this morning. They didn't expect you to be there, that's for sure."

The elevator settled on their floor, and they exited. Sue got her card out when they reached the room and slid it home. She poked her head inside before widening the door for Hunter and his bag. "Just making sure nobody is here before us."

"They were good last night, but not that good." He wheeled his suitcase into the corner and then bounced on the edge of the king-size bed. "Plenty of room for the two of us—your side and my side."

No time to burst his bubble now. She curled her lips

into a perfunctory smile. "Should we get to work on the phone now before it's deactivated?"

"Do you have any tricks of the trade to find out or bypass the password?" He fished the would-be kidnapper's phone from his pocket and tossed it onto the bed beside him.

"I might have a few tricks up my sleeve." She wedged a knee on the bed and scooped up the phone. "In the meantime, why don't you have a look at Jeffrey's picture just in case? We could send it in for facial recognition—if I were still in good standing with the CIA."

"Yeah, I was counting on you having all the Agency's resources at your disposal. Now I'll just have to do this the sneaky way."

She paused as she drew her phone from her purse, holding it in midair. "Are you telling me you have a contact in the CIA? Someone to do your bidding?"

"Do my bidding? I wouldn't put it like that, but yeah, I have a little helper."

Shaking her head, she said, "That agency has more leaks than a colander."

She tapped her photos to bring up Jeffrey's picture. "Give me your number and I'll send it to you."

"I can just look at it on your phone." He snapped his fingers.

"It's better if we have a copy, anyway." She held her finger poised above her display. "Number?"

"Is this your sneaky way of getting my cell? You could just ask, you know." He rattled off his cell number and she entered it into her phone.

Actually, it was just her sneaky way of keeping him away from her phone. She didn't keep pictures on her cell, but she didn't need Hunter looking at her text messages.

She tapped her screen with a flourish. "There. The picture is on its way. Now, I'll get to work on this phone."

She dragged a chair to the window and kicked up her feet onto the chair across from it. She powered on the stranger's cell, which they'd turned off to avoid any tracking, but turning it back on couldn't be helped.

"This guy your type?" Hunter held up his phone with Jeffrey's mug on the display.

"Tall, dark and handsome?" She snorted. "You could say that."

Hunter brought the phone up to his nose and squinted. "How tall was he?"

"Tall enough." Sue eyed Hunter's lanky frame stretched out on the bed, his feet hanging off the edge.

With a smile curling her lip, she hunched over the cell phone again.

Sue clicked through the phone to access a few of the backdoor methods she'd learned at the Agency for bypassing a password to get into a phone. These worked especially well for burner phones like this one—and she knew a thing or two about burner phones.

She glanced up as Hunter swung his legs off the side of the bed, hunching over his phone, his back to her. Seconds later, his cell buzzed and he murmured a few words into his phone.

He must've reached his secret CIA contact—one who hadn't been suspended from the Agency. She just hoped he knew to keep her name off his lips.

A few taps later, the gunman's phone came to life in her hand. She slid another glance toward Hunter's back and launched the man's text messages and recent contacts.

Hunter ended his own call and stood up, stretching his arms to the ceiling. "I'm going to grab a soda from the machine down the hall. Want something?"

"Something diet, please." Tucking her hair behind one ear, she glanced up and pasted a smile on her lips.

When the door closed behind Hunter, Sue began transferring the data from the stranger's phone to her own—contacts, pictures, texts and call history.

When she reached the last bit of data, Hunter charged into the room, a can of soda in each hand. "Any luck with that?"

She slumped in her chair, clutching the phone in her hand. "Not yet."

Then she tapped the display one last time to erase everything the man had on his burner phone.

Chapter 4

Hunter snapped open Sue's can of soda and leaned over her shoulder, placing it on the table in front of her. The click of the aluminum against the wood made her jump and flush to the roots of her dark hair as she jerked her head around.

"Did I scare you?" He dropped his hand to her shoulder briefly.

"I didn't realize you were right behind me."

"You were too engrossed in that phone." He opened his own soda and sank to the edge of the bed. "It's a bummer you can't get anything from it."

She placed the phone facedown on the table and spun it around. "None of my tricks are working. Phones are getting more and more sophisticated now and harder to break into. I think the CIA needs to get its cyber division on this to come up with some methods to bypass the new security measures."

"Speaking of the Agency and security measures, my contact thinks he can run Jeffrey's picture through face recognition. If he's on the intelligence radar, we should get a hit."

"He?" Sue twisted the tab off her can. "Is he stationed here in DC?"

"Oh no, you don't. I don't give up my sources, not even to other sources." He leveled a finger at her. "And that should give you some sense of comfort."

She tucked one long leg beneath her. "Did you ever tell anyone about us? I mean our brief affair in Paris?"

Brief? Had their affair been brief? He'd been so lost in Sue, lost in Paris that the world had seemed light-years away, and he'd felt suspended in time. Ever since then, he'd measured everything in terms of before Sue and after Sue. And everything before seemed to be a pale imitation of what came after.

Under her penetrating dark eyes, he felt a flush creep up from his chest. "I did tell a few people—my Delta Force team. That's all. It's how Major Denver knew to task me with contacting you."

"I see." She braced one elbow on the table and buried her chin in her palm.

"Did you?" He held his breath for some reason.

"No."

The word didn't come out as forceful as the expression on her face. She *had* told someone.

"Our affair was a mistake." She sat back in her chair and crossed her arms over her chest.

Hunter gulped down his soda until it fizzed in his

nose and tears came to his eyes. So much for getting Sue into bed tonight.

He wiped the back of his hand across his tingling nose. "Two people, even someone from Delta Force and someone from the CIA, enjoying some R and R in Paris, off duty. As far as I remember, our pillow talk didn't include any state or military secrets. Why is that a mistake?"

She drew her bottom lip between her teeth and hunched her shoulders.

"Oh." He crushed his can with one hand. "You weren't off duty, were you?"

Her eyes narrowed. "You need a haircut."

"What?" He skimmed the palm of his hand over the top of his short hair. "Where did that come from?"

"I know just the place." She sat up ramrod straight and snatched her cell phone from the desk. She tapped her screen and nodded. "It's called T.J.'s Barbershop, and it's downtown."

"Does this have something to do with what happened this morning?"

Sue stood up, tilting her head to the side. "Do you trust me, Hunter?"

Did he? She'd indulged in a fling with him while she was on an assignment in Paris, without telling him, and then left him high and dry in their love nest without a backward glance and disappeared. He never heard from her again. She wouldn't take him back to her place here in DC. And she'd just been suspended from the Agency.

Her dark lashes fluttered as the sun from the window set fire to the mahogany highlights in her hair. Her lips parted, waiting for his answer.

"Yeah, I trust you, Sue."

"Good." She reached across the table and tugged her jacket from the back of the chair. "Haircut at T.J.'s. They take walk-ins and you're going to ask for Walid."

Hunter drummed his thumbs against the steering wheel as he waited for Sue outside her townhouse in Georgetown. She neglected to invite him in, claiming she'd be just a few minutes.

A few minutes later, true to her word, she appeared on her porch, wheeling one bag behind her, another slung over her shoulder. She waved to someone coming up the steps, clutching a small child by the hand, exchanged a few words with this person and then jogged across the street to his rental car.

He popped the trunk and hopped out of the car.

"Bad idea to leave the car. Parking enforcement love giving tickets on this block." She nudged up the trunk.

"I haven't gone anywhere." He collapsed the suitcase handle and hoisted the bag into the car. "This, too?"

"Got it." She swung her shoulder bag into the trunk on top of her suitcase.

When they got back into the car, he glanced at her as he started the engine. "I suppose you're coming inside with me for the haircut I don't need."

"Of course."

"Are you going to tell me what this is about?"

"I'm pretty sure this barbershop is connected to the group I've been tracking, the same one Denver was looking into before he went AWOL, if his intel is correct."

Hunter's pulse ticked up a few notches. Progress. "You're *pretty* sure, not positive?"

"I got a tip about T.J.'s, but apparently it couldn't be verified."

"And now I'm going to try to verify again. Walid?" He made the turn she indicated onto an even busier street than the one they'd left.

"He's the key." She tapped on the window as they crawled through traffic. "You're going to make a right in a few miles at Sixteenth Street. There won't be any parking on the street at this time of the day, so we'll leave the car in a public lot."

"Are we doing anything in the barbershop, whether or not Walid is there?"

"I am." She dug through her purse and cupped a small black device in her palm.

Hunter raised his brows. "A camera? A bug?"

"Both video and sound. I'm leaving it there, regardless of what happens."

"Do you need me to do anything?"

"A little distraction wouldn't hurt, but don't go overboard and make them suspicious." She poked his thigh with her knuckle. "I know you D-boys like to come in with guns blazing, but this is a little subtler than that."

He raised two fingers. "I'm the height of discretion. I didn't even chase after you after you dumped me in Paris."

"I didn't dump you, Hunter." She folded her hands in her lap. "The affair had run its course. I had somewhere else I needed to be."

"There's nowhere else I wanted to be." He squinted at the brake lights of the car in front of him.

She turned her head to look out the window, her dark hair creating a silky veil over her face. "It was… nice."

Nice? Not exactly the word he'd use for the passion they'd shared, but he'd take it for now.

Rapping on the window, she said, "Next right."

He maneuvered the car around the corner into a bustling business district missing the genteel leafiness of Georgetown but making up for it in sheer energy.

"Is that it?" He pointed to a revolving barbershop pole on the next corner.

"Yeah. Look for a lot."

Almost two blocks away, Hunter pulled the car in to a public parking lot and paid the attendant. As he and Sue trooped up the sidewalk back toward the barbershop, he shoved his hands into the pockets of his jacket, against the chill in the air. Spring had sprung, but nobody had told the DC weatherman yet.

Sue's low-heeled boots clicked beside him. She'd done a quick change of clothes at her place, replacing her black slacks with a pair of black jeans that hugged her in all the right places. Every place on Sue's body was the right place, as far as he was concerned.

When they reached T.J.'s, Hunter swung open the door, causing a little bell to jingle wildly. Three barbers turned their heads toward the new customers.

The one on the end paused, clippers in the air. "Can I help you? Cut?"

"Just a cleanup." Hunter ran a hand over his head, the short ends tickling the palm of his hand. "Edge the neck."

"Sure, have a seat."

As he perched on the edge of a worn love seat, Sue remained standing, facing a rack of magazines, her hand clenched lightly at her side.

Hunter cleared his throat. "Is Walid around? My friend recommended Walid."

Did two of the barbers stop clipping at the same time?

"Walid?" The man on the end who'd welcomed him shook his head. "He doesn't work here anymore. Hasn't been here for a while."

"No problem. Thought I'd check."

"I hope this doesn't take too long, James." Sue grabbed a sports magazine and leafed through it.

"You're the one who wanted me to get the cut, honey. We can leave right now if you want."

The barber in the middle chuckled as he handed a mirror to his customer. "I'm ready for you. Shouldn't take long. Step over to the sink."

The last thing he wanted was some dude washing his hair. He held up his hands and took a step back—right into Sue.

She drilled a knuckle into the center of his spine. "Go ahead, James. I saw a drugstore down the block and I have a few things to pick up. Take your time."

"You're not in a hurry anymore?" He shuffled toward the barber holding out a white towel.

"You might as well get the full treatment." She tapped him with the rolled-up magazine in her hand, and it slipped out of her hand and fell to the floor at the feet of the barber at the first station.

Hunter followed his guy toward the row of sinks, leaving the magazine on the floor.

The first barber set down the hairdryer he'd just picked up and bent over to retrieve the magazine.

Sue reached out, wedging one hand against the magazine rack as she reached with the other. "Oh, thank you."

Hunter figured she'd just placed her device and got confirmation a minute later when she called from the door. "Meet me at the coffeehouse next to the drugstore when you're done."

He lifted his hand before he went under the warm spray.

Thirty minutes later, he managed to get out of T.J.'s with a little off the sides and a cleaned-up neckline. He loped down the street and ducked into the coffeehouse.

Sue looked up from her phone and wiggled her fingers.

He ordered a coffee on the way, when what he really wanted was lunch, and pulled out the chair across from her. "I'm guessing you did what you went to T.J.'s to do."

"Nice cut." She peered at him over the top of her cell phone and then turned it around to face him, showing him a video of the barbershop in real time. "But then I already knew that."

"What did you make of Walid's absence? Do you believe them?"

"I'm not sure, but the fact that they knew Walid was a plus. I know that's the barbershop that featured in my intel." She tapped her phone on the tabletop. "And now I'll have an eye on what goes on there."

"Is that why you dropped by your place—to pick up spy gadgets?"

"That and to change clothes and pack a bag. I meant it when I said I was going to stay with you at the hotel."

"Déjà vu all over again."

She opened her mouth, probably to correct him, but the barista saved him by calling his name.

"My coffee." He pushed back from the table and picked up his drink.

When he returned, she was hunched over her phone again. "Any activity?"

"Plenty, but not the kind I'm interested in." She swirled her cup and took a sip.

"What about the other phone?"

"The other phone?" Her paper cup slipped from her hand and rolled on the table.

He picked it up and shook it. "Lucky it's empty. The phone I took off the intruder."

"I turned that off for now. I'm afraid it can be tracked or pinged." She folded a napkin into a small square. "I wasn't having any luck with the password, anyway."

"We still have his fingerprints on that gun. I'm hoping to get some help with that."

"Yeah, that gun." She dropped her phone into her purse. "Sounds like you have more contacts at the Agency than I do. Maybe your contacts can get me my job back."

"You weren't fired."

"Not yet." She twisted up her mouth on one side. "Now I know how Denver feels."

"You think you're being set up?"

"I don't know what to think." She stuffed her napkin inside her cup. "Are you ready?"

He drained his lukewarm coffee from his cup and stood. "Let's go."

He guided Sue through traffic on the sidewalk, as her phone engrossed her and she barely looked up.

When they got to the car, he opened the passenger's

door for her. "I hope you don't walk around the city with your nose in your phone like that all the time."

She held up her cell as she slid onto the seat. "Just when I'm watching surveillance video."

"Do you know what you're watching for?"

"Not really. I'll know it when I see it."

"And then you'll let me know, right?" He caught the door before slamming it. "Right?"

Sue answered without looking up. "Of course."

Hunter scuffed back around to the driver's side. Why did he feel like he just got used in that barbershop? He didn't even need a haircut.

As he got behind the wheel, his phone buzzed. He checked the display. "Perfect timing. My contact has some info on Jeffrey."

"Did he send it through?" Sue finally glanced up from her phone, her eyes shining.

"No. He doesn't want to expose the information by emailing or texting it. He's going to leave it for me in a mailbox."

A laugh bubbled from her lips. "You're joking."

"Why would I be joking? He sent me the address of a vacant house in Fredericksburg, Virginia, and he's leaving the information in the mailbox." He tapped his phone to bring up his GPS and then tossed it to Sue. "Can you enter the address for me?"

"Fredericksburg? That's at least an hour away." She held his phone in front of her face.

"You don't expect him to leave it outside the gates of Langley, do you?"

"No." She turned down the news on the radio. "I take it back. It's an ingenious method of communication. I'll have to remember that ploy for my next covert operation."

"This *is* your next covert operation." He gave her the address of the house and then headed out of town, following the GPS directions south.

The landscape rolled out the green carpet as they hit the highway to Virginia. The recent rains had created a verdant emerald border along either side of the highway that rushed by in a blur.

"Pretty, isn't it?" Sue had slumped in her seat, resting the side of her head against the window.

"I was just thinking that, myself." Hunter glanced at his rearview mirror and furrowed his brow. "That truck's coming up fast on my tail."

"We have two lanes. He can go around." Hunching forward, Sue peered into the side mirror. "Idiot."

"He must've heard you."

Hunter tracked the truck as it veered into the left lane and started gaining on them. He eased off the gas to give the behemoth plenty of room to pass and move over.

As the truck drew abreast of his car, it slowed down.

"Jerk. What does he want? I'm not getting into a road rage situation with him."

Gripping the steering wheel, Hunter glanced to his left and swore. "He has a gun!"

Chapter 5

Sue threw out a hand and wedged it against the dashboard as Hunter slammed on the brakes and the car fishtailed on the road. Her gaze flew to the side mirror and an oncoming car blowing its horn and swerving toward the shoulder.

She hunched her shoulders and braced for the impact. Instead, the car lurched forward as Hunter punched the gas pedal. Her head snapped forward and back, hitting the headrest.

The truck to their left had slowed down when they had, and as the little rental leaped ahead eating the asphalt beneath it, the truck roared back to life.

Hunter shouted, "My gun! Get my gun under the seat."

Sue bent forward, her hand scrabbling beneath the driver's seat between Hunter's legs. Her fingers curled around the cold metal and she yanked it free.

When she popped up, she screamed as Hunter zoomed toward the car in front of them.

He pumped the brake pedal, and their tires squealed in protest. The truck had pulled up next to the car in front of them, veering to the right, almost clipping the left bumper and then jerking back, probably realizing he had the wrong target.

"He's gonna hang back and wait for us again." Hunter's gun nestled in her hand and she slipped her finger onto the trigger.

"You know what to do." Hunter held his body stiffly, pressing it against his seat back.

Sue released her seat belt with a click and leaned into the driver's seat, practically resting her chest against Hunter's.

As the truck drew level with them, she thrust the barrel of Hunter's gun out the open window.

She caught a glimpse of the face in the window, eyes and mouth wide open, before the driver of the truck suddenly dropped back, tires screeching.

The car behind the truck honked long and hard, and Sue retreated to her seat, the gun still clutched in her hand, finger on the trigger. "Someone's gonna call 911 and report this, report our license plates."

"Then it's a good thing that sap Roberts is renting this car and not me."

"Unless the cops respond to the scene and pull you over."

"Not. Gonna. Happen." Hunter cut in front of the car ahead of them and accelerated onto the off-ramp, checking his rearview mirror.

"Is the truck following us?"

"If he can see what we're doing, he will."

They curved to the left, and Hunter blew through the stop sign at the T in the road, making the turn. He pointed at the windshield. "Shopping mall ahead. We're going into that parking structure."

Sue twisted her head over her left shoulder, scanning the road and the off-ramp behind them.

"Is he coming?"

"I can't see around the bend in the road. It's no longer a straight shot."

"Good." Hunter wheeled into the structure and climbed a few levels. He parked between two SUVs, pulling the car all the way in to the parking slot.

He left the engine idling and closed his eyes, drawing in a deep breath. "Should we stay here or go inside?"

"I don't like the idea of being a sitting duck." Her gaze darted to the side mirror for the hundredth time since they'd parked, and they'd been here just about thirty seconds.

"If we head into the mall and they locate the car, they can stake it out. Wait for us."

"We don't know what kind of firepower they have." She licked her dry lips. "They could come up behind us and blast the car. We can't hold them off with one gun."

"Where's yours?"

"It's in my bag in the trunk."

"Bad place for it, Chandler."

She smacked her hand against the dashboard. "I have an idea. I have another camera in my bag of tricks. I can stick it on the back window of the car. That way, we can see if anyone approaches the car while we're inside. If not, and we give it enough time, we'll make our escape."

"I can live with that." He peeled her fingers from his gun still in her grip and wedged by the side of her hip. "I'm packing this and you'd better take yours. We still need to get to Fredericksburg and that mailbox."

She flicked the door handle and Hunter raised his hand. "Hang on. Let me check the area first."

When he finished his surveillance, he tapped on her window. "All clear...for now."

She got out of the car and immediately grabbed Hunter's forearm as her knees gave out.

Curling an arm around her, he asked, "Are you all right?"

"Didn't realize that wild ride had shaken me up so much." She stomped her feet on the ground. "Just need to get my bearings."

"Take all the time you need." His fingers pressed the side of her hip through her jeans.

"Thanks, and thanks for getting us out of that mess...whatever that mess was."

"I'm not convinced they were going to shoot us."

"Really?" She shifted away from him and tilted her head. "He had a gun."

"So did the guy in the hotel room. He could've shot both of us the minute he walked in with the laundry—had a silencer and everything. He didn't." Hunter tugged on his earlobe. "What do you think they want? An interrogation?"

Sue lifted her shoulders up and down in a quick movement. "I'm not sure, but let's not stand around here any longer than we have to."

He popped the trunk for her and stood guard as she rummaged inside her duffel bag and pulled out her weapon and a small plastic bag containing the same type of camera she'd stuck in the barbershop. Was that where they'd been picked up? Had asking about Walid marked them as hostile intruders?

When she finished, Hunter slammed the trunk closed and said, "I know what I want to do in that mall while we're killing time."

"See a movie?"

"Not a bad idea as long as we get hot dogs and popcorn. I'm starving." He patted his flat stomach. "Evasive driving always works up my appetite."

"I'm glad someone can eat. I feel like I'm gonna throw up." Sue zipped her gun into the side pocket of her purse and strapped the purse across her body.

They took the elevator to the third floor and a pedestrian bridge that crossed to the mall.

The normalcy of people shopping, having coffee and eating made Sue blink. The world still revolved and people still lived their lives while others, like her and Hunter, had to protect them from the harsh truths. She'd been aware of those truths for far too long, thanks to her father.

Hunter tipped back his head and sniffed. "Ahh, mall food—cinnamon, grease, cookies and pizza—what more could you ask?"

"Some real food." She tugged on his sleeve. "There are a couple of restaurants upstairs. We need some privacy."

They rode up the escalator together, which gave her a better view of the indoor mall—and the people in it. Hunter couldn't fool her. Beneath his joking manner—and hers—the tension simmered like a live wire.

She dragged him into a chain restaurant with a five-page plastic menu, and they both ordered ice tea after they sat down.

Sue sucked down some tea, and when she came up for air, she asked, "Do you think they were trying to run us off the road by shooting out our window or tire?"

"Or they were trying to warn you. Maybe someone saw us at the barbershop or the guys at the barbershop placed a call and set someone on us. Where'd you get the barbershop tip?"

She ran a finger across the seam of her lips. "That's top secret stuff. You have your sources and I have mine."

"Yeah, but my source is one of your fellow agents. Who's your source?" Hunter picked up a couple of menus and tapped them on the table before sliding one across to her.

"Can't tell you that." If she started down that road with Hunter, there's no telling where it might end— probably with Drake.

"Then only you know if the intel about the barbershop is legit—seems that it was, if five minutes after my haircut we're being chased down the highway."

Why would The Falcon tell her the barbershop hadn't panned out? Had someone there recognized her, realizing she probably knew all about the barbershop, anyway?

Hunter pinged her menu and she glanced up.

"Are you feeling better? You're going to order something?"

She ran her fingertip down the page of items. "Probably just some soup."

When the waitress came over, Sue ordered some

cream of broccoli soup and Hunter went all out with a burger and fries.

"You haven't checked the barbershop." He prodded her phone with his knuckle. "Maybe we'll see someone making a call or coming inside."

"And let's not forget your rental car." She picked up her phone and tapped the display to toggle between the two camera views. "I'm not going back to that parking lot if there's any suspicious activity going on."

She turned the time back on the barbershop video and hunched forward on the table to share the view with Hunter. "There's you getting your haircut."

"Don't remind me." He huffed out a breath. "You can skip that part because, I can tell you, one other guy came in after me and spent the entire time complaining about his prostate."

"Sounds fascinating." She flicked her fingers at the images. "Did you give him a good tip? Maybe that's why they were chasing us in that truck."

"That's a good sign."

"What?" She stopped the video.

"You can sort of laugh about it after you nearly collapsed getting out of the car."

She smacked the back of his hand. "I didn't almost collapse. My knees were a little wobbly. That's all."

"That's right. You're the badass agent who escaped from a gaggle of terrorists in Istanbul. You never told me about that whole incident, and that's what I should've been asking you about all this time because that's really the connection to Denver."

"Well, we did get sidetracked." And with any luck she'd sidetrack him again. Her so-called abduction was the last thing she wanted to discuss with Hunter...second to the last thing.

Sue clapped her hands together. "Our food's here."

"I thought you weren't hungry." Hunter thanked the waitress and asked for ketchup.

"I recovered." She dipped her spoon into the soup and blew on the liquid.

As they ate lunch, they kept checking back and forth between the two videos on her phone and nobody went near Hunter's rental in the parking lot.

"I guess we lost them." Sue broke up a cracker between her fingers. "I just wish I knew who they were and what they wanted."

"Maybe they just wanted to warn you away from the barbershop."

"How'd they know we were there?"

"They could have their own surveillance devices there if it's a hotbed meeting place for terrorists. They made you when you went into the shop, and someone came out to track you...warn you."

"That's some warning—a gun out the car window."

"No shots fired when they could've easily taken one at the window." He dragged a fry through the puddle of ketchup on his plate. "Same with the guy in the hotel room this morning. They don't seem very eager to kill you. They want something else from you."

"I can't imagine what." She picked up her phone and studied the display. "I'm okay with heading back to the car now. We want to get to that mailbox before someone beats us to it."

On the ride to Fredericksburg, Sue sat forward in her seat, her spine stiff, her gaze darting between the side-view mirror and out the window.

"I think we're in the clear." Hunter adjusted the rear-view mirror, anyway. "However they got onto us, it wasn't through GPS or we'd have a tail right now."

"If it's GPS, they can afford to keep their distance and ambush us at the mailbox." Her fingers curled around the edge of the seat. "Do you think they put something on your car?"

"When could they have done that? They wouldn't have been able to identify this car at the hotel."

"Unless Jeffrey watched you pick me up from the gutter and load me into your car."

"Didn't happen, and even if they did ID you in the barbershop, which seems likely, they couldn't have known which car was mine or where we parked before we got there."

"So, you think they caught me on surveillance at the barbershop and followed us to our car from there and then tailed us and made their move on the highway?"

"That seems the most probable to me. What they wanted?" He scratched his chin. "I still don't have a clue, but then you haven't been completely open with me, have you?"

Sue's stomach flip-flopped. "What do you mean?"

"Why that barbershop? What do you know about it? Who's there? What are they doing there? Who gave you the tip?"

She released a slow breath through parted lips. "I just can't tell you some of that, Hunter, and some I don't know. Can you be patient?"

"I've waited this long."

He mumbled the words under his breath and she gave him a sharp glance. Did he mean he'd waited long enough for the information or for her?

She felt like she'd been waiting for him, too, but she'd had her orders.

She pinched the bridge of her tingling nose. Hunter was here under an assumed name on unofficial duty. The Falcon didn't have to know, did he?

"Are you okay?" Hunter brushed a hand against her thigh.

Sue blinked. "I'm good. We're almost there."

Hunter followed the voice on his phone's GPS to a leafy neighborhood in an upscale suburb. He spotted the house for sale on the left and drove to the end of the block to make a U-turn.

As he rolled to a stop at the curb, he said, "Sit tight. I'll run around and get it."

"You're driving. I'll hop out and grab it."

"I don't want you to." He put a hand on her shoulder.

Goosebumps raced down her arms. "You just got through assuring me we weren't followed from the mall."

"I don't think we were, but why expose yourself?" He grabbed the handle and popped the door. "This is my contact, my setup."

"Knock yourself out, Mancini." She slumped down in her seat just in case his concerns came to fruition.

He bolted from the car and strode to the curb. He flipped open the mailbox and reached inside. Waving a cardboard tube in the air, he hustled back to the car and tossed the package into her lap. "Got it."

As Hunter peeled away from the curb and punched the accelerator, Sue stuck her eye to one hole in the tube. "There's stuff rolled up in here."

"Can you get it out?"

"Hang on." She licked the tips of two fingers and

stuck them inside the cardboard roll. She pressed her fingers against the paper inside the tube and dragged them toward the opening. "I think I have them."

When the rolled-up papers peeked over the edge of the tube, she pinched them between her thumb and forefinger and worked them out.

She unrolled the slick photograph paper first and flattened the pictures on her lap. "It's Jeffrey."

The first photo showed the man who'd chatted her up at the bar last night in conversation with another man, whom she recognized.

She held up the picture to Hunter. "Here's Jeffrey meeting with a known terrorist, proving you were right about him and his motives."

She flipped through a few more pictures in that sequence and turned over another batch. She gasped as her gaze locked onto Jeffrey's companion in the next picture.

"What is it? Who's that?" Hunter pumped the brakes to slow the car.

She knew the identity of the man in the picture with Jeffrey, all right.

But if she told Hunter how she really knew this man, she'd reveal the truth about her real function with the CIA—that she was a double agent, had been one for years and wouldn't be able to help him clear Denver without blowing her own cover.

So, she did what she'd been doing with Hunter ever since the day she met him in Paris—she lied.

Chapter 6

Hunter's gut twisted as he glanced at Sue's face. This had to be bad. Denver?

He careened to the side of the road and skidded to a stop on the soft shoulder. "Show me."

Pinching the photo between her thumb and forefinger, she turned it around to face him. "H-he's a known terrorist."

Hunter squinted at the picture of Jeffrey talking to a man in the shadow of a building, a hoodie covering his head and half his face.

"You recognize him?" He flicked his finger at the photo, hitting it and causing it to sway back and forth. "How can you tell who he is?"

"I just know. I've seen him before…in other surveillance photos." She stacked the picture on top of the others in her lap.

"What does my guy say about these pictures? Any commentary or am I supposed to know what this all means?"

Sue stuck the tube to her eye. "There's a piece of paper in here."

Hunter threw the car into Park as Sue fished the paper from the tube.

She shook it out and started reading aloud. "Face recognition matched with these pictures in our database. The guy with the dark jacket is Amir Dawud, who's gone underground since the bombing in Brussels. We don't know the guy in the...hoodie, but if he's with Jeffrey, he's probably involved in terror activity."

"The entire CIA doesn't know that guy and doesn't have a file on him, but you recognized him from a half-profile shot?"

Sue shuffled through the pictures in her lap and held the photo in front of her again, her head to one side. "Well, I thought it was someone we had ID'd from a previous campaign, but I could be wrong."

"Regardless—" he put the car in drive and rolled away from the side of the road "—Jeffrey is definitely connected to a terrorist organization and his meeting with you last night was no coincidence."

"I'm just glad nothing happened to Dani." Sue busied herself rolling up the pictures and paper again and stuffing them inside the tube.

"I wanna get ahold of one of these guys who keeps threatening you and ask him what he wants." Hunter clenched the steering wheel with both hands. "Did they ever get around to interrogating you when they kidnapped you?"

"No." Sue closed her eyes and sighed. "I guess my

connection to Major Denver is tenuous unless we find out what they want from me—and I'm not going to give them that chance."

"This could all be related to your suspension. Do you think someone's trying to set you up at work to discredit any information you might have about Denver?"

"But I don't have any information about Denver." She tapped on the window. "Are we going back to the hotel now?"

"I was, unless you have somewhere else you need to be." He nodded toward her purse on the floor. "You should check the barbershop camera for any developments. Since we left there, we were shot at and almost run off the road."

Sue hesitated before bending forward and plunging her hand into her purse.

He quirked an eyebrow in her direction. "Are you okay?"

Clasping the phone to her chest, she slumped in her seat. "Just tired."

"Do you want me to look?" He held out his hand.

"You're driving. Keep your eyes on the road." She scooted up in her seat and tapped her display several times. "I'll review the footage from earlier—about the time we lost the car following us and turned in to that mall."

Hunter glanced in his rearview mirror. "Nobody tailing us now."

"That's good. It means someone picked us up at the barbershop as opposed to putting a tracker on your car, or something like that." She raised the phone in the air and tilted it back and forth. "They're cutting hair. That's all I see."

"What did you expect to see? What's supposed to be going on at the shop?"

"I'm not sure it's a *what* so much as a *who*."

"And you don't see the *who* there?"

"No."

"And you'd know him if you saw him because you never forget a terrorist's face. You're good."

"I've been at this awhile, Hunter. I've studied pictures, video, been involved in interrogations."

"That's why I think you can help clear Denver's name." He flexed his fingers on the steering wheel. "If we can match up his contacts with your knowledge of these groups and their personnel, I think we might get a few hits. He seems to think so. That's why he sent me out here to connect with you."

Not that anyone had to twist his arm. He'd wanted to contact Sue so many times over the past few years, but she'd left him and he was done chasing after women who didn't want him.

Sue studied her phone for a few more minutes and then slipped it back into her purse. "Nothing but haircuts."

They drove the remaining miles to the hotel in a silence heavy enough to fog the windows of the car.

Hunter shifted a glance to the side at Sue's profile. She'd had her eyes closed for the past thirty minutes, but she didn't fool him. The pretense of sleep had allowed her to avoid conversation with him. Maybe she'd just shut down, unable to process any more of the information coming at her from all directions.

She'd escaped a kidnapping a few months ago, had just been suspended from her job, narrowly missed another abduction from the bar last night, had been held at gunpoint this morning and had literally just dodged a bullet this afternoon. She deserved the downtime.

He sucked it up, turned on the radio and drove back to DC Metro content with his own thoughts for company.

When he swung into the valet parking area of the hotel, he nudged Sue's arm. "We're here."

She blinked and stretched, putting on a good show. "That went fast."

"I almost didn't want to wake you up."

"Oh." Her cheeks turned pink. "I wasn't really sleeping. Just recharging."

Two valets opened their doors at the same instant, and Hunter plucked the ticket from his guy's fingers and went around to Sue's side of the car. "Are you sure you're feeling all right?"

"I'm good." She stretched her arms in front of her, flipping her hands up and down. "Look, no visible scratches."

"It's a miracle we got out of that." He rested his fingertips on the small of her back. "When we get up to the room, I'm going to start putting some of this information together."

"We don't have much."

"It's more than Denver has right now."

They swept into the hotel and made it back to their room without incident.

Hunter opened the door cautiously, his gaze scanning the room. "Everything's just as we left it."

"That doesn't always mean it's safe."

"Spoken like a true spook." The door slammed behind them and Hunter threw the top lock. He stood in the middle of the room, hands on his hips, turning in a circle.

Sue threw herself across the bed and buried her chin in her palm. "What are you doing? Planning a remodel?"

"I wish I could repaper these walls."

"Huh?" She widened her eyes, blinking her lashes.

He spread out his hands. "I'd like to tack up the pictures and info we have so far and start making some connections, but I don't think the hotel would appreciate it."

"Whiteboard?"

"I think I'm just gonna have to go digital and create a file on my laptop. I can scan in the pictures we have, add the barbershop, the incidents, and put you and Denver at the top of it all. I'll even add your kidnapping and his setup."

"You're so sure he and I are linked?"

"He is." He flipped open his laptop. "That's all I need."

"Do you want my help over there, or are you better on your own?" She rolled onto her back and crossed her arms behind her head.

"You know what you can do?"

"What?"

"Get back to work on the phone we took off that guy this morning."

"None of my tricks worked earlier, and I'm worried about turning it on. He probably knows we have the phone and they can ping it for our location."

"I get it, but information from that phone could be invaluable." Hunter started a new file and entered Major Denver's name at the top on one side and Sue's name on the other. "Maybe we can try it when we're not at the hotel, and then move on to another location—keep 'em guessing."

"That's an idea." She wiggled her fingers at him. "You keep going. I'm going to make a few phone calls downstairs."

His head jerked up. "I'll be quiet."

"It's not that—CIA business." She shrugged and left the room, her phone cupped in her hand.

Hunter stared at the door for a few seconds after Sue clicked it shut behind her, then returned to his file.

By the time Sue returned to the room, he had all his actors set up in his file and crooked his finger in the air. "Have a look at this and let me know what you think."

The slamming of the bathroom door answered him and he spun around in his chair and called out, "Are you all right?"

"Fine. I'll be right out."

Several minutes later, she emerged patting her face dry with a towel. "How's it going?"

"It's going." He shoved his laptop in front of the empty chair at the desk and kicked out the chair with his foot. "Have a look."

She shuffled toward him, the towel still covering her face. Whipping it off, she plopped into the chair.

Drawing his brows over his nose, he studied her makeup-free face and the red tip of her nose. "Bad news from the Agency?"

"Just that they don't know when they're going to lift the suspension." She draped the towel over her shoulder. "Show me what you've done."

He got out of his chair and leaned over her shoulder, inhaling the soapy scent from her skin. With her hair over one shoulder, the back of her neck exposed damp tendrils of her hair.

His fingers itched to run the pad of his thumb over the soft strands. He reached past her and jabbed his finger at the display. "You and Denver are at the top, with the inciting incident right beneath you."

"The point when Denver went AWOL and my kidnapping in Istanbul."

"Right." He trailed his finger down the screen. "Then we have Pazir, Denver's contact in Afghanistan. The group that grabbed you, Jeffrey and Mason. The gunman whose phone we have. The barbershop. And the two men in the truck."

"What are your initial thoughts? You have to have more than Denver's belief that the guys who snatched me are connected to the group he was investigating before he was set up."

"Denver's word goes a long way with me." He dragged himself away from her realm and sat back down in his own chair. "And then there's the timing. As soon as Denver makes contact with me to look you up, all these events occur."

"So, your presence here in DC is the trigger and I can blame you for everything?" She began typing on the keyboard.

"What are you entering?"

"My suspension from the CIA. Don't forget." She tapped a key with a flourish and spun the laptop around to face him. "That was in the works before you got here."

"Your abduction prompted that, didn't it?"

"Correction." She held up one finger. "Some bogus emails prompted that."

"Just like for Denver—emails to the CIA." Hunter scratched his chin. "I think someone may have hacked into the CIA's computer system, unless it's someone on the inside."

"It could be both." She stretched out her long legs, crossing them at the ankles. "The only entity I know even remotely capable of that is Dreadworm, but those hackers are not in the game of setting up people."

"We don't know that. They're in it to cause trouble."

"I thought they were in it to shed the light of truth on some dark corners of the government."

He raised his eyebrows. "You sound like a convert."

"I just don't think Dreadworm is responsible for the content of those emails, even if they may have been the conduit." She wound her hair around her hand. "Do you want something to eat? I have to go out anyway to run a few errands, and I can pick up something and bring it back to the room, unless you want to order room service."

Hunter's pulse ticked up a few notches, but he schooled his face into an impassive mask. "Pizza? Chinese? Whatever's easy for you to carry out. Do you need my rental car?"

"No, thanks." She waved her hand. "I can walk."

"Are you sure it's safe out there for you?" She would expect him to ask that, wouldn't she?

"I have my weapon, and I'll take it with me." She tossed her hair over one shoulder and pushed back from the desk. "I—I won't be too long."

"Keep me posted. You should be okay. I don't think they tracked us to this hotel, so nobody would be following you from here."

"Exactly." She grabbed her purse from the bed and

hitched it over her shoulder. "Do you trust me on the food?"

"Yeah...on the food."

The hotel door slammed before the last words left his lips—and maybe that was a good thing.

He waited two beats before springing from his chair and grabbing a gray hoodie from the closet. He stuffed his arms into it and zipped it up. Yanking up the bottom of the sweatshirt, he snapped his fanny pack containing his gun around his waist.

He gave the room a last look before slipping into the hallway and heading for the stairwell. He jogged down the nine flights of stairs and peeked through a crack in the fire door, watching the lobby.

He spotted Sue's long stride across the floor, flipped up his hood and edged through the door. He fell in behind her as she exited the hotel, keeping out of sight.

He might trust Sue Chandler with picking out dinner, but that was about the extent of it.

She'd been hiding something from him since the minute she woke up in his hotel room—and he was about to find out what it was.

Chapter 7

Sue took a quick glance over her shoulder before slipping into the ride-share car she'd ordered on her phone.

Leaning forward in her seat, she asked, "You have the address, right?"

"I know where the park is."

On cue, his GPS spit out the first direction, and the driver pulled away from the curb.

Sue pressed her hands on her bouncing knees. If they needed to talk to her, she'd have to pretend she had no problem meeting with them. Regaining their trust had to be her first step.

She didn't know how she'd lost that trust in the first place. Did they already know Hunter Mancini was in DC and why? Could she help it if the guy rescued her?

She fished her latest burner phone from a pocket

hidden inside her purse and placed a call to The Falcon. His phone rang and rang and rang.

She'd have to do this on her own. She could brief The Falcon later. Surely, he'd agree that she had to make this move.

She could be back at the hotel, Chinese food in hand, within an hour, with Hunter none the wiser.

Collapsing against the back seat, she covered her eyes with one hand. Why couldn't she have had the good luck to have met Hunter under normal circumstances? Why couldn't he be a DC doctor? An animal trainer? A ditchdigger?

She'd take any of those over what he was—a Delta Force soldier and a man on a mission.

She ran a hand beneath her nose and straightened her shoulders. She just had to convince Hunter her circumstances had nothing to do with Major Denver's and get him out of her life again...out of Drake's.

Hearing her son's voice tonight had given her strength. She had to do this for him—just as she'd always done everything for him the moment she found out she was pregnant.

"Where do you want me to drop you?" The driver met her eyes in the rearview mirror.

"The road nearest the band shell."

"There's a concert tonight?"

"I'm meeting a bird-watching group there." Not that she owed her driver an explanation of why she wanted to be dropped off near the band shell at Creek Run Park, but she didn't like leaving loose ends—like Hunter Mancini.

The driver pulled over on one of the park's access roads, and she cranked open the back door. "Thanks."

"Be careful out there."

She slammed the door and placed her hand on the outside pocket of her purse that concealed her weapon, putting her one Velcro rip between her hand and the cold metal of her gun.

Another car drove by on the access road, and she held her breath but it kept going. She crept forward on the path that led to the band shell.

Voices echoed from the stage and she drew up behind a tree and peered around the trunk at the band shell.

Clutches of kids…high school kids…were scattered across the stage practicing dance moves or projecting their voices into the night air. A teacher or director shouted instructions from the seats.

She eased out a breath. At least she wouldn't be meeting her contact in a deserted place in the park— unless he led her away from the lights and action.

A twig cracked behind her and she spun around, a gasp on her lips.

"Shh." Jeffrey, in the flesh, held up his hand. "It's just me."

"Yeah, that's why I'm freaked out." She wedged a hand on her hip and widened her stance. "Why the hell did you try to drug me last night and then send some goon to take me by force?"

"Who's your companion?" Jeffrey slid a hand into the pocket of his jacket.

"M-my companion?"

Jeffrey tilted his head to the side with a quick jerk. "Let's walk."

Her tennis shoes squished the mulch beneath her feet, damp with night dew, as Jeffrey took her arm.

She resisted the urge to shake off the pincerlike hold he had on her arm, advancing their status as comrades, two people on the same side.

He led her down a path, away from the performing teens, away from the comfort their voices brought. As she started to turn around, he shoved her against a tree and yanked her purse from her arm.

"Hey!" She spun around and made a grab for it, but he held it out of her reach and she didn't want to jump up and down to get it back.

"Do you have a weapon?"

She swallowed. "Of course I do."

He tossed her purse under a bush, several feet away. "Your companion?"

"That guy in the hotel room? He's a friend, an ex-boyfriend." She didn't want to stray too far from the truth. "He followed me and my friend out that night, saw me flailing around in the gutter after you slipped me the mickey and took me back to his hotel."

"If he's an ex, why does he have a hotel room and not a place of his own?" His dark eyes glittered through slits.

She rubbed her stinging palms together, dislodging bits of bark. "He doesn't live in DC. What does he matter, anyway? Why are you guys trying to bring me in by drugging me and holding me at gunpoint? You don't have to put on an act...unless you think someone is watching me here."

The pressure in her chest eased as she blew out a breath. Maybe that was it. They knew she'd been suspended and figured the Agency was watching her. Maybe the assaults were just another staged kidnapping like the one in Istanbul.

"The CIA has suspended you." He pointed a finger at her. "Do they know?"

"Know about us? No." She folded her arms, pressing them against her chest. "Just more follow-up from Istanbul. Is that what this is all about? You think the CIA is onto me?"

A bird chirped from the darkness and stirred some leaves with its night flight.

Jeffrey held a finger to his lips and cocked his head. Then he took the same finger and sliced it across his throat. "If they make you, you're no longer of any use to us."

"Obviously." She straightened her spine against the chill making its way up her back. "That's not what happened. They don't have a clue. Do you think I'd do anything to jeopardize what we have going?"

"How do I know you're not bugged right now?" He waved a hand up and down her body.

She spread her arms out to the sides. "You're welcome to check. I initiated this meeting because I wanted to know why you were trying to take me by force. Do you really think I'd meet with you to try to entrap you?"

Clamping a hand on her shoulder, he forced her to face the tree and shoved her against it again.

The rough trunk bit into her palms again and she sucked in her bottom lip as Jeffrey reached under her shirt and thrust one hand between her breasts. She held her breath as his hands continued their impassionate but thorough search of her body. Thank God she hadn't decided to go rogue and show up with a listening or tracking device.

The Falcon had always given her explicit instructions to show up to meetings clean…but she hadn't been able to reach The Falcon. In fact, he hadn't given her an opportunity to even tell him about her suspension, which made her think he might be behind it.

Jeffrey's strong hands spun her around. "You've made it easy for us. You're coming with me."

"What do you mean? Where are you taking me?" This time she *did* shrug out of his grasp. "I can't just disappear from my life. It's one thing to do that in Istanbul, but it's not happening in DC."

He whipped his gun from his pocket and jabbed her in the ribs. "It's not up to you. We own you."

"I told you. Everything's on track. The CIA doesn't suspect a thing. I haven't been suspended because they're suspicious about any of my activity. That's all you need to know." She wrapped her fingers around the barrel of his gun. "I'll be delivering another piece of information soon."

"You don't get it." He put his face so close to hers she could smell the garlic on his breath. "We don't trust you anymore."

"That's ridiculous. I haven't given you any reason not to. The suspension is not my fault." Her knees began to buckle beneath her, but she widened her stance. Now was not the time to crumble. If she couldn't convince Jeffrey of her loyalty to the cause, he'd take her away and then the interrogation would begin…for real.

"Barbershop." He spat out the word between clenched teeth. "What were you doing at the barbershop? Did you think nobody would recognize you there?"

"I was hoping you would. I was reaching out and

Rahid had mentioned the shop at our last meeting in Istanbul. I didn't expect you to try to run us off the road."

"If you knew that was us, why'd you pull a gun?" He nudged her again with his weapon.

"I was with my friend. He doesn't know anything about any of this."

"And then you contacted us with the phone you took off…our guy in the hotel room. Why didn't you do that before the barbershop?"

Sue swallowed. "I couldn't access the phone before. It took me a while to break into it. Give me another assignment. Let me prove myself."

Jeffrey kicked at a rock in the dirt. "This is not what we had in mind for an interrogation. You're coming with me—now."

He shoved her away from him with one hand, while he kept the gun trained on her with the other.

She stumbled and fell to her hands and knees. A wild thought came into her head to scramble for her purse and get her weapon.

A second later, Jeffrey grunted and crashed onto the ground next to her.

She twisted around and growled at Hunter looming above her, "What the hell are you doing? You just signed my death warrant."

Chapter 8

"Not now." Hunter crouched beside the man he'd knocked out, the man who'd been threatening Sue, and searched his pockets. He had nothing on him, not even a phone.

Hunter pocketed the man's gun and reached down to grab Sue by the arm. "Let's get out of here before his backup arrives. He must have someone waiting in a getaway car."

Sue threw him off and launched to her feet. "Didn't you hear what I said? If I escape now, they're gonna kill me."

"They were going to kill you, anyway. Don't make me drag you out of here by force—because I will to save your damn life."

She blinked at him, brushed off her jeans and

stomped past him. She stopped several feet in front of him and spun around. "Don't kill him, for God's sake."

"I have no intention of killing anyone." He spread his hands in front of him. "But let's get out of here before I *do* have to kill someone."

They tromped down the access road in silence, both breathing heavily. He didn't know what the hell Sue was involved in, but it was putting her in danger and he wasn't going to stand by and watch her get manhandled…or worse.

When they reached the sidewalk bordering the park, Hunter pulled out his phone and ordered a car from the same app that got him here.

Fifteen minutes later, Sue finally broke her silence when they pulled up to an Italian restaurant in Georgetown, not far from her place. "What are you doing?"

"I'm going to eat. I was starving waiting for you to come back with food. I'm also going to conduct my own interrogation—but you'll like mine a lot better than the one you were facing."

Her lips twisted as she got out of the car. "You wanna bet?"

He opened the door for her and the whoosh of warm garlic scent that greeted them made him feel almost comforted. He couldn't help it. The smells of Grandma Mancini's family dinners lived deep in his soul.

He raised two fingers at the hostess scurrying to greet him. "Table for two, please."

She seated them at a cozy, candlelit table with a checkered tablecloth, obviously laboring under some false impression.

Hunter waited until they'd ordered their food and a bottle of Chianti and a basket of garlic bread sat between them on the table before hunching forward on his elbows and saying, "Now, you're going to tell me what the hell is going on."

She plucked a piece of bread from the basket and ripped it in two. "I can't. It's top secret, and I'm not even kidding you."

"I know it's top secret. You wouldn't be meeting with a terrorist in the park in the middle of the night if it weren't. But, hey, you can tell me anything. I happen to have a top secret clearance."

He poured two glasses of wine from the bottle encased in wicker and held one out to her.

She dropped the bread onto a plate and took the glass by its stem. She tipped it at his. "Here's to top secret clearance."

He tapped her glass and took a long swig, the red wine warming his throat.

After taking a dainty sip from her own glass, Sue cupped the bowl with one hand. "What did you overhear?"

"Enough to know you're working with Jeffrey and his cohorts. For whom and how deep is something I aim to discover."

"Why can't you just leave it? Just know that I'm doing my job."

"I can't ignore it. I know it has something to do with Major Denver…and it looks like your assignment has gone haywire and you're in danger. I can't allow that to happen."

"Why is that?" Sue traced the rim of her wine glass with the tip of her finger.

He snatched her hand and squeezed her fingers together. "You know damn well why. I wasn't the one who slipped out of that Paris hotel room in the early morning hours. I wasn't the one who ended our whirlwind affair. I never would've ended it. Those few weeks with you…"

He dropped her hand and gulped back the rest of his wine.

"I—I didn't realize…" Her cheeks flushed the same color as the wine.

"That I'd fallen so hard, so fast?" He snorted. "I thought I'd made enough of a fool of myself for you to figure that out."

"You were just coming out of a marriage—a bad marriage. I figured I was the rebound girl." Her dark eyes glowed in the soft light, making her look nothing like a rebound girl.

"The first couple of days I would've agreed with you, but the more time I spent with you…" He broke off. He was *not* going to open himself up to her again. "Look, I wanna keep you safe. It's the only way I'm going to find out how your group is connected to Denver."

Sue pursed her full lips and nodded. "My cover has probably already been blown. I'm not sure it matters anymore."

They stopped talking when the waitress arrived with their steaming plates of food. She looked up after she sprinkled some grated Parmesan on their pasta. "Can I get you anything else?"

Hunter raised his eyebrows at Sue, who answered no, and he shook his head.

He plunged his fork into his linguine. "I have a question."

"Of course you do."

"Did the Agency suspend you so that you could go deeper undercover with this group?"

"Before I answer that—" she directed the tines of her fork, dripping with tomato sauce, at him "—why did you follow me tonight? How did you know?"

"Lots of little things that added up to a great big thing—your reluctance to work on that phone when it could've been a treasure trove of information, your quick ID of the man in the photo with Jeffrey, even though the CIA didn't have a name for him." He shrugged. "The feeling ever since I got here that you've been keeping something from me."

Dropping her lashes over her eyes, she balanced her fork on the edge of the plate. "Then to answer your question, the CIA *did not* suspend me to allow me deeper access to this group. The CIA doesn't know about this group and doesn't know I'm working with them."

Hunter coughed, almost choking on his pasta. "Who are you working for if not the Agency?"

"It *is* the Agency—they just don't know about it."

"Black ops? Deep undercover?"

"That's right." Sue's shoulders dropped and she stuffed a large forkful of food into her mouth, closing her eyes as she chewed.

"It looks like a big weight just slipped off your shoulders." He cocked his head. "Have you ever told anyone that before? Does anyone know?"

"My dad."

Hunter steepled his fingers, resting his chin on the tips. Sue had told him about her father, the retired spook who had encouraged his daughter to follow in his footsteps, once she'd shown an affinity for languages and martial arts. Hunter wasn't sure he'd urge any daughter—or son—of his to enter the high-stakes and dangerous game of spying, but Sue had taken to it with a flair.

Not that he had children to urge one way or another—his ex had decided, after they were already married, she didn't want any. Julia must've known before he did that their marriage didn't stand a chance.

"He must be proud of you."

"I'm not sure about that." She pushed away her plate and folded her arms on the table.

"You're kidding, right? It's what he wanted for you from the beginning—not only a CIA agent but a double agent, someone working in the bowels of the machinery."

She dug her fingertips into her forearms. "I'm not sure I did things the way he would've wanted me to."

"It's crazy the amount of pressure we allow our families to exert on us." He reached around his own plate and brushed his fingers across the back of her hand. "I'm sure your father thinks the world of what you're doing."

"I've got a bigger problem now, don't I?" She uncrossed her arms, dislodging his hand, and picked up her wine glass, swirling the remnants of the Chianti. "My contacts within this terrorist cell don't trust me anymore—and they're planning to take me captive to interrogate me."

"What about your first kidnapping?" Hunter leaned back in his chair and flagged down their passing waitress. "Check, please."

"What about it?"

"That wasn't real, was it? That was a preplanned meeting with your contacts."

"Ah, you don't believe I escaped, either."

He drilled his finger into the tabletop. "I'm convinced you know how to look after yourself, but it makes sense now. You orchestrated a kidnapping with them to make things look good on your side of the fence. Am I right?"

"You are." Sue whipped the napkin from her lap and dropped it onto the table next to her plate. "But now they want to kidnap me for real, and this time I don't think they're gonna offer me tea and cakes."

"How long have you been working undercover?"

"Over four years now."

Hunter rolled his eyes to the ceiling and counted on his fingers. "You were doing this when we met in Paris."

"I was."

He dropped his gaze to her face. "Is that why...? Never mind."

He snatched up the check the waitress dropped off and reached for his wallet. "You're going to need some protection."

"I thought I had it." She leveled a finger at him. "You dropped poor Jeffrey before he even knew what hit him."

"I mean someone official, someone at the Agency."

"I don't have anyone at the Agency—just my contact. The person who recruited and trained me. He's the only one, as far as I know, who knows what I'm doing. In fact—" she slid her jacket from the back of her chair "—I believe I'm on suspension for the very activities I've been doing undercover, only the CIA doesn't know I'm undercover."

"That's a dangerous game, Sue." He couldn't help the way his heart jumped at the thought of Sue in the middle of all this intrigue—even though he knew better, knew she could handle herself. "You need to contact him right away."

"I tried earlier through our regular channels, and he's not picking up."

"But this has hit critical mass now." He smacked his fist into his palm.

"You don't need to tell me that, although I may have figured a way out, a way to keep working this group."

He raised one eyebrow. He hadn't intended on coming out here and playing bodyguard to a badass spy, who was way more hooked in than he realized, but she'd just pushed his protective instincts into overdrive. "You don't need to keep working with this group. Call it a day and fold your hand."

"This is almost five years of work, Hunter. You don't give up on five years of blood, sweat and tears—and sacrifices. You wouldn't. You can't even give up on Denver. You won't give up on Denver." She shrugged into her jacket and flipped her hair out of the neckline. "Don't tell me what to do."

He held up his hands. Where had he heard that before? "What's your plan?"

"I'll run it past my contact first, but since Jeffrey never saw what hit him and I was just about to go off with him, I can make the case that you followed me without my knowledge—which you did—and were just playing the protective boyfriend."

"Which I was." He felt heat prickles on his neck. "Except for the boyfriend part."

She ignored him.

"I can arrange another meeting for them to pick me up."

"No!" The word was out of his mouth before his brain could stop it. He coughed. "I mean, they're not going to believe you and you know what's waiting for you on the other side of a so-called meeting with these guys. They're gonna want to make you talk and they'll use any means necessary. You know that, Sue."

She lifted her shoulders. "I have to try to salvage my mission."

"Wait and see what your contact has to say. I can't believe he'd be willing to sacrifice an asset like you for a compromised mission."

"I have my burner phone back at the hotel." She jerked a thumb over her shoulder. "I'll try to call him again when we get back."

Hunter had to keep his fingers crossed that this guy was reasonable and would see the futility in having Sue continue with a group that clearly didn't trust her anymore.

Through all this, he couldn't deny that Sue's position gave her an even better perspective on the web entangling Denver—the same web had her in its sticky strands.

"Let's go, then." He added a few more bucks to his cash on the tray for the tip and pushed back from the table.

When they stepped outside, Sue huddled into her jacket. "The hotel's not far. We can catch the Metro."

"No way." He held out his phone. "I already ordered a car."

As they waited, he rubbed her back. "We don't have to figure this all out here in DC. You're suspended. The Agency doesn't expect you to sit around waiting for them to call you back. We can get out of here, someplace safer for you."

"I need to stay right here. Besides, where would we go?"

"We could go to my place."

She twisted her head to the side. "Colorado?"

The fact that she remembered where he lived caused his mouth to slant upward in a ridiculous smile. "Clean air, wildflowers for days and mountain views for miles."

"I really can't leave DC, Hunter. It's impossible." She waved at the approaching sedan. "This is our guy, right?"

"Yeah." He lunged forward to get the door for her. "Why are you so wedded to DC? You don't even have family here, right? Dad, mom and sister's family all in South Carolina?"

Sue tripped getting into the car and grabbed onto the door. "Good memory. Yes, but I have things to do here."

Good memory? She had no idea the things he remembered about her—the way her brown eyes sparkled when she laughed, the curve of her hip, the hitch in her breath when he entered her.

"Are you getting in or planning to push the car?"

Hunter blinked and ducked, joining her in the back seat. They kept their mouths shut during the brief ride back to the hotel, but once outside the car they both started talking at once.

Tucking her hand in the crook of his arm, she leaned her chin against his shoulder. "There's no use trying to talk me out of anything, Hunter, until I contact The Falcon."

"The Falcon?"

"That's his code name—and I've never told anyone that before."

"Does that mean you're ready to trust me now? Tell me what the two of you have been busy infiltrating all these years?"

She pressed a finger to her lips as they got into the elevator with another couple.

Hunter shifted from foot to foot on the ride up to their floor.

When they got to the room, Sue made a beeline to the hotel safe in the closet. She crouched in front of it and entered the code she'd plugged in earlier. Cupping the phone in her hand, she sat on the edge of the bed with a bounce.

"You just call each other on cell phones?" He sat beside her and the mattress dipped, her body slanting slightly toward his.

She scooted forward to straighten up. "It's a little more complicated than that."

She tapped the display to enter the number and held the phone to her ear. A few seconds later, her body became rigid and she sucked in a quick breath.

Hunter watched her face, as her brows collided over her nose.

"Two, eight, three, five, six." She spit out the numbers in rapid succession.

She jumped to her feet and repeated. "Two, eight, three, five, six."

The phone slid from her hand and she spun around to face him. "He's gone. The Falcon has been compromised."

Chapter 9

She paced to the window, twisting her fingers in front of her. She chanted under her breath, "This is bad. This is bad."

"How do you know? What just went down?" Hunter leaned forward and scooped the burner phone from the floor. "Was that a code between the two of you?"

"We have a number code that changes for each phone call. We answer calls from each other with random numbers, and the caller returns with the appropriate sequence of numbers based on the original set. It's a calculation The Falcon made up. Nobody knows it but us." She clasped the back of her neck beneath her hair and squeezed.

"What happened this time?" Hunter retrieved a bottle of water from the minifridge and handed it to her.

"When I placed the call, someone said hello with the

voice alteration program on. We're not supposed to answer with a hello, but I guess he could've slipped up."

"You've never even heard The Falcon's real voice?"

She shook her head and her hair whipped back and forth across her face. "I have no idea who he is or where he resides—or who else works on the team."

"He answered hello and you threw a random code at him, right?"

"Yes, but he couldn't respond. He paused. He recited some numbers, but I knew by then I didn't have The Falcon on the other end of the line." She pressed two fingers to her right temple. "I don't know what could've happened."

"Maybe he lost the phone and some random person picked it up and was fooling around."

Digging her fist into her side, she tilted her head. "I know you're trying to make me feel better, Hunter, but just stop. We both know something's wrong. Jeffrey tried to take me in for questioning and now this."

"They could've stolen the phone off him, trying to find another way to reach you."

"How do they know The Falcon? *I* don't even know The Falcon."

The thought of The Falcon, her lifeline, disappearing from the other end of that burner phone suddenly hit her like a sledgehammer and she collapsed onto the bed before her knees gave out beneath her. She flung herself facedown on the mattress and stared at the comforter inches from her nose. "M-maybe The Falcon figured we were made and dropped out of sight for a while."

The bed sagged as Hunter sat beside her. "Sure, that could be it. If he's running a black ops organization, the guy has skills. He's gonna lay low until it's safe for him to poke up his head."

"The timing couldn't be worse. I'm under suspicion at work, and I always thought The Falcon would be able to rescue me if things got too heated. Someone in his position would be able to tell the investigators to back off." She buried her face in the crook of her arm. "What if the CIA actually believes I've been working with this terrorist group and there's no Falcon to bail me out?"

"It's going to be okay, Sue. We're going to clear you and Denver at the same time." He squeezed her shoulder. "But you have to help me out. You have to give me something—something more than fake kidnappings and barbershops and shadowy black ops commanders. I wanna know what you know."

She squeezed her eyes shut. Should she really tell Hunter what she knew? If she told him her biggest secret, he might walk away from her forever. Last night she would've welcomed that prospect, but now? She'd found her shoulder to lean on.

Rolling onto her back, she sighed. "The group we've infiltrated has ties all over the world. That's why the people I met in Istanbul are connected to a cell here in DC. In the past years, we've become aware that they're planning something big here in the US, but they're being coy."

"This group has tentacles in Afghanistan? Syria? Nigeria?"

"Yes, yes and yes." She narrowed her eyes. Hunter knew more than she thought. "Why did you mention those places?"

"Because Denver has been tied to all those places,

as well—he was placed at a bombing at a Syrian refugee center, he was inspecting suspicious arms at an embassy outpost in Nigeria and he went AWOL in Afghanistan—and some believe he's still there."

"It sounds like he's tied into the same structure. Who does he know in Afghanistan? Who was his contact there? Do you know?"

"Pazir—that's the only name I have."

Sue drew her bottom lip between her teeth. "I don't know that name, but I'm going to do a little research tomorrow."

"Thatta girl. Let's meet this thing head-on and be proactive. No point in sitting around waiting for things to happen."

She rolled off the bed and stamped her feet on the carpeted floor. "You mean like intruders, car chases and abductions?"

"Exactly." Hunter formed his fingers into a gun and pointed at her.

"Where's Jeffrey's gun?"

"In my jacket pocket. I'll lock it up in the safe if there's room. In a day or two, I might have as many guns as you do cell phones." He plucked his jacket from the back of a chair. "What did you get off that phone?"

"The number to set up that meeting tonight."

"What did you hope to accomplish by sneaking away to the park to meet with Jeffrey?"

"The chance to convince them that I'm still on their side, maybe persuade them to stop attacking me." She yawned, a heavy lethargy stealing over her body. "Can we pick this up tomorrow? I'm going to brush my teeth and hit the sack."

"We'll be thinking more clearly in the morning,

anyway." He grabbed a couple of pillows from the bed and tossed them onto the sofa. "You take the bed, and I'll stretch out over here."

She eyed the sofa, wrinkling her nose. "You're not going to be stretching out on that, Hunter." She patted the bed. "This is big enough for both of us."

His gaze shifted to the bed and his Adam's apple bobbed in his throat. "I don't want to crowd you…or make you uncomfortable."

"It's not like we haven't shared a bed before."

"Yeah, but we weren't sleeping in *that* bed." He thrust out a hand. "Sorry, had to put that out there."

She grinned, a punch-drunk laugh bubbling to her lips. "Oh, I remember."

She turned her back on him and weaved her way to the bathroom to escape the intensity of those blue eyes. When she'd safely parked herself in front of the sink, she hunched over the vanity and stared at her flushed cheeks.

Must be the Chianti…and the fear. Sharing a bed with Hunter Mancini was a dangerous proposition— no telling where that pillow talk might lead.

She brushed her teeth, wound her hair into a ponytail and washed her face. If he were as exhausted as she was, he'd be out already.

Opening the bathroom door, she peered into the room, spying Hunter in front of the room safe.

He twisted his head around. "You wanna share the combination with me, so I can lock up my weapon collection?"

She reeled off the numbers. "Bathroom's all yours. I'm ready to black out."

Once he secured the guns in the safe, Hunter stepped into the bathroom and closed the door behind him.

Sue let out a breath and stripped out of her clothes in record time. She pulled on a pair of pajama bottoms and a camisole and crawled between the covers.

Hunter had already turned off all the lights except for one over the bed. Sue reached over and flicked it off, leaving the flickering blue light from the TV as the only illumination in the room.

When the bathroom door clicked open, she squeezed her eyes closed and then relaxed her face muscles. She deepened her breathing. As long as she pretended to be asleep, she'd be safe from Hunter…or rather her own desire for him. She'd always be safe with Hunter. She'd known that from the moment she met him in Paris.

He'd been wounded by his ex. She'd cheated on him while he'd been deployed, and Sue's heart ached knowing she'd added to his love battle scars.

Her lashes fluttered and she watched him undress through the slits in her eyes. The glow from the TV highlighted the flat planes and smooth muscle of his body.

He'd stripped to his boxers, and she held her breath as he crossed the room to his suitcase in the corner. He glanced over his shoulder once, then plunged his hand into his bag, dragging out a pair of gym shorts—as if those could hide the beauty of his body and dampen the temptation that coursed through her veins at the sight of him.

He crept past the foot of the bed and tugged at the covers behind her. The bed squeaked as he eased into it.

The mattress bounced a little and it sounded like he was punching pillows. Then the TV station changed from the news to a cooking show, and every muscle in Sue's body seized up.

She'd been hoping he'd fall into an exhausted sleep, but no. The man had more energy than Drake high on sugar at a bouncy house birthday party.

She covered her mouth. She'd been avoiding making those comparisons between her son and Hunter.

A soft whisper floated over her. "Is the TV keeping you awake? I'll turn it down."

"I'm sorry, Hunter."

"Don't worry about it. I can watch the cooking shows without sound—unless it's the light that's bothering you."

She turned toward him, pulling the covers to her chin. "No, I meant I'm sorry that I left you in Paris like that."

He lifted one bare shoulder, and the sheet slid from his chest, exposing his chiseled pecs. "It's all right, Sue. It was a fling—a totally hot, unforgettable fling—and I don't regret it, even though it ended the way it did."

"I—I always meant to look you up later."

"Don't." He lifted a lock of her hair and wrapped it around his finger. "You don't have to pretend."

"I wasn't pretending then—" she scooted closer to his warmth "—and I'm not pretending now."

A low light burned in his eyes, and it sent a shudder of anticipation through her body. She knew they'd wind up here together—the moment she woke up in the bed of his other hotel room. At the time, she didn't know how or where, but she knew she had to have this man again, regardless of the consequences.

His fingers crept through her hair until he loosened

the band holding her ponytail together. He pulled it out and scooped one hand through her loose strands.

"As long as you want this now, I'm not even going to ask for a tomorrow."

She placed two fingers against his soft lips. "Let's not talk about tomorrow."

"Let's not talk." He slid down until they were face-to-face. He cupped her jaw and pressed his lips against hers. His tongue swept across the seam of her mouth, and she sucked it inside.

They hadn't even kissed since he'd walked back into her life, so this intimate invasion left her breathless. How many times had she dreamed about Hunter's kisses?

His soft lips carried an edge of greedy urgency, as if he couldn't get enough of her—or maybe he was taking what he could get before she disappeared from his life again.

And she'd have to disappear.

Without breaking his connection to her, he shifted his hands beneath her pajama top and caressed her aching breasts. Would he feel the difference in her body? The new softness since her pregnancy and the birth of Drake?

A sigh escaped her lips as he rolled her nipples between his fingertips. Men didn't notice things like that—even men like Hunter, who had a surprisingly tender side despite the rough edges.

She placed a hand on Hunter's hip, her fingers tucking inside the waistband of his boxers. Resting her forehead against his, she whispered against his mouth, "I've been waiting so long for this."

He turned his head to the side and growled in her

ear. "Same. Never forgot you. Never wanted to forget you."

He slid his hands to her shoulders and pulled her camisole over her head. He dipped his head and let his tongue finish what his fingers started, teasing her nipples to throbbing peaks.

The tingling sensation curled in her belly and zigzagged down the insides of her thighs. She hooked a leg over his hip and rocked against him.

His hands slid into her pajama bottoms and her underwear at the same time and he caressed her derriere. He hissed between his teeth. "So smooth."

She yanked down his boxers and skimmed her hand down the length of his erection. "So smooth."

His breath hitched as he nibbled her earlobe. "Take those off."

"You don't have to ask me twice." She dragged his underwear over his muscled thighs and down the rest of his legs, dropping them onto the floor.

Before he asked, she stripped off her bottoms and tossed them over her shoulder. "Now we're even."

With a smile lifting one corner of his mouth, he encircled her waist with his hands and pulled her toward him.

He always did like her on top first. She straddled him and folded her body to smush her breasts against his chest as he dug his fingers into her bottom.

She laid a path of kisses from the curve of his shoulder to the side of his neck and his strong jaw. She gasped as his fingers probed the soft flesh between her legs.

As he rhythmically stroked her, she rocked against him, closing her eyes. The passion built from the tips of her toes and raced up her legs, pooling where his fingers teased her and then clawing through her belly.

She caught her breath and held it, every muscle in her body tensing, awaiting her release.

As her climax claimed every inch of her body, her lids flew open and her gaze met the flickering blue light in Hunter's eyes. He plunged his fingers inside her wet core and he rode out her orgasm with her, holding her gaze with his. She couldn't break that connection even if she wanted to—and she didn't want to.

Her body shook and trembled as she came down from her high only to have Hunter enter her slowly and deliberately. He steadied her movement by placing his hands on her hips, guiding her onto his erection as he thrust upward.

They hit their stride and she rode him hard, controlling how deep he went and how fast. He soon tired of her game.

Pinching her waist, he flipped her onto her back and wedged one hand against the headboard as he continued to plunge into her.

Her desire for him burned once again in her pores, and she wrapped her legs around his hips.

He stopped moving and his voice came out in a strangled whisper. "Are you close?"

"Don't wait for me. It feels like you're ready to explode."

"Waited for you for almost four years. I can wait."

His words sent a river of electric current across her flesh. She arched her back and undulated against him where their bodies met.

He sucked in his breath and braced his hands on either side of her head as he pressed and rubbed against her, his face tense, his jaw tight.

He was a man of steel.

She puffed out a breath, which started the avalanche. Her orgasm rolled through her, turning her muscles to jelly.

Feeling her release, Hunter picked up where he'd left off, driving into her, lifting her bottom off the mattress with the force of his thrusts.

He exploded inside her and kept pounding her until they both lay drained and exhausted.

Totally sated, Sue let out a squeak. "You're squishing me."

"I'm sorry." His body slid off hers, slick with sweat and boneless.

"I can't move."

He rolled his head to the side and opened one eye. "I can barely move."

"Water?"

"I thought you couldn't move?"

She snorted. "I'm afraid if I don't move now, I'll never get up from this bed."

Brushing his knuckles against her hip, he said, "That doesn't sound so bad to me right now. Here, we're in a bubble. Out there…"

"It's a whole different kind of bubble out there, but the night is young—sort of."

His eyebrows jumped. "You mean you're going to require more of me?"

"If you play your cards right." She smoothed her hand across his damp chest and rolled from the bed. "There's still water in the minibar, right?"

"I can get it."

She swept her camisole from the floor and pulled it over her head. "You stay right there and keep that bed warm."

"Impossible without you in it, and how come you look even sexier with that top on and your bare bottom peeking from the hem?"

"Because you have sex on the brain now." She bent forward in front of the fridge to grab a bottle of water, mooning him.

"You don't play fair, woman." He threw a pillow at her but missed.

"I sure hope you have better aim with a gun than you do with a pillow." She spun around, holding out the bottle of water.

As Hunter grabbed another pillow to chuck at her, a soft knock at the hotel door had them both suspended, the look of shock on Hunter's face surely mirroring her own.

"Wait." He leaped from the bed, snagging his boxers from the floor.

She dropped the bottle of water onto the floor and crept toward the door, hugging the wall in case someone decided to shoot point-blank into the door.

The knock sounded again—louder, stronger.

Hunter appeared beside her, thrusting her behind him as he leaned to the side to peer through the peephole. "It's someone in a dark hoodie. I can't see his face. Too short to be Jeffrey."

A woman's voice called through the door. "The code. Give me a code, Nightingale."

Chapter 10

Sue pressed a hand against her heart. "It must be someone working in The Falcon's unit. Maybe she brought news of The Falcon."

Hunter held up his hand. "Hang on."

As he turned to the safe in the closet, Sue called out. "One, five, two, two, seven."

The woman coughed and rested her forehead against the door, but she answered the correct sequence of responding numbers.

Hunter sidled up next to her with a gun pointed at the door.

"She's legit, Hunter. I'm opening the door."

"Slowly." He stood behind the door as she eased it open.

The woman fell against the door with a thump, and as Sue widened the door, the woman fell into the room, landing in a heap on the floor.

"Oh my God." Sue dropped to her knees beside the woman. "What's wrong?"

"I hope she wasn't followed here." Hunter poked his head out the door and then shut it, throwing the top lock in place.

Sue had loosened the woman's sweatshirt and pushed the hoodie back from her head. She gasped and fell back on her heels. "She's been beaten."

Hunter crouched beside her. "What happened? Who did this?"

The woman's lashes fluttered and her slack mouth hung open, a trickle of blood seeping from the corner.

"I think she lost consciousness."

"Let's get her on the sofa. Get some towels." He slid his arms beneath the woman's small form and lifted her in a single motion.

As he carried her to the sofa, Sue pulled on her underwear and rushed to the bathroom to collect the extra towels. She grabbed a hand towel and ran it beneath the faucet.

Had The Falcon's entire unit been blown wide open? Were they all targets now?

When she returned to the room, Hunter was seated on the floor next to the sofa checking the woman's vitals.

"Is she still alive?"

"Barely." He peeled the woman's blouse back from her chest. "She has multiple wounds. These look like stab wounds."

"God, what happened to her?" Sue pressed a towel against the woman's bleeding head.

"The same thing that would've happened to you had you gone along with Jeffrey tonight."

Sue clenched her teeth as she used the wet towel to clean up some of the blood on the woman's face. "How did she get here?"

"God knows." Hunter clasped his hands behind his neck. "She needs medical attention, Sue. We can't do this here. We're losing her."

"If she wanted to go to the hospital, she would've gone to the hospital—she came here instead."

"Maybe just to warn you, and she's done that." He rose to his feet. "We have to get help. She's somebody's daughter, sister, wife, mother. My God, if this were you, I'd want immediate medical care for you, regardless of any other circumstances."

"Of course, you're right." She smoothed the corner of the towel across the woman's mouth. She might have a son, just like her.

"I'm calling 911, and then I'll call the front desk of the hotel. We can say we don't know her. She came up to our room like this, knocked on the door and collapsed. We don't know anything."

"Does she have ID? Did you check?"

"I didn't." He held up his phone. "You do that while I call."

Sue searched the woman's pockets and scanned the floor inside the room and in the hallway in case she'd dropped something.

When Hunter ended his call, Sue spread her hands. "Nothing. She has nothing."

Ten minutes later, Sue waved at the EMTs as they came off the elevator. "Over here. She's here."

For several chaotic minutes, the EMTs stabilized the injured woman and got her onto a stretcher as the police questioned Sue and Hunter.

The questions continued even after the EMTs had taken away the patient, but Sue had years of lying under her belt and she maintained her ignorance without blinking an eye.

Maybe Hunter didn't have quite the same skills in mendacity as she possessed, but his military training had given him an erect bearing and poker face that was hard to pick apart.

In the end, the cops had no reason to believe she and Hunter had injured the woman or even knew who she was—and the hotel's CCTV would back them up.

Sue clicked the door closed behind the last of the police officers and braced her hands against it, hanging her head between her arms. "I wonder who she is."

"Hopefully, she'll regain consciousness and tell us... and tell us why she came here." Hunter traced a line down her curved spine. "She must've used every last ounce of her strength to get here and recite that code to you."

Sue turned and nestled her head against Hunter's chest, just because she could. "How did she know I was here? How did she even know about me? The Falcon has never even implied I was part of a group."

"Different plans for different people. Maybe you're the only CIA agent and The Falcon has different rules for you." He squeezed her shoulders. "Let's get back to bed for the remaining hours we have left in this morning."

"We're going to try to see her at the hospital tomorrow, right?"

"I don't see how we're ever going to get any information out of her if we don't—and I'm sure she wanted you to have info or she never would've shown up here."

He leaned over her to put his eye to the peephole in the door. "I hope nobody followed her. We've been secure at this hotel so far."

"We *think* we have. How did she find us?"

Hunter yawned and flicked off the light in the entryway. "We'll ask her tomorrow."

On the way to the bed, Hunter peeled off the T-shirt he'd hastily thrown on when the EMTs arrived and stepped out of his jeans and boxers at the same time. He slid his naked body between the sheets and patted the bed beside him. "Has your name on it."

Sue shed her pajamas and underwear and crawled in beside him. She didn't know if she could do another round with Hunter, but if he wanted her again she wouldn't mind one bit—and she owed him.

Instead, he pulled her back against his front and draped an arm over her waist. He nuzzled the back of her neck. "Would you think I'm heartless if I told you I'm glad that wasn't you bloody and beaten, looking for refuge?"

"No. I know what you mean. You're not happy it happened to her, either, but…yeah." She threaded her fingers through his and planted a kiss on his palm. "I'm glad you're here, Hunter. I've never had a bodyguard before."

"I'm here and I'm not leaving."

She squeezed her eyes shut. *Don't be so sure about that, Hunter.*

The following morning, Hunter slipped from the bed, careful not to disturb Sue. He'd lain awake most of the night as much to soak in feeling Sue's body next to his as to keep watch over her.

He crept to the bathroom and shut the door behind him.

He didn't like the fact that the woman had shown up at their hotel room, hanging on to consciousness by a thread. How did she know she hadn't been followed? She could've led her assailants right to Sue's doorstep.

Or maybe that's what she planned. Who knew where she learned that reciprocal code? Sue had no idea whether or not this woman was connected to The Falcon and the work they were doing.

He couldn't have left a battered woman in the hotel corridor anyway, but he didn't trust her. Hell, he still didn't trust Sue. He knew she'd been hiding something from him. Why not just come out and tell him she was a double agent, a mole embedded with a terrorist group? Why sneak around when they were on the same side... or at least he assumed they were.

Sue had told him she was black ops working for the other side, but what if she were just working for the other side? People turned all the time for money, ideology, revenge. The CIA seemed to have its suspicions.

If he were honest with himself, he didn't know much about Sue's work or life. He'd heard about the CIA father, the overbearing stepmother, the beloved sister. He hadn't fallen for her based on anything she'd told him about herself.

He'd gotten in deep because of the way she made him feel. Rebound. He turned his face to the spray of water in the shower.

He'd clicked with her so quickly because she was nothing like his ex-wife, Julia—except for the secrets and now the lies.

Sue had wanted him at a time when he'd no longer felt wanted. Powerful stuff to resist.

He shut off the water and snatched a towel from the rack next to the shower. Maybe this time, he needed to be the one to walk away—but not before he got everything he could about Major Denver out of her.

She could be lying about what she knew about Denver, too. Once you caught a woman in one lie, you never knew how many more could be on her lips.

The knock on the door caused him to drop his towel. "Did I wake you?"

"Just by not being in bed when I reached for you." Sue knocked on the door and jiggled the handle. "Have you gotten modest all of a sudden? I've seen it all, Mancini...and I'd like to see it again."

He left the towel on the floor and reached over to let her in.

The dark gaze that meandered over his body from head to toe felt like a caress. When she met his eyes, she licked her lips. "Thought we might shower together this morning."

He stepped back, whipped aside the shower curtain and turned on the water again. "Great idea."

As she joined him under the warm spray and he kissed her wet mouth, all his doubts disappeared... or rather receded into one small corner of his brain.

After breakfast in the hotel restaurant, Sue called the hospital, but once the nurse who answered the phone determined that Sue was not related to their visitor from last night, she refused to give her any information at all.

Sue shook her head at Hunter and raised her voice. "I'm the one who called 911. She stumbled to my hotel room."

A few seconds later, Sue slammed the phone to the table, rattling the silverware.

"No luck?"

"She refuses to tell me anything."

Hunter drained the coffee from his cup and clicked it back into the saucer. "If the nurse is that closemouthed, we don't stand much of a chance getting in there to talk to her, even if she does regain consciousness."

"The nurse wouldn't even tell me if she was awake or not." Sue broke a crust of toast in two and crumbled it between her fingers.

"I'm thinking not. If she used the last bit of energy she had to make it to our hotel and give you that code, I think she'd want to talk to you when she comes to."

"Maybe, maybe not, but there are ways to get into hospitals and see patients, whether you're family or not."

"Yeah, I almost forgot…you're CIA." He winked and pulled his laptop from its sleeve and placed it on the table. "You ready to look at everything I have on Denver?"

"Go for it." She raised her hand as the waitress walked by. "Can I get a refill on my coffee, please?"

Hunter brought up the spreadsheet and file he'd been populating since yesterday while Sue had been making her mysterious phone calls and attending her mysterious meetings with terrorists.

He swung the computer toward her. "You and Denver are at the top, and my goal is to connect you by the time we reach the bottom of the tree."

"Have his contacts told him about an impending attack on US soil, too?"

"Yes, that's what he believes is happening. The

problem is that the attack is not being carried out by one group—or even the usual suspects. This group is scattered, has no defined leader—and may have connections to the US government."

Sue's heart skittered. "Traitors on the inside?"

"It's the only way to explain the setup of Denver. It's widespread and there seems to be no urgency to clear Denver's name, even when charges against him have been shown to be false."

Sue's phone buzzed on the table beside her, and she shot him a glance beneath knitted brows. "It's my manager."

"Are you going to answer it? Maybe you've been cleared to go back to work."

"I doubt it." She lifted the phone to her ear. "Hi, Ned."

She cocked her head as she listened to the voice on the other end of the line. "What are you doing on the sidewalk in front of my place? I'm not home, Ned."

Sue's eyes widened in her suddenly pale face, and Hunter's insides lurched.

"Okay, okay. I'm at the Hay-Adams in the coffee shop." She ended the call and tapped her chin with the edge of the phone. "Ned's coming over. He wants to talk to me."

Hunter swallowed. "He couldn't do it over the phone?"

"Apparently not."

"He just wants to update you." Hunter shrugged, feigning a nonchalance that didn't match the rumblings in his belly. He tapped his laptop's display. "Did the group you infiltrated ever mention weapons from Nigeria? Apparently, there was a secret stash there that Denver knew about or suspected."

"I'd have to retrieve all my notes, which I pretty much turned over to The Falcon."

"You kept copies?"

"I have copies of all my reports on my laptop. I can definitely go through them with you, and you can tag anything that relates to Major Denver."

They went through another cup of coffee each as they discussed Hunter's spreadsheet, and he really felt that they were making some progress. If they could get to the bottom of this plot and link it to Denver's findings before he went AWOL, the army would have no choice but to exonerate the major.

Sue had been keeping an eye on the entrance to the restaurant, and she lifted her hand and waved at a compact, balding African American man charging toward them.

When he reached their table, Sue stood up and pulled out the chair across from her. "Have a seat, Ned. This is Hunter Mancini. Hunter, Ned Tucker."

Hunter had risen from his chair and stuck out his hand to the other man.

Ned looked him up and down before releasing his grip and taking his seat. "Military?"

"Delta Force. You?"

"Air Force." Ned leveled a stubby finger at Sue. "Are you helping her out?"

"I'm trying. Why?"

"Because she needs it." Ned turned to Sue and covered one of her hands with his. "Sue, what have you been up to? There is no way I believe you've been spying for the other side, but I'm hearing about evidence against you that's giving me pause. Enlighten me."

"You enlighten me." Sue wiggled her fingers at the waitress. "Do you want some coffee, Ned?"

"I'm wired enough as it is." He turned to the approaching waitress and asked her for a glass of water. "I can't tell you much, Sue."

"Bogus emails again? Emailing classified documents?" She pinged her coffee cup. "None of that is true, Ned. It's been planted, just like those emails about Major Rex Denver were fakes."

"It's more than that, Sue." Ned glanced over his shoulder and ducked his head. "The investigators have pictures—pictures of you meeting with known terrorists."

Sue dropped her spoon onto the saucer with a clatter that further jangled Hunter's nerves. Those pictures could definitely be in existence, but who could've taken them?

"That's absurd. Any photos of me with terrorists would be meetings with informants."

Ned wiped his brow with a napkin and then crumpled it in his fist. "Okay, that makes sense, and any of those meetings would be documented as protocol dictates, right? Right, Sue?"

"Of course. Protocol."

"Speaking of protocol." Ned thanked the waitress for his water and downed half the glass in one gulp. "You never saw me here. We never had this conversation. I have my own sources within the Agency and someone gave me a heads-up, but if anyone found out I relayed this info to you, I'd be in almost as much trouble as you're in now."

"I appreciate you're going out on a limb for me, Ned. This is going to come to nothing, but even if it doesn't, I'll leave you out of it." She patted his arm. "Don't worry."

Ned raised one eyebrow to his bald pate. "You're always telling me that like you have some secret guardian angel. I hope you don't mean your old man, because as revered as he is in the Agency, not even he could get you out of this mess if it's true and you don't have the documentation to support those meetings."

"Don't worry." She slid a plate with a half-eaten pastry on it toward Ned. "Have a Danish."

"That's even worse." He patted his rounded belly. "My wife still has me on that diet."

"Thanks for the intel. We can handle it."

Ned rose from the table and said his goodbyes. Then he snatched the Danish from the plate and waved it in the air. "Now you have two secrets to keep."

Hunter watched Sue as she kept the smile plastered to her face long enough for Ned to get sucked into the lobby.

Then she turned toward him and smacked her palm against her forehead. "Who's taking pictures of me at my meetings?"

"The Falcon?"

"And then sending them to the CIA? For what earthly reason?"

"Sue…" Hunter took both of her hands. "The Falcon is gone…disappeared. Maybe his information was also compromised. Maybe someone else has those pictures and then fed them to the CIA to discredit you."

"Discredit?" She disentangled her hands from his and raked her fingers through her hair. "Those pictures can send me to federal prison. Of course, I didn't document those meetings. They were secret. The Falcon always assured me that he had everything covered—even in the case of an emergency."

"Like this one?"

"Exactly." Sue grabbed her purse and smacked down the lid of his laptop. "Let's get going."

He smoothed his hand over his computer. "If you insist. Where?"

"We're going to talk to the one person who just might know what happened to The Falcon."

Hunter wheeled his rental car into the hospital parking lot, climbing up to the top floor of the structure. He cut the engine and folded his arms. "Are you sure you know what you're doing?"

Sue had already popped open her door and cranked her head over her shoulder. "We need to get in there and talk to this woman. She knew the code. She knows The Falcon. And she knew where to find me. She probably knows where The Falcon is, too. She's the only hope I have right now...or you can forget about helping Denver. If I'm locked up, you're never going to discover the link."

"I will leave it to your covert ops hands to get us into that hospital room when the nurse wouldn't even tell you if the woman regained consciousness." He yanked the keys from the ignition and opened his own door. "What if she hasn't?"

Sue slid out of the car and ducked her head back inside. "We'll have to come back."

Sue strode into the hospital like she owned the joint. Might as well come in with confidence.

They reached the elevator and she scanned the directory for the correct floor.

Hunter leaned over, touching his head to hers. "Do you know where you're going?"

"When the operator transferred me this morning, the nurse answered with the department—and this is it." She poked at the glass directory with her fingertip and then jabbed the elevator call button. "I just hope this elevator doesn't dump us out in front of the nurses' station."

"If it does?"

"We don't get off on that floor. We'll ride it up to the next."

"Tell me you've done this before." Hunter followed her into the elevator and then held the door for a woman with a tearful, sniffling baby.

Sue nudged Hunter's shoe with her toe. "Something like it."

Hunter ignored her in favor of wiggling his fingers at the baby, who gave him a watery smile and kicked his legs against his mommy's hip.

Sue pressed a hand against her belly. Hunter had wanted children with his ex, but she put him off and then dropped the bombshell that she didn't want kids at all.

When the elevator settled on the woman's floor, she nodded to Hunter. "Thanks for entertaining him right out of his fussiness. You must be a dad."

"Nah, babies just think I'm funny." He touched his finger to his nose and then the baby's. "Must be my nose."

When the doors closed, Sue cleared her throat. "When the doors open on our floor, if you see the nurses' station, press the button for the next floor up and we'll circle back down via the stairwell."

Hunter saluted. "Got it, chief."

"Don't get smart." She elbowed him in the ribs just as the doors whisked open on a short corridor, not a nurse in sight. "We're good."

Sue stepped from the elevator with Hunter close behind her and made a sharp right turn. Seconds later, she tugged on his sleeve and tipped her head toward a door marked Maintenance.

Hunter eased open the door and they both slipped inside the dark room, cluttered with cleaning supplies—and coveralls.

"This is you." She tugged a blue coverall from a hook and tossed it to him. "Slip into that and grab a mop."

"You're kidding."

"I'm not. Do you think the hospital staff knows the entire custodial staff or keeps track of the turnover?"

"What are you dressing up as for Halloween?"

"I'm going to try to snag myself a lab coat." She pinched his cheek. "This will work."

She cracked open the door and put her eye to the space, checking the hallway. She scooted out and checked on the offices and rooms on the corridor before heading upstairs. She had more luck on the research floor where there were no patients.

She lifted a lab coat from a hook just inside a lounge area and stuck her arms into the sleeves. She jogged back downstairs and had even more luck on the way back to the custodians' closet when she ducked into an examination room and swiped a stethoscope from a silver tray.

As she continued down the corridor, she hung it around her neck and then dipped into the maintenance room.

She almost bumped into Hunter, the blue of his coveralls matching his eyes, holding a mop in one hand and a clipboard in the other.

"Hello, doc." He held out the clipboard to her. "Look what I found."

"See, you're catching on. I'll put in a good word for you at the Agency when you get cashiered out of Delta Force."

He leaned on his mop. "You're assuming *you're* going to have a job."

Turning the doorknob, she bumped the door with her hip. She held her breath as two nurses walked by.

She stepped into the hallway and whispered over her shoulder, "Give me a few minutes to find her room. I'll wait in front of her door and you can follow me inside."

Sue tucked her hair behind one ear and peered down at the clipboard in her hand that contained a cleaning rotation schedule instead of someone's vitals—but nobody had to know that.

It took her two passes down the stretch of hall with patient rooms before she located the double room the mystery woman occupied with another patient.

Hunter turned the corner, pushing the mop in front of him. Their eyes met for a split second before Sue crept into the room.

An African American woman hooked up to monitors and devices snored slightly from the first bed.

Sue jumped when the door creaked, and Hunter held his finger to his lips.

Sue said, "Our patient is in the next bed on the other side of the screen."

"Lucky for us, she's out of view of the door. If anyone comes in while we're here, you called me in for a cleanup."

"Got it." Sue tiptoed past the first bed and around the screen. She grabbed onto the footrest of the other bed where the woman from last night breathed through tubes.

"She looks worse than the other woman." Sue sidled up next to the bed. "Hello, it's me. It's Nightingale. Where's The Falcon? What do you know?"

The woman's eyelids flew open, and Sue jumped backward, gasping and dropping her clipboard.

"What happened?" Hunter materialized by her side, mop in hand.

Sue touched the woman's cool, papery arm. "She's awake."

"She can't talk, Sue." Hunter pointed to the mask over the woman's face.

"She's all I have right now, Hunter." She squeezed the woman's arm. "What can you tell me? You came to our hotel room, and you recited the code. Who are you? Where's The Falcon?"

The woman managed to roll her arm over and blink her eyes once.

"I don't know what you mean. Do you think you can write something?"

"Sue, she can't write. She can't grip a pen."

The woman turned her arm again and blinked.

"She can move her arm." Sue stroked the woman's flesh. "I'm sorry. I don't know what you mean. Maybe you can communicate to the nurses that you want to see me and when you're able to talk I'll come back."

The woman blinked her eyes twice and rolled her arm over again.

"She keeps moving her right arm."

"Maybe it's the only thing she can move right now."

The woman blinked without moving her arm this time and Sue glanced down. "Wait, Hunter."

"What?"

"She has something on her arm." Sue turned the woman's arm, so that her palm was displayed, and squinted at the tattoo on the inside of the woman's elbow.

She skimmed her thumb across the dark blue falcon imprinted on the woman's skin, then raised her gaze to meet the woman's glittering eyes above her mask.

"She's The Falcon."

Chapter 11

Before Hunter could respond to this news, the machines keeping The Falcon alive began to beep and whir.

"We'd better get out of here."

He grabbed Sue's hand and tugged, but she seemed rooted to the floor, her mouth working as she mumbled.

"A woman. I can't believe you're a woman." Sue grabbed a handful of white sheet. "Why? Why would you do that to another woman?"

He had no idea what Sue was rambling about, but they had to get out of here. He yanked on her lab coat. "Let's go."

Swinging around, he claimed his mop and pushed it in front of him out the door, almost colliding with three nurses in the corridor on their way to the distressed patient.

He cranked his head over his shoulder and let out a breath as he saw Sue following him. Without waiting for her, he careened around the corner and dumped his disguise in the maintenance room.

He made his way to the elevator, where he found Sue, head tilted back, watching the lights above the car as it descended, the lab coat still over her clothes.

They stepped into the elevator with several other people and continued to pretend they didn't know each other—not that it would've mattered to these strangers.

When they hit the parking structure, Hunter slowed down to let Sue catch up with him. Her white face and huge, glassy eyes caused his heart to bump in his chest.

He took her hand on the way to the car. "Are you sure she's The Falcon?"

"Positive." She chewed her bottom lip. "Didn't you see her tattoo?"

"Maybe she just got that to mark herself as someone in The Falcon's unit."

Sue turned on him and thrust out her arm, wrist turned outward. "Do you see one of those on me? That was not required—other things were required, but not that."

When they reached the car, Hunter opened the door for her but blocked her entrance into the car. "What's wrong, Sue? Why are you so shocked The Falcon is a woman? You yourself know women in the CIA can be as good as any man."

Her lashes fluttered. "I—I just never pictured The Falcon as a woman. I'm shocked…and I'm shocked that she showed up at my hotel room beaten and bloodied. How did that even happen? She's always worked behind the scenes—giving orders, issuing ultimatums."

Hunter stepped aside and Sue dropped to the car seat, covering her face with her hands.

He closed the door and shook his head on his way to the driver's side. It must be disconcerting to discover someone you assumed was one gender was another. He didn't get the big deal, but maybe it was a female thing—and he'd never voice *that* to Sue.

He slid behind the wheel and smoothed a lock of hair back from Sue's forehead. "At least The Falcon is still alive."

"As far as we know." She peeled her hands from her face. "She looked bad, and what happened at the end? That didn't sound good."

"How'd you get out of the room with all those nurses rushing in? Sorry I left you, but I figured it would look even weirder for a doctor and a maintenance guy to be in a patient's room while those bells and whistles were going off."

"That's okay. I would've expected you to get out while you could." She powered down the window and took a deep breath. "When I heard them coming, I waited until they were in the room, and then I stepped behind the screen. They never saw me."

"Thank God for that. I wouldn't want to see you accused of tampering with a patient on top of everything else you're going through."

Sue clasped her hands in her lap. "I think my very survival depends on finding a link between the terrorists The Falcon and I have been tracking and the ones Denver was onto. If I can uncover a terrorist plot here in the states, the CIA will have to believe I was working deep undercover—whether or not The Falcon survives."

"Maybe she'll out herself now and the whole operation before she takes a turn for the worse."

"Before she takes a turn for the worse?" Sue flung out her hands. "What were all those beeps and hisses from her machines? That sounded like a turn for the worse to me."

"The nurses were in there in a split second."

"If The Falcon dies..." Sue ended on a sob and covered her eyes with one hand.

"I know she's been someone important in your life, a mentor. Even if you hadn't met her, I'm sure it was hard to see her like that." Hunter rubbed his knuckles on the denim covering her thigh. "Now maybe you can understand what I'm going through with Denver in the crosshairs."

Sue's voice hardened along with her jaw. "The Falcon can rot in hell for all I care. She'd just better not take me down with her—again."

Hunter snatched his hand back and jerked his head to the side. "Whoa. Do you blame her for getting compromised? For comprising your position?"

"I blame her for a lot of things, Hunter." Sue dragged her thumb across her jaw. "And to think, all this time The Falcon was a female—a coldhearted, cold-blooded one."

Hunter braced his hands against the steering wheel and hunched his shoulders. "Why does it matter to you so much that The Falcon is a woman? Professional jealousy?"

He bit his tongue, literally. Did he just say that out loud?

Sue snorted, the nostrils of her longish nose flaring. "Yeah, that's it. Professional jealousy because I aspire to be a cold fish just like The Falcon…or is that a cold bird?"

Hunter gave up on the conversation and concentrated on the road. He didn't want to open his mouth again and blurt out the wrong thing, and Sue wasn't making much sense, anyway.

She descended deep in thought for the rest of the ride back to the hotel, her chin dropped to her chest.

At least she seemed more on board with his agenda, which seemed to have taken second place to all the drama swirling around Sue. But he'd lay odds that her drama was Denver's drama.

By the time they reached the hotel, Sue had climbed out of her funk—mostly.

"Pazir, huh?"

"What?" He pulled the car up to the valet stand.

"Denver's contact is Pazir, some Afghani who's working both sides over there?"

"That's right. Sound familiar now?"

"Not yet, but by the time I'm finished researching him, he's gonna be my best friend in the world." She shrugged out of the lab coat and tossed it in the back seat.

Back in the hotel room, Sue made a beeline for her laptop. "I have most of my files on here. It's secure. Email is encrypted. And my password is my fingerprint."

"All the latest and greatest stuff, but can you get to everything you need?"

"I can, but if your CIA buddy who likes to leave you gifts in mailboxes wants to play, I might need his help."

"I can get him on board. He knows Rex, and he wants to help."

"Rex?"

"Denver."

As Sue attacked her keyboard, Hunter crossed his arms and studied her from across the room. The Falcon's identity seemed to energize her, fueled by her puzzling resentment that The Falcon was a woman.

Sue raised her eyes from her laptop. "What? Why are you staring at me? Shouldn't you be on the phone to your CIA contact to see if he wants to play ball?"

"When we met in Paris, you said you were on assignment, although I didn't know it at the time."

"That's right." She planted her elbows on either side of her laptop, joined her hands and rested her chin on them. "So?"

"I'm not trying to grasp at straws here—or maybe I am—but is that why you had to leave me without a word, without a backward glance, without warning?"

"Technically, I left you word. I put a note on your pillow."

"Cut it. You know what I mean." He wedged a shoulder against the window, wondering again what they were doing in this hotel room instead of Sue's townhouse in Georgetown.

She closed her eyes for a second. "Yes, that's why. Do you think I wanted to leave you? Did last night feel like I wanted to leave you all those years ago?"

His jaw tightened. "The Falcon made you leave me. She's the one who told you never to contact me again."

"Bingo." Sue stared off into space. "I'd already been warned not to get personal with anyone while on a mission, but—" she shifted her gaze to him "—we couldn't help ourselves, could we?"

Warmth flooded his veins, washing away all the

doubt and regret that had dogged him since his affair with Sue. After his divorce and his abandonment by Sue, he'd felt toxic.

His shoulders slumped and he sagged against the window.

Sue jumped up from her chair and flew toward him. Wrapping her arms around his waist, she choked, "I never wanted to leave you, Hunter. Never wanted to give up on you, on us, b-but my job depended on it. Maybe even my life."

He rested his cheek on top of her head. "And people think the military demands blind allegiance. Was the job important enough for you to give up…love?"

"I didn't know it was love." She pulled back from him and cupped his jaw with her hand. "Not then. We had a crazy chemical attraction for each other. When we weren't making love, we were talking to all hours of the morning, strolling along the Seine. It was like a magical dream, wasn't it?"

"It wasn't a dream. It was real." He thumped his chest with his fist. "I knew it then. Knew we had something special. The setting, the circumstances might have supercharged what we were feeling, but there was no denying what we were feeling."

"You'd just gotten out of a marriage. I knew it had been hard on you." She brushed her thumb over his lips. "I thought maybe I was just a rebound for you, someone to hold on to and make you feel again."

He raked a hand through his dark hair. "I can understand that. I can even understand slipping away when ordered to by The Falcon, but I can't understand the rest."

Her body stiffened. "The rest?"

"Never calling me, never reaching out." He snapped his fingers. "All it would've taken was one phone call. I would've followed you anywhere. Surely, even The Falcon realizes that CIA agents have relationships, marriages."

Sue broke away from him and stepped back. "I'm more than an agent. You know that now."

"So, once you join a black ops organization, you give up your personal life? I find that hard to believe." He flattened his hands against the cool window behind him.

She pressed the heel of her hand against her forehead. "You might find it hard to believe, but you see how I live—racing from one thing to another, always living on the edge, never knowing whom to trust."

"You're giving up on marriage, kids…love?" He reached out and captured a lock of her hair, slowly twisting it around his finger. "You're made for love, Sue. I see it."

Her cell phone buzzed on the table behind her, and she shifted her gaze to the side as he tightened his hold on her hair.

She jerked her thumb over her shoulder. "That might be important."

Expelling a long breath, he released his hold on her, maybe forever. Her priorities lay elsewhere and he couldn't change that.

She lunged for the phone. "It's the hospital. I'll put it on speaker."

Cradling the phone in her hand, she tapped the display and returned to him by the window, but their connection had been broken. She'd broken it.

"Hello?"

"Is this Sue Chandler?"

"It is."

"I'm calling about the injured woman who came to your hotel room last night."

"Yes?" Sue grabbed his arm.

"She's conscious and she's asking for you. Do you know who she is? She won't tell us her name, she had no ID on her and we can't fingerprint her without her consent. We're going to have to get the police involved, as she was a crime victim."

"I don't know who she is, but I'm curious to find out why she came to my room and why she wants to see me now. Maybe it's just to thank me, but could you hold off on calling the police until I talk to her? Maybe I can discover who she is."

"She just came to in the past few hours after a turn for the worse. She's still not out of the woods, so we have no intention of calling the police yet."

"Okay, I'll be there within the hour. Tell her I'll be there."

"Thank you."

Sue ended the call and then backed up, falling across the bed. "Thank God she's awake and okay."

"It doesn't sound like she's okay. The nurse said she's still in bad shape, but at least she's asking to see you." He sat on the edge of the bed. "I hope she plans to tell you how she was compromised and can set things right with the Agency."

"I hope she can tell me a lot of things."

They made the drive back to the hospital—a little faster this time and with more confidence. At least he had more confidence. Sue had never had any doubts they could get into The Falcon's hospital room.

This time they checked in at the nurses' station and were given the room number, which they pretended they didn't already know.

The same patient, hooked up to the same machines, in the same position greeted them when they entered The Falcon's hospital room.

Hunter hung back as Sue poked her head around the screen and said, "Are you awake?"

When Hunter heard a slight intake of breath, he followed Sue around the screen. The Falcon didn't look much like a falcon.

The beating had taken a toll on the older woman in the bed. Two dark, penetrating eyes stared out from a worn face, crisscrossed with life's miseries and triumphs.

She rasped out one word. "Nightingale."

She could barely get out that name as it cracked on her lips, and Hunter's high hopes took a nosedive. How much could Sue get out of The Falcon in this condition? The woman looked as if she were on death's doorstep.

Sue dragged a chair over and sank into it while she took the older woman's hand. "What happened? How'd they get to you?"

The Falcon pointed a clawlike hand at the plastic water cup on the bedside table, and Hunter retrieved it for her and held the straw to her lips.

She drank and then waved him away. "Ambush."

"They ambushed you? How did they find you? The CIA doesn't even know who you are. I didn't even realize you were here in DC."

The Falcon coughed. "Whole mission over."

"No." Sue scooted her chair closer. "I don't believe

that. I can't accept it. I gave up…everything for this mission."

The Falcon's gaze darted to Hunter and pierced him to his soul. She coughed again, and the beeping on her machines picked up speed. "Over. Too dangerous."

"Tell me what to do. I'll finish it." Sue reached for the water cup again as The Falcon went into another coughing fit.

"Over, Nightingale. Someone inside."

Hunter hunched forward. "Are you telling us there's someone on the inside of our own government working with terrorists against US interests?"

The Falcon placed her thin lips on the straw. When Sue pulled it away, a few drops of water dribbled from the corner of The Falcon's mouth.

"Deep. Someone deep. Major Rex Denver."

"No!" Hunter shouted the word. "He's not involved."

The Falcon reached out, and with unexpected strength, she wrapped her bony fingers around his wrist like a vise. "Someone inside setting up Denver. My shoe, Nightingale."

Sue's eyebrows arched. "Your shoe? What are you talking about? This isn't over, Falcon. I'm gonna see this through."

"Danger. Stop."

"There's always been danger. I'm not stopping now." Sue jumped from the plastic chair and it tipped over. "Why did you do it? Why did you ruin my life if you're going to give up so easily?"

"Necessary."

"Necessary but now it's over?"

Hunter drew his brows over his nose. How did The Falcon ruin Sue's life? If she was talking about their relationship, that wasn't over—and he had no intention of allowing Sue to end it now, black ops or no black ops.

"Had to do it, Nightingale. For the best."

"The best? Really? The best that I gave up the man I loved and our...son?"

Chapter 12

A sudden fog descended on Hunter's brain activity. What the hell was Sue talking about? Son? She didn't have a son. They didn't have a son.

Another coughing fit seized The Falcon, and her face turned blue while the machines went crazy.

This time the nurses arrived even faster, and as they swarmed the room and clustered around the bed, Hunter tugged on Sue's arm.

"Her shoe. Get The Falcon's shoe."

Sue turned a blank face toward him as one tear seeped from the corner of her eye.

He dived past her and yanked open the door of a cabinet. He plunged his hand into the folded stack of The Falcon's bloodstained clothes, and his fingers curled around a pair of sneakers. He clasped them to his chest, unnoticed by the nurses and by Sue herself, still rooted to the floor, in a daze watching the medical efforts to save The Falcon's life.

Hunter grabbed her hand and pulled her out of the room, past a doctor rushing in to take their place.

He propelled Sue to the elevator and out to the car, where he tossed The Falcon's shoes in the back seat. He'd deal with those later. There was so much more to deal with in the seat next to him.

His throat tight, he closed his eyes and he took a deep breath. "Sue, what was all that about our son?"

She slumped in her seat and clasped her hands between her knees. "It's true. I'm sorry, Hunter. I got pregnant in Paris and had a son. Drake is almost three."

Her words punched him in the gut and for several seconds he couldn't breathe. For the second time in his life a woman had lied to him about children—but this was much worse than his ex changing her mind about having them. He'd had a son out there for three years and never knew.

A wave of rage overwhelmed him and he punched the dashboard, leaving a crack—like he felt in his heart right now. "Why?"

"Do I have to tell you that after what you just heard?"

He rubbed his knuckles. "You kept my son from me because The Falcon told you to?"

"Yes. I had to. I had to comply."

"Your job was more important…is more important, than anything else in your life?" He snorted. "What a sad life you lead."

Sue sniffed and the tears she seemed to be holding back spilled over and coursed down her cheeks. "You don't think I know that?"

"Where is he now? Where's... Drake?" The unfamiliar name stuck on his tongue and the rage burned in his gut again.

"He's with my dad and my stepmom."

Hunter whistled through his teeth. "That's great. He's with a woman who detests you and a father who groomed you for a soulless, empty career with the CIA. Don't tell me. It was your father's idea for you to go black ops. His little girl fulfilling everything he hadn't in his career."

Sue pressed her fingers against her temples. "Drake lives with my sister, Amelia, and her family in South Carolina. They went to the Bahamas and I didn't want Drake to go, so he spent some time with me first and then I sent him with my parents."

"Our son doesn't even live with his mother." Hunter bowed his head and rested his forehead against the steering wheel. How did this happen?

He felt Sue's hand on the back of his neck, and he stiffened, his first instinct to shrug her off—this woman who'd tricked him and lied to him at every turn.

But her touch turned to a caress as she stroked his flesh with her fingers. "I'm sorry, Hunter. I thought it was best for Drake to live with my sister while I'm involved in all this. Can you imagine if he lived with me and I failed to return home one night? Or worse, what if I were home with him and someone broke in with a weapon, like how someone stormed our hotel room the other night?"

"Why even have him if you weren't going to keep him?"

Her hand trailed down his back. "There was never any question that I'd have your baby, regardless of how I chose to care for him later. I was thrilled with my pregnancy and never thought about my situation until… I told The Falcon."

He lifted his head. "She's the one who told you to send Drake away."

"Yes."

"Is she the one who told you not to tell me about the baby?" He tried to swallow the bitterness filling his mouth.

"Ordered me. She ordered me to keep quiet and explained the difficulties of raising a child for someone in my position."

"And then she sent you off to Istanbul and Berlin and God knows where else to make the point, right?" He cranked on the car engine, and Sue went back to her own side of the car.

"Do you think she kept me busy on purpose?" She dragged her hands across her face and peered at him through her fingers.

"She must've had a lonely, desolate life herself. She wanted to make sure you had the same." He pulled out of the parking garage so fast the car jumped and Sue grabbed the edge of her seat. "Isn't that why you were so angry when you found out The Falcon was a woman? You could understand a *man* telling you to give up your child, keep him from his father, be a part-time mother. But coming from a *woman*? That must've felt like betrayal."

Sue crossed her arms. "I guess so."

"I'm taking us back to the hotel, or do we even need the pretense now? You did keep me away from your townhouse because there's evidence of Drake all over that place, isn't there?"

"There is and I did." She dropped her chin to her chest. "But that's not the only reason. I really did believe we were safer at the hotel."

"Do you want me to take you home now? Forget this whole thing? Go back to your life?"

She whipped her head around. "Go back to my life? This *is* my life now. Like I told The Falcon, I have sacrificed too much to walk away now. I can't walk away, anyway. I'm under suspension and suspicion at the Agency, and I'm going to be cleared there only when The Falcon speaks up. Besides, didn't you hear The Falcon? There's someone on the inside and that someone is responsible for setting up Major Denver and probably for outing The Falcon's operation."

He nodded and squeezed the steering wheel. "I want to see my son, Sue. I want to meet Drake."

"You will." She traced the corded muscle on his forearm. "Can we wait until this is all over? We can go down to South Carolina together. He's just starting to ask about his father, and I can't wait to introduce him."

"I could've taken him, you know. I could've taken care of him."

"Hunter, you're in the army still getting deployed."

She was right, but he'd be damned if he were going to admit anything. He pulled in front of the hotel and said with a grimace on his lips, "Home sweet home."

She pointed into the back seat. "Don't forget the shoes. Why did you take her shoes?"

"Didn't you hear her? She mentioned her shoes. She distinctly said something about her shoes when half of what she said wasn't distinct at all, but that I caught."

"I'm glad you grabbed them. I was just so consumed by my anger at the time."

"I know how you feel."

They landed in the console, and Hunter picked up one of the small size sixes and shoved his hand inside. He peeled back the insole and ran his finger around the edge of the shoe.

Sue's phone buzzed in the cup holder, and as she picked it up, Hunter picked up the other shoe and repeated the process. "Go ahead."

She glanced at her phone's display. "It's the hospital."

As she spoke in monosyllables, Hunter removed the insole of the second shoe. He peeled up a small piece of paper stuck to the bottom inside of the shoe and unfolded it.

He whispered, "This is it, Sue—The Falcon left an address and a code."

She ended the call and cupped her phone between her hands. "That's good…because The Falcon is dead."

Chapter 13

Sue dropped the phone in her lap and tilted back her head. "Can this day get any worse?"

"I'm sorry." Hunter touched her hand.

He must still be under the impression that The Falcon represented some feminist mentor to her or something, when all she'd felt for the frail woman in the hospital bed was contempt and anger. And now the woman had failed her again.

"How am I going to prove anything to the Agency without The Falcon? I have no idea what umbrella she was under or where she was getting her orders."

Hunter held up a shiny piece of paper pinched between his fingers. "I told you. There's an address and a code on this piece of paper. It was hidden beneath the insole of her shoe. She told you to get her shoes, and this is why."

"An address to what? A code for what?" Sue scooped her hair back from her face. "She left me flapping in the breeze. I'll have no explanation for the investigators when they ask me about those photo ops with terrorists—unsanctioned."

"We'll get there, Sue, and we're gonna start with this slip of paper."

Hunter's blue eyes bored into her, shoring her up, giving her strength. And she'd just rocked the foundation of his world.

"Okay, I'll try to have as much faith in that info as you do." She squared her shoulders. "I'm sorry I didn't tell you about Drake. It was cruel and wrong."

"You were just…" He pocketed the precious piece of paper. "Hell, I don't know what you were doing. You've told me so many lies, I don't know what to believe about you, Sue."

"Just believe I have regrets, and we'll leave it at that for now." She pointed out the window. "The valet has been champing at the bit to park your car and get it out of the way."

"Then let's give him that opportunity. We'll regroup, get lunch and find this address." He patted his front pocket.

Back in the hotel room, Hunter entered The Falcon's address on his laptop. He smacked the table. "It's a storage unit in Virginia. There could be a treasure trove of information in there."

"Why would she keep hard copies?"

"Laptops—" he pinged the side of his "—can get stolen."

"Even if my laptop disappeared, whoever took it

would have a hard time accessing any data on it. We have so many layers of security on our stuff."

"Really? Because I'm pretty sure someone used that hacking group, Dreadworm, to access CIA emails to get the ball rolling against Major Denver."

"Maybe, maybe not." She reached into the mini-fridge and snagged a bottle of water. "If what The Falcon said is true, there's someone on the inside pulling the strings for this terrorist group. He…or she could easily cover his…or her tracks."

Hunter snapped his laptop shut. "Are you ready to head over there now, or do you want to stop and get something to eat?"

"I don't think the storage unit is going anywhere and you look like you could use some food—and some pictures."

"Pictures?"

"Of Drake." She grabbed her purse. "Let's go back to my place before we eat. I have to collect my mail and water a few plants."

"I was going to ask before, but I figured you might not want to carry any pictures of him." Hunter slipped his laptop into its sleeve and tucked it under his arm. "You don't have any pictures on your phone?"

"I don't keep pictures of Drake on my phone—just in case."

"The Agency must know you have a child. You can't keep that kind of information a secret from your employer—especially a government employer like the CIA."

"My employer knows. The pregnancy and birth were covered by my insurance, of course, but I took a leave of absence for five months. None of my coworkers know I have a child. They know I'm close to my nieces and...nephew, but that's it."

"That's crazy, Sue." He rested one hand on her shoulder. "You know that, right?"

"I know, but it makes sense—or made sense for me."

"And it was something The Falcon suggested."

"Working a black ops team is special, Hunter, different. We follow different rules, live different lives." She folded her arms over her purse, pressing it to her stomach. "I'll bet you Major Denver isn't married, is he? No children? No long-term relationships for him. He's not only your Delta Force commander. Someone is using him for intel. He's no different from me."

Hunter blinked his thick, black lashes. "Major Denver's wife and child were killed by a drunk driver. It gutted him. He changed after that, became harder, fiercer and more determined."

"A man with nothing to lose."

"That's right, but you..."

"My mother died from an aggressive form of breast cancer at a particularly vulnerable time in my life. I suffered from depression. I even made a half-hearted attempt to commit suicide, but my father rescued me."

"I had no idea." He touched her cheek. "I'm sorry. How did your father help?"

"I had already shown an aptitude for languages, so he encouraged me, sent me to boarding school in Switzerland for a few years, where I picked up more languages...and a purpose in my life." She lifted her shoulders. "So, your interpretation of my father's grooming me to fulfill his CIA dreams may be true, but it saved my life."

His mouth lifted on one side. "I don't know what

the hell I was talking about. I just wanted to strike out at you."

"Understandable and deserved." She took his hand and kissed the rough palm. "Now, let me show you those pictures."

As they got into the car, he leaned over and tapped the phone in her hand. "You haven't looked at the barbershop video in a while. You said Jeffrey admitted we landed on their radar the minute we walked into that barbershop. That means you did have the right barbershop all along. Are you ready now to tell me how you heard about the shop and Walid?"

"Drive." She snatched his phone and entered her address in the GPS, although he probably already had it in there. "When my terrorist contacts pretended to kidnap me in Istanbul, they did so in order for me to pass them information about a raid, which of course was completely made up. The most valuable time I spend with my contacts is when they speak among each other in their own language. They have no idea I know their language, and it's the best way for me to pick up information."

"No wonder The Falcon wanted to keep you on her team by any means necessary. Go on."

"There I was, drinking tea and rubbing a rope against my wrists to prove I'd been held captive instead of turning over intelligence—even if it was fake intelligence." She smoothed a finger over her skin, which had long since healed but looked raw enough after her so-called escape. "They weren't paying much attention to me. They'd already paid me off."

"They thought you were doing it for the money?"

"Oh, yeah. The Falcon had manufactured some

gambling debts for me…and several illegal prescriptions for drugs."

"Sue—" the steering wheel jerked in his hands "—would the CIA internal investigators see those things, also?"

"I'm pretty sure they would." She held up one hand. "I know. Don't say it. I already know I'm in big trouble if The Falcon's storage unit doesn't yield any proof of our deep undercover operation."

"I didn't mean to interrupt. Go on. They were ignoring you and talking among themselves without a clue that you could understand everything they were saying."

"That's right. And what they were saying had something to do with picking up materials from a barber named Walid at the shop on that corner. Like a dutiful little spy, I passed that info along to The Falcon. Two days ago, she called me and said the information was false and that there was no Walid at the shop."

"How did she know that?"

Sue spread her palms in front of her. "I was not privy to that sort of information. The Falcon told me it was the wrong barbershop."

"Maybe that's how they made The Falcon…and you. It was some kind of trap. They became aware somehow that you knew their language and they set you up, just like you'd been setting them up with your fake intel."

"Maybe you're right, but it's hard to believe The Falcon would expose herself like that. She was a pro." Sue pressed her fingers against her lips.

"What's wrong?"

"A pro. That's what she always used to call me. She knew she'd asked a lot of me—giving you up for good and then turning my son over to my sister. It was her ultimate compliment, but she was just playing me as surely as she played those terrorists."

"Nice neighborhood you have here." Hunter pointed out the window to the cherry trees lining her block, their pink blossoms preparing to explode with the next spring shower.

"But you've been here before." She tilted her head at him. "Why didn't you come up to my door that night? You'd come to DC specifically to contact me, right? Why skulk around and follow me to bars?"

He pulled up to the curb and put the car into Park. "The truth? I didn't know what I'd find when I got here—husband…children."

She coughed. "Little did you know."

"When you left me in that hotel room, I considered calling you anyway, even though you'd asked me not to contact you. I even looked you up once or twice."

"Let me guess—your CIA friend. Because my address and phone number are not easy to find."

"Don't be too hard on him. I never got your phone number, which is a good thing because it would've been less stressful to place a call or, better yet, leave a voice mail."

"What stopped you from looking me up in person?"

"Pride, I guess. I'd spent enough time trying to make things work with my wife. I didn't want to face any more rejection."

"I half expected you to show up on my doorstep one day."

"And you would've slammed that door in my face?"

"I would've thrown it open and fallen into your arms."

He snorted. "That's not exactly what you did when you woke up in my hotel room."

"Different circumstances." She tapped on the window. "You can't park here. You'll get a ticket. You can park behind my car in the garage."

She directed him around the corner to her parking spot. "You can block me in for now. I'm not going anywhere."

With her key chain dangling from her fingers, she led him through the garage to her back door, which faced an alley. She unlocked the door and pushed it open.

"No killer cats going to spring on me?"

"No, but Drake loves animals and I'm going to get him a puppy…one day." She stepped into the kitchen and wrinkled her nose at the mess on the counter. "I didn't leave…"

Hunter wrapped an arm around her waist and dragged her backward into the alley, hissing in her ear, "Someone's in your place."

Sue arched her back. "I'm done with this. If they're in there, let's find out what they want."

Hunter cocked his head. "I don't hear any doors slamming or cars starting. Wait here and I'll check it out."

"Are you kidding?" She practically ripped the zipper from the outer pocket of her purse, which concealed her weapon.

"At least let me go in first."

She huffed out a breath, her nostrils flaring.

"Humor me." He withdrew his own gun and crept back into the kitchen with Sue's hot breath on his neck.

Leading with his weapon, he crossed the tile floor.

The kitchen opened onto a small dining area, the round table adorned with a lacy tablecloth and a vase full of half-wilting flowers. He turned the corner and caught his breath.

Sue swore behind him at the upended drawers and bookshelves in disarray. Colorful pillows from the sofa dotted the floor.

"Looks like they didn't plan to keep their visit a secret."

"Shh." He nudged her shoulder as she drew up beside him.

"If they don't know we're here yet, they're too dumb to surprise us now." She waved her gun around the living room. "There's a half bathroom down here and then two bedrooms and a full bath upstairs."

Hunter glanced at a few photos of a child strewn across the floor, but he didn't have time to look yet.

As Sue placed a foot on the first step, he squeezed past her to take the lead. She'd done enough on her own these past three years. She had nothing to prove.

He made his way up the staircase, then checked both rooms, swallowing hard as he entered the room with the pint-size bed shaped like a car and the puppy-themed border of wallpaper ringing the room.

He checked out the closet, crammed with toys, and then backed out to join Sue in the bathroom, which had also been ransacked.

He wedged a foot on the edge of the tub, brushing aside the shower curtain dotted with red-and-blue fish. "What the hell were they looking for in here?"

"Maybe all my illegal meds."

Sue backed out of the bathroom and returned to her

bedroom where she smoothed a hand over her floral bedspread. "Bastards. What do they think I have?"

Hunter crouched down beside the bed and stirred the shards of broken glass on a framed picture of a small boy hugging a rabbit. "He has black hair."

"And the bluest eyes ever—just like his dad." Sue perched on the end of her bed. "This is not how I wanted you to see him."

"But then you never wanted me to see him, did you?"

Biting her lip, she rubbed the back of her hand across her stinging nose. Of course, Hunter wouldn't get over her deception as fast as his casual attitude made it seem he had. The resentment toward her burned deep inside him.

But working with her to clear Denver had to take precedence over any lashing out against her. He couldn't afford to alienate her now. He had to put his work first, too; maybe not to the degree that she'd put hers, but he had to understand what had been at stake for her.

She'd disobeyed direct orders by having a fling in Paris while she was on assignment—and a fling with a military man had just made the infraction worse. She'd doubled down with the pregnancy and her decision to keep the baby—as if she could've come to any other.

When The Falcon had told her to forget Hunter and keep her baby a secret, she'd finally complied—but what a price she'd paid.

She sighed. "Do you want to help me clean up?"

Cranking his head from side to side, he asked, "Is anything missing?"

"Anything of importance? No. I have my laptop with

me, my phones. Anything else?" She shrugged. "Don't care. They didn't come here to rob me, did they?"

He straightened up with the frame in his hand. "Do you have a trash bag for this glass?"

"I'll grab some." When she returned upstairs with two plastic garbage bags, Hunter had another photo of Drake in his hands.

"He looks like a happy boy."

"Amelia and Ben live on Shelter Island off the coast of South Carolina. Drake loves it there, loves his two cousins, loves the beach." Her voice hitched. Did she have to tell Hunter that sometimes Drake cried for his mommy in the middle of the night or that he'd started saying the word *daddy* with alarming frequency? Time enough for that.

"But he'd rather be home with his mother?"

"Here." She shoved a plastic bag at him. "You can dump that glass in here. I'll take care of my clothes."

As Sue yanked open her drawers and folded and replaced the clothing that had been tossed, Hunter walked around the room straightening the furniture and picking up books, pictures and knickknacks.

Once her bedroom had been put together again, they moved on to Drake's room. The intruders hadn't spared her son's belongings. Whatever they suspected her of hiding, they'd figured that among kids' toys might just be the perfect spot.

This room took longer to set right as Hunter spent much of his time examining Drake's toys and testing them out. Finally, she trailed downstairs and got to work on the living room.

As Hunter picked up pillows and tossed them back onto the couch, she organized her shelves. Had they been sending her a message by having a total disregard for her possessions? Breaking items? Scattering things across the floor?

She stooped to pick up a frame lying facedown on the floor. The picture had slipped out, but she knew what had been in here.

Sue dropped to her hands and knees and scoured the floor, checking beneath the coffee table.

Hunter tousled her hair as he walked by. "I'll start tackling the kitchen."

Sue passed her hand beneath the sofa and then sat back on her heels, her heart fluttering in her chest. "You know how I told you upstairs I didn't think anything of importance was missing?"

"Yeah." Hunter stopped at the entrance to the dining area, his hand braced against the wall.

"I was wrong."

"What's missing?"

"They took a picture of Drake."

Chapter 14

Hunter tripped to a stop as a shot of adrenaline spiked through his system. "You're sure? Did you check under the sofa?"

She held up an empty picture frame. "It was in here—a shot of him at the beach just a few months ago. It was my most recent picture of him."

When Hunter thought his legs could function properly, he pushed off the wall and joined Sue on the floor. Shoulder to shoulder, they searched the floor for the missing picture.

He even pulled all the cushions off the sofa to check behind them. "We don't know if they took it on purpose or it was stuck to something else they took out of here, or maybe it's still lost in the house somewhere."

Sue remained on the floor, legs curled beneath her.

"Why would they take a picture of Drake unless they wanted to know what he looked like?"

"They have no way of knowing where he is, right?" He stretched out a hand to Sue and helped her to her feet, pulling her into his arms.

He'd wanted to remain angry at her for keeping Drake from him and a core of that anger still burned in his gut, but she was the mother of his son. He had a son, and the joy of that reality blotted out every other negative feeling.

"You're going to call your parents ASAP and tell them to keep an extra eye on Drake. Your father, at least, will understand the significance of that, won't he?"

"I'll make him understand." She broke away from him and pounced on her purse, dragging her cell phone from an outside pocket.

"You make that call, and I'll work on the kitchen. Hell, I might even locate that picture. On the beach, right?"

She dipped her head, wide-eyed, and tapped her phone to place the call.

As Hunter banged pots and pans back into what he hoped were their right places, he strained to hear Sue from the next room, but all he got was worried murmurs. He hoped the old CIA man was up to the task.

When she joined him in the kitchen, her face had lost its sharp angles. "My dad's on it. I think it'll be fine. They live in a pretty small town, and it's not like Drake is even school-age and out of their sight."

"That sounds good." He swung open a cupboard door. "Is this right?"

They finished putting the house back together and

Sue watered her plants and collected the mail that was at least in a locked mailbox in the front—not that the intruders couldn't have broken into the mailbox. They'd done a bang-up job of breaking into Sue's house and wreaking havoc without raising any suspicion in the neighborhood.

When they were back in the car, Sue turned to him as she snapped her seat belt. "Should we head straight to the storage unit and skip lunch?"

"Are you kidding?" He patted his stomach. "That breakfast seems like a long time ago."

"It was. It's still not daylight saving time and this lunch is more like dinner and it might be dark by the time we get to the storage unit."

"People check on their stuff at all hours of the day and night. I checked their website, and they're open twenty-four hours, as long as you have the code for the gate—and we have it."

"She wrote down two sets of numbers. Do you think one set is for a lock?"

"I hope so, because we don't have a key, and I don't feel like breaking into a storage unit. The company probably has those units under CCTV surveillance, and we wouldn't last long trying to break into her unit."

"Then lunch—or dinner it is. Luckily, the place I had in mind for lunch serves dinner, too, and it's not too fussy, so we can get a quick bite and head out to the units."

They did just that, and as Hunter shoveled the last forkful of mashed potatoes into his mouth, Sue waved down the waiter for their check.

She pulled out her wallet before he could even wipe his hands on his napkin. "I'll get this one."

Hunter dragged the napkin across his face. "You seem like you're in a big hurry now when before you acted like we had all the time in the world."

"Yeah, that was before those lowlifes broke into my place and trashed it, stole a picture of Drake." She waved the check and her credit card at the waiter.

Sensing her urgency, the waiter returned with the receipt in record time and Sue stood up and scribbled her signature. "It's still somewhat light out."

Hunter dragged his jacket from the back of the chair. "Why are you so hell-bent on getting to this storage place before dark?"

"Storage units are creepy enough without having a pack of terrorists dogging your every move."

"There's no way they know where this place is. That paper was hidden in The Falcon's shoe, and they didn't find it when they searched her."

"I don't know. They seem to be everywhere we are."

As she headed for the door, Hunter gulped down the last of his water and followed her out to the car. He'd already put the storage unit address into his phone's GPS, and he turned it on when they got into the car.

"Just forty minutes away."

Sue cranked her head over her shoulder. "I hope nobody followed us from my place."

"Did you notice anyone? You had your eyes on your mirror the whole way over here."

"I didn't, but then I didn't notice anyone following us from the barbershop, did you?"

"Wasn't looking." He adjusted his own rearview mirror and watched a white car pull out behind them. He eased out a breath when the car turned off. "Now you have me jumpy."

"Good." She punched his arm. "You should be."

"You know, we've been going a mile a minute since I found out I had a son. You were supposed to fill me in at your place, but we were otherwise engaged there, and then we spent our meal talking about The Falcon's storage facility." He drew a cross over his heart. "I promise—no recriminations. I know I don't need to repeat how disappointed I am or...upset."

"That sounds like recriminations to me." She set her jaw and turned her head to stare out the window.

"I'm sorry." He rolled his shoulders. "Did I also tell you how happy I am to have a child? I can't wait to meet him, and I want to play a role in his life—including financial. I'll pay child support or whatever the courts order."

"I hope we don't have to go that route. We can figure this out together without lawyers or courts, can't we?"

"I'd like that. Now tell me about Drake. Does he have a middle name?" His head jerked toward her. "What's his last name?"

"I-it's Chandler. I had to do that, but we can change it to Mancini. I don't have a problem with that."

She slid him a sideways glance, probably to see if he planned to slam his fist into the dash again. He didn't. Drake Mancini.

"Middle name?"

"It's Hunter."

He swallowed the lump that had suddenly formed in his throat. "Thanks for that."

"It was the least I could do."

Then she launched into a history of Drake Hunter Mancini—his likes, his dislikes, his first everythings.

He raised one eyebrow at her. "Does he ask about a daddy?"

"He's practicing the word. Amelia's husband is his father figure—for now—but he calls him Uncle Ben, not Daddy." She twisted her fingers in her lap. "I always figured those questions would come once he started school and saw all the other dads. Now we can avoid that."

Too soon, he took the turnoff for the storage units, located in a light industrial area of Virginia. He'd already memorized the address and the two codes, and as they pulled up to the security gate, he leaned out the window and entered the first code The Falcon had written on that slip of paper.

The gate glided open, and Hunter turned to Sue to share a fist bump. "First hurdle."

Sue pressed her nose to the window glass. "This first row has units in the hundreds. Hers is in the five hundreds."

He rolled to the end of the first row. "Right or left?"

"There's a sign up ahead. Drive forward."

As the headlights illuminated the sign, they both said at the same time, "Left."

Hunter swung the car around the corner. "These are three hundreds and the numbers are getting bigger."

"They just jumped from three to five. This is our row."

Hunter slowed the car to a crawl as Sue called out the storage unit numbers until she recited The Falcon's.

He parked vertically in front of unit number 533, leaving on his headlights. "Just in case the unit doesn't have a light inside."

"Great. We're going to have to fumble around in there in the dark?"

"We'll see." Hunter scrambled from the car, the second code running through his head. He punched it in to the keypad, and the lock on the big silver sliding door clicked on the other side.

He grabbed the handle and yanked it to the side. The door opened with a squeal, and he rolled it wide.

Tipping his head back, he said, "Looks like there's no light source inside."

"Why are they open twenty-four hours if they don't provide lighting in the units?" Sue brushed past him to step inside the chilly space. "Or heating."

Hunter jerked his thumb over his shoulder. "I guess you have to provide your own. You have about twenty cell phones on you now, don't you? We can use all those flashlights."

She tapped the phone in her hand and a beam of light shot out from it. "I have just my own phone right now, but yours and mine should be able to do the trick, and once you move out of the way, those headlights should at least let us see what's in here."

He shoved the door to the end and shifted to the side to allow the lights from the car to flood the unit.

Sue lifted her nose to the air. "At least she didn't stash any dead bodies in here."

"That doesn't mean there aren't a few skeletons in her unit...or her closet." He kicked the bottom box of a stack. "I hope these aren't files."

"One way to find out." Sue attacked the box on the top, lifting the lid and knocking it to the floor. She sneezed. "Kind of dusty."

He sidled up next to her, aiming the light from his phone into the box. "What's in here?"

Sue reached inside and pulled out three passports. She fanned them under the light. "Two US, one Canadian."

Hunter plucked one from her fingers and thumbed it open. "It's not The Falcon. It's a man. Recognize him?"

Sue rubbed her finger across the picture. "Nope."

Hunter flipped open the other two passports. They featured the same man, his appearance slightly altered with glasses, facial hair, different colored contacts... and a different name.

Sue dug through the rest of the box's contents. "Same stuff. Passports, some birth certificates—everything you need to establish a fake identity for purposes of travel."

"These must be all the agents The Falcon used for her black ops missions."

Sue rapped on the second box. "This proves she *did* have black ops missions, anyway, doesn't it? Helps me out."

"Let's keep looking for something more recent." Hunter kicked another box and crouched down to paw through some gadgets. "This is regular spy stuff here—old cameras, listening devices."

"Why would she want me to see all this stuff?" Sue hoisted the box on top and settled it on the floor. She replaced its lid and dived into the second box. "More of the same."

"It proves she was running an operation, for sure, or several operations."

Sue gasped. "Oh my God."

Hunter spun around. "What is it?"

"My father." She held up a passport in each hand and waved them. "These are my father's. He must've worked with or for The Falcon himself."

"Is there any doubt now he got you into the unit?"

She fired the passports back into the box. "He had to know the price I had to pay. He was allowed to have a family and a home life before opting into that unit."

"You're done with that now, Sue. The Falcon is dead. The mission is over. You need to get your life back."

She waved her arm at the stacks. "And all this is gonna help me. I need my job...and my reputation back."

Hunter tripped over a metal filing cabinet. He flipped it open and rifled through the contents. "This is more like it. Paperwork on some of her missions. Forget the passports and spy gadgets. This is the stuff we need."

Sue stepped over a stuffed suitcase and crouched before another filing cabinet. "At least this one doesn't have two inches of dust coating it."

"Yeah, those are the ones we need to be looking at. I'm sure she directed you to this storage unit for a reason—and it wasn't to find your father's fake passports."

"Okay, minimal dust." Sue's muffled voice came from the back of the unit.

Still in a crouch, Hunter moved two steps to the side and ducked into another filing cabinet. The headlights beaming into the unit flickered.

He called out to Sue. "I hope my car battery's not dying."

"That's all you need. You already cracked the dash."

The lights flickered again and Hunter twisted his

head over his shoulder. A flash of light illuminated the space, blinding him.

An explosion rocked the unit and then the sliding door squealed closed—trapping them inside with the blaze.

Chapter 15

The explosion had thrown Sue backward, and she clutched a stack of folders to her chest as she fell to the floor.

As the acrid smoke burned her eyes and lungs, she screamed for Hunter. He'd been behind her, closer to the source of the blast...and now the fire that raged, blocking their exit from the storage unit.

"Sue, are you all right?"

At the sound of Hunter's voice, she choked out a sob. "I'm here. I'm okay."

The boxes provided fuel for the flames and they licked greedily at their sustenance as they danced closer to the back of the unit. Sue flattened her body on the cement floor, the files digging into her belly.

Hunter appeared, crawling through the gray smoke. "Thank God you're not hurt. You're not, are you?"

"No. You?"

"Fine." He even scooted forward and kissed the tip of her nose. "Don't worry. I have a plan."

"The fire's blocking the door, isn't it?" She rubbed her stinging eyes. "What kind of plan could you possibly have?"

"All those spy gadgets I was making fun of?" He reached behind him and dragged a box forward that looked as if it contained wet suits.

"We're trapped in a room with fire. We're not underwater." Her gaze shifted over his head and her nostrils flared. "It's bad, Hunter."

He pulled one of the wet suits from the box. "These aren't wet suits, Sue. They're fire-retardant suits. They'll allow us to literally walk through flames—if they're not too old and decrepit."

"Why'd you have to add that last part?" She snatched the suit from his hands and shimmied into it while she was on the ground.

"Pull up the hood and put on the gloves." A crash made her jump but Hunter didn't blink an eye. "Hurry! There's netting that drops over the face but cover your face with your gloved hands. Make sure your hair is all tucked in and hang on to me."

Suited up, they crawled across the floor for as long as they could. Then Hunter gave her the command to stand up in the fire.

Sue's mind went blank as she covered her face with one hand and kept the other pressed against Hunter's back. She had a moment of panic when they reached the door, but Hunter yanked it back.

As the air rushed into the storage unit, the flames

surged, but Hunter dragged her outside. He pulled her several feet away from the blazing unit and then left her.

Seconds later, she heard the car idling beside her. As she lurched to her knees, Hunter came around behind her and hoisted her to her feet, half dragging, half carrying her to the car.

With her door still hanging open, Hunter punched the accelerator and they sped from the facility. Once outside, he pulled over beneath a freeway on-ramp. "Call 911 from your burner phone."

She reached for the phone on the console, but her thick gloves wouldn't allow her to pick it up.

"I've got it." Hunter yanked off one of his gloves and made the call to 911 to report the fire.

Then he flipped back his hood. "Are you all right? Did you get through okay?"

Sue pounded her chest through her suit. "I think so, but my lungs hurt."

"Mine too. Let's take these things off and see if they worked."

"We're sitting here talking to each other." She reached out and smoothed a thumb over one of his eyebrows. "Outside of some singed hair, I'd say we made it."

Hunter got out of the car and tugged at the suit, kicking it off his legs. He ran his hands over his arms, legs and head. He poked his head into the car. "Do you like that thing so much you plan to wear it?"

Sue hugged herself. "I love it. It saved our lives."

Hunter walked around to the passenger's side and opened the door. "I'll help you."

As she slid out of the car, sirens wailed in the distance. "At least the fire engines are on the way, but the cops are going to wonder why we left the scene. Your rental car is going to be on camera, along with our activities."

"Along with the activities of the people who tossed that explosive device into the unit?" Hunter ripped at the Velcro closure around her neck. "Do you really think they would allow that?"

"What do you mean? You think they disabled the security system?"

"I'm sure of it. They're professionals. There's no way they would be seen on camera—even disguised."

As she stepped out of the suit, Sue ran a hand through her tangled hair, which seemed to have a few crispy ends. "How'd you get that door open? I thought they'd slid it closed, trapping us inside."

"That door won't close without the code. They could slide it shut and maybe they even thought they were locking us in, but you need the code to do that."

"Thank God." She clung to him for a second to steady herself. "I—I thought we were going to die, although really my mind was numb. Looking back, I realize we could've died."

"That's the important thing...but I felt that we were getting so close to finding what we wanted. I suppose if everything's not burned to a crisp, we could try to get back in there."

"We might be okay."

"Yeah, I suppose if you can get us into the hospital room of Jane Doe patients, you can get us into burned-out storage units."

"No, I mean I think we might be okay." Sue pulled up her shirt and gripped the edge of the file folders stuffed into her pants.

Hunter took a step back. "What the hell?"

"You thought we were getting close—we were." She waved the file folders at him. "Do you know how these are labeled?"

"I'd have to get my phone to see. Don't be a tease."

She held the folders in front of her face and kissed the top one. "Denver Assignment."

Hunter wrapped his arms around her and swung her through the air. "I could kiss you."

"Do it."

He set her down and grabbed her face with his hands. He puckered up and pressed a kiss against her mouth that nearly swept her off her feet again.

Back in the car, she shuffled through The Falcon's notes. "Let's not get too excited. We need to find out how they tracked us to that storage unit. We know they didn't follow us there."

"We also know they didn't have a clue about that place before we got there, or they would've already paid it a visit." He drummed his thumbs on the steering wheel. "They tracked us there."

"They know this car." Sue flipped down the visor and jerked back from her reflection in the mirror. "You could've told me I looked like a raccoon with black circles of ash under my eyes."

He reached across her and grabbed a tissue from the glove compartment. "When would they have had time to bug this car? At the hotel? I don't think they ever knew we were there."

"Maybe not until The Falcon showed up on our doorstep. Don't forget, they know where I live. They could've been bugging your car when you were parked at my place when we were in there cleaning up."

"If they were there when we were, they would've made a move." Hunter scratched the sexy stubble on his chin. "We never found a phone on The Falcon, did we?"

"Nope. We found very little except for that piece of paper in her shoe. Do you think the people who ambushed and beat her have her phone?"

"Makes sense. It also makes sense that The Falcon would have a tracker on every burner phone you picked up, so that she could keep tabs on you."

Sue snatched up the phone in the console, buzzed down the window and tossed it outside onto the highway. "Not anymore."

"It was just a suggestion."

"A damned good one." She patted the dashboard. "But this car is next. Too bad you didn't snag any bug finders in the unit, but I'll get my hands on one and we can sweep this car."

"I'll do one better." He swerved off the highway and pulled in to a gas station. He parked next to the air-and-water station. "Give me some light while I check."

She followed him out of the car and crouched beside him as he scanned the undercarriage. The beam of light from her cell phone followed his hands while he felt for a device.

He rose to his feet, brushing off his jeans. "Nothing."

"They can be pretty small these days. We'll do a more thorough check when we have a device."

"Or I can just swap the car out tomorrow and own up to the cracked dashboard."

"Either way." She pointed to the convenience store. "I need something to drink to soothe my throat. How about you?"

"A couple of gallons of water should do the trick." He coughed and spit into the dirt. "Hotel, right? Unless you want to go back home."

"I'm not going back home until we settle this issue. I feel safer in the hotel—I feel safer with you."

As they drove back to the hotel sipping on their drinks, Sue flipped through the folders on her lap. "It doesn't look like Denver was working with The Falcon, but she definitely knew what he was up to."

"I wonder why she didn't come forward in some way and clear him?"

"We're talking about The Falcon here." Sue gripped her knees. "This is the person who told me to walk away from you forever and then ordered me to send my son away. If it served her purposes to hang Denver out to dry, then she'd do it. The ends justified the means for her."

"I wonder if the hospital and the police identified her yet. Would her fingerprints come back to the Agency?"

"I don't know. If someone's that deep undercover, I can't imagine their ID is going to be easy to ascertain in a situation like this." Sue's fingers curled into her jeans. "It's kind of sad, really. She must have family somewhere—even if that family doesn't include a spouse and children."

"She was at least your father's age. Maybe she had the family first, and with her children grown, she went undercover."

Sue shrugged. "Obviously, I'm not the one to ask. I didn't even know The Falcon was female."

Hunter pulled in to the hotel and left the car with the valet. On the ride up the elevator, he asked, "Do you think our arsonists believe we're dead and gone?"

"I'm sure that was their intent. They must've realized when we went to that storage unit that we were after The Falcon's files—and we led them right to it."

"I'm wondering what they were going to use that explosive device for originally. They couldn't have known before they arrived about the storage unit."

"That's why I'm glad we're here." Sue stepped off the elevator. "It's a little more complicated for them to bomb a whole hotel than one townhouse in Georgetown."

As she flicked out her key card, Hunter cinched his fingers around her wrist. "Wait. It's not that difficult to wire one room in a hotel."

She stepped back while Hunter crouched down and inspected the space under the door. He ran his finger along the seam where the door met the floor and then put his eye to the doorjamb.

"If they think we're dead, they wouldn't be rigging our hotel room, would they?"

"Do they think we're dead?"

Hunter slipped his card into the door and Sue found herself holding her breath as the green lights flashed.

Again, Hunter blocked her entrance, stepping into the room before her. "Looks fine."

Sue followed him in and strode to the window and yanked the drapes closed. "They've upped their game. They're no longer interested in questioning me. They know I've been on the other side all this time, and now they want me dead."

"They also want any information you and The Falcon collected on them all these years. And thanks to your quick thinking—" he drilled a knuckle into the file folder she'd placed on the desk "—you have it and they don't."

Sue rubbed a spot of soot on her jeans. "I'm going to take a shower and wash the smoke and ash away, and then let's see if The Falcon's information can clear me and Denver at the same time."

"And stop whatever this group has planned because that's why both of you got involved in the first place." Hunter pulled out his wallet. "I need another soda. Do you want one?"

"Yes, please. Do you think hot tea would be better?" She stroked her neck and swallowed.

"I don't know about you, but I don't think I could take a hot drink right now."

"You're probably right. Diet for me." She grabbed her pajamas and went into the bathroom.

In the shower, she turned her back to the warm spray and let it pound her neck. She'd been on such a roller coaster these past few days, she couldn't wait for the ride to stop. And when it did, would Hunter be interested in being more than just Drake's father?

Today he'd talked about custody and child support as if they'd be living apart instead of together as a family, which was what she wanted. She'd already wasted too much time with her misplaced priorities, robbing Hunter and Drake both of a relationship with each other.

She loved Hunter. She'd felt ridiculous admitting that to herself years ago when she'd left him. But the years hadn't dissipated her feelings, and when she saw him again in that other hotel room, she knew they were for real.

He'd made it clear—up until the point when he

found out about Drake—that he still had strong feelings for her, had never forgotten their time together in Paris. But now?

He seemed to have settled down. The anger had left his blue eyes, but it might return when he met Drake and realized all that he'd missed.

And he'd take out that anger on her—rightly so. She'd been duped, manipulated, and with her puppet master dead, she may also be charged with treason.

The bathroom door cracked open and Hunter stuck his hand through the space, clutching a can of diet soda. "What are you doing in there?"

"Thinking." She shut off the water. "I'll be right out."

She dried off quickly and slipped into her pajamas. Hunter hadn't made a move to join her in the shower or even joke about it. Yeah, that resentment still simmered beneath the surface of his seeming acceptance of her deception.

She entered the other room, drying her hair with a towel. "You should've seen the drain in the shower— black. We're lucky to be alive."

"Amen." He snapped the tab on her soda can and handed it to her. "I was looking through the files and The Falcon's shorthand is kinda cryptic. I hope you can make more sense out of it than I can. She liked codes, didn't she?"

"Always felt memorized codes were the safest way to communicate." She sat on the bed cross-legged, fluffing a couple of pillows behind her. She patted the space beside her. "Bring those over here and let's have a look. Can you bring our laptops, also? I want to compare any notes I have with hers, and maybe we can fill in more of your chart."

He plucked his T-shirt away from his body. "It's only fair that I shower, too, now that you're all fresh and clean."

"How considerate of you." She crooked her finger. "Can you drop off the files and my laptop on your way to the bathroom?"

He complied and shut the door behind him.

Sue stared at the closed door—another sign that he wanted to keep his distance.

She took another sip of soda, allowing it to pool in the back of her throat, before opening the top file marked Denver Assignment.

As she ran her finger down The Falcon's notes, someone pounded on the hotel door. Her finger froze midpage.

This had better not be another member of the housekeeping staff with laundry.

The pounding resumed before she could even roll off the bed. On her way to the door, her gaze darted to the bathroom, her step faltering.

A split second later, Hunter burst through the door, tucking a towel around his waist. "Don't answer it, especially without your weapon."

He made a detour to the credenza and swept up his gun. He approached the door from the side, his weapon at the ready. Bracing his hand against the door, he leaned in to peer through the peephole. His shoulders dropped. "It's Ryan."

"Who?" Sue stood behind Hunter's broad back, her arms folded, hands bunching the sides of her pajama top.

"Ryan Mesner, my CIA contact."

With his gun still raised, Hunter eased open the door. "You're alone?"

"Not for long. Let me in, Hunter. This is important."

Hunter swung open the door and a tall man with cropped dark hair and a full beard pushed past him.

He leveled a finger at Sue. "Are you Sue Chandler?"

"Yes."

"You'd better get the hell out of here. CIA internal investigations is on its way—and they're prepared to charge you with treason."

Chapter 16

Sue's legs wouldn't move. Her brain wouldn't work. The only thing racing through her mind was that if she were arrested, she'd lose Drake. She couldn't lose Drake.

"They're on their way now?" Hunter dragged some clothes from his suitcase and stepped into a pair of jeans underneath his towel, dropping it to the floor.

"They were just at her place in Georgetown, and now they're triangulating her cell phone."

Sue lunged across the bed and ripped her phone from its charger. She turned it off and stuffed it into her purse.

Hunter pulled a shirt over his head and stuffed his feet into his shoes. "Do they know she's with me?"

"As far as I know they do not, but they've been questioning Ned Tucker. Does he know about you?"

"Ned won't tell them anything. If they went to my place first, Ned didn't tell them I was at this hotel. He's not going to tell them about Hunter."

As she and Hunter shoveled their clothes and toiletries into their bags, she turned to Ryan. "Why are you doing this for me? I don't even know you."

"I've had to watch Major Rex Denver, the most honorable man I know, get dragged through the mud and set up. I'm not going to stand by and watch it happen again to someone who might be able to clear his name."

"And we're not going to allow you to take the fall for this, Ryan. Get the hell out of here now." Hunter clasped Ryan on the shoulder and gave him a shove toward the door.

As Ryan grasped the door handle, Sue grabbed his arm. "Is there any way they can track you here or find out you warned me?"

"I don't have my phone on me, I took a taxi over here and paid cash, and I made sure my face was hidden as I went through the hotel—just in case they decide to check the footage."

"You're a good agent, Ryan. Thanks—you won't regret this. I'm no traitor."

"Neither is Major Denver." He flipped up his hoodie and slid out the door.

"The files." Hunter tipped his head toward the bed. "For God's sake, don't forget those files."

Sue gathered them up and shoved them into the outside pocket of her suitcase. She waited at the door with their bags, as Hunter cleared out the safe and gave the room a once-over. "If they decide to run prints on this room, they're going to ID me."

"Maybe you should stay here and wait for them. I

can knock you on the head, and you can pretend you know nothing about any of this." Her voice hitched in her throat. "Drake's going to need one parent who's not in federal prison."

"Nobody's going to prison, and I'm not gonna allow you to bash me over the head." He joined her at the door and held it open. "Now let's get the hell out of Dodge."

They avoided the lobby on their way down to the car and Hunter waved off the valet to load their bags in the trunk himself.

As he pulled away from the hotel, he said, "I'm returning this car now. I don't want anything to be traced back to me, but we can't use your car, either."

"Thanks to The Falcon, we have some options. I've never had to use it before, but there's a safe house near Virginia Beach. I think we'll find everything we need there for a quick getaway."

"How far is Virginia Beach?"

"About four hours."

"We can't drive for four hours in this car. The rental car company most likely has a GPS on this vehicle, and once the CIA shows up, they'll track the car for them."

"I have a plan for that, too." She held up one of her many burner phones. "I'm going to call a friend of mine to pick us up at the airport after you leave the car there. She'll let us have her car and she can take a taxi home."

"Is this Dani from the bar?"

"Dani's on a road trip. This is another friend who owes me and I'm about to collect, big time."

While Hunter drove to the airport, keeping one eye on his rearview mirror, Sue placed a call to her friend.

Jacqueline answered after three rings, her voice sleepy and befuddled. "Hello?"

"Jacqueline, it's Sue. I need your help."

Her words worked like a slap to the face. Jacqueline's voice came back sharp and urgent. "Anything."

"Meet me at Reagan as soon as you can. I'll be at parking lot D, the main entrance. Bring your junker. I'm going to take that car and you'll take a taxi home. I'll pay you for everything—the car, the ride home, your time."

"I'll do it and you don't owe me a dime. You know that, Sue. I'm leaving now."

"And if anyone comes by later and asks you about me…"

"I never got this call."

Sue closed the phone and tossed it out the window. "Like you said—Jeffrey and his gang probably have The Falcon's phone and she may have put trackers in all my burner phones."

"What did you do for this woman that she's willing to leave her home in the middle of the night, drive to the airport and give you her car?"

Sue lifted her shoulders. "I saved her life."

She directed Hunter to the parking lot where he plucked a ticket from the machine. He parked on an upper level, and they emptied the car.

Hunter pulled a T-shirt from his bag and wiped down the inside of the car for good measure. "They don't have to know you were in this car."

Sue grabbed his wrist as he stuffed the shirt back into his suitcase. "You don't have to do this, Hunter. I can take it from here."

"I'm not leaving you to finish this on your own." He kicked the side of her suitcase. "Besides, you finally have what I came here seeking—information about Denver, and I'm not giving up on that, either."

She pressed her lips against the side of his arm. "I knew you were someone I could count on the minute I met you. I'm just sorry you couldn't count on me."

"I'm counting on you now. I'm counting on you to get us out of this mess and to that safe house."

They dragged their bags and the rest of their gear to the elevator and got off on the ground level. They stationed themselves near the parking arm, turning away each time a car rolled through.

Thirty minutes later, a small compact flashed its lights and pulled to a stop in front of them.

"That's her?" Hunter squinted into the back window.

"That's Jacqueline."

Jacqueline hopped out of the car and ran to Sue. She threw her arms around her, and Sue hugged her back with all her might.

"Thank you so much, Jacqueline."

She flicked her long fingernails in the air. "What else would I do when you call?"

"Jacqueline, this is my friend—no names, just in case."

Jacqueline extended her hand. "Bonjour, no name."

Hunter sketched a bow and kissed her long fingers, befitting the Frenchwoman. "Bonjour. What exactly did Sue do to warrant this loyalty?"

"This?" Jacqueline flicked back her dark hair. "This is nothing compared to what she did for me. She saved my life."

"Okay, I won't ask." He held up his hands. "Could you please open the trunk…if it opens?"

"The remote doesn't open it anymore, but there's

always the old-fashioned way." Jacqueline shoved the key into the trunk and lifted it.

As Hunter loaded their bags, Sue took Jacqueline's hands. "Everything still okay with you?"

"Perfect." Jacqueline lifted her delicate brows. "I won't ask the same, but it looks like you have a big, strong man on your side now."

"I do. I'll call you when this is all over."

"Is it ever over for you, Sue?" Jacqueline shook her head. "You give too much."

"This time you gave to me and saved *my* life." She kissed Jacqueline's cheek. "Now call up a car so you're not waiting out here alone. We can't wait with you."

"I'll be fine. I've faced worse than a dark corner at night, and you know it."

They hugged again and Hunter waved. He got behind the wheel of the little car that could, and Sue slipped into the passenger's seat.

Sue directed Hunter back to the highway, heading south, and they drove in silence for a few minutes before he turned to her. "Are you going to tell me how you saved her life, or is that top secret, too?"

"Jacqueline was seeing a dangerous, violent man. The more she tried to get away from him, the more ferociously he went after her, and protective orders did nothing to stop him because he had diplomatic immunity here. But I finally stopped him."

"How?"

"I knew he'd been supplying information about some of his country's dealings to sources who were then using that intel against his country to strike favorable deals." She shoved her hands beneath her thighs. "I told his country."

"What happened to him?"

"I don't know. He disappeared and Jacqueline never heard from him or saw him again."

Hunter whistled. "Do you think he was killed? Was it one of *those* countries?"

She glanced at him out of the corner of her eye. "*Any* country can be one of those kinds of countries."

"I suppose you're right. The US has had our share of spies working against us, but it looks like we're dealing with corruption at the highest levels here. I guess anything is possible." He held out his phone to her. "Are you going to put the address in my GPS or am I going to drive blindly into the night in a car that's on its last legs...wheels?"

"There is no address, or at least not that I'm aware of, but I have the directions up here." She tapped her forehead.

"Then take me home, but when we stop for gas, I'm going to need some coffee and some food. We haven't had anything to eat since that late lunch, and we've been through an explosion and a whirlwind escape from the hotel."

"Let me know if you want me to drive." Sue curled one leg beneath her. "I hope The Falcon's files have enough to prove my innocence. Someone at the Agency *has* to know what she was doing. With all the money and support we had, she couldn't have been running a rogue operation."

"And her black ops contact at the CIA can't be our insider, or he never would've allowed her to compile the information she got."

Sue shivered. "That's a scary thought—the one person who can verify The Falcon's existence is the one working with this terrorist group."

"I have a feeling the insider is terrified of black ops groups like The Falcon's. Those groups are the very ones that could uncover a leak or a spy within."

"There's just one problem."

"What?"

"Why hasn't this person stepped forward yet?"

"The Falcon just died this afternoon. Her contact may not even know that yet." Hunter squeezed her knee. "It'll be okay, Sue. I'm not gonna let this end any other way—I've got a son to meet."

They drove through the night, stopping for gas, coffee and snacks. As they began to head east, toward the coast, Sue studied the road signs and the landmarks.

She'd never been to this safe house before, but The Falcon had drilled its location along with countless other details into Sue's head for so long, she felt as if she'd been this way before.

"Here, here, here." She hit the window with the heel of her hand. "Turn right here."

"Are you sure?" Hunter turned the wheel, anyway. "It looks dark and deserted. I hope you're not directing me right into the water."

"The isolation is the point...and the water is farther out with a few more houses scattered out there." She hunched forward in her seat, gripping the edge of the dashboard. "Turn left at the big tree. It should be a gravel road—not quite unpaved."

The little car bounced and weaved as they hit the gravel, but the headlights picked out a clapboard house ahead with a wooden porch.

"That's it. I think you can park around the back."

The car crawled around the side of the house and Hunter cut the engine. "Let's leave the stuff in the car so we can check it out first. I suppose you know where to find the key."

"Exactly." She took his cell phone because she was running out of ones of her own and she hadn't had a chance to charge the temp phone she'd picked up at the gas station. She turned on the flashlight and stepped from the car.

Several feet from the house, she spotted the rock garden and she lit up the ground below her to avoid tripping over the uneven surface. She counted three rocks from the left and crouched before it, digging her fingers in the dirt to tip it over.

Bugs scurried at the invasion while she sifted the dirt with her fingers. "Got it."

She pulled the key free from its hiding place and wiped it clean on the thigh of her jeans.

She returned to Hunter waiting by the car, his gun drawn. She pointed to the weapon dangling by his side. "Expecting company?"

"You never know."

She held up the key in the light. "I think this works on the back door, too."

Hunter dogged her steps as she walked to the back of the small house and unlocked the back door.

She pushed open the door, clenching her jaw. Something had to go right. This had to work. Creeping to the front of the house with Hunter right behind her, she held the phone in front of her. She sniffed, the musty odor making her nose twitch.

Hunter voiced her thoughts. "Hasn't been used for a while, has it?"

"Doesn't smell like it, but then I think this particular place was sitting in reserve for me and I never needed it...until now." She twisted on the switch for a lamp centered on an end table and a yellow glow illuminated the comfortable furniture.

"Looks more like my nana's place than a spy hideaway." Hunter picked up a throw pillow, punched it once and dropped it back onto the sofa.

"That's the point." Sue wandered into the kitchen and flicked on the light. "It's supposed to be stocked—with all kinds of things."

Hunter crowded into the kitchen next to her and tugged open the fridge. "Not much in here. Bottled water, which I could actually use right now."

Sue reached past him to open the cupboard door. She shuffled through some cans of food and freeze-dried pouches. "This is more like it. Stuff for the long haul. I don't know how often these safe house supplies are replenished."

Hunter leaned over her shoulder and picked up one of the packets and threw it back into the cupboard. "Ugh, looks like an MRE. I'll pass on these for the local pizza joint."

Sue returned to the living room and turned in a circle, her hand on her hip. She'd seen this room and knew just where to look.

"Do you have a knife on you?"

Hunter reached for his belt and produced a switchblade. "What do you need?"

Sue knelt in front of the fireplace and lifted the braided rug. She placed her hand on the wood slats and rocked back and forth. When she felt some give, she pounded the board with her fist. "Here. Try here."

Hunter crouched beside her and jimmied the blade of his knife between the two slats. When he got a lip on one, he pulled it up to reveal a cavity in the floor.

He scooted onto his belly and put his face to the space. "There's a canvas bag in there, along with a few spiders. We'll need a bigger space to bring it up."

Sue curled her hand around the next slat and yanked it free. They had to dislodge one more before they were able to lift the bag from the space beneath the floor.

Hunter swung it out and plopped it onto the floor.

Sue eyed it, wrinkling her nose. "Are those spiders gone?"

"Badass spy like you worried about a few spiders?"

"Yes."

Hunter kicked the bag a few times. "That should do it. Are you sure it's not booby-trapped?"

"Why would there be a booby-trapped bag in a *safe* house?"

"I have no idea how you people operate, but just in case, I'll let you open it first."

"What a man." She pinched his side.

Leaning over, she unzipped the bag and peeled back the canvas. She clicked her tongue as she ran her hands through the stacks of cash. "Nice. Having all this means never having to use your credit card."

She dug in deeper and pulled out a gun. "Untraceable I'm sure."

Hunter dived in next to her and withdrew handfuls of minicameras, GPS trackers, a small flashlight. "This is a mini stash of the same stuff she had in the storage unit."

"Minus the fire suits." Sue rubbed her arms and

looked around the room. "I hope we don't need those here."

Hunter scooted back, sitting on the floor and leaning his back against the sofa. "We can stay here for a few days and catch our breath. Really look over The Falcon's files on Denver and this whole assignment and get your name cleared once and for all. Get you back to Drake where you belong."

"Which reminds me." Sue held up one finger. "I need to get that phone charged so I can call my parents tomorrow morning, just to make sure everything's okay. I suppose I'm going to have to tell my father that I'm under investigation. I'm sure the CIA investigators are going to pay them a visit."

"Maybe not. They might be afraid of tipping off your parents and having them shield you and hide you."

"Funny thing is? They probably wouldn't."

"It's late, Sue. I'm going to bring in our bags and then you're going to get some sleep."

"You, too."

"Yeah, of course."

She narrowed her eyes. "Right. You have no intention of sleeping, do you? You're going to be on guard all night long."

"I'll catch some shut-eye. Don't worry about me." He stood up and made for the back door.

Sue zipped up the bag and dragged it next to the fireplace. The day's events caught up to her and she sank onto the sofa. She didn't even blink when Hunter came through the back door, hauling their suitcases.

The sofa dipped as he sat beside her, pulling her against his chest. "Do you think the beds are made up?"

She murmured against his shirt, "I don't care at this point. I'm going to fall asleep right here."

He kissed her temple. "Stay right here."

Sue must've drifted off. It seemed like hours later when Hunter returned and took off her shoes, lifted her legs to the sofa and spread a blanket over her body.

He sat back down in the corner and shifted over so that her head nestled on his lap, as he stroked her temple.

A smile curved her lips. Whatever happened now, she could endure it as long as Hunter stayed right by her side.

Chapter 17

Her lashes fluttered, and she reached for Hunter. When her hand met the sofa cushion instead of the warm flesh she'd expected, she bolted upright.

"I'm in here." Hunter waved from the kitchen across the room. "I'm making oatmeal if you're interested, but we have to skip the bananas, blueberries, almonds, brown sugar and everything else that makes it remotely tasty."

"Breakfast?" Sue rubbed her eyes, running her tongue along her teeth, which she'd been too tired to brush last night. "I didn't even realize it was morning."

"You slept soundly."

"Did you sleep at all?" She gathered her hair into a ponytail.

"A little." He held up the burner phone she'd bought

yesterday. "It's fully charged, and better yet, it's not being tracked by The Falcon."

She yawned and shrugged off the blanket. "I wonder who pays the utility bills for this place to keep the gas, water and electricity running."

"Probably comes from some supersecret spy slush fund."

She joined him in the kitchen and watched him stir hot water into some instant oatmeal. "Not bad. I'll have some of this coffee first, though."

She leaned her elbows on the counter and plucked the phone from the charger. She entered her father's cell phone number, although at this point it might be worse talking to him than Linda.

"Hi, Dad."

Hunter held a finger to his lips. He didn't want her to give Dad the lowdown on her situation in case the CIA hadn't contacted them yet.

"Hi, Sue." Her father didn't even ask her about the new phone number. He knew. "Drake's just fine, although he misses his...cousins."

Sue's shoulders sagged. For a minute, she thought Drake had been missing her. "I hope you're keeping him busy. He likes blocks and he loves riding his tricycle."

"He sure is an active boy." Dad cleared his throat. "We had a surprise this morning."

"Oh?" Sue's heart picked up speed.

"A friend of yours named Dani Howard called and asked if she could stop by for a visit. Says her daughter plays with Drake there in DC?"

Sue patted her chest and sucked in a breath. "That's

right. She told me she was driving down to Savannah to visit her folks and said she'd stop in to see Drake."

"Okay, just checking. She's going to call back, and I'll tell her it's fine."

"Thanks, Dad." She threw a quick glance at Hunter, pouring a cup of coffee. "Sh-should you put Drake on the line? I'll say a quick hi."

"He's outside on that trike already, Sue. Maybe later. This a new number for you?"

"For the time being. Don't program it in your phone or label it."

"I know better."

Sue's mind flashed back to her father's fake passports in The Falcon's storage unit. *I bet you do.*

"Okay, then. Just keep me posted. Everything else… all right?"

"Everything's just fine. We'll have Drake back at Amelia's just as soon as they return from the Bahamas."

"Maybe he'll be returning to me instead."

Hunter's hand pouring the condensed milk jerked and he splashed milk on the counter.

Her father paused for several seconds. "Why would you say that? Mission over? Won't there be another?"

"We'll talk about it later. Just keep my little boy safe." She ended the call and tucked the phone into her purse.

"Drake's okay?" Hunter shoved a cup of coffee at her.

"He's fine. Apparently, he's always just fine without me." She blew on the coffee before sipping it.

"You meant what you said to your father? That Drake will be going back home with you?"

"The Falcon's dead. These assignments, this lifestyle I have is too dangerous for a parent. As soon as I'm clear, I'm done."

He scooped up a spoonful of oatmeal and studied it. "I'm not arrogant enough to tell you what to do, but I think it's a good idea—if you can manage it."

"I have to get out of this mess first, or Drake will be visiting me behind bars—both of us."

After two more tastes, Hunter gave up on the lumpy oatmeal and dropped the bowl into the sink. "Who's driving down to Savannah and stopping in to see Drake?"

"My friend Dani Howard. She has a daughter around Drake's age."

"Is she the one you went out with the night you ran into Jeffrey?"

"Same. Thank God he left her alone. Jeffrey's cohort must've had orders not to hurt her."

"Does Dani know what you do for a living?" Hunter rinsed out the bowl and held out his hand for hers.

"I'm willing to give it a try." She yanked the bowl back and held it to her chest. "Dani? Yeah, she knows I'm with the Agency but not much more, of course."

"And what does she do?"

"She's a nurse." Sue wrapped her hands around her bowl and walked to her suitcase. She unzipped the outside pocket and pulled out the file folders she'd rescued from fire and mayhem.

"I think it's time for me to have a good long look at these and try to decipher The Falcon's notes. They're my only chance right now."

She brought the files to the kitchen table, and as she dropped them, the contents spilled out of one of them.

She pinched a newspaper clipping between two fingers and she waved it in the air. "From a French newspaper, but it looks old. Probably nothing to do with Denver."

"You read French, don't you?"

"Oui, oui." She pulled up a chair and scooted under the table. She brought the article close to her face, translating out loud a story about a bombing in a Paris café that took the lives of four people, one a child.

When she finished reading, Sue pressed the article to her heart. "How awful. This sounds familiar."

"It's all too familiar." He leaned over her shoulder and plucked up another article. "Looks like it could be the same story."

She took it from his fingers and scanned it. "Yes, the same story, different newspaper or maybe a follow-up."

Straddling the chair next to her, Hunter asked, "Why was she keeping this story in particular? She must've worked a lot of these types of cases."

"Maybe she has more articles on more cases, but I didn't happen to pick those up."

"But these were filed in the same cabinet as the Denver material." Hunter rubbed his chin and shuffled through the folder. He slid another article toward him with his forefinger. "This one has an accompanying picture."

He squinted at the two women and one man, grimfaced, looking away from the camera. "What's this one say, Sue?"

Her gaze flicked over the words. "They're the victims, or the victims' family members."

"Sue," Hunter bumped her shoulder with his as he

ducked over the article. "Doesn't that look like a young Falcon? And I don't mean the bird."

"What? No." She smoothed her thumb across the pinched face of a woman, her sharp chin dipping to her chest. "This one?"

"Exactly." He circled her face with his fingertip. "You said The Falcon didn't have a family. How'd you know that?"

"When she was telling me how I needed to leave you and then give up Drake, she implied that this job and a family didn't mix. I just assumed she was speaking from experience."

He tapped the picture. "Maybe she *was* speaking from experience. Maybe she lost her daughter in that explosion."

"And her husband." Sue pressed a hand against her roiling belly. "The child killed in the blast had the same last name as one of the men who died."

Hunter blew out a breath that stirred the edges of the clippings. "It makes sense, doesn't it? If she lost her own family to a terrorist attack, maybe one that was directed at her and her loved ones, she'd want to warn you away from that possibility."

"I feel sick to my stomach."

"I wonder why she put this personal stuff with the Denver notes."

"Maybe it's more than personal. Do you think The Falcon has been tracking this group for—" she glanced at the date on the newspaper "—twenty years?"

Hunter pointed at the articles. "Did they ever find out who was responsible? Or more likely, did anyone take credit for the attack?"

Sue flipped through the rest of the articles. "Nidal

al Hamed's group claimed responsibility. That group is the precursor to Al Tariq, but more importantly al Hamed's son broke away from Al Tariq a few years ago to form his own organization—an international organization that finds common bonds with terrorists across the globe, no matter what their agenda."

"The Falcon's entire investigation could be a personal vendetta."

"You can frame it that way, but this group has hurt more than just The Falcon's family."

"Nidal's dead, right? What's his son's name?"

Sue cranked her head to the side, her eyes as big as saucers. "Walid. Walid al Hamed."

"From the barbershop." Hunter slapped his hand on the table.

"It's not an uncommon name. Don't jump to conclusions."

"Could the leader of this new group be hiding out in plain sight in the middle of DC, mere miles from CIA headquarters?" Hunter swung his leg over the chair and paced to the window, the drapes firmly pulled across them.

"And this could be the same group Denver is tracking. The two investigations must converge somewhere in here." She fanned out the pages of the Denver folder on the table.

"You worked with The Falcon, knew her fondness for codes. Get on it, girl." Hunter strode toward his laptop on the coffee table. "I'm going to research something else that's been bugging me."

"What?"

"How long have you known Dani Howard?" Hunter sat on the sofa and flipped open his laptop.

The pen Sue had poised over a blank piece of paper fell from her fingers. "What? Why? I've known Dani for almost two years."

"Where did you meet her?"

Sue forgot about the articles and her research and turned around, fully facing Hunter. "At the pediatrician. We both had our kids in at the same time. Drake had an ear infection. Why are you asking these questions about Dani? You were probing me about her before when I got off the phone."

"I just thought it was unusual for her to take a detour from her trip to Savannah to see your parents. I mean, if you were there, I could see it."

"Sh-she just thought a familiar face from home would be nice for Drake."

"Why? He's at his grandparents', and excuse me for saying this, but isn't he more at home in South Carolina than he is here?" He held up a hand. "I don't mean to poke at you or criticize."

"Yeah, but I didn't think her offer was weird. Do you?" She scooted to the edge of her chair, her heart beating double time. "How long have you been thinking about this?"

"It niggled at me after your conversation with your father." He tapped his keyboard, and without looking up, he asked, "Whose idea was it to go out that night and who picked the bar?"

"Dani, but she was always the one issuing the invitations and she goes out more than I do, so it's only natural for her to pick the spot."

"And who noticed the two men that night?"

Sue sprang from her chair, gripping her arms, her

fingers digging into her flesh. "Stop it. You're scaring me."

"Who noticed the two men, Sue?"

"Dani." She locked her knees so they'd stop wobbling. "Of course she did. That was her thing."

"Was it also her thing to leave with men when you two were out together, or was that an unusual move for her that night?"

"It was atypical, but that was a different kind of night. We were drugged. I don't think she realized what she was doing." Sue pressed a hand against her forehead. "This is crazy. She has a young daughter. I've been in her home. She has pictures of…of…"

Hunter glanced up sharply from his laptop. "Of what?"

"Of her daughter."

He hunched forward on his elbows. "And what else?"

"I don't know." She sat next to him on the sofa. "Maybe it's what she didn't have, or maybe you're just making me crazy for no reason at all."

"What didn't she have?"

"She had pictures of Fiona but nobody else—no family photos. I know she didn't get along with her mother." She flicked her finger at the computer screen. "What have you been looking up?"

"Did a general search of Dani Howard, and I didn't find much. What hospital does she work at?"

"She doesn't work at a hospital. She works for a medical group."

"Do you know the name of it? I'll look it up." He gestured to her phone on the kitchen counter. "Call it."

"It's Mercer Medical. I've picked her up there before." She jogged across the room to grab her phone.

"Out front or did you go inside?" His fingers moved quickly across his keyboard.

Sue licked her dry lips. "Outside only, but she had a lab coat on."

"You mean like the one you stole in the hospital yesterday? Call." He swung his computer around to face her. "The website doesn't list any personnel."

"I know Dani. You don't. I think you're on the wrong track here." She entered the number on the website with trembling fingers.

Hunter said, "Speaker."

She tapped the speaker button just as someone picked up the phone. "Mercer Medical, how may I direct your call?"

"I'm trying to reach a nurse there, Dani Howard."

The pause on the other end seemed to last a lifetime. "What doctor does she work for? He?"

"Dani is a she. Dr. Warner."

"She doesn't work for Dr. Warner. Is she new?"

Sue squeezed the phone in her hand. "C-could you check. Maybe it's not Dr. Warner. Could she be in another office?"

"I'll check, ma'am, but this is the only Mercer office in the DC area."

Sue heard some clicking on the other end, which sounded like pickaxes against rock. Her gaze met Hunter's, but if she expected reassurance, what she saw was grim confirmation instead.

The receptionist came back on the line. "I'm sorry, ma'am. There's no Dani Howard here. Perhaps you…"

Sue didn't hear what she should perhaps do because

she ended the call and dropped to the edge of the coffee table. "Oh my God. What have I done?"

"You've done nothing." Hunter placed a steadying hand on her bouncing knee. "Call your father right now and warn him against Dani. He'll know what to do."

Sue went back to her phone and called her father for the second time that morning, this time putting the call on speaker for Hunter.

"Hello?" Leave it to Dad to know not to assume it was her calling just because it was the same number from this morning.

"Dad, it's Sue again."

"Don't worry. Drake is fine."

She flattened a hand against her fluttering belly. "I need to tell you something very important. That woman who's supposed to come by..."

"Yeah, Dani. Nice girl."

The blood in Sue's veins turned to ice. "She's there? Dad..."

"No, they're not here. Dani and her little girl Fiona took Drake to the park down the street."

Chapter 18

A sharp pain pierced the back of his head, but Hunter didn't have time to succumb to it. Sue had dropped the phone and let out a wail.

Her father was shouting into the phone. "Sue? Sue? What's wrong?"

Hunter scooped up the phone. "Mr. Chandler, I'm with Sue right now. Dani Howard isn't who she says she is. When did they leave? Can you catch up to them?"

Sue's father swore. "We didn't know. How were we supposed to know? They left over thirty minutes ago."

"Did you see her car?"

"Of course I did. Who the hell are you, anyway?"

"I'm Sue's...friend. I'm trying to help her, and she needs help. The Falcon is dead and Sue's been implicated. She has no one to vouch for her and now they've taken Drake."

"The hell they have. I'll get him back. You tell my little girl. Tell her I'll get him back. I'm going out right now. Our town isn't that big. Someone must've seen them."

"While you do, stay on the phone with me and tell me everything you remember about Dani and her car."

As Mr. Chandler gave him the details of Dani's visit, Hunter squeezed Sue's shoulder. She hadn't moved since getting the news from her father, except to drop her head in her hands.

Sue's stepmother interrupted her husband.

"What are you saying, Linda? Phone number?"

"What is it, sir?"

"My wife said that snake, Dani, left her a new phone number for Sue. Said she'd lost her phone on the road and picked up a temporary one. She wanted Sue to have the number." Chandler snorted. "I'll bet she did."

"Give me the number. It's probably the contact phone for Sue's instructions."

Sue's father recited the number to him. "What do they want with Sue, anyway?"

"I think they just want Sue."

Sue moaned. "They can have me as long as they let Drake go."

Sue's father yelled into the phone. "Don't be ridiculous, Sue. Do you know what they'll do to you? Someone who betrayed them? Someone who has information about them?"

"I'd rather have them do it to me than Drake."

Hunter knelt beside her and brushed the hair from her hot face. "We'll get him back. Don't worry. Your father gave me some good information."

Mr. Chandler said, "I'm already in my car. I'm going to find her. I'll keep you posted."

Hunter ended the call and ran his hand over Sue's back. "We're going to rescue him, but we'll play along. Call Dani now. She won't be expecting you to call her for a while—not until your parents notify you that she never brought Drake home."

Sue straightened her spine and pulled back her shoulders. "Catch her off guard."

"Exactly."

Sue snatched the phone from his fingers and tapped in the number as he recited it to her from memory. He didn't have to tell her to put it on speaker.

This was his son—a son he'd never even met. He'd go to hell and back to bring him home.

"Yes?"

A woman answered the phone. There was children's laughter in the background, and Hunter ground his teeth. What kind of a mother could kidnap a child from another mother?

Sue's nostrils flared and her cheeks flushed. "Where's my son, you bitch?"

Dani drew in a sharp breath, audible over the line. "That was fast."

"You've had him for half an hour. You can't be far. My father's out looking for you."

"How did he find out?" Dani laughed. "I guess he's a better CIA operative than you are. You didn't have a clue for almost two years."

"Why would I think another *mother* would be plotting against me?"

Dani clicked her tongue. "Oh, Sue. You don't have to play the outraged mother with me. You're never with

Drake anyway, but I hope you care enough to turn yourself over to us to keep him safe."

"Keep your commentary to yourself and tell me what I need to do."

"I'll call you back with instructions. I really didn't expect you to call so quickly—and make sure your parents know that if we detect any police involvement, you'll never see Drake again."

Sue covered her mouth with her hand but didn't let the fear seep into her voice. "Why did you move in on me two years ago? Did Walid al Hamed's group suspect me then?"

The silence on the other end of the line proved that they'd been right about Walid's group being behind the plot.

Dani cleared her throat and recovered. "Nobody knew for sure, but you really should've been spending all that money we'd funneled to you. Once we realized someone was checking out that barbershop, we knew we had you…and your boss, too."

"You killed her."

"We left her for dead. She must've been a tough old bird. We never imagined she'd pull herself together and go see you. And we never imagined you'd get out of that storage unit alive."

"I guess you underestimated both of us."

"Who's your sidekick? Who's helping you?"

Sue reached out and squeezed Hunter's hand. "I work alone. You should know that by now."

"It doesn't matter who he is. You'll be on your own for sure now. Any interference and Drake is gone."

"What does that mean, *gone*?" Sue's body seemed to vibrate.

"You don't want to find out. I'll be in touch."

Dani cut off the call, and Sue's shoulders rounded. "They're going to interrogate me—torture me to find out what I know about the organization, and then they're going to kill me."

Hunter laced his fingers with hers. "Do you think I'm going to allow that to happen? We'll find a way to get Drake back and keep you safe."

"We have to be able to use The Falcon's files to lure them into a change of plans. They don't know what we have, if anything, from that storage unit."

He pushed off the sofa and pulled her along with him. "Then let's get back to those files and see if we can trade anything for Drake."

Sue shuffled the papers from The Falcon's personal folder and closed it, setting it aside. "That's The Falcon's motivation for bringing down this group and now I have my own personal reasons."

"Then let's do it." He slid her notebook and pen in front of him. "What do those notes say about the group Denver is investigating?"

"Looks like The Falcon picked up on Denver's activities a while ago. There was a bombing at a Syrian refugee camp designed to derail the negotiations between the Syrian government and the rebels—it worked. So, Walid's group is all about fomenting dissent in the Middle East…and Africa." She tapped the paper with her finger. "Denver discovered a cache of weapons at an embassy outpost in Nigeria. He's putting these events together like nobody else is and The Falcon is paying attention."

"Someone else was paying attention, too, and that's

why he was set up. There has to be someone on the inside."

"At what level?" She skimmed her fingertip down a list of agencies and names. "The Falcon was on that track, also."

"Walid's group, which doesn't even have a name, is dependent on this insider and they're desperate to keep him a secret."

"Then we need to pretend we know who this insider is and that we have the proof to bring him down—and we'll do it unless we get Drake back."

"That won't work, Sue. We can't offer the people who took Drake any insurance that we didn't pass along this info to someone before we collect Drake, or any assurance that we didn't take pictures of the proof with our phones." He rubbed a circle on her back. "The only thing we have as a bargaining chip—is you."

Sue folded her arms and buried her face in the crook of her elbow. "Then it has to be done. My life for Drake's. It's a no-brainer."

"It's a no-brainer that you're going to show up, but I'll figure out a way to get you both out alive." He put his head close to hers and his warm breath stirred her hair. "I found you again and discovered we have a son together. Do you seriously think I'm going to let anything come between me and everything I ever wanted?"

She raised her head and kissed his chin. "How did I ever let myself get talked into leaving you and keeping Drake from you?"

Tapping the notebook with his knuckle, he said, "This is how. The work. Your work."

"And where has that work gotten me? Estranged

from you, Drake kidnapped, my career and my very life in jeopardy."

"Make it worthwhile."

"You mean instead of wallowing in self-pity?" She picked up the pen and resumed her examination of The Falcon's notes.

"I know what your problem is, and it's not self-pity." He stood up and made a move toward the kitchen. "You need to eat something. You never finished that awful oatmeal. I'll make us something else awful."

While Hunter banged around in the kitchen, Sue put together a time line of all the events that linked Major Denver with their undercover work with Walid. "It's here. This is it, Hunter. Walid's group is the same one Denver has been tracking and the same one The Falcon had me infiltrate. But for what purpose?"

"What purpose?" He walked toward her carrying two bowls of something steaming.

She sniffed the air. "Chicken noodle soup? Drake loves noodles."

"Must be genetic. This stuff is homemade, straight from the can." He set the soup at her elbow, a spoon already poking up from the bowl. "What purpose are you talking about?"

"The connection between Denver's investigation and the one I was doing with The Falcon is evident, but I don't know why either investigation is so important. This group—" she thumbed through the pages "—really hasn't been up to much of anything. Outside of the Syrian bombing and another in Paris, the group has been operating under the radar."

"Denver seems to think they're plotting something big, and obviously The Falcon thought so, too."

"In the US." Hunter blew on his soup before sucking a noodle into his mouth. "Yeah, I know that."

She shifted her gaze from Hunter's lips and glanced down at the page in front of her. "The Falcon does have *GB* several times on the page. Could there be an impending attack in Great Britain, also? It just doesn't make sense in the context of her notes, which really couldn't be more confusing if she tried."

"GB?" Hunter dropped his spoon and snatched the notes from her hand. "That's what the military calls sarin gas."

Sue choked. "My God, Hunter. That's it. A weapon in the context of these notes makes so much more sense than a place. They're planning a sarin attack. But where?"

She scrambled through The Falcon's notes again, drawing a blank. Slumping in her chair, she dropped the notes onto the table. "Do you think these are enough to clear me with the CIA? There are references to the people I met and why. The Agency can't accuse me of collaborating with the enemy once they see The Falcon's notes. Someone has to come forward at some point to claim The Falcon. She didn't work in a vacuum."

"They'll go a long way toward proving your innocence."

"Then maybe I should turn myself in now. Maybe they can help us get Drake back."

"That would be the worst thing we could do for Drake right now. If there's an insider, and these notes—" he smashed his fist against the papers "—indicate there is, how long do you think it's gonna take him, or her, to report back that the Agency is aware of the kidnapping?"

"Not long at all." She plowed her fingers through her hair and dug her nails into her scalp.

Her cell phone rang and she froze.

Hunter picked up the phone and checked the display. "It's your father."

Sue lunged for the phone. "Dad?"

"I couldn't find her, Sue. I don't know where she took him, but he's gone."

"We'll handle it, Dad. I'll get Drake back."

"At what cost?"

"Whatever it takes."

When her conversation with her father ended, Sue finally picked up her spoon and took a few sips of soup. She'd hoped that The Falcon's notes would contain a blueprint to clear her, clear Denver, give her something to use to bargain with Drake's kidnappers, ID the mole and map out the plan for Walid's attack. It only hinted at some of those things, leaving the rest just out of her grasp.

She cared only about Drake now. His safety was more important than all the rest. It always was and she hadn't been able to see that until now.

Her phone rang again, and when she looked at the calling number, she inhaled her soup so fast it went up her nose. "It must be Dani."

She put it on speaker and answered. "Yes?"

Dani answered, a slight accent creeping into her voice that Sue had never noticed before. "Are you ready?"

"I'm ready for anything."

"You'd better be." Dani spoke away from the phone

in a muffled voice and then continued. "We're going to pick you up on a street corner in DC at midnight tonight. If anyone follows us or we see any police presence, helicopters, drones or any other suspicious activity, your son will disappear."

"Are you bringing him with you when you pick me up? How will I know he's safe?"

"We'll let you video chat with him on the phone before we pick you up. We'll even let you see him before...before we take you away for interrogation."

Hunter jumped up from the table, his hands clenched into fists.

Sue met his gaze. "How do I know you'll let him go once you have me?"

"You'll just have to trust us. We're working out a plan for your father to pick the boy up."

"I need more than that." Hot anger thumped through her veins and she pressed two fingers against her throbbing temple.

"What choice do you have, Sue? Are you going to be at the meeting place tonight or not?"

Hunter came up behind her and stroked the side of her neck.

Sue took a deep breath and swallowed. "Of course I'll be there. Give me the instructions."

As Dani reeled off the steps, Sue wrote them down on a piece of paper. When the call ended, she dropped her head to that paper and banged her head on the table. "What are we going to do? There's no way to find out where they're going to take me. You can't follow us. She already said they're going to divest me of any cell phones, purses, bags, and they're even leaving clothes for me to change into so I can't sew anything into my clothing. And I don't even know if Drake will be safe at the end of this. They might kill us both."

Hunter braced his hands on the table, his head drooping between his arms. "That's not going to…"

His head jerked up. "Where's the bag from the floor with all the cash?"

"By the fireplace." She jerked her thumb over her shoulder. "Why?"

Crossing to the fireplace in three long strides, he said over his shoulder, "The Falcon had every conceivable spy tool in that storage unit. She also had some in that bag."

"GPS tracker? They'll find it, Hunter."

He knelt before the bag and dived into it, dragging out stacks of money and throwing them over his shoulder. His hands scrabbled through the items in the bottom of the bag, and then he sat back on his heels, with a smile that showed all his white teeth.

"Got it. God bless The Falcon."

"What do you have?" Sue sprang up from her chair like a jack-in-the-box and launched herself at him.

He waved the package in front of her nose. "You're going to swallow the GPS."

Chapter 19

Hunter tugged his hat lower on his forehead as he watched Sue across the street in her ill-fitting jeans and baggy T-shirt. She still looked incredible, regal even, as she awaited her fate—and Drake's.

They'd made the four-hour drive back to DC that afternoon and had lain low in a chain hotel outside the capital until it was time to leave. They'd come separately, he in a disguise, so nobody would make the link between him and Sue.

She'd followed their instructions to the T, picking up a bag at the front desk of the specified hotel, changing into the clothing in the bag, stashing her own clothes, along with any personal items, in the bag and checking it back in with the bellhop.

Now she waited on that corner with no guarantee that her sacrifice would spare Drake. *He* was her guarantee. He finally had the family he'd dreamed of having and he wasn't going to let it—or them—slip out of his grasp so easily.

He brought up the GPS app on his phone and entered the code for the tracker in Sue's belly. She appeared as a stationary green dot.

Sensing movement, Hunter shifted his gaze from his phone to the street. A blue van pulled up alongside Sue and she hopped in. Just like that, she disappeared from his sight, and a wave of panic clutched at his innards for a few seconds until he got his bearings.

They could search her all they wanted; they'd never find the tracker. But he—and they—had to act quickly. It was good for only a few hours, and he couldn't be seen following the van.

He swallowed the fear bubbling up from his gut and paid for his coffee and apple pie. He hobbled out of the twenty-four-hour café and made a sharp turn toward the parking garage where he'd left the car borrowed from Sue's friend.

Nobody knew that car. Nobody knew the bearded man in the Nationals cap with the slight paunch and the stiff leg. He limped toward the elevator, passing a few tourists out on the town, maybe going to their nighttime monuments tour.

When he got behind the wheel of the car, he checked his phone again. Sue and the van were headed out of the city, south toward Virginia.

He followed their path. At this rate, he'd be pulling in to the destination ten minutes after they did. If her captors acted quickly and whisked her or Drake away as soon as they got there, he didn't stand a chance.

They didn't even know if Drake would be waiting at the location. He might be somewhere else completely.

He pounded his hands against the steering wheel. He couldn't let himself think that way. He had to be Delta Force right now. He had to remove the personal feelings from this mission and focus on the objective. Rescue the targets and kill the enemy, if necessary.

With his phone propped up on the dashboard, he followed the green bull's-eye. Forty-five minutes passed before the van made a move off the highway. Hunter checked the map and saw farmland. A rural area would expose him, but it would expose them, too.

And he had all the gear he needed to conduct a raid—Delta Force–style.

When the target stopped moving, Hunter caught his breath. He was eight minutes out. As he continued to drive, he pulled up another map on his phone and switched to a street-view image. The location of the green dot matched up to what looked like a barn of some sort.

His mind clicked into action. A barn—high ceilings, wooden structure, possible fire hazard, maybe a hayloft, horse stalls. Places for concealment.

He parked his car a half mile out, hiding it behind a clump of bushes. He secured his backpack, the weight of his equipment solid on his shoulders. He stumbled onto a dirt access road—no trees or cover-up to the structure, but high grass, high enough to conceal a man in a crouching position.

He waded into the grass, hunching forward, his pack bouncing on his back. The vegetation whispered beneath his feet, and he could imagine it said "Sue, Sue" with every step closer to the barn.

Just as he was close enough to emerge from the grass and hit the ground in an army crawl for the ages, Hunter almost plowed into a man standing on the edge of the grass.

Hunter fell to the side just as the guard cocked his head. Hunter circled around to the side, grateful for the wind that kicked up and fluffed the grass, making it sigh.

The man on duty didn't know which way to look, and when he cranked his head in the other direction, away from him, Hunter made his move.

He came from the side, hacked his hand across the man's windpipe to silence any cries, shoved his gun beneath his left rib cage and pulled the trigger.

The silencer made a whooshing sound and the man collapsed to the ground, his blood already soaking the dirt. "That's for Major Denver, you bastard."

Hunter searched him for a walkie or cell phone and found the latter. Hopefully, Hunter would be in that building before anyone decided to check with the guard on watch.

Stashing the dead guard's weapon in his backpack, Hunter dropped to the ground and crawled toward the barn. He paused next to the van and hitched up to his knees.

He pressed his ear against the side of the van, which rumbled with the sound of a radio. Damn—someone waited inside. He'd never make it to the barn without being seen.

He scanned the ground and scraped his fingers through the dirt to collect some pebbles. He tossed these up in the air and they showered down on the top of the van. Then he scrambled beneath the van and held his breath.

The driver's door opened and one booted foot landed in the dirt. Another followed, and the driver emerged from the van, facing it, probably trying to see the roof.

As the man's boot heels eased up off the ground, Hunter rolled out from beneath the van and bashed the guard in the kneecaps.

The man gave a strangled cry and swung his weapon down to point it at his surprise attacker. The same look of shock was stamped on his face when Hunter shot him. "That's for Sue, you bastard."

His path now cleared to the barn, Hunter returned to the ground and snaked his way to the building. When he heard the high, clear tones of a child's voice, his heart lurched.

He was here. His son was here.

The barn's windows were too high to see into and he couldn't charge through that swinging front door without knowing the situation inside first. He crawled around to the side of the building and swung his pack from his shoulder.

He rummaged through the contents, feeling each item with his fingers, identifying each gadget from memory. When his fingertip traced around a small, round object encased in plastic packaging, he withdrew it from the backpack.

This little device could be his eyes inside the barn, give him some situational awareness. He slit the package open with his knife and programmed the spy cam into his phone. He rose, creeping up the side of the barn, and swung his arm at the window above him a few times to judge the distance.

As long as this didn't land on someone's head, he should be able to slip it inside without anyone knowing they were being watched.

Saying a silent prayer, he tossed the minicam through the window and into the barn. He held still for several seconds, his muscles taut. No screams, shots or people came from the barn, so he turned to his phone and brought up the app.

The camera had landed almost against the wall, but it gave him a clear view of a small area encircled by farm equipment—and made his heart ache.

Sue sat on the floor with Drake, his dark head against her shoulder. Were they allowing her to say goodbye to her son before they tortured and killed her? Would they do the same to Drake?

A cold dread seeped into his veins as he thought about all the ways they could use Drake to get Sue to talk. But he was here now—watching everything they did.

Sue and Drake sat on the farthest side away from the door. A woman, he assumed Dani, and a man, who looked like Jeffrey, stood close to the door. They both had weapons, but they hung loosely in their hands. They figured their trusty guards would warn them of any trouble.

Hunter eyed the van with the dead man next to it, just feet from the front door. The construction of the barn wasn't very solid, and a heavy vehicle wouldn't have too much trouble crashing through that door.

Would Dani and Jeffrey react to the van's engine starting? Why wouldn't the guard start the van if he were cold and wanted the heat on? Would Sue realize what it meant? She had to know he had successfully tracked her and was planning her rescue.

Hunter shook his head and squeezed his eyes closed. Too much second-guessing. Too much indecision. Act. Move. Now.

He pushed away from the side of the barn and crawled toward the van. He stepped over the dead guy and settled behind the wheel, leaving the driver's door open. The keys in the ignition jiggled as his knee hit them.

He held his phone in front of him and propped it on top of the steering wheel. Dani and Jeffrey had their heads together, their guns at their sides. Sue had Drake in her lap. Good. Keep him safe.

He'd do the rest.

Without another thought clouding his brain or instinct, Hunter dropped the phone and replaced it with his weapon. In one movement, he cranked on the engine and stomped on the accelerator.

The van roared to life and barreled toward the barn door. As it crashed through and splintered the wood, he got a glimpse of Dani's face, eyes and mouth wide open. Jeffrey had rolled up onto the hood.

Hunter didn't relent, as he kept his foot firmly on the gas pedal. He heard a scream. A thud. A crunch.

He didn't hear any gunshots.

When the van reached the other side of the barn, Hunter bolted from the driver's seat. A twinge of fear brushed across the back of his neck when he didn't see Sue or Drake across the room where they'd been when he started his assault, but he had to neutralize the enemy first.

He kicked aside the debris and wreckage in the barn

and stumbled upon Jeffrey, his crumpled body thrown up against some heavy machinery, his head at an odd angle. Hunter felt for a pulse—there was none.

As he turned from Jeffrey's dead body, he almost tripped over Dani's legs protruding from beneath the van's wheels. He crouched down, his gaze meeting her lifeless eyes, still wide-open. He growled, "And that's for my son."

"Hunter? Is it safe?"

Sue's voice calling out to him sent a rush of warm relief through his body, and for the first time that night, his rigid muscles lost a little of their tension.

He lurched to his feet and spotted her across the room, standing on a tractor, Drake clutched to her chest.

"It's safe. They're both dead."

They started toward each other at the same time, and for the first time, Hunter wrapped his arms around his son, safe in his mother's arms.

Epilogue

Ned dangled Sue's badge in front of her. "You're not out of the woods yet, Sue. Hunter took out several of Walid's cell here in DC, but we don't know how many are left and if they're going to be out for revenge."

As Sue hung her badge around her neck, she glanced at Hunter. "And we still don't know who the mole is—but we can all agree there is one."

Ned ran his finger along the seam of his lips. "The intel stays in this room…and with The Falcon's replacement."

"Who is?"

Hunter touched her hand. "I guess you'll never find out. You're off undercover duty."

"Your choice, right, Sue?" Ned raised his brows at her.

"Absolutely. I have a son to raise. Even my father's good with that."

"We've got plenty of analysis duty for you right here at home, but we're extending your leave for a little bit longer." He held up his hands. "For safety reasons only."

"That's fine. I need a break, and I know exactly where I'm going to take it."

Hunter extended his hand to Ned. "Thanks for guiding Sue through the process of coming out from under her undercover assignment."

"Once we got The Falcon's notes, it was easy." Ned crossed his arms. "Do you think you can get Major Denver to come in now?"

"I doubt it. He wants assurances before he surrenders, and the army is not ready to offer him those assurances yet."

"The Falcon made it clear that Denver's investigation was dovetailing with hers."

"Until the mole can be ID'd, I think Denver will remain in hiding."

Sue hitched her bag over her shoulder. "We'd better get going. Our son is with Peter right now and probably has him climbing the walls."

Sue and Hunter collected their son from her co-worker and exited the building, with Drake cuddled into Hunter's arms. After Hunter had saved them from the scary barn with the scary people, Drake had been clinging to his father as if he'd known him all his life.

They drove back to her place and Sue hesitated on the threshold. Her space, her life had been violated and the terrorists she'd been tracking for over three years were still out there…and Hunter had another deployment around the corner.

Hunter returned from his brief survey of her condo and nodded. "All clear."

Sue put Drake down and tousled his hair. "I think we should order pizza—one cheese and one with everything on it."

"Sounds good to me." Hunter patted his stomach.

Drake scampered to the packed suitcases in the corner of the room and tackled one. "Mama going?"

Sue's eyes stung and she sniffled through her smile. "You're coming with me this time, cupcake. I already told your aunt and cousins, and maybe they can visit us. We're going to Hunter's home in Colorado. He even has horses."

Drake skipped to Hunter and threw himself at his legs. "Horses."

Hunter scooped him up in his arms and flew him around the room a few times before settling on the sofa with him in his lap. Hunter touched his nose to Drake's. "You'd like a daddy, wouldn't you, Drake?"

Drake nodded and grabbed the buttons on Hunter's shirt. "Daddy."

Sue put a hand over her heart. It was as if he already knew.

"Well, I am your daddy. Is that okay? You can call me Daddy instead of Hunter. All right?"

Drake snuggled farther into Hunter's arms, burrowing against his chest. Still hanging on to the shirt button, he said, "Daddy."

"I guess that's settled." Hunter rested his chin on top of Drake's dark hair, a look of serene satisfaction softening the hard line of his jaw.

"And after Colorado? After your deployment?"

"I'm still gonna be Drake's dad…and your man, if you'll have me."

Sue meandered to the sofa where her two guys, her two heartbeats, cuddled together. She sank down next to Hunter and rested her head on his shoulder.

"If *I'll* have *you*? My concern is the other way around. I abandoned you. Lied to you. Kept your son from you and lied again."

"And I still love you. What does that say about me?" He pressed his lips against Drake's temple.

"That you're loyal and forgiving and a little bit crazy." She rubbed her knuckles against his chin. "You *did* crash headlong into a barn."

Dragging his fingers through her hair, he said, "My life was in that barn. My family. And I'm not gonna give up on my family—not now, not ever."

And just like that, Sue had her job, her man and her son back in her life.

* * * * *

He'd recognize that voice anywhere, even though he'd heard it live and in person just a few times and never so...forceful. He believed her, but he had no intention of letting her off the hook so easily.

He raised his hands. "I'm LAPD Detective Jake McAllister. Are you all right?"

A sudden gust of wind carried her sigh down the trail toward him.

"It...it's Kyra Chase. I'm sorry. I'm putting away my weapon."

Lowering his hands, he said, "Is it okay for me to move now?"

"Of course. I didn't realize… I thought you were…"

"The killer coming back to his dump site?" He flicked on the flashlight in his hand and continued down the trail, his shoes scuffing over dirt and pebbles. "He wouldn't do that—at least not so soon after the kill."

When he got within two feet of her, he skimmed the beam over her body, her dark clothing swallowing up the light until it reached her blond hair. "I didn't mean to scare you, but what are you doing here?"

"Probably the same thing you are." She hung on to the strap of her purse, her hand inches from the gun pocket.

"I'm the lead detective on the case, and I'm doing some follow-up investigation."

"Believe it or not, Detective, I have my own prep work that I like to do before meeting a victim's family. I want to have as much information as possible when talking to them. I'm sure you can understand that."

"Sure, I can. And call me Jake."

Love Harlequin romance?

DISCOVER.

Be the first to find out about promotions, news and exclusive content!

Facebook.com/HarlequinBooks

Twitter.com/HarlequinBooks

Instagram.com/HarlequinBooks

Pinterest.com/HarlequinBooks

YouTube.com/HarlequinBooks

ReaderService.com

EXPLORE.

Sign up for the Harlequin e-newsletter and download a free book from any series at **TryHarlequin.com**

CONNECT.

Join our Harlequin community to share your thoughts and connect with other romance readers!
Facebook.com/groups/HarlequinConnection